Bloody BRITAIN

Bloody BRITAIN

ANNA TABORSKA

Shadow Publishing

BLOODY BRITAIN

ISBN: 978-0-9572962-9-9

Shadow Publishing, Apt 19 Awdry Court, 15 St Nicolas Gardens,
Kings Norton, Birmingham, B38 8BH, UK

david.sutton986@btinternet.com

For Charles Black

ANNA TABORSKA is a British filmmaker and horror writer. She has written and directed two short fiction films, two documentaries and an award-winning TV drama. She has also worked on twenty other films, and was involved in the making of two major BBC television series: *Auschwitz: the Nazis and the Final Solution* and *World War Two Behind Closed Doors – Stalin, the Nazis and the West.*

Anna's short stories have appeared in over thirty anthologies, including *Best New Writing 2011, The Best Horror of the Year Volume Four, Best British Horror 2014, Year's Best Weird Fiction Volume 1* and *Nightmares: A New Decade of Modern Horror.*

Anna's debut short story collection, *For Those who Dream Monsters*, published by Mortbury Press in 2013, won the Dracula Society's Children of the Night Award and was nominated for a British Fantasy Award.
Anna's other books include *Shadowcats* – a micro-collection of feline horror stories published by Black Shuck Books in June 2019.
Bloody Britain includes the Bram Stoker Award nominated novelette *The Cat Sitter.*

You can watch clips from Anna's films and check out her full biography at: https://annataborska.wixsite.com/horror

Contents

INTRODUCTION:

WHY I'M A LITTLE BIT SCARED OF

ANNA TABORSKA

Robert Shearman

Sometimes I worry about what would happen if I woke up as a character in a horror writer's story. (I can't be the only one. Reassure me on this.) And I know my first concern would be to ascertain which particular writer's world I'd fallen into. If I discovered I was in a Stephen King, I'd be wary – but so long as it was one of his more sprawling community novels, I'd try to stay generically nice and hide somewhere in the background, and I should be okay. If it were a Clive Barker, I'd be doomed – but at least I'd be fairly sure there'd be opportunity for some interesting transgressive fun along the way. Realistically, I think I'd take my chances in most horror reasonably well. I understand the conventions. I'd keep myself safe.

But God protect me from being a character in an Anna Taborska story. Anything but that. Please.

Anna is one of my best friends. We lunch together sometimes, and she's always very kind to the waitress when she gives her order. (I always think – oh, if only they knew!) It's one of the clichés of horror writers that people always worry about where all our darkness comes from, we seem so charming and nice on the exterior, but what depravity are we hiding? It's only with Anna Taborska that I sometimes find myself wondering the same thing. I peer at her cautiously over the French onion soup starter. Most writers who dabble with the grotesque feel a little shame about the way the genre is perceived – myself included; we redefine horror as something else, as if by changing the words we can claw back some respectability. Anna has no shame whatsoever. Her tales are frequently very violent, and unforgiving, and brutally extreme. I'd say it was almost gleeful – I can certainly imagine Anna's naughty

1

face breaking into a smile as she plots out her latest nightmare – but what's so powerful about her work is how little glee there is in it – there's none of the self-mocking wink and chuckle that reassures us that horror is something to laugh with. And the punishments meted out to her characters are, just as in real life, nasty and random; the wicked get their just desserts, but the innocents are never spared either. Anna Taborska stands over her characters like a cruel god, and no amount of special pleading is going to spare them.

When I read a story by Anna, I frequently need to put the book down afterwards and go for a long walk. They're very moreish, the tales of Taborska, but very heady too. Gobbling too many at once can do temporary damage to your taste buds.

There are many horror writers out there who can splash out the gore, but the result of that is usually numbing. Anna isn't about gore (though I have a particularly high squeamishness threshold, and she can certainly ladle it out when she wants to). The reason why her stories are more effective – and so disquieting – is that she writes with the empathy of someone who expects that life is cruel and unfair, but still has enough hope in the world to be dismayed by it. Horror stories regularly invite us to engage with the victim, with the character under threat – it's why, I'd argue, horror is among the most empathetic genres out there, as over and over again the reader bonds with people in terrible danger, and subjects themselves to that danger by doing so. Anna Taborska stories do something slightly different. It's not simply that she invites us to identify with the monster instead – that's a trick we've all been using since Mary Shelley. It's more that she refuses to draw a distinction between the monster and the victim – they are both equally damned. And as you read her work you get the slightly sickened sensation that you can no longer quite work out where your sympathies lie, which one is the hero, with whom you should identify. (Which one is the safest, and most likely to be left standing at the end. As I said – God protect me from being any character in a Taborska.)

Most horror is suggested by something external. An everyman character finds his life and world view under threat from a new outside menace. Anna's threats grow from within. Ordinary people destroy their lives – and other hapless lives in the process – because of growing mad obsessions, or uncontrolled ambition, or greed, or curiosity. Characters like you and me fall in love with the idea of killing, and take new guiltless delight in it, that seems gruesomely at odds with their recognisable sanity. I think, unavoidably, there is a political point to this, made all the more acute by a collection being called Bloody Britain. Anna has been writing these stories over many years, and they are not inspired by recent events per se – but she has accurately, and with withering eye, been watching and chronicling how this country has become progressively colder and more uncaring. The most terrifying thing about Anna's horror is how nonchalant it is. That we've let it become normal.

The first story of Anna's I ever read was 'Little Pig', which Ellen Datlow had reprinted in 'Nightmares', a collection of the best horror published over the past decade. It had a reputation already as something of a classic – and it's an untypical tale that nonetheless is typical of Anna's work, showcasing the way good people can find it in themselves to do unspeakable things under duress. Her biography revealed that Anna made films, and this seemed immediately obvious – there's a visual immediacy to her stories that often borders on pure cinema. I watched her work. There is a short in Polish called 'The Sin' (Grzech) that is hauntingly beautiful, and is about the way a childhood act of petty destruction resonates throughout a man's life as the Devil's work. Perhaps more telling still, 'The Rain Has Stopped' features a shy and awkward salesman going door to door and encountering all manner of British eccentrics, before finally being transformed into a terrifying psychopath during a rain storm. This, Anna says, is what is happening in the houses and in the hearts of the people you meet, and take for granted every day. Anyone can succumb to an evil that is all the more unnerving for being so banal and so cold.

Anna Taborska invites her readers to peer into the darkness with her – but looking too hard has its own dangers, and there may be dreadful consequences. My favourite stories of 'Bloody Britain' act like horror stories within horror stories. An Oxford undergraduate who becomes insanely addicted to translating a series of tales of torture and rape, even as they disgust him, even as they are killing him. A rock star who starts performing anonymously delivered songs that celebrate violence, cruelty and death. Anna's great skill is that she fully understands the seductive pull of the dark and the profane – that's entirely its appeal, and why by degrees its impact is blunted, and why we live in such a corrupted amoral world as the one depicted in 'Bloody Britain'. She doesn't judge us for being excited by it. As I say, she loves horror. As I say, she feels no shame whatsoever.

Every chance I get to spend any time with Anna feels like a dangerous treat – because she is that most interesting of artists, she is an enigma, she is a contradiction. I love her company, and her kindness, and her great generous humour. Even as I try to square it with the dispassionate anger I see in her best work. She is a great friend, and a great talent. Occasionally she tries to lure me to the cinema with her, to watch strange new horror movies she has discovered. Even though she knows they frighten me, even though she knows I don't have the same stomach for pure dread blackness that she has. "Come on," she smiles, "it'll be fun," and it's in those moments that I see the other Anna Taborska, the writer who unnerves me so much. And I refuse to go.

NIGHT OF THE CRONE

NIGHT OF THE CRONE

A weight of Awe, not easy to be borne,
Fell suddenly upon my Spirit – cast
From the dread bosom of the unknown past,
When first I saw that family forlorn.
Speak Thou, whose massy strength and stature scorn
The power of years – pre-eminent, and placed
Apart, to overlook the circle vast –
Speak, Giant-mother! tell it to the Morn
While she dispels the cumbrous shades of Night
Let the Moon hear, emerging from a cloud;
At whose behest up-rose on British ground
That Sisterhood in hieroglyphic round
Forth-shadowing, some have deemed, the infinite
The inviolable God, that tames the proud!

William Wordsworth

TEK CARE
LAMBS
INT ROAD

THE HOME-MADE SIGN toppled to the ground as the SUV swerved into it, then ran it over. The three youths in the back of the Range Rover tumbled from one side of the vehicle to the other, cursing profusely.

"Ten points if you hit a lamb!" Zed grinned at the driver from his prime position in the passenger seat, then ran his hand through the thick dark blond hair that covered his ears and almost reached his chin in a kind of matted, over-grown bob. Had his nose been a bit smaller, and his eyes a bit bigger, he might almost have passed as attractive. There was no doubt he had a certain charisma and menacing charm, which probably contributed to the unquestioning loyalty he inspired in his friends. None of them had the slightest idea that Zed (christened 'Brian' by his doting mother) only kept them around for his own amusement and to help him get what he wanted from life.

"No problem!" responded Johnny. At twenty he was the eldest, but also the smallest of the youths, and the only one to have once held a driving licence. What Johnny lacked in size and wit he made up for in unpredictability and violence. He'd gotten by in school by being a total psycho and he got by with girls by forcing them. His drug of choice – in which he indulged at every given opportunity – was speed, which no doubt contributed to his regular bouts of mania and over-excitement. A casual observer might have described him as something of a killer-dweeb.

"Unfortunately, it might actually *be* a problem," Zed grinned. Johnny glanced at him quizzically. "You only get lambs here in spring," Zed explained.

"Oh yeah... But you said... oh, it was a joke!" Johnny finally got it. Anybody else would have had their nuts ripped off and shoved down their throat for making a joke at his expense, but as far as Johnny was concerned, Zed was God.

"Don't worry about it, man," Zed told him. "It's twenty points for a granny."

The short drive from Langwathby, through Little Salkeld, was uneventful. The yuppie couple they'd stolen the SUV from must have alerted the police by now, but Zed figured that they could safely drive as far as the stone circle without getting caught. Once there, they'd ditch the vehicle under the tree in the small parking space to the side of the path. It would be dark soon and nobody would think to look for it at a heritage monument off the beaten track. Besides, if anybody asked, they would deny all knowledge of the theft.

They followed the signs for *The Druid's Circle* and were soon turning left off the road onto the narrow track. As they drove through a small copse of trees, the first stones came into view, but so did a pink Mini Metro tucked neatly under the tree where they'd planned to park.

"Stop here," Zed told Johnny.

"Where?"

"Pull in behind that pussy wagon."

Johnny obliged and the five of them got out.

"Looks like we have company," said Zed, moving swiftly in search of the intruders, followed closely by Johnny and Franko – Zed's friend since primary school, as intelligent as Zed, but the least secure in the group due to his ill-disguised distaste for vandalism, theft, cruelty to animals, and the odd attempted rape or mugging. A plain-looking, quiet boy of eighteen, Franko was grateful for the sense of belonging he got from the group, and still retained something of his schoolboy crush on Zed. Although the recent escalation in the group's violence made him feel increasingly uneasy, he enjoyed all the drink and drugs, and these got him through the worst of it. Besides, he had the distinct feeling that leaving was not an option. At least tonight they weren't going after anything that had a pulse, so Franko felt relatively relaxed as he hurried after Zed and Johnny.

Spike – an overweight and singularly unpleasant-looking skinhead – was the last to scramble out of the car. He came to a halt beside Rizla, a swarthy youth with long black hair, who had produced a penknife from his jacket pocket and was busy carving away at the front of the SUV.

"What yer doing?" asked Spike.

"Wait and see." Rizla skilfully cut out the top of the first 'R', the first 'E' and the second 'R' from the 'RANGE ROVER' sign above the grille. He finished his handiwork and stood back, then cast Spike an expectant glance, but Spike didn't get it.

"What?"

"Hangover, man," explained Rizla. "Look, it says 'HANG-- OVER'."

Spike peered at the vandalised sign. "Oh, yeah. I see it now."

"Spike! Rizla!" Zed's voice reached them from the field beside the track. "Come and meet our new friends!"

Spike and Rizla hurried over, hardly noticing the spectacular stone circle they were entering in their hurry to do Zed's bidding. Cornered by Zed, Johnny and a despondent-looking Franko, next to an enormous pale grey, crystal-streaked stone, were two teenage girls: a skinny little blonde and a girl with dyed red hair. The redhead was probably not much older than her girlish friend, but her shape was already impressively curvaceous. Zed figured that at least one of them had to be seventeen, as the pink Mini couldn't have belonged to anyone else.

"This is Spike," Zed nodded in the direction of the panting skinhead, "and this is Rizla – so known for his unparalleled ability to roll a Camberwell Carrot in under ten seconds." The red-haired girl giggled self-consciously, and her friend tried to smile, but both looked distinctly frightened. "This is Trish," Zed introduced the redhead to Rizla and Spike, "and this..." Zed smiled at the little blonde, who blushed and lowered her eyes, "is Amy."

There was something about frightened little girls that rocked Zed's world, and his jeans were already starting to get a little too tight around the crotch. Judging by the unsavoury glint in Spike's eye, he evidently felt the same, while Rizla couldn't take his eyes off Trish's chest, and extended his hand to the girl, who shook it reluctantly.

"I've just been persuading the ladies to join us for the evening," Zed explained to the latecomers.

"Cool," Rizla commented, his eyes still glued to Trish's boobs; the outline of her nipples visible through the tightly stretched pink fabric of her top as a cold breeze stirred around the stones. Trish pulled her jacket around herself self-consciously.

"We've got to go," she said.

"You're very brave to be camping this time of year." Zed ignored Trish, focussing his attention on the petite blonde. "So where exactly are you ladies staying?"

"North Dy..."

"Amy!" Trish quickly silenced her friend. Amy blushed, upset at herself for falling into Zed's charm-trap and almost giving away their location for the night. "We've got to go," repeated Trish, trying to push her way past Zed.

"Not so fast!" In a split-second Johnny had Trish firmly by the arm and was leering at her in a way that made her nauseous with fear. She could feel Johnny's stale cigarette breath on her face, and for a moment she froze. Amy made a move towards her friend, but the huge skinhead barred her way, grinning lecherously.

"It's okay, Johnny," Zed surprised his friends, much to the girls' – and Franko's – relief. "We have business to attend to, but I'm sure we'll catch up with the ladies later." Sick with disappointment, Johnny let go of Trish; Zed was right – they had a plan to stick to, but surely a half-hour digression couldn't hurt?

"Catch you later, ladies," Zed crooned after the pair as they fled for their car.

"Yeah, catch you later," echoed Spike.

"What's the matter, Johnny?" teased Zed, sensing his pal's growing tension.

"Man, how could you let a chance like that get away?" whined Johnny, looking increasingly as if he were about to re-enact the head explosion scene from *Scanners*.

"Relax man, you heard what the blonde bitch said," soothed Zed.

"What?"

"They're at North Dyke Farm."

"What? How d'yer know?" demanded Johnny, the angry scarlet already draining from his face.

"She said."

"She started to say something, but she never finished coz the other bitch stopped her."

"She said 'North'," Zed continued patiently. "Well, they said they were camping, and there's only one campsite around here that's open in October, and that's North Dyke Farm. It's just past Great Salkeld, and it's a piece of piss to get to. Once we're done here it will be night, everyone will be in bed. We'll drive round and surprise them."

Rizla and Spike stared at Zed in admiration, Franko eyed him with trepidation and awe, while Johnny's shoulders slumped with relief.

"Don't worry, man!" Zed patted Johnny on the back, "You'll get to have your little party. We all will."

"Zed, man," Johnny's mood – ever volatile – went from barely suppressed rage to deep affection in under a second. "You're the best!"

"I know," grinned Zed. "Now let's get the stuff out the car."

As they followed Zed back to the Range Rover, Franko paused for a moment and took in the eerie beauty of the desolate place. The track the youths had driven in on cut through one side of the Bronze Age stone circle known as Long Meg and Her Daughters, and carried on past a nearby farm, now dark and deserted. The Daughters were vast rhyolite boulders placed in a flattened oval almost 360 feet in diameter at its widest point. Twenty-seven of the stones still stood; thirty-two had toppled over or sunk into the ground, leaving only flat, lichen-covered grey slabs in the grass; the others that had once made up the original number of about seventy had vanished – below the earth perhaps. Sixty feet southwest of the circle stood Long Meg herself – an imposing twelve-foot-high megalith of brooding red sandstone, watching over the smaller stones and the fields beyond. Its four corners faced the points of the compass, and three clearly visible spiral, ring and concentric circle patterns had been cut into its northwest face thousands of years ago. The sun had just set and a bloody glow still lingered above the horizon, enhancing Long Meg's ruddy hue.

"Trippy, huh?" Rizla stopped by Franko and followed his gaze.

"There's a story about the stones," Franko told him. "A landowner once tried to blow them up, but a massive storm broke out and his workmen refused to carry on with the demolition."

"Just as well we're only here for the treasure then, isn't it?"

"I think that's what the landowner was after too," said Franko, but Rizla was already halfway to the Range Rover. Something about the hunched, human-like form of the towering sandstone unnerved Franko, and when the cold breeze started to whisper among the stones he hurried after his friends.

They pulled out their supplies – spades, pick-axes, torches and beer – from the car, and prepared to return to the circle.

"Let me torch it," Johnny got out his Zippo and turned back to the vehicle with a look of unhealthy excitement.

"Yeah, man, let's torch it!" Spike joined in. He looked round at Zed, like a dog waiting for its owner to throw it a stick.

"Not yet," responded Zed. "A fire here would be visible for miles. Besides, we'll need it to pay the bitches a visit. When we're done, you can torch it."

"Oh, okay." Zed's genius never ceased to impress Johnny. He put away his lighter, and he and Spike followed Zed, Franko and Rizla back to Long Meg.

Life in Langwathby did not suit Zed and his friends. The tranquil beauty of the village with its stone and slate cottages, and eighteenth century church, all surrounded by rolling green fields, did nothing for them. They were frustrated and skint. After all, what can you do when you've been banned from the only pub, and the main attraction on offer is *Eden Ostrich World* (at which you also happen to be less than welcome after throwing stones at the llamas and traumatising a chipmunk)? Zed had long thought about raiding St. Peter's, but they'd probably have gotten away with no more than the contents of the collection box, and besides, the church was too visible, and they were notorious in the village already. The only options open to the youths were preying on unsuspecting tourists – of whom there were not that many, particularly in autumn and winter – and the occasional raid on nearby Penrith, but even that wasn't easy without a car.

Zed often wondered why on earth his parents had left London; certainly the move hadn't done them any good. Zed's mother had taken to her bed soon after, rapidly developing an affinity for prescription painkillers and tranquilisers. Zed's father tried to bring up his son to be a decent human being, but any attempts at discipline inevitably led to recriminations and attacks from his wife, and ultimately failed, at which point he upped and left while Zed was still at school. Zed blamed his useless bitch mother for his father's departure and their subsequent lack of money. He never expressed his true feelings to her, and always addressed his mother in a warm, if somewhat calculated and patronising manner, but nevertheless he saw her money and her drugs as fair game, and regularly stole them from the top drawer in her bedside cabinet. But the pittance that she had stashed was not enough for a decent life – and certainly not one away from Langwathby – so when he read something on the internet about treasure buried under Long Meg, he latched onto the idea a bit too fast and a bit too uncritically, immediately hatching a cunning plan, which his friends would put into practice for him.

"Don't piss on them!" Rizla snapped at Johnny who'd wandered a little way off and was urinating on one of the fallen boulders. The others looked at Rizla like he'd just gone mad.

"What did you say?" Johnny had that *Scanners* look again.

"Don't piss on them, man. It's unlucky."

"What the fuck are you on about?"

"It upsets the dead."

"What the fuck have you been smoking, you fucking hippie fuck?" Johnny zipped up his jeans and strode over to Rizla with clenched fists. The long-haired youth stood his ground.

"I've been smoking the same stuff as you. I'm not a hippie. And it upsets the dead."

"Rizla!" Amused by the entire situation, Zed nevertheless decided to break things up before they got out of hand. "They're not gravestones," he said, leaning on the spade he'd been using to dig under Long Meg. Franko and Spike had also paused in their work and were observing events with some interest.

"They're not?"

"No, man."

"Oh, okay." Rizla turned away from Johnny and directed his attention back to Long Meg. Johnny started after him, but Zed held him back.

"Let it go; we've got work to do."

Johnny took a deep breath and nodded at Zed. They re-joined the others at the megalith, and resumed digging – all except Rizla, who took out his penknife, chose a prime spot to the right of Meg's circular 'cup and ring' pattern, and began carving his name. He twisted the point of his knife into the sandstone. A faint rumble of thunder growled somewhere nearby. Rizla stopped short; a thick viscous substance had seeped out onto his knife.

"What the fuck?" Rizla inspected the tip of his blade.

"What is it, man?" Zed stopped digging.

"Blood... I think." Rizla smelled the muck on the blade, then tasted it and winced.

"Be more careful," Zed told him.

"It's not mine."

"Whose then?" Zed put down his spade and walked over to Rizla. Soon all of them were gaping and dabbing at the oozing spot.

"It's bleeding." Franko shone his torch onto the stone as a thick globule of what undeniably looked like blood trickled from the tiny hole that was Rizla's attempt at the letter 'R', and started to pool in the dips and grooves of the spiral pattern.

"It's a mineral deposit of some sort," said Zed. "You must have exposed it to the air and it's reacted with the oxygen or something."

"It tastes of blood," Rizla protested.

"It's probably made of the same stuff as blood," Zed told him. "Probably iron oxide or something. Now leave it and help us dig."

They carried on digging at the base of the stone. Spike was strong, but his weight and general lack of fitness were starting to take their toll. He swung his pick-axe increasingly wildly, almost hitting Rizla.

"Watch it!"

"Fuck off!" Spike swung the pick-axe once more, but instead of breaking the earth, it connected hard with Long Meg's side. Spike winced from the unexpected contact with the rock.

"Jesus!" Johnny covered his ears against the jarring thud. Blood-coloured dust rose into the air from where the pick-axe had struck, and a small fracture appeared in the stone. Just then a flash of lightning lit up the sky, accompanied by a deafening crack of thunder. A second lightning bolt followed almost immediately, striking and splitting a tree at the edge of the field with a loud bang, and sending half of it toppling to the ground in flames.

"What the fuck?!" Rizla dropped the spade he was holding, and Spike stared at his pick-axe in disbelief. A peal of thunder cracked directly above the stone circle, a violent wind arose out of nowhere and rain started to pour from a sky that had suddenly turned pitch black.

"What's going on?" shouted Johnny.

"I don't know," Zed struggled to be heard over the howling wind. "But we need to take a break."

"Whadda we do?" yelled Spike.

"We go to plan B."

"What's plan B?" shouted Johnny.

"Bitches!" Zed managed to grin despite the hail stones that had started pelting the ground all around him. "Grab the tools and meet at the car!"

"Shit!" Franko's house keys fell out of his pocket as he grappled with a spade and torch, while trying to do up his jacket at the same time. "Wait up!" he shouted as he fumbled around on the ground. He switched on the torch and swept the beam over the grass. A mist had crept over the ground, and bounced Franko's torchlight back at him. Finally his fingers connected with metal. He stuffed the keys into his jeans pocket and got up to follow his friends. But the mist had become a thick, drifting fog, and even with the torch on he could see nothing. "Hey, wait up!" he yelled, but his words were devoured by the wailing wind.

Franko headed in the direction where he thought they'd left the car. As he moved the torch's beam around in front of him, his heart suddenly skipped a beat. Directly ahead of him in the eddying fog, Franko thought he saw two malevolent red eyes staring at him. The torch fell from his hand and went out. He cried out in alarm, then cursed himself for having smoked too much weed earlier. He picked up the torch and set off for the car, then realised that he'd lost all sense of direction in the shifting fog and had no idea which way to go.

"Hey, guys!" Franko shouted into the night, but his voice was carried away by the storm. There was no way his friends could hear him. His only option was to go back to Long Meg; if he fixed the location of the huge stone in his mind, he should be able to navigate the short distance to the dirt track and the car without too much trouble. But when he looked back to where he'd just come from, all he could see were wind-driven banks of milky fog, punctuated by bouts of rain and hail, and occasional glimpses of the profound darkness beyond. Confused, he staggered the few paces to where Long Meg should have been, but there was nothing there. The fog must be playing tricks on his sense of distance. He kept going until he almost fell over a boulder – but it wasn't Meg; it was one of the smaller stones that made up the circle some sixty feet from Meg. He must have walked right past the megalith in the miasma.

The lashing rain was beginning to soak through his jacket, and a hailstone the size of a grape hit him on the arm, causing Franko to cry out in pain. Desperate and cold, he moved away from the circle again, in another attempt to locate Long Meg. As he staggered first one way and then the other, he became aware of another sound over the howling of the wind and the pounding of the hail. It was like the flapping of giant wings, as if a colossal bird were flying overhead. Then a shadow fell over him.

Franko looked up and saw a hovering shape – black against the pale fog.

"Shit!" Terrified now, he started to run, falling a couple of times, smearing himself in mud and cow dung. He fled through the stone circle, the creature in pursuit – once above him, once behind him, then beside him – gliding effortlessly on the storm. As Franko dodged past one of the tumbled stones, the thing was suddenly in front of him. As the youth came to an abrupt halt, he saw the creature clearly for the first time. It was humanoid in form; hunched over, unnaturally twisted, and smaller than Franko had originally thought. It wore a tattered black cloak that swirled around it in the gale, giving it the impression of being larger than it actually was. Its gaunt face was scarred and craggy – like ancient rock. Its bloodshot eyes glowed with an age-old malevolence that spoke of torment and rage, of knowledge of the lowest depths of hell, and of a need for vengeance that would never be satiated.

Despite the corrupt hideousness of the visage before him, Franko somehow knew that whatever it was, it had once been female.

The crone extended her arms to the youth, as if inviting a lover to share an embrace. Her skeletal fingers ended in long, curved talons, like those of a bird of prey. She reached out for Franko, and he staggered back, tripped on the edge of a toppled stone, flailed around wildly in an attempt to regain his balance, then fell over backwards, hitting his head on another boulder. As he lost consciousness, the last thing he was aware of was the crone gliding towards him, and then a familiar voice shouting over the wailing wind.

"Franko!"

The crone turned her attention away from the unconscious youth and headed for the second desecrator.

"Where the fuck are you?" Rizla moved the feeble beam of his torch around the stone circle. How typical that Zed should pick on him to go looking for that moron in the middle of a storm. "Franko!" And then a lighting flash lit up the sky, and Rizla saw it – a monster from hell bearing down on him from above, framed by whirling fog and blinding rain. Rizla didn't even have time to yell 'What the fuck?' as the thing swept down and clasped him in its bony, but inhumanly strong arms. His lungs filled with the stench of sulphur and putrefaction, then emptied of breath entirely as the crone's embrace squeezed all the life out of him and shattered every bone in his body.

"You might as well turn off the engine."

Johnny did as Zed told him. "Can't we just leave those hippie fucks behind?" he asked.

"You never know, we might need them," said Zed, without really meaning it.

"We can handle two bitches between the three of us," urged Johnny. Spike grinned in the back seat.

"Spike?" Zed turned to the oversized thug. "Would you mind...?"

"Sure Zed. I should've gone in the first place. No point sending a boy to do a man's job."

"Thanks... man," replied Zed, smiling at his own wit. Spike pulled his hood over his head, took a torch, and clambered out into the storm. He didn't mind doing things for Zed; if it wasn't for Zed he'd have ended up in prison a long time ago. Thanks to how smart Zed was, he could indulge in his two great passions – hurting people and damaging property – with little risk to himself. And Zed's inventiveness when it came to aberrant and criminal behaviour was truly admirable. Spike would never forget how Zed helped get him off arson charges when he'd burnt his grandmother's house down – with his grandmother in it – by some very quick thinking, careful planning and framing the ginger-haired kid they'd hated at school. Yes, Spike would do anything for Zed, and retrieving some hippie fucks from the stone circle was the least of it.

With all these loyal thoughts milling around in his head, Spike found himself in the middle of the circle. A little surprised, he looked around for the massive red boulder they'd been digging under, but Long Meg was nowhere to be seen. Spike shrugged his shoulders.

"Rizla! Franko!" he yelled and took a step forward. His foot connected with something soft, but offering enough resistance to send him sprawling. He fell heavily, landing on the offending object. It was wet and sticky, lumpy and broken.

"Shit!" Spike scrambled up with difficulty and stared at the crumpled form at his feet. It had jeans, a black leather jacket, and long black hair. "Fuck!"

Spike started to back away in horror from what was left of Rizla, then thought better of it and, after casting a quick look around, turned the body over and went through the corpse's pockets until he found Rizla's wallet and drug stash. He took the drugs, pulled all the money out of the wallet, which wasn't much, then discarded the wallet and turned to go – and came face to face with a wizened old hag dressed in a ragged cloak and stinking of decay, mustiness and a choking, cloying odour like rotten eggs.

"What the fuck?" The monstrosity reached for Spike, and he swung his torch at her, connecting with her head. A trail of what looked like blood-coloured dust rose from where she'd been hit, but the crone hardly winced.

"Shit!" Spike hit her again, the impact sending the torch flying from his hand. This time she let out a snarl and a low, creaking moan – like the sound of shifting, breaking rock. He turned and ran, making sure to avoid tripping over Rizla's corpse again.

Spike panted through the fog, rain and hail; his sweat hot, then cold; steam rising off him as though from an over-taxed cart-horse. Within seconds he was wheezing with exertion, his lungs felt like they were on fire, and his heart seemed to be thumping somewhere in his throat, ready to explode. As he turned around to see if the obscenity was gaining, the crone was upon him, her talons clawing his face. Then she had him in her arms, and Spike managed a feeble squeal as her grip tightened, and all the fat surrounding his organs was mashed into a reddish-white jelly, and his stomach, his spleen, his liver, lungs and all his other organs were compressed and ruptured like blood-filled sacks. A gurgling sound emanated from the youth's pain-distorted mouth, then his bulging eyes popped right out of their sockets as the crone crushed his insides into a steaming, gelatinous mass.

"Man, this sucks!" Johnny was getting angry again, and Zed was starting to worry about the others.

"Something's up," he told Johnny.

"They're just pissing around. Let's just go." Johnny didn't share Zed's concerns. "You can have the blonde bitch and I'll take the redhead." But even as he said it, he knew that Zed wouldn't leave Spike. Besides, Rizla had all the drugs; Rizla always had drugs. If it wasn't for the fact that Rizla's cousin was an acid chemist, and Rizla was always generous with his cousin's handouts, Johnny would have had the hippie fuck's balls before you could say 'lysergic acid diethylamide'.

"Something's wrong. Let's tool up and sort things out." Zed climbed out of the car and grabbed a pick-axe from the trunk. Johnny produced a chain from an inside pocket of his jacket. It was his regular weapon of choice – not strictly illegal, and in the right hands it could inflict a hell of a lot of damage. And his were definitely the right hands.

Johnny turned up his collar against the raging storm, and he and Zed strode side by side to the circle.

"Where's Long Meg?" Zed looked around, bemused, and figured the thick fog must be impairing visibility and sense of space.

"Huh?"

"The stone we were digging under." Zed raised his voice over the wind. "I don't see it!"

Meg had stood for thousands of years, rooted to the desolate spot by a man of magic more powerful than her own. She'd tried to break free; she had used all of her will and power and spirit to tear herself from her craggy prison. She'd writhed desperately, and her determination was so great that she'd even managed to lift herself in the air so that when the stone jail finally set around her, it was several times the size of her slim body. Trapped within the jagged prison, her youthful skin, her beautiful face, her bones and hair, and even her soul had turned to cold, unfeeling rock. And yet she'd been aware of every year that passed, of all the elements battering her overblown, twisted form; doomed forever to gaze upon the members of her coven, entrapped too because they had followed her.

It was said that if someone counted the same number of rocks twice, the spell would be broken, and Meg and all her 'Daughters' would be released. While she waited to be set free, the torment she suffered and the passing centuries caused Meg's youth and beauty to fade. Within the rock, Meg's skin withered, her body became wizened, her face weather-beaten and eyes rheumy. But the magician had made sure that the stones changed and shifted, and no one could count the same number twice. Meg and her sisters would never regain their rightful lives, but Meg's blood had been spilt, and that granted her freedom for just one night. She could not avenge herself and her sisters by taking the magician's life, for he was long dead. But at least she could have a small revenge – on the men who'd cut her and made her bleed.

And there they were – grasping their pathetic weapons, as if they thought they could break her. Meg raised her arms in anger, her rage lifting her high off the ground and into the storm. With a shriek like the wind blowing through a hollow cave, she swooped down on the pair.

Zed and Johnny saw her at the same time. Zed froze, but Johnny raised his right hand and, chain held firmly, threw himself forward to meet the atrocity that lunged at them from above. With his own yell of rage, Johnny swung his chain, connecting heavily with the hardened lump that was the thing's left breast. Dust rose from the wound and the creature hissed, wrapping itself around the youth, clinging and squeezing with all four limbs and shrivelled, craggy body. Johnny fell to his knees, screaming to Zed for help. Zed took one look at the obscene tableau before him, and fled for the Range Rover.

As the crone crushed Johnny's body to a pulp, Zed started the engine and put his foot down. The tyres spewed up mud as he tried frantically to turn the car around on the narrow track. His customary composure had evaporated – much at the same time as the unfortunate Johnny's last breath – and his desperate manoeuvrings to get the car to do what he wanted were becoming increasingly frenzied. Finally he got the vehicle to point in the right direction and then he floored it ... straight into a tree.

Before he could recover from the whiplash, the windscreen imploded – spraying him with thousands of tiny glass fragments – and the monster had a hold of him and was pulling him out and up. Then Zed was flying through the air, bleeding from where the creature's talons pierced his skin; flying, screaming, through the night sky, the icy fog, and the biting wind and rain. Beneath him he could just make out the grey-white forms of Long Meg's Daughters – paler than the fog that pooled around them. Then he was falling – not from a great height, but far enough to dislocate his shoulder as he made contact with the ground. When he looked up, the crone's rheumy, bloodshot eyes stared into his own, and then she pounced. As she crushed the life out of the violator, she realised that breaking his bones would not satisfy her. She ripped into his flesh, gulping down the blood that spurted from his face and neck. When she was satiated, she sensed something stir in the darkness behind her.

Franko regained consciousness to find the crone crouched nearby, watching him closely. She bared her teeth at him, and he saw that they were small and razor-sharp, like those of a lamprey he'd seen on a wildlife documentary. Some of them had rotted away and the spaces that were left oozed putrescence, but those that remained looked lethal enough, and were stained with blood.

Franko scrambled backward, twisted round and with a single deft movement – with which he rather surprised himself, as he was no great athlete – leapt up and ran. The back of his head felt cold and clammy from where he'd cut it open during his fall, but he didn't feel pain as adrenaline coursed through his body. The crone too was taken by surprise at the unexpected flight of the last desecrator – her bloodlust and killer sense dulled after feasting on the one before – but she threw herself after him in pursuit.

Franko ran blindly, not caring which way he went. He broke clear of the stone circle and ran across the open fields, heading for trees and shelter. Once he ran straight into a barbed wire fence, but managed to disentangle himself, and kept going despite bleeding from his hands and head. The crone seemed less sure of herself away from the circle, but still pursued him. She almost caught up with him in the open, but then he was under trees and running, stumbling, through the woods that stretched to the old gypsum mine and the River Eden beyond. The gold and russet splendour of the beech and oak trees was obscured by the darkness and fog, and Franko had to be careful not to trip on a root or knock himself out on a protruding branch. The trees also slowed down his pursuer, but never stopped her, as she glided silently, her eyes fixed on her fast-tiring quarry.

Exhausted and breathing heavily, Franko half ran, half slid down a steep embankment, managing to stop just in time to avoid plunging down a precipitous set of slippery steps. He realised where he was: just above the sealed entrance to the abandoned gypsum mine – a creepy place at the best of times. He wanted to turn back rather than risk falling on the steps in the pouring rain. But as he looked back, he saw the crone behind him, gaining. He ran, stumbling and sliding down the steps. Remarkably he survived the descent, turning right and heading past one of the eerie boarded-up mine entrances, along the path that led to Lacy's Caves.

As he hobbled along, Franko prayed not to fall into the river, which – fed by the staggering amount of rain that was pouring down – now raged to his left. If he could only get far enough ahead for the creature to lose sight of him for a few moments, he could hide in the caves until morning, and then try to make his way back home, or to the nearest farm.

Franko cast a desperate glance over his shoulder and saw that the crone had indeed fallen behind – he knew that she was following, but she was far enough away for him not to see her in the dense fog. Mustering the remains of his strength, he climbed the short steep path up to Lacy's Caves and crept inside. Feeling his way carefully along the walls in the pitch blackness, he moved to the farthermost chamber and slumped against a wall, close to one of the other entrances, which opened directly out of the embankment onto the wild, rainwater-swollen river below. There he half crouched, half lay in the darkness, trying to still his racing heart and quieten his breathing.

Franko knew Lacy's Caves well, but not the details of their inception. Had he been familiar with their history, the irony of his choice of hiding-place would have been lost on him in any case, given his current predicament.

Lacy's Caves had been created on the orders of the same man

who'd tried to blow up Long Meg and Her Daughters. Colonel Samuel Lacy, an eighteenth century dandy who seemed hell-bent on perfecting nature (and the work of anyone who'd gone before him) had – presumably after his failure to destroy the several thousand year old stone circle that stood on his land – ordered five chambers to be hacked out of the living rock overlooking the River Eden, for the amusement of himself and his fashionable friends. Samuel Lacy was long gone now, but his caves remained; making a lasting mark on the local landscape was perhaps what the Colonel had wanted all along.

Franko listened closely, but couldn't hear anything apart from the hissing river. As his breathing slowed, and the adrenaline in his body gradually dissipated, he realised how cold and tired he was, and not a little faint from the blow to his head and the dizzying chase through the woods. He started to wonder whether, in fact, getting hit on the head had caused him to imagine the whole insane episode with the monster – either that, or maybe Rizla's cousin hadn't been able to resist adding a little something extra to the Super Skunk that Rizla had scrounged off him. Just as Franko started to let his guard down, a shuffling noise in the darkness startled him. He pressed himself against the wall of the cave and tried to be as quiet as possible. But it was no use – a triumphant, rattling shriek pierced the silence, and the crone came leaping out of the shadows, straight for the terrified youth.

Franko stumbled back and, as he did so, his head spun; he lost his balance, and fell – right through the chamber opening, his body plunging into the wind and rain, and the raging river below. Had he held out a moment longer, Franko would have seen the first light of dawn fall into the cave, and the hideous crone writhe and transform into a young woman of delicate, unsurpassed beauty, then fade away to nothing and disperse in the early morning light.

Franko's body wasn't found and will probably wash up in the Solway Firth one day. His friends, on the other hand, were discovered by shocked tourists visiting the third largest stone circle in Britain. The police pathologist had no explanation as to why every bone in the young men's bodies was broken; he only commented that it was as though they'd been pulverised by the weight of a huge boulder. But the fact that the twelve-foot sandstone megalith commonly known as Long Meg was dripping with blood and other human tissue led officers to conclude that a Satanic cult was most likely involved. The site of Long Meg and Her Daughters was closed to the public, but further investigation revealed – nothing.

CYRIL'S MISSION

CYRIL'S MISSION

"**I** NOW PRONOUNCE you man and wife."

The sun streamed through the stained-glass window, painting the bride's dress blood red. Cyril wondered whether it would have bothered the newlyweds to know that the priest who'd just married them didn't believe in God. He guessed that it might have done, but fortunately they'd never find out. He cast a quick glance at the window responsible for the light that was bloodying the bride's white gown – his favourite panel, as it happened. It portrayed what at first glance appeared to be Saint George slaying the Dragon, but under closer scrutiny turned out to be a mounted knight, brandishing a flaming torch, and confronting something that resembled a giant earthworm. The bizarre group was silhouetted against a vast expanse of bright red sky.

Cyril blessed the congregation and led the happy couple and their witnesses to the sacristy, to sign the register. He hadn't been invited to the wedding reception, which suited him just fine. It would probably be a subdued, awkward affair in any case. Since the disappearance of little Mary Croft at the beginning of the month, and then Ollie Frampton a fortnight later, the village of Mortkirk had become a melancholy and fearful place.

Once the wedding party left, Cyril drank the rest of the communion wine and headed to the rectory – in which he lived – to re-acquaint himself with the whisky bottle that was waiting for him in the cupboard. The disappearance of the children only six months after his re-assignment to Mortkirk had hit Cyril hard, and when things hit him hard, Cyril hit the bottle.

The world was a bad place, Cyril knew that. Always had been. Always would be. Perhaps it was meant to be that way. Cyril would never be able to change the way things were or make the world a better place, but as long he was in it, he would do the best he could for his parishioners. And if the best he could do involved feeding them lies about a benevolent God who would forgive them their sins and welcome them with open arms into a better place, then so be it. If he could listen to their woes, comfort them in their times of need, and offer help to the homeless and hungry among them, then it was worth him living his 'little lie', and staying in the priesthood, where he had access to funds that enabled him to help those who needed it most. Besides, what else would he do? He was nearing sixty now. His alcoholism had rendered his nose a puffy red and his face a battleground of tiny broken blood vessels. His drinking habit did nothing for his psoriasis either, and his itchy scalp flaked, so that dandruff-like skin coated his cassock a manner that put off even the most desperate of his female parishioners. No, there was no doubt about it: the Church was his home. Always had been. Always would be. Perhaps it was meant to be that way. But when it came to the possibility of some bastard abducting children, Cyril's carefully constructed philosophy of life fell apart.

Cyril hadn't always lived in Mortkirk. He'd come from Ireland originally, where, as a young boy he'd fallen into the hands of the Jesuits. They'd educated him well – he'd been sent to a seminary in Rome, and later completed doctoral studies in philosophy and theology at Greyfriars College, Oxford. Despite his aptitude for academia, Cyril decided that a scholarly and monastic life was not for him. He was ordained to the priesthood, where he hoped that he'd be able to fulfil what he'd come to recognise as his mission in life: to ease the suffering of society's most vulnerable souls.

Through contacts made at university, Cyril soon became pastor of a London parish, but his questioning attitude and maverick outlook alienated him from his fellow priests and put him on the wrong side of the local bishop. His liberal views on everything from women priests to contraception, and his staunch belief in tolerance and forgiveness, rather than the fire and brimstone sermonising favoured by many of his colleagues, isolated him from his peers and bosses, and eroded his faith in the Church. When a priest from a neighbouring parish was caught abusing children and the bishop swept the whole despicable business under the carpet, Cyril stopped believing in God. He drank himself into a rage and threatened to go to the police and the press. Cyril's dissent proved too much for the bishop. Excommunication was not an option, so Cyril's punishment was exile to a small and isolated village in the northeast of England.

Despite a population of over one thousand, Mortkirk had the atmosphere of a ghost town. Once it had been a thriving community coalesced around the alum mines owned by the Huntley family. When old Lord Huntley died childless in 1956, his nephew John inherited the house, grounds and mines. Not wishing to leave his home in the United States, John Huntley sold off the family estate, and the mines were duly closed. The Mortkirk community collapsed. Those still able to work drifted to Newcastle and other major cities, taking their families with them. Members of the older generation gradually died out or were coerced to move away by developers whose task it was to tear down the old cottages and build a new town of cheap housing that would serve to remove immigrants and other undesirables from the more picturesque and profitable areas nearby.

It was into this social and spiritual void that Cyril arrived, to find a displaced, discordant populace of lost souls, with no sense of history, culture, identity or self-worth. The only shared experience of Cyril's new flock was that of the daily struggle to make ends meet. But they had one other thing in common, thought Cyril: the astonishingly beautiful Mortkirk Church, which the original village had been named after and which, in comparison to the ugly, style-less new build developments nearby, looked like a stunning exotic bird that had been swept from its natural habitat by cruel winds and found itself in a barren wilderness.

Mortkirk Church had somehow survived the Reformation, when Henry VIII's troops swept through Britain, gutting Catholic monasteries and churches, and killing priests. Its stained glass dated back to medieval times and rivalled anything Cyril had seen in Rome. Cyril recognised the saints portrayed in the panels, and knew their histories, but the story of the giant worm, and the identity of the knight doing battle with it, eluded him. None of his congregation could enlighten him as to its origins, the local library had been closed due to financial cuts, and the internet yielded nothing either, so he put the mystery out of his mind and concentrated on his master plan: Cyril was determined that Mortkirk Church should become a haven and social centre for all of his parishioners – whatever their creed, colour, gender or sexual orientation.

All had gone well with Cyril's plan. In the brief time since his arrival, he had lobbied for funds and opened a soup kitchen. His Sunday school quickly became famous for its sandwiches, cakes, and the opportunity for children to spend the afternoon drawing and blowing up balloons. Hidden away from the disapproving scrutiny of his bosses, he had even managed to devise his own course on comparative theology, in which he taught children, and anyone else who wished to turn up, about the many great ideas their different religions shared, and how they could all live and even pray together, while remaining true to the ideals of their own particular doctrine – a feat, you would agree, truly astonishing for a non-believer. But Cyril believed in people and he believed in Love.

Then Mary Croft went missing. Cyril had been one of the last people to arrive in the parish, so he was one of the first on the police list of possible suspects when it came to the disappearance. It had taken the priest an unprecedented amount of effort to get the villagers to open up to him, and, when Ollie went missing too – after last being seen playing in the vicinity of the church, some of them started eyeing Cyril with mistrust, and stopped their children from attending his lessons, meals and services. Others, however, continued coming, and Cyril's Sunday school was still the highlight of his week. But today was Saturday, and he had to get ready for the more serious business of preparing the Catholic children for their First Holy Communion. With a sigh, he replaced the bottle of blended whisky in the cupboard and started looking for his notes.

As he rummaged around in the top drawer of the large antique chest of drawers in which he'd placed the manuscripts of his sermons and other useful documents, he felt something solid right at the back. It was an old, leather-bound volume, tied with a piece of string that disintegrated as Cyril attempted to untie it. He was surprised to see a list of names and dates and couldn't understand what a register of births and deaths was doing in the rectory rather than being locked away in the small archive in the sacristy, along with other important church documents. But a closer inspection revealed that the list was not an ordinary register.

The first sequence of dates – presumably copied from a much older book – spanned March, April and May 1114. Each date was preceded by a name and a number. Occasionally the annotation 'months' appeared next to the number. The numbers did not exceed 12, and most of them ranged from 5 to 10. Cyril figured that the numbers corresponded to the ages of children. Where a child was less than a year old, the figure given referred to months. Cyril felt the whisky he'd drunk earlier turn to acid in his stomach. He could only think of two occurrences that those dates might signify – the children's deaths or... their disappearance.

Cyril studied the dates closely. They started off about a fortnight apart, then increased to one a week, two a week, three a week. This pattern culminated in one child a day in the final week of May 1114, and then nothing. The occasional date, but nothing out of the ordinary. Until March 1414. Cyril knew that child and infant mortality was high in the Middle Ages. So the sparse entries between May 1114 and March 1414 could not be deaths. They were disappearances. Then in March 1414 the same pattern: dates starting off spaced apart, increasing in frequency and reaching a climax in the final week of May. Another three hundred years of the odd disappearance – nothing alarming. Then another spate of child disappearances in 1714. None of this made any sense. Then Cyril had a horrible thought. Seven-year-old Mary had disappeared on the third of March 2014, and nine-year-old Ollie on the seventeenth. Today was the twenty-fourth. Incomprehensible as it was, the pattern was undeniable and, if it was anything to go by, the disappearances of the two children could be the first of many, and the next one could occur any time now.

Cyril's mind raced. He could go to the police, but what would he tell them? They already had him down as a potential child abductor and possibly a paedophile. Adding 'delusional psychotic' to the list would only get him locked up and wouldn't help anyone. He could contact the church hierarchy, but they considered him an alcoholic and a loose cannon. And what good would telling anyone do in any case? Sick to his stomach, Cyril glanced at his watch and grimaced. It was too late to stop the children from coming to their Holy Communion lesson. He had to get back to the church and get ready for their arrival. He had no time to look for his notes; he'd deal with the matter in hand and then work out what to do next.

Preoccupied and upset, Cyril hastened to the church. There was a car parked outside and, as he got closer, a woman and a little boy got out.

"Mrs Jones!" Cyril smiled warmly as he recognised the pair. "Good to see you both!"

"Hello, Father Cyril." The woman's smile was slightly strained. "Father, I'm running a bit late. Is it okay if I leave Timmy with you?"

Cyril had a soft spot for Timmy. No, he had a soft spot for all his young parishioners, but Timmy did hold an extra special place in his heart. The eight-year-old had lost his hearing as a toddler – the result of a serious ear infection, and had never learnt to speak properly. He could use sign language and, thankfully for Cyril, lip-read a little as well. Timmy was a brave boy, though, and determined to receive his First Holy Communion with his classmates.

"Of course it's okay," Cyril assured the woman. "We'll have a grand old time, won't we Timmy?" Cyril bent down to the boy and signed a greeting, ruffling the child's hair. Timmy grinned broadly and signed a hello back.

"Thank you, Father." Mrs Jones hugged her son and got back in the car.

There was still half an hour before the class was due to start. Timmy enjoyed laying out hymnbooks and looking at the artwork adorning the church walls, so having him around while Cyril prepared the church would be no problem.

Cyril unlocked the church and led Timmy inside. He usually held his classes in the church hall, and occasionally even allowed the children into the exceptionally large sacristy, but the Eucharist lessons seemed to work best inside the church itself. Cyril could point out paintings and carvings of the saints, and show the children the tabernacle, which housed the Communion host. But as he now headed for the altar, Cyril heard a noise coming from the staircase that led to the crypt. He paused and listened, disturbed by the prospect of an intruder. The noise came again: a shuffling, slithering sound, as though something large was moving around down there.

Timmy had stopped when Cyril stopped, and now eyed the priest expectantly. Cyril turned to the boy, speaking slowly, and articulating each word as clearly as possible.

"Timmy, please go to the back of the church and sit down near the door. Wait for me. I have to check something. Please wait over there." Cyril pointed to the entrance door. "Okay?"

Timmy nodded and did as he was told. Cyril cautiously descended the stone stairs leading down to the crypt and unlocked the door, opening it slowly. The sounds stopped.

"Hello?" Cyril called out. "Who's there?" Silence. Cyril reached for the light switch and flicked it on. The sight that greeted him rooted him to the spot. It took a moment before he could fathom what he was looking at. Silhouetted in the dim light of the crypt was a huge, monstrous, wormlike creature. Its skin was brownish-pink and membranous. Stretched out on the floor, the abomination extended from one end of the crypt to the other. As Cyril stared at it, the beast reared up, its front half towering above him. The priest watched as a gaping maw opened in its featureless snout, exposing a halo of slavering flesh-coloured tentacles surrounding a set of sharp, lamprey-like teeth. A rush of air escaped the cavernous mouth, creating an angry hiss, like a violent gust of wind blowing through a cave. The beast drew back its head further still and prepared to strike.

Cyril came out of his stupor just as the thing lunged forward. He jumped back and tried to pull the heavy wooden door of the crypt shut behind him. But it was too late – the creature's head was through the door. In a split-second it extended its front half along the ground, then swiftly pulled up its latter half, moving forward and out of the crypt. Cyril cried out as the tentacles brushed his skin and the razor-sharp teeth snapped shut inches from his face. He ran up the steps, the thing slithering after him, and looked around for a makeshift weapon, shouting to Timmy to get out of the church. The boy was standing in the nave, transfixed by a painting of a man tied to a tree and gazing painfully up towards heaven, a dozen arrows protruding from his bleeding flesh. He didn't notice the commotion near the altar.

Cyril grabbed a heavy candlestick and swung it at the monster. He struck it hard, but made no discernible mark on its flank, and didn't appear to hurt the creature in the slightest. The beast's body was almost translucent; the blood vessels running the length of it partially visible through the skin. And yet the skin was hard, almost like an exoskeleton, and evidently extremely difficult to penetrate. The creature reared once more, and Cyril threw the candlestick at it and ran towards the entrance door.

"Timmy!" He spotted the boy by the painting of Saint Sebastian and headed towards him. Unfortunately, the worm had also seen the child, and was slithering towards its preferred, bite-size prey more rapidly than Cyril would have thought possible. "Timmy!"

Cyril reached the boy first and grasped his arm, planning to drag the startled child to the exit. But the creature blocked their way, rearing up and weaving its monstrous bulk form side to side. Cyril tried to pull Timmy past it, but the thing was incredibly fast, jerking its head to the side and blocking their escape route. Timmy screamed and Cyril seized him by the hand, pulling him back towards the sacristy. They ran as fast as they could and the worm followed, expanding and contracting its muscles as it rapidly propelled itself forward.

Cyril yanked open the door of the sacristy and pushed Timmy inside, slamming the door shut behind them. He fumbled with the key, but managed to lock them in. There was a loud thud as the beast threw its weight against the ancient wood on the other side. The door shuddered visibly and Timmy screamed again. Cyril pushed his back against the door and tried to work out what to do next. Timmy was staring past him, pale and shaking, eyes impossibly wide. Cyril put an arm on his shoulder.

"Timmy, look at me. It's going to be okay."

The door buckled as the creature slammed into it again. Cyril rushed over to an oak table that stood against the wall and managed to push it in front of the door. Then he snatched the telephone from the desk and dialled 999.

"Emergency services. Which service do you require?"

"Police!"

"Where are you calling from?"

Another thud, and the lock on the sacristy door gave way.

"Mortkirk Church!" Cyril shouted, then dropped the receiver and ran to the door again, pushing the table against it as hard as he could and leaning on it. But it wasn't going to hold.

Grabbing Timmy by the hand, Cyril ran to the cupboard in which he kept his secret stash. He reached into the back and pulled out a cigarette lighter and the two bottles of rectified spirit that a Polish priest had brought over as a present for him when he was still living in London.

"You must dilute it with vodka," his Eastern European colleague had told him.

Cyril hadn't drunk the gift; he had kept the 190-proof alcohol as a kind of challenge, to prove to himself that no matter how bad his drinking got, he hadn't yet hit rock bottom. When he moved to Mortkirk, he took the bottles with him and hid them in the sacristy, for 'emergencies'. Well, one could certainly say he was having one now – thought Cyril, as he pulled a handkerchief out of his pocket, unscrewed one of the bottles, took a swig, gagged, then thrust the end of the handkerchief into the remaining liquid. He stuffed the other bottle as deep into his jacket pocket as he could, just as the creature burst into the room.

Cyril gripped Timmy by the shoulder and spun him round to face him, so the boy could read his lips.

"Stay behind me!" he shouted into the terrified child's face. Then he flicked the lighter on and held it to the protruding end of the handkerchief until it caught fire. The creature, which had advanced to within several feet of them, paused and raised its front half so that it loomed over the man and boy. But rather than preparing to strike, it seemed to pull its head away from the small flame, swaying from side to side, as if looking for a way around the fire. Cyril brandished the bottle in front of the monster's snout and, making sure that Timmy was behind him, sidled away from the beast, backing slowly towards the door leading back into the church. But before Cyril and Timmy reached the doorway, the flame reached the neck of the bottle. Cyril just managed to throw it in the direction of the beast before the glass exploded. The hastily thrown vessel missed the creature, and shattered on the floor by the window, sending the curtain up in flames. The worm was momentarily distracted, and the priest and boy managed to make their way past the overturned table and out of the door before it lunged forward again.

Cyril and Timmy made it out of the sacristy just as the other children started to arrive for the Eucharist class. Some of the parents dropped off their children and left, but most hung around at the back of the church for the duration of the class. Cyril spotted the group of seven- to ten-year olds and their parents before they spotted him. A couple of children were already heading for pews in front of the altar.

"Dear God!" moaned Cyril – out of habit rather than any trauma-induced resurgence of faith. He had to destroy the creature before it got out of the sacristy and went for the children. He quickly turned Timmy around to face him. "Run to the others!" he gasped. "Right now. Run!" Cyril gave the child a shove and turned back to face the beast. It had paused in the sacristy doorway, ascertaining the direction taken by its prey. It seemed to sense Timmy fleeing, but before it could react, Cyril had flicked on his lighter and managed to distract it. He pulled out the other bottle of spirit and unscrewed the top, only to realise that he had nothing to use as a fuse.

The lighter heated up quickly and Cyril's hand opened in a reflex reaction. The lighter fell to the floor and Cyril dropped to his knees, fumbling around until he found it again. The creature lunged forward and almost knocked the bottle out of the priest's hand, spilling some of the liquid onto itself. Cyril quickly backed away, allowing a rivulet of the alcohol to trickle onto the floor as he went. Then he threw the rest of the bottle at the beast, bent down to the near end of the stream of spirit, and set it alight.

Cyril's arm went up in flames, but so too did the creature. It reared up and fell crashing back into the sacristy, where it was engulfed in the fire that had spread rapidly through the wood-panelled room. Crying out in pain, Cyril managed to put out the flame that had shot up his arm, and stumbled in the direction of the waiting parents and children, just as Timmy fell crying into the arms of one of the mothers.

The sight of the dishevelled, terrified, wailing little boy running towards them had upset the parents and frightened the other children, some of whom had also started crying. Police officers had arrived on the scene and were making their way past the parents, towards the fire at the far end of the church. Static crackled from a police radio, as one of the officers radioed in to headquarters.

"Morris here. We need a fire engine out at Mortkirk Church."

Now all eyes fell on the abomination that was weaving its way erratically towards the officers and civilians from the direction of the sacristy. It was burnt, bloody, stinking and horrible to behold. And this monster – the one who had fooled them all with his kind words and warm smile, with his bible classes, his meals and his charity; the one from whom the little deaf-mute kid had miraculously escaped, scared out of his wits – how obvious it now was to all of them, that this was the monster that had been taking their children. Just another filthy paedophile priest, but this one was worse – this one was a child killer.

As the officers approached Cyril, they drew their weapons.

"Stop where you are!" WPC Morris warned Cyril. Even at a

distance of several metres, and through the smell of smoke and scorched flesh, she could smell the booze coming off the priest. "Put your hands in the air!"

"What? No! You don't understand!"

"Hands in the air!"

Cyril tried to raise his blistered hands out in front of him. Tears rolled down his soot-smeared face, and he swayed on his feet as the adrenaline left his body, and exhaustion, pain and distress threatened to overwhelm him.

"Is there anyone back there?" the policewoman demanded.

"No. Yes. The worm," Cyril stuttered. He yelped in pain as WPC Morris and another officer got hold of him and handcuffed his raw, bleeding hands behind his back. A third officer made an attempt to reach the sacristy, but the flames forced him back.

"I don't see anyone else," the officer called back to his colleagues. "But it's an inferno back there. Where's the fire brigade?"

"Cyril Downey," WPC Morris and a colleague led Cyril towards the exit as she informed him of his rights. "I am arresting you for the attempted abduction of a minor. You do not have to say anything, but it may harm your defence if you do not mention when questioned something which you later rely on in court."

"You've got it wrong! Ask Timmy. Timmy will tell you."

"Timmy?" WPC Morris's tone was brimming with sarcasm. A resident of Mortkirk, she'd never warmed to the new priest. He looked creepy and acted too good to be true. "You mean the little boy who can't speak?" She exchanged a smirk with her male colleague. "Don't worry, Father, we'll be sure to take a full statement from Timmy."

The looks of hatred from the parents and fear from the children pierced Cyril's heart as surely as any weapon would have done. As he was led past Timmy, he cried out to the little boy.

"Timmy!"

But Timmy was being comforted by a couple of the mothers and a police officer, and had his back to the unfortunate priest and the officers who were leading him away. As Cyril was marched out of the church, something – instinct perhaps – made Timmy look to the church door. He caught sight of Cyril just as the priest disappeared from view beyond the doors of the church. Timmy broke away from the adults he was with, and raced after the departing group.

"Father Cyril!" he tried to shout, but the words came out as usual: mumbled, unintelligible and virtually inaudible. "Father Cyril!"

One of the dads saw the distressed little boy running for the exit and intercepted him, holding him firmly by the shoulders and trying to calm him down.

"Hey, little guy. Where you going?"

"Father Cyril!"

"What's that you're saying?" The child was completely incoherent, but the man could sense his distress. He held the boy tight so he couldn't run off in a panic and hurt himself. "Don't worry," he soothed. "He can't hurt you anymore. Let's see if we can find your mum."

Several of the parents had followed the disgraced priest out of the church.

"I hope you die and go to hell!" someone shouted as Cyril was bundled roughly into a police car.

Cyril didn't believe he'd be going to hell when he died. He was already in it.

TEATIME

TEATIME

THE CHILD'S BEDROOM was dark, lit only by a magic lantern night-light, which rotated large, blurred, coloured animal shapes on the walls. Cold moonlight fell through the window, illuminating the tear-stained face of a little girl with light blonde hair and pale blue eyes. Fear distorted the child's pretty face and, although her lips trembled, she remained completely silent. With one hand she pulled the duvet to her chest, with the other she clutched an old toy rabbit with long, floppy ears.

The handle on the bedroom door rattled. The girl sat up, terrified. The door started to open, and the child pushed back against the headboard, clutching her toy even more tightly.

As the door opened, some dim light spilled in from the corridor, silhouetting the man who now entered the room. The girl started sobbing as the man approached. She shook her head in protest and mustered all her courage to send the intruder away.

"Go away!" she cried as the man came closer, "I don't want to play with you!"

"It's all right, darling," the man soothed as he reached the bed, "Daddy loves you."

"No, Daddy! No!" The little girl lost her grip on her toy and the rabbit dropped out of sight, into the darkness.

Eighteen years later and the early autumn sun lit up the tree-lined suburban street. The houses were large in this part of Cardiff, each with an ample front garden or a driveway. On a corner of the street, at its intersection with another, larger one, a young engineer was repairing a telephone junction box. A sudden gust of wind whipped up some russet and blood-coloured leaves and blew them along the pavement. The engineer shivered and turned around, thinking for a moment that he heard the click of a woman's high-heeled shoes hurrying past, but there was nobody there. He turned his attention back to the job at hand, peering closely at the multi-coloured tangle of spaghetti that were the telephone cables he was supposed to sort out. He paused for a moment to wipe his brow and that was when he heard the voice behind him.

"Bad one?"

The engineer looked up to see a well-dressed man of about thirty smiling down at him. The man wore an elegant suit with a neatly buttoned shirt and tasteful tie. He was carrying a leather briefcase. It was too early in the afternoon for him to be a businessman coming home from work, and the engineer guessed that he was probably a door-to-door salesman of some sort.

"Not really," replied the engineer. "Just one line messed up. Shouldn't take more than forty minutes."

The man nodded understandingly – one working man to another.

"Well I'm off. Take care."

The engineer nodded a goodbye and turned his attention back to the wires. He didn't notice the man pick up a tiny piece of discarded wire that had been lying on top of the junction box and put it in his pocket.

Victor was twenty-six, but looked older. He'd taken his mother's death badly – very badly. Ever since his father had passed away – an event that Victor had been too young to remember – it had been just Victor and his mother. She'd been Victor's number one fan and had been beside herself with pride when her golden boy was offered a place at Oxford University to study Experimental Psychology.

Victor was a very promising student. He particularly impressed his tutors when he expressed his intention to study the effects of fear on animal behaviour. There was no doubt that Victor was a bright and capable young man. His only problem seemed to be his lack of interpersonal skills – no, that wasn't quite it. He did have interpersonal skills because he could be very charming when he wanted to. It was the fact that he seemed to glean a perverse enjoyment from talking to people about subjects that made them feel uncomfortable. Once he struck upon – or teased out – what it was that someone didn't want to talk about – and this was particularly true when the conversant was a young woman – Victor seemed unable to change the subject. A peculiar glint appeared in his eye and he would insist on delving further and further until his conversation partner made her hasty excuses and left. This may have explained why handsome, intelligent and charming Victor never seemed to keep a girlfriend. This, and the fact that no woman would ever adore Victor unconditionally the way his mother did.

Victor's supervisor certainly lavished no unconditional adoration on him. At thirty-six, Dr Gilby, who looked ten years younger, was respected by some of her colleagues, avoided by others. Holding her own in the predominantly male world of Experimental Psychology, she had turned down a number of propositions from male colleagues in no uncertain terms and made it clear that she was not someone to be messed with. Her hard, untouchable stance had made her a few enemies in the Psychology Department and even student opinion on her was divided. The students from her college – Oxford's last remaining women's college – appreciated her 'firm but fair' approach and benefited from her warmth and support. Students from other colleges, especially arrogant young men, found her a little cold and critical.

Victor didn't like Dr Gilby – she had failed to be taken in by his friendly smile and charming ways. She was a frigid bitch, probably a dyke – thought Victor – despite all the photographs of her smiling husband and three enthusiastic children that she had pasted ostentatiously all over her lab. And now she was to be Victor's supervisor. She was the only member of the Psychology Department who specialised in Animal Behaviour and, rather than handing Victor over to a tutor from the Zoology Department, it was decided that Dr Gilby should supervise Victor's research.

Victor's research would test how fear affected the responses of rats to novelty. The experimental group of rats would be conditioned to expect a mild electric shock every time a buzzer sounded. They would then be familiarised with a group of objects – small toys of different types – by daily exposure to these items. Then their reaction to a novel object – a toy they hadn't seen before – would be tested with and without the concomitant sounding of the buzzer which they had learnt to associate with electric shock and hence to fear. A computer connected to the rats' maze would track all the movements made by the animals and process them, ready for analysis. The responses of the experimental rats to the novel object would be compared with those of a control group that had not been given electric shocks and therefore had no conditioned fear. After the various random influences that could be acting upon the rats' behaviour were factored out, an analysis of the results would show how rats' responses to novelty – normally cautious exploration – were affected by fear. Victor had come up with the idea for this research himself and was the only student in his year studying this topic. His experiment would give him lots of extra credits towards his practical work score. But unfortunately he needed Dr Gilby and her laboratory equipment.

Victor decided to go to work on Dr Gilby. He turned up one day in the lab with two cups of strong tea from the canteen; this was Dr Gilby's favourite beverage. He knocked on the lab door.

"Come in."

"Good morning, Dr Gilby. I got us these." Victor held out a cup of tea like a peace offering.

"Thank you, Victor, but you know there's a kettle in the lab. You shouldn't waste your money." Dr Gilby took the drink. She'd been poring over some paperwork and didn't notice the sudden flash of ill-concealed anger in Victor's eyes.

"I know, Doctor, but you don't have *these* in your lab." Victor smiled, producing two fresh donuts in a paper bag and holding them out to his supervisor.

"Oh, Victor, you really shouldn't have." Dr Gilby got a couple of plates out of a cupboard and placed the donuts on them, gesturing for Victor to sit down next to her. The young man's efforts to win her over melted her somewhat and she wondered whether she'd been wrong about him, but there was something about him that didn't seem quite right.

Victor beamed at Dr Gilby over his polystyrene cup. Now that she'd let her guard down, he'd make sure she never put him down again.

"So, how come you work with rats?" he asked.

Dr Gilby looked surprised. "Well, they are the easiest animals to work with in a laboratory. White rats, as you know, are bred to be passive – not to bite humans, and so on. They are relatively cheap to keep, they reproduce rapidly and their DNA is close enough to humans' to render them valid test subjects in place of people."

Victor laughed. "No, I mean, how come you're not afraid of them, like so many women... er... people?"

"What's there to be afraid of? They don't bite, they don't scratch; they're not poisonous even if they did. They're not dangerous in any way."

"But people are afraid of animals that aren't dangerous. There aren't any dangerous spiders in Britain, for example, but many people are afraid of spiders."

"Well, yes," Dr Gilby agreed. "The common phobias do seem to have been useful to humans in an evolutionary sense, such as fear of darkness in a time when men lived in caves and to venture out at night meant possible death from a wild animal, a fall, etc. Now, in the age of technology, these phobias persist, but are no longer particularly useful to mankind."

"Some still are," argued Victor. "Like blood phobia; the phobic person sees blood, their blood pressure drops and they faint. The fainting isn't particularly pleasant, but the drop in blood pressure can lessen bleeding, which might save a person's life."

"Sure. I'm not saying all phobias are useless, but most of them have outgrown their usefulness to mankind and tend to hinder rather than help."

"So, what are *you* afraid of?" asked Victor, catching Dr Gilby by surprise. Dr Gilby didn't like to get personal – with colleagues or with students. But she also believed in directness and honesty.

"Snakes," she said simply.

"Oh." Victor could barely disguise his sense of triumph. "Yes, snakes are pretty nasty. The way they move – slither – and the way their tongues flick in and out. And of course, many of them are deadly. And they have so many ways of killing you. They can poison you, or suffocate you, or paralyse you and swallow you whole, breaking all your bones, and then digest you while you're still alive."

"Well, I think we've chatted long enough," interrupted Dr Gilby. "I believe you have some work to do."

"Oh, yes. I'd best be getting on with it." Victor smiled sweetly and went to get his rats.

Dr Gilby watched him go. She'd been right about him after all. He really was a little creep.

Several days later Dr Gilby forgot to pick up her car keys from the top drawer of her desk and had to go back to the lab after a staff meeting that had ended late. She was getting increasingly worried about Victor's research; a number of rats had died – an unprecedented occurrence in the Psychology Department, in which all the rats used in experiments were young and healthy. Sure, animals were humanely disposed of when the experiments they were involved in had been completed, and animals did die occasionally after brain surgery or drug tests, but never during simple, non-invasive experiments. Perhaps a disease had somehow spread among the rats – now, that would be a major cause for concern – but unfortunately Victor had disposed of the bodies before she'd had a chance to look at them.

She'd had words with Victor and he had smirked at her in his usual way and made all the right noises, "Yes, Dr Gilby. I'll make sure you see the body if another rat dies" and so on. But his sincerity left much to be desired.

As Dr Gilby approached the lab door, she heard the tiny high-pitched scream of a small animal. She immediately recognised it to be the scream of a rat, although she'd never heard a rat scream before. The animal was evidently in great pain. Besides, there shouldn't be any rats in the lab. The animals were all kept in special living quarters – a large room stacked full of cages – and were only brought out for a couple of hours a day when required for a particular experiment. Perhaps that idiot Victor had accidentally left a rat inside the maze and the creature had somehow got itself caught on something. Dr Gilby rushed into the lab. She stopped short as she caught sight of Victor, who'd been working with his back to the door and was now staring at her, a startled expression on his face.

"What the hell is going on?" demanded Dr Gilby.

"I was just trying to get ahead..." But Dr Gilby had already pushed past Victor and was staring in horror at the scene before her. On the large laboratory table that served as the base for Victor's maze was a mini torture chamber for rats. One little creature was hanging by its throat from a tiny gallows, its back paws twitching their last. Another rat had been nailed using tacks onto a small wooden cross, a vast number of pins sticking out in all directions from its blood-matted fur. Mercifully, these two animals were dead now, but the terrible stench of burning flesh was coming from a third rat – one that was still alive. The helpless creature was connected via a number of electrodes to the electric shock generator used to condition fear in rats by giving them small shocks. The electricity had been set to maximum and it was apparent that the creature had been systematically electrocuted with bouts of electricity that had been great enough to burn right through its fur and into its flesh. One of its eyes had been burnt out and now bubbled slightly in the neon glare of the laboratory lights. Dr Gilby stared in horror – and then relief – as the rat gave out a final whimper and breathed its last. She turned slowly to look at Victor.

"After I'm through with you, no reputable university will touch you with a barge pole."

And Dr Gilby kept her promise. After a week-long suspension, the Proctors of Oxford University decided to send Victor down for good. And it was made abundantly clear that he should be grateful not to have been handed over to the police.

Victor's mother took his expulsion badly – very badly. She never blamed Victor. Instead, she cried and cried, and cursed the slut who'd had Victor expelled. A month later she was diagnosed with cancer, and Victor blamed the cancer on his expulsion, and his expulsion on Dr Gilby.

Victor nursed his mother with great devotion. He fed her and bathed her and listened to her voice her bloodcurdling fear of the disease raging silently inside her. Victor listened as his mother spoke of the fear and the pain, and the fact that she would die slowly, eaten inch by inch, cell by cell, until her devastated body could stand it no longer. Victor held his mother's hand as the cancer, which had finally reached her brain, took away her speech and threw her emaciated frame all over the hospital bed in one last life-ending spasm. When his mother's pain-filled life was finally over and her body buried in the local cemetery, Victor locked himself in the home they had shared and planned his revenge. Six weeks later Dr Gilby was found crushed to death by the Oxford University Zoology Department's giant python – it took staff twenty minutes to pull the python's jaws off the tutor's face – and Victor set up his own cancer research charity, going door-to-door and offering raffle tickets for holidays and other prizes in return for a few pounds.

Five years had passed. Victor now walked away from the telephone engineer at a leisurely pace and pressed a couple of doorbells on the tree-lined street. The houses were large and it was hard to tell if there was anyone in.

He had enjoyed watching Dr Gilby die. He had enjoyed it very much, but he had enjoyed telling her how she was going to die even more. Dr Gilby's eyes had become impossibly wide – so wide that Victor thought they were going to burst out of their sockets. And the woman's heart had beaten so fast he thought she'd have a heart attack. But she didn't. She stayed conscious as the giant python wrapped its coils around her and squeezed. Sure, she passed out a couple of times, but Victor slapped her and she came to, only to be thrown into a world of fear and pain all over again. Eventually her bones started to break and the breath was squeezed out of her lungs.

It was good – death was good – but nevertheless it was something of an anti-climax after dying. And as Victor sat for a few minutes, watching the python try its damnedest to fit the woman's head into its mouth – sadly he could only allow himself a few minutes before making himself scarce – he realised that killing Dr Gilby would never be enough.

As Victor moved from one house to the next, an elderly woman passed by with a small dog. The dog growled at Victor.

"Coco, stop it!" cried the old lady, genuinely appalled, it seemed, at her baby's behaviour towards the nice young man in the elegant suit. "I'm terribly sorry," she told Victor.

"Oh, it's perfectly all right." Victor smiled charmingly. "He's obviously a great guard dog,"

"Oh, no. He's perfectly harmless, you know. He wouldn't even hurt a killer if he were trying to murder me."

Victor beamed. "Well, he's a lovely dog just the same."

"Thank you. Come on, Coco." The old lady dragged the growling dog away down the street and Victor turned his attention back to the doorbell at hand.

Camille could hear the doorbell ringing. She stood in the middle of the large sitting room – a small, dark haired figure, pretty in a tired sort of way, with an anxious look on her face. She didn't like opening the door to strangers, but the doorbell kept ringing and whoever this was didn't seem to be about to go away.

Camille glanced into a huge wall mirror, adjusted her hair and made her way slowly into the hall. There was a sudden burst of rain and the stranger outside started banging on the door. Camille put the chain on the door and opened it.

"Yes?" the woman spoke with a slight foreign accent.

"Good afternoon, madam. Sorry to disturb you. I'm here on behalf of the Cancer Research Charitable Fund."

"Just a moment," the woman interrupted him. "I'll get some money for you."

Camille closed the door and retreated into the house. Victor waited on the doorstep, trying to peer between the garden bushes that obscured the front window and get a view into the sitting room.

Camille came back with a handful of coins. She opened the door and went to put the coins in a collection box, then realised that Victor wasn't holding one, and backed off a little, somewhat flustered. Victor noticed her suspicion and opened his briefcase.

"Oh, I'm sorry. I haven't given you an envelope." Victor produced a small envelope with 'Cancer Research Charitable Fund' written on it, together with a competition entry form. He held the envelope out to Camille, who put her coins into it.

"Thank you very much. And here's a competition for you to enter."

"Oh." Camille hesitated. "I'm not very good with things like that."

"Don't worry, Madam." Victor managed his best smile despite the rain. "It's very simple." He shut his briefcase and showed Camille the entry form.

"All you need to do is answer a few simple questions and you can win a holiday for two to Paris."

"I haven't been to Paris for a long time," mused Camille, "but I never win anything."

"Well, maybe today your luck's going to change."

There was a distant rumble of thunder and the rain started to fall more heavily.

"I can help you answer the questions if you like," carried on Victor, the rain increasingly interrupting his salesman's banter. "Oh, this rain..." he commented. "... For example, here you have to..."

Camille relented.

"Maybe you'd better come in for a while, out of the rain."

"Yes, why not? Thank you." Victor smiled triumphantly and followed Camille into her home.

The stranger soon put Camille at ease with his charming manners and the compassion with which he told her all about the cancer charity he was running. Before Camille knew it, they were on first name terms and they were sitting together, sipping tea and eating the cake that she'd baked for her husband.

Victor helped Camille fill out a simple questionnaire, which was a prerequisite of entering the competition. One of the questions asked about the interviewee's greatest fear.

"That's a strange question," Camille was concerned.

"Oh, don't be alarmed," soothed Victor. "The question is very important for the research we carry out. You see, more people than is commonly known have a strong fear of something. Sometimes the phobia is so bad that it affects the person's life, such as being afraid to leave the house. And it is a little-known fact that many people actually have a phobia of getting cancer, which can affect what they eat and where they go."

Camille still didn't see how answering a question about phobias would help in cancer research, but Victor seemed very keen for her to answer all the questions and she wanted to please him. He was being so nice to her, even though he didn't need to be once she'd given him the money he was after. Reluctantly Camille admitted that since earliest childhood she'd been terrified of choking while swallowing even the smallest tablet. This had been a constant source of friction in her household. Her parents had been furious with her every time she was ill and refused to take her medicine. She'd been traumatised for many years by her father's attempts to make her swallow pills, until some sympathetic doctor had displayed an unmitigated stroke of genius – alas, so rare in the medical profession these days – and suggested that Camille's parents should crush her tablets and dissolve them in water or sprinkle them in food if there was no syrup medicine alternative.

Victor listened to Camille's tales of childhood woe with a growing excitement. Camille seemed quite emotional as she finished confessing all to Victor and, when she fell silent, he took his cue and started spinning a tale of his own. He told Camille how in his youth he'd assisted a sword swallower in a circus. He then vividly described how he himself had swallowed knives, live rats and neon tubes. Camille listened with growing alarm. She asked Victor to stop several times, but he went on to describe various accidents that he'd seen occur when handles had come off knives during swallowing acts, how neon tubes had burst in people's chests and how snakes had slipped through their handlers' grasping fingers and slithered "all the way down the gullet and into the guts".

Victor's expertise on the subject seemed inexhaustible and his stories endless, and Camille's requests for him to leave fell on deaf ears. The woman became progressively more hysterical and eventually threatened to call the police. Camille went for the phone and Victor went for Camille, getting between her and the telephone. Camille started to panic and, as Victor moved in on her, she grabbed a golf club from her husband's golf bag and brandished it at her attacker. Strong and nimble for his relatively small size, it took Victor seconds to overpower Camille. He held her down, relishing the terror in her eyes, and slowly forced a golf ball into her mouth and then, ever so slowly, down her throat. Camille struggled and gagged, but Victor was stronger and she didn't stand a chance. Eventually the terrible pain ceased as the golf ball stopped all air getting into her lungs and Camille suffocated.

Victor let Camille's body fall back on the floor and sat by her, waiting for his erection to subside. Then he dropped the little piece of telephone wire by her body, finished his tea and took his teacup to the kitchen. He put on a pair of thin latex gloves, washed his teacup and wiped it carefully, replacing it among similar cups. Finally he returned to the sitting room, carefully wiping off any fingerprints he might have left on the golf club and anywhere else he could think of, took a final look at Camille's puffy face, gaping mouth and bulging, tear-filled eyes, picked up his leather case and let himself out.

Victor swiftly slipped off the gloves and returned them to his jacket pocket. He was still tingling with pleasure and figured that he'd go home and relive his tea with Camille in his mind. How unimaginative must those people be who took trophies from their victims, or recorded their crimes with a smartphone or camera. Surely, humans were intelligent enough not to need such props. They had the wonderful gift of memory – of being able to recall and relive experiences in the mind alone.

Victor, it seemed, was already starting to relive his last house visit in his mind, when he was startled by a woman's piercing scream. The scream came again, and Victor moved swiftly in the direction from which he thought it was coming. Sure enough, he turned a corner to find a young woman in her front garden, pruning scissors in one hand, screaming and pawing frantically at her hair.

"Madam, what's wrong?" called Victor, eventually succeeding in distracting the woman long enough to ascertain what the problem was.

"Spider!" the woman managed to squeal, before resuming her violent hand gestures.

"Don't move. Please stay still and I'll get it," Victor moved towards the woman and she froze long enough for him to pull the offending creature out of her hair.

"Don't look, madam," warned Victor. "It's a big one. I'll get rid of it."

He carried the stunned spider around the corner and let it loose in a neighbouring garden. The spider sat uncertainly on the ground. Victor looked at it, feeling magnanimous about sparing its life, then changed his mind and brought his shiny black shoe firmly down on the cowering creature. He wiped his shoe on the pavement and hurried back to the young woman.

"It's gone," he said proudly, giving the woman his winning smile.

"I can't thank you enough. You must think I'm so stupid." The woman was in her late twenties, with thick auburn hair and bright green eyes.

"Not at all," Victor reassured her. "I know quite a lot about phobias; they're more common than you think. In fact, I might even be able to help you."

"Oh, I think I'm beyond help." The woman smiled, then, taking a good look at Victor, added, "But you're welcome to try... Would you like to come in for tea?"

"I'd love to, but I'm afraid I can't today. I have some important business to attend to, related to my charity. It's a cancer charity," he explained.

"I see." The woman actually looked disappointed. God, these housewives really were desperate sluts, thought Victor. This leafy suburbia was nothing short of paradise. Victor couldn't understand why every horny postman, milkman, door-to-door salesman and delivery boy in South Wales wasn't packing his bag, briefcase or milk float and hightailing it into the area. Still, the fact that they weren't was all the better for him.

"Perhaps I could come back on Thursday?" Victor ventured shyly.

"Yes, why not?" The woman seemed pleased.

"Say about four?"

"Four would be fine. I don't think I'll be doing any more gardening for a while, so just ring the doorbell when you arrive."

"Great," said Victor. "Perhaps you could have the kettle on?"

He left the woman smiling and hurried to the anonymity of an Internet café, to surf the net.

It was late evening and a cold wind stirred the fallen leaves outside the large house. Inside, a small female figure sat alone in the shadows, watching a news report on the television.

It seemed that two women had been killed in broad daylight in their own homes in the local area. One had been suffocated with a golf ball; police ruled out accidental death because of defensive marks and bruises on the woman's body. A British Telecom engineer had been arrested in connection with the crime.

Force had also been used to restrain the other dead woman. She had been tied up and apparently tortured with a variety of large spiders. There were many bites on her body from a number of different spiders, none of them native to Britain, but just one of them had been venomous enough to kill her – that of the Australian funnel web spider, found only in the greater Sydney metropolitan area. The police had been forced to bring in the spider expert from Bristol Zoo to capture the arachnids, which had spread throughout the victim's house. It was uncertain whether all of them had been caught, and local residents were warned to keep an eye out in their gardens, sheds and even inside their homes for any furry friends that might have got away.

The owner of a specialist spider and reptile online pet store had been arrested for the illegal supply of dangerous animals, but the address to which he had delivered the spiders, with strict instructions to leave the package containing them behind a bush in the front garden, had turned out to belong to an elderly lady who knew nothing of any spiders and had no idea what the Internet was. The police were trying to work out if the two crimes were connected and how smart the BT engineer really was. Of course, not all the details of the investigation had been released to the public – just enough to shock local residents and disturb the rest of the nation.

The woman in the shadows switched off the television. Her silhouette momentarily reflected in the black screen as the moon appeared from behind a cloud and threw some scant light in through the large window. Then the wind outside grew in force, battering against the window and letting out a high-pitched whine as it curled its way around the house. A wind-blown cloud obscured the moon once more and the woman was plunged into darkness.

Victor sat in the doctor's waiting room, worried about his cough. He'd had a dry scratchy cough for a few days now, and he wondered whether perhaps it was cancer. With his mother it had been different; she'd started feeling breathless and the condition had gradually worsened until she'd been forced to go to the doctor. Victor was not experiencing breathing difficulties, but he wasn't going to leave anything to chance.

He sat quietly; the collar of his jacket pulled up around his mouth so he wouldn't catch any germs from the people around him. He didn't want to be drawn into any conversation, so he pretended to read a ludicrously out-of-date magazine on home furnishings and tried not to make eye contact with anyone.

"I'm here for a tetanus jab." A young woman had sat down next to Victor. He tried to ignore her, but she carried on regardless. "The doctor said I have to have one, but I think I'd rather get tetanus than have an injection."

"Is that so?" Victor turned to study the woman. She was probably in her late twenties, with short brown hair and coral-coloured lipstick.

"Well, maybe that's a slight exaggeration, but I *am* really scared of needles."

"Are you scared of the blood?"

"No, not the blood. It's more the needle going in. Just thinking about it makes me feel funny. Oh – that's me. Wish me luck."

"Good luck," said Victor, suddenly feeling a whole lot better.

Victor left the surgery without waiting for his appointment and sat on a nearby bench until the woman with the short brown hair came out. A sudden gust of wind brought with it a flurry of brown and gold autumn leaves and the click of high heels on paving stone. Victor was so preoccupied with following his quarry that he failed to notice the other woman who kept pace on the far side of the road, a wisp of pale blonde hair escaping the hood of her long black coat.

"But we're not strangers," Victor explained. "We met yesterday."

"I don't remember any such thing." The woman with the short brown hair peered at the man on her doorstep through the narrow opening allowed by her door-chain.

"You sat next to me at the doctor's surgery. You were having a tetanus jab and you were really nervous about it. By the way, how was it? Not too bad, I hope."

There was a pause as the woman reached back in her mind.

"Oh my God, you're right. We did meet yesterday." The woman's tone changed. Despite the shadowy hallway in which she was standing, Victor imagined that he could see her blush. "I'm so sorry. I didn't recognise you."

"Oh, don't worry about it. Your mind was on other things yesterday."

"What a coincidence, you knocking on my door. Please, come in; tell me more about your charity."

The woman unchained the door.

"I'm sorry about the mess." She smiled nervously as Victor glanced quickly up and down the street and slipped past her into her home. "I was just about to clean the house when you rang."

"Oh, please, there's nothing to apologise for; you have a lovely home," enthused Victor, hiding his disgust at the dusty sitting room, the withered flowers in the vase on the mantelpiece and the dead fly on the windowsill. He told himself that a filthy trollop who obviously sponged off a hard-working man and did nothing all day, who couldn't even be bothered to keep the house clean for her husband to come home to, deserved to die slowly and painfully; deserved to die in exactly the manner that he had planned for her. He couldn't be bothered with idle chatter today; he just wanted to drink his tea and get to the enjoyable part of the proceedings as quickly as possible.

"Please, sit down." The woman smiled at Victor and motioned to a leather armchair, sitting herself down opposite. "I made such a fool of myself yesterday. I feel so stupid. It's just that I've always had this thing about needles."

"I understand," reassured Victor. The woman smiled in response. "No, really, I *do* understand," continued Victor. "I'm scared of needles too."

"Really?" The woman looked at Victor incredulously.

"Yes. I've been afraid of injections ever since I was a child." The woman nodded sympathetically and Victor carried on, "I remember being vaccinated for the first time when I was little."

"Wow," said the woman. "You must have been *really* little."

"Oh yes, I was. I was tiny, and the needle was huge." The woman winced, much to Victor's delight. "Those were the days when they still used really large needles. I remember it piercing my skin and poking around, looking for my vein."

"But I thought vaccines were injected into muscles, not into veins." The woman looked puzzled.

"Not that one," retorted Victor. "Anyway, my veins were very small, you see, and the doctor had to make several attempts to find one, what with the needle being so large." The woman frowned and Victor felt the first wave of excitement growing in his stomach. "I was screaming and the nurse was holding me down, and the doctor was sticking the needle into my arm again and again – you know, the soft part of the arm, in the bend on the underside of the elbow..."

"It sounds horrible." The woman interrupted Victor's story. She felt sorry for him; poor man – he seemed to be even more frightened of injections than she was. But he wasn't helping himself by obsessing the way he did. These things were best not dwelt on. "But it was a long time ago, perhaps you should try to forget about it," she concluded, hoping her comment would close the subject. It did not.

"Do you remember the first injection you had?" asked Victor. His tenacity was beginning to make his hostess uncomfortable.

"Just talking about it makes me feel faint. Perhaps you could tell me about your charity."

"Oh, but it's very important to talk about one's phobias; that's the only way to cure them, you know. Why don't you tell me about the first time you had an injection; it will help, you know." Victor smiled at the woman encouragingly.

"I really can't remember. And I'd rather not talk about it, if you don't mind."

"Oh no, no, of course not," responded Victor. "You know, I still can't work out what's worse: the sting when the needle goes in or the poking around to get the vein, or the cold feeling when the liquid goes into the vein and you can feel it spreading through your arm..."

"Look, I'd really rather not talk about this."

"I'm just trying to help you. You don't think I enjoy talking about needles, do you? I just want to help you. I know what it's like to be afraid. I was afraid too, but I cured myself. Would you like to know how I did that?"

"I..." The woman held up a hand in protest, but there was no stopping Victor.

"I took a needle – a large sewing needle – and I stuck it through the skin on my arm, all the way through the skin, like body piercing, you know. And then I took another one and I..."

"Look, I'm sorry. I don't think..."

"I put it all the way through my skin, just above the other one. It hurt a lot, my arm bled, but I took the entire packet of sewing needles and I..."

The woman got up from her seat, visibly upset.

"I'm sorry, but I think it's best if you left now," she told Victor, her voice shaking.

"Leave?" Victor remained seated. "But we haven't even had tea yet."

"Tea?" The woman sounded confused. "Look, I'm sorry. This was a mistake. Maybe we can do this another time, but right now I'm not in the mood to talk."

"Not in the mood to talk? *You're* the one who started talking to *me*. Maybe *I* wasn't in the mood to talk *yesterday*, but I was nice to you. I tried to make you feel less scared about your injection. And now I've taken time out from my busy schedule to try to help you overcome your fear, and you tell me that you're not in the mood to talk."

"I'm sorry..."

"You will be."

"What?"

"I said, you will be."

"I want you to leave... right now!"

"I'm going," said Victor. He picked up his briefcase and moved towards the front door. The woman followed nervously, ready to lock the door behind him the second that Victor was out, but as he got to the front door Victor paused and, placing his briefcase on the floor, slipped his right hand into his pocket.

"What is it?" The woman stopped behind him.

"Just putting my gloves on," Victor explained.

"Can't you do that outside?"

His latex gloves on, Victor spun round and punched the woman in the face.

"No," he said.

The woman went down hard, her broken nose bleeding all over the carpet in the hallway. Before she managed to make a sound, Victor had produced a roll of gaffer tape from his briefcase, ripped a piece off and stuck it over his victim's mouth. He grabbed her by the arm and dragged her back into the sitting room.

Tears flowed from the woman's terrified eyes as Victor secured her hands and feet with the gaffer tape. She tried to struggle and Victor punched her again. She inhaled rapidly and sharply through her nose, and Victor checked that her nasal passages weren't blocked from the breakage lest she suffocate before he was through. He made sure the woman was securely tied, then sat back in the armchair, watching her. Something wasn't right. Victor became increasingly agitated. Finally he got up and stormed off in the direction of what he assumed to be the kitchen. Bitch; she didn't even have the basic manners to make him a cup of tea. He couldn't believe that he was having to make his own tea. He boiled the kettle and found a mug and a teabag. He got some milk from the fridge and helped himself, replacing the carton before taking his mug back to the sitting room with him.

The woman had been struggling to free herself and was breathing even harder than before. Blood had dripped onto the gaffer tape on her mouth and looked disgusting. The woman stopped moving as Victor came into the room, and lay very still, only her sharp breathing giving away the fact that she was still alive.

Victor sat down and took a sip of his tea. He gagged, spitting the hot liquid back into the mug.

"You stupid bitch," he told the woman. "The fucking milk's off. I can't believe what a lazy filthy slag you really are."

The woman's eyes opened wide in terror.

"I bet you don't clean your drains either, do you?" asked Victor. "Well, never mind. I have a little something for you. It will clean your drains good style." Victor opened his briefcase and took out a bottle of drain cleaner. "You know what happens when drain cleaner enters your veins?"

The woman was rocking on the floor in terror.

"It burns. It burns like hell." Victor studied the woman closely, then reached down into his briefcase and took out a syringe complete with hypodermic needle. The syringe was the disposable type that you can buy from the chemist when you're travelling to some obscure country with dubious healthcare. Victor had hoped to get one of those great big glass syringes that they used in the old days, or at least a very large plastic one like he imagined a country vet would probably use on a horse or a cow, but time had been of the essence, and the small plastic one would have much the same effect in any case. He walked up to the woman and held the syringe out before her eyes. The woman started to struggle again. Victor opened the bottle of drain cleaner and filled the syringe.

"As soon as the needle pierces your skin, you'll feel a stinging. Then, as the drain cleaner enters your vein, it will start to burn. The burning will make you want to tear apart your flesh and dig into your own veins to relieve the pain, but I'm afraid you won't be able to." Victor looked down at the woman's bound hands and smiled. "Let's see if we can find a vein."

The woman started to struggle violently again, but Victor threw her into one of the leather armchairs and taped her to it, exposing the soft flesh in the bends of her arms. The woman's face was smeared with blood and tears; her nostrils flared like a terrified animal's as Victor brought the syringe closer.

"Now, which arm would you prefer?" Victor asked the gagged woman. "You're not sure? Okay, I'll decide. Eeny meeny miny mo..." Victor pointed with the syringe from one arm to the other. "Catch a bitch by the toe..." Victor gazed into the woman's face. Her bloodshot eyes pleaded with him; her torment unimaginable. The warm glow between Victor's legs grew until the pleasure was almost unbearable. He needed release. "If she screams, let her go. Eeny meeny miny mo."

Victor needed all his willpower not to stab the syringe into the woman's arm. Instead he held the arm tightly and pushed the needle in little by little, squeezing the liquid ever so slowly into the woman's vein. The look of terror in the woman's eyes turned to one of agony. So excruciating was the pain that the woman's back arched right off the armchair, all but breaking the bonds that held her in their sticky grip. Victor sat back, gazing in wonder at the woman until her agony ended and his climax subsided. Then he went to the kitchen, poured the remains of his undrinkable tea into the sink and washed any traces of saliva off the mug.

Victor peered out of the window, making sure the street was empty before leaving the woman's house. As he hurried down the street he thought he heard the tapping of a woman's high-heeled shoes, but when he turned around there was nobody there.

Annie Bell's husband found her at seven p.m. when he got back from work. He was still in shock when the police arrived and was unable to tell them anything that would help them with their investigation.

Detective Chief Inspector Pryce was by now convinced that the recent spate of murders was the work of a serial killer, and the unfortunate British Telecom engineer presently being detained at Her Majesty's pleasure was not the man. It was time to move on to suspect number two.

The police had been aware of Victor for some time. They knew that he was working the area in which the murders had taken place. They'd even questioned him after the first two killings, as he'd been mentioned by a number of local people spoken to by police officers making door-to-door enquiries. The women had all said that the cancer charity man was quite charming, and the elderly woman who'd met him while walking her dog had insisted that he couldn't hurt a fly. Such high praise didn't fool Pryce, who knew that psychopaths could turn the charm right up when it suited them, but the neighbours had also mentioned a British Telecom engineer in the area, and the tiny piece of wire found in the dead French woman's house had led them to him and not to the charity man.

Now the time had come to take a closer look at Victor. There was no physical evidence linking him to any of the crime scenes, and a search of his house revealed nothing untoward. Victor, who lived less than a mile away from where the first murder had taken place, had been friendly and polite when Pryce had paid him a visit with one of his men. The charity man had offered them tea, and had agreed to a thorough search of the house. The officers found nothing to link

Victor to the dead women. Indeed, the only strange thing about Victor's house was how clean it was; Pryce could have sworn that there wasn't so much as a speck of dust in the entire place. But you couldn't arrest a man for keeping his house clean. Or for having an exceptionally large number of photographs of his mother on display. Not in this day and age. So Pryce decided to do what he did best: set a trap.

WPC Bryant matched the profile of the killer's victims. She was in her late twenties, reasonably attractive, with shoulder length dark blonde hair and brown eyes. The police would set her up in a house in Victor's target area. She'd wear a wire, and would be informed when Victor was spotted in a nearby street. She would then ostensibly go for a stroll and initiate a friendly conversation with Victor, express an interest in his charity and invite him back to the house. As soon as Victor made a move on her, Pryce and the other officers would move in and make their arrest.

Pryce's colleagues were not impressed with the Chief Inspector's latest plan. He'd only transferred in from the Met eight months ago, but ever since day one he fancied himself as John Wayne – chasing the bad guys out of town and running things in a manner more suited to the Wild West than sleepy Welsh suburbia. But the Chief Inspector was convinced that drastic times called for drastic measures and he had a good feeling about his trap. The only weak link was WPC Bryant; not so much the policewoman herself – she was hard-working and conscientious – but her inexperience: she'd only been in the police force a couple of months and had never been used as bait.

Victor knew that he should slow down – give himself some time off perhaps – but he couldn't forget the rush he'd experienced with the needle phobic. He kept reliving it in his mind, and for a couple of days that was enough, but then the craving returned and settled in his stomach once more, allowing him no peace. His obsession with finding a new victim, with a new phobia, and a new way to kill, sent him back out onto the streets.

Victor was tense. He was finding it hard to be nice to all the lonely old ladies he was encountering on his charity round today. He'd sold a record number of raffle tickets and turned down four cups of tea; it was five o'clock already and still he hadn't found the right woman. Soon it would be past teatime, and he couldn't bear the thought of going home with the hunger still raging in his belly.

He stood for minutes outside a large dark house, dreading the prospect of having the door open and being confronted with another old lady or unemployed youth peering at him with disdain or outright hostility.

As he stood there, he heard a woman's voice behind him.

"I think she's out."

"Excuse me?" asked Victor, turning around to see a young woman with dark blonde hair smiling at him nervously.

"I think the lady who lives there is out."

"Oh, thank you. That's really very kind of you." Victor gave the woman his best smile.

"Are you a friend?" she asked. Victor couldn't tell whether the woman was attracted to him or just being friendly.

"No, no. I'm collecting for charity."

"Oh, how nice. What charity is that?"

"The Cancer Research Charitable Fund."

"Oh, what a noble thing to do. My uncle died of cancer," said the woman.

"I'm so sorry," responded Victor. "So did my mother."

"I'm sorry," said the woman. "It must have affected you very much, for you to get actively involved in a cancer charity."

"Yes, it did."

"Look, I'd like to donate something, but I just popped out to post a letter and I don't have any cash on me. Would you mind coming back to my house for a moment and I'll get some money? It's just a couple of streets from here."

"It will be a pleasure," smiled Victor, not quite believing his luck.

Once they got to her house, the woman invited Victor in. Detective

Chief Inspector Pryce and his officers were listening intently in their surveillance van across the road.

The woman offered Victor a cup of tea and the killer sighed with relief, convinced now that his luck had turned. He just needed to find out the woman's deepest darkest fear; he hoped it would be something simple – something he could put into practice straight away, without having to leave the house in order to obtain elaborate props.

Victor presented the woman with a copy of his questionnaire.

"I'll help you go through it if you like," he told her, "to speed things up." The woman looked at him blankly. "I don't want to take up too much of your time," he explained.

"Oh it's no problem," the woman told him, "and I *would* appreciate your help."

The woman made Victor a cup of tea, and he guided her through the questionnaire. They came to the question, 'Do you have any fears/ phobias? If so, please state what you are afraid of.'

For a moment the woman seemed taken aback, but she quickly hid her surprise and said nothing. Victor figured that she was trying to please him.

"Is there anything that you're particularly afraid of?" he prompted.

"Well, er..." the woman paused for a moment, then seemed to make up her mind about something. "I guess I'm claustrophobic," she said finally. A massive smile spread over Victor's face.

"Really?" he asked incredulously. The woman nodded.

"That's amazing!" Victor enthused. "What I mean to say is, so am I."

"Really?" the woman asked.

"Yes. I have this overpowering fear of enclosed spaces. I can't even go in a lift, you know. I try not to work tower blocks simply because of all the stairs I'd have to climb." The woman nodded in sympathy.

"It must be hard," she said.

"Well, I'm lucky, I guess. I can choose where I work. Although it's not always possible to avoid small tight spaces. So how did you discover that you were claustrophobic?"

"My brother locked me in a coal bunker." The woman smiled at Victor nervously.

"What a horrible thing to do."

"I don't think he really meant any harm. I don't think he realised just how much it would frighten me. Neither of us did."

"What was the worst thing about being locked in there?" asked Victor. The woman gave him a surprised look. "Was it the dark? Or the damp?" he prompted. The woman thought for a moment.

"The worst thing was that I couldn't breathe. Well, I guess I could breathe, but I felt like I couldn't. And my heart was beating so fast I thought it would explode. But the worst thing was the feeling that I'd suffocate if I didn't get out immediately." Victor nodded, his eyes sparkling. He felt happy.

"So what happened?" he asked.

"Oh, I started screaming and my brother let me out."

"You were lucky," said Victor. "When I was a kid, one of the girls from my class got locked in a coal bunker. A boy locked her in for a joke, but he got hit by a car before he had time to let her out. He hadn't told anyone, and by the time they found the girl she'd starved to death. Her fingernails were all ripped up and her fingers were worn down to the bone; she'd tried to scratch her way out. When they opened the coal bunker, it was teeming with rats. They were all over the girl's body; they'd eaten her eyeballs and chewed their way inside her. She had to be identified by her dental records." The young policewoman looked at Victor in disgust. "Can you imagine," he asked, "being stuck there, in the dark, breathing in the foetid air, with hungry rats nipping at your heels?" Victor smiled at the woman. "Could I use your bathroom, please?" he added. The woman blinked, surprised.

"Sure," she said "It's..."

"That's okay." Victor smiled. "I'll find it." He left the room and moved swiftly and quietly to the kitchen. He knew the layout of these big suburban houses by now. The sitting room was almost always at the front of the house, leading onto the dining room, which would have windows or a door onto the back garden. Off to the side, also leading onto the garden was usually the kitchen.

Victor wasn't mistaken. He walked quickly into the kitchen and looked around for the trap door leading down into the cellar. For a moment he didn't see it, but then he spotted a large rectangular cut in the linoleum with a ring on one side – the tell-tale rectangle that showed the opening to the cellar and the hoop that one lifted and pulled to open the door in the floor. Victor quickly went to the small toilet that had been installed under the stairs and flushed it before returning to his hostess.

As he approached the sitting room, Victor thought he heard the woman muttering something in a quiet voice. He stopped short, wondering whether someone had arrived without him hearing or if the woman was crazy enough to be talking to herself knowing that her guest could come back into the room at any minute. He listened for a moment. He couldn't hear what was being said, but he thought he caught the phrases "gives me the creeps" and "I think he's the one". Victor couldn't be sure that those were the words the woman had whispered, but he suddenly had a terrible feeling in his gut. The way the woman had approached him, the way that *she* had initiated a conversation with him and persuaded him to come back to her house. It had all been too good to be true.

Victor went back into the sitting room and sat down.

"Thank you," he said and took a sip of his tea.

"You're welcome," the woman responded nervously.

"Did you know," asked Victor, "that the Nazis used to torture prisoners at Auschwitz by putting them in standing cells?"

"No, I didn't."

"They had these tiny little dark cells. They were too low to stand in and too narrow to sit in, so the prisoners had to half crouch in excruciatingly uncomfortable positions for days, sometimes weeks. It was pitch black in the standing cells and in summer the temperature would soar to over forty degrees Celsius. People really *did* suffocate in there. Not to mention the lice and other bugs that crawled all over you, and you couldn't move your arm to get them off."

The young policewoman was speechless, as were Pryce and the other officers in the surveillance van. Victor eyed the young woman closely.

"You know, they say that the best way to get over one's phobias is to face them – 'exposure therapy' they call it." The woman sat very still, returning Victor's gaze. "When I was looking for the toilet, I noticed you had a trap door to the cellar in your kitchen floor. Well, I was thinking, perhaps we could go down there together and sit for a while in the dark with the lid down. It wouldn't be so bad if we were in there together and we'd be helping each other overcome our phobias. It's a good idea, don't you think?"

This was something that WPC Bryant hadn't prepared for. The prospect of going into a cellar with the prime suspect in three murders was more than she'd signed up for when she joined the force. Should he try anything, the other officers wouldn't be able to get to her in time to stop him. She was starting to feel scared.

In the surveillance van, DCI Pryce was also getting very worried about his WPC; he wanted to go in and get her out of there, but Victor had done nothing so far but talk. Pryce didn't want to blow the whole operation by going in too early.

"Shall we go?" Victor smiled sweetly at the woman.

"I'm not sure that would be a good idea," the woman responded.

"No, me neither," Victor laughed. "I'm sorry. It was a stupid joke. You know: from one claustrophobic to another. Maybe it wasn't as funny as I thought. Please forgive me. I'm afraid I have to go now. I promised my next-door neighbour that I'd cook for her today; she's eighty-two, you know." Victor got up to go. "Don't worry about the rest of the questionnaire; I can fill it in for you. Here's your raffle ticket. There's no need to pay me for it." Victor handed the raffle ticket to the woman. He took out three pounds from his wallet, placed the coins in one of his charity envelopes and sealed it. He put the envelope back in his briefcase. "It's a thank you present for the tea and the lovely afternoon. I've taken up a lot of your time. Please don't get up; I'll see myself out."

Victor got his things together and left quickly. Bryant breathed a sigh of relief. So did Pryce, although he was very disappointed that his trap had failed. He sent a couple of officers to tail Victor, but he wasn't going to hold his breath waiting for results. He wondered what had got Victor spooked.

Victor stayed at home for as long as he could bear, which proved to be a couple of days. When he finally went out, he made sure that he lost the officers who were following him by hopping on a bus, changing onto another bus, then slipping back to his original point of departure, free to go where he pleased.

Even though he'd shaken off the cops, Victor decided to concentrate on his cancer charity. He was a highly intelligent human being (or so he told himself); he could relive his past murders in his mind. He didn't need to commit any new ones – not just yet. True, the world still needed to be purged of bitches – parasitic useless women who lived off their hard-working husbands and cheated on them with the postman or gardener when their backs were turned, pushy arrogant career women who stole men's jobs just to make a point about how 'equal' they were. They weren't equal – they were scum and they needed to be dispatched screaming to the next world. Victor would purge his neighbourhood of filth, but it would have to wait until the police lost interest in him. For now he would distract himself by selling raffle tickets to old ladies.

Victor's face fell when he rang a doorbell and a beautiful woman of around thirty opened the door. Something about her tied Victor's stomach in knots. He felt himself getting tense and angry standing there on the doorstep, gazing into the woman's big green eyes. He should have walked away right then, but he'd already switched to automatic pilot and was trotting out his usual spiel, "Good morning Madam, sorry to disturb you. I'm here on behalf of the Cancer Research Charitable Fund..." Before he knew it, Victor was inside the woman's house, being ushered into her sitting room. Then it hit him: the woman bore just the slightest resemblance to Dr Gilby –

something in the shape of her mouth and the way her eyebrows arched when she spoke. It wasn't much, but it was enough to start that hungry, angry, excited feeling in Victor's gut.

"Would you like a cup of tea?" The woman smiled at Victor.

There was a long pause as Victor struggled with his inner demon – not through any moral scruples or pangs of conscience, of which he had none, but to prove to himself that he had the strength to stick to a plan of action that he'd chosen; to show the demon who was in control.

"No thank you." Victor smiled back politely. "I just had a cup."

And that was when it happened. In an effort to clear the coffee table, the woman picked up some sheets of paper. She let out a hiss of air and dropped the paper back down, staring at her finger. A thin red line of blood slowly appeared from the paper cut.

"Oh God!" said the woman, turning white as a sheet. Victor gazed at her in fascination.

"I think I'll have that cup of tea after all," he said. The woman made a valiant effort to stop herself fainting.

"I'm sorry, what did you say?"

"I said, I'd like to take you up on your offer of tea."

The woman tried to shake off the waves of blackness that were descending before her eyes. She knew that once the feeling started it was almost impossible to stop. She leaned her head back against the sofa.

"I'm sorry," she said. "I don't feel very well. Please could we do this another time?"

"Another time?" For a moment Victor's annoyance got the better of him, but he quickly got a hold of himself. After all, it wouldn't be the first time he'd had to make his own tea. "Don't worry about a thing," he said. "You just sit back and relax, and I'll make us both a nice cup of tea." He flashed the woman a charming smile and eventually she smiled back. "How do you take it?" he asked.

A few minutes later Victor brought in two mugs of tea and handed one to the woman. She smiled up at him gratefully and they sat in silence for a moment, Victor sipping his tea and observing the woman closely.

"I'm sorry," the woman spoke first. "You must think I'm really pathetic."

"Oh no," said Victor. "Blood phobia is more common than you'd think and, actually, passing out when you sustain an injury is a very smart thing to do. Do you know what happens to a blood phobic when they see blood?" The woman shook her head. "Well, the subconscious mind tells the body that there is a risk of bleeding to death and in response your blood pressure drops, and you pass out. You find it upsetting, but, by passing out, your body thinks it's saving your life by limiting the amount of blood you lose. It's really very clever. Of course, if you lose enough blood, even passing out can't save you."

The woman looked at Victor uncertainly. All this talk of passing out was making her feel faint again. She hoped Victor would drink his tea and leave. Victor's own blood was beginning to sing a song of joy within his veins.

"How are you feeling?" he asked the woman.

"I'm okay," she lied.

"Oh, that's great," said Victor. "Well, in that case you won't mind if I do this..." He pulled a Swiss army knife out of his pocket, opened it and proceeded to cut his thumb. He looked at the thumb until it started to bleed and then presented it to the horrified woman.

By the time Jacqui Campbell regained consciousness, she was lying on her back in a bath full of water.

"Welcome back." The voice made her sick to her stomach. She looked up and saw Victor kneeling over her, casually brandishing his penknife in a latex-clad hand. This time he pulled out the scissors accessory. Jacqui tried to scream, but her mouth was sealed with gaffer tape. She grabbed the side of the bath and started to pull herself out. In a single swift move, Victor prised her hand off the bath and snipped off one of her fingers. Jacqui's eyes widened in terror and pain; she froze, stared at the bleeding stump and slumped back in the bath in a dead faint. Victor sat and watched her, making sure her head didn't go under water.

A few minutes later Jacqui came to and tried to pull herself out of the bath again. This time Victor grabbed her by the leg, yanking it upwards so that she fell back in the bath. She kicked at Victor, but he held her fast and snipped off her little toe. Jacqui thrashed around for a moment, then passed out again. Victor got bored waiting for her to regain consciousness and splashed some bloody water on her face, bringing her round.

Victor amused himself for the best part of an hour. By the time Jacqui's torment was over, she had only one finger and three toes left. Victor switched on the Jacuzzi function and giggled as Jacqui's blood bubbled in the bath. He really was having too much fun, and it was time to go, before the woman's husband got home.

Victor went to the sink to wash his gloved hands. As he glanced in the mirror above the sink, he recoiled in horror. There was a large thick globule of blood on his tie. Victor took off the tie and stuffed it in his pocket, but this didn't help. There was blood on his shirt as well.

Victor scrubbed at his shirt as best he could, but only succeeded in making matters worse. Damn! He'd got carried away again and hadn't even noticed the woman's blood spurting onto his clothes. How could he have been so stupid? Victor's agitation grew and he decided to get out of the house as soon as possible. One last glance at his handiwork – just looking at the blood-soaked woman in the bath was enough to give him another erection. He chastised himself for wasting time, made sure he hadn't left any physical evidence of his presence, gathered up his things and left.

Victor slipped quietly out of the house, making sure that nobody was watching. He pulled up the collar of his jacket, hiding the bloodstains as best he could. As he hurried off in the direction of his house, he heard footsteps behind him. He looked over his shoulder, but saw nothing – only blood red leaves picked up by the autumn wind and carried along the pavement with a harsh rustling sound.

Victor headed home, slowing down as he approached his street. As he rounded the corner he stopped and ducked into a doorway.

There was a dark blue car parked across the road from his house, and the two men sitting in it, sipping what Victor guessed to be coffee out of polystyrene cups, could only be plain-clothes police. Victor panicked. He spun round, planning to return the way he'd come and figure out what to do next, and bumped headfirst into a young woman in a long black coat. A strand of pale blonde hair had escaped from the hood pulled tightly around her delicate-featured face. Autumn leaves swirled around the woman's slim form. Her pale, ghost-like skin and the way she'd appeared behind him out of nowhere made Victor jump.

"What the hell?" he blurted out before he had time to regain his composure.

"I'm Lucy," said the woman in a soft, cold voice. She smiled at Victor, but her smile didn't reach her eyes.

"You're a cop." It was a statement more than a question.

"No," said Lucy. "I'm a fan of yours – of the work you've been doing. Your charity work, that is."

Victor stared at the woman uncomprehendingly. She stared back, and Victor made a self-conscious attempt to cover up the bloodstain on his shirt.

"Come with me," Lucy told him.

"I don't think now's the time." Victor glanced back over his shoulder, in the direction of his house.

"You can't go back there," said Lucy. "Your house is being watched."

"I know," said Victor.

"I live just a couple of streets away. You can get cleaned up at my place and decide what you're going to do next."

Victor weighed up his options. The police had nothing to pin on him except the blood on his clothes. If he cleaned himself up, he could walk right past the cops and, even if they stopped him, they wouldn't find anything they could use against him.

"Okay," he said.

Lucy led Victor to a particularly large house with big windows. He'd worked this street recently and even stood outside the building itself, but he'd never rung the doorbell because the house looked so dark and uninviting.

"Why are you helping me?" he asked as Lucy locked the front door behind them.

"I told you, I'm a fan of your work. Collecting money for charity, helping others – it's a wonderful thing to do."

"Thanks," said Victor, not quite sure what to make of his hostess.

"The bathroom's upstairs, first door on your left. Why don't you have a shower and I'll find you some clean clothes. Use any towel you like; they're all clean."

"Thanks," said Victor, still feeling uneasy.

He mounted the stairs, but didn't go into the bathroom straight away. He stood silently for a few minutes, listening to see if Lucy would call the police. She didn't, and eventually Victor got into the shower.

Victor savoured the sensation of the warm water on his skin. He relaxed and ran through the day's events in his mind. What a day it had been – and it wasn't over yet. He wondered what Lucy wanted from him. She was a strange girl. She was beautiful in an unearthly sort of way. Her skin was so pale it was almost translucent; her hair the colour of a ripe cornfield and her eyes a pale but intense blue. She said she was a fan of Victor's – and God knows, he needed a fan at this point in time – but the way she spoke was so cold, almost lifeless. She was what people might call 'an ice maiden'. Victor wondered what it would take to put some expression in those unfathomable eyes. He wondered what she was afraid of. He wondered how red her blood would look on her pale, milky flesh. He... felt a sharp blow to the back of his head and the world went red, then black.

When Victor came to, he found himself strapped naked to an armchair in a child's bedroom. The curtains were drawn and the only light came from a magic lantern night-light, which threw flickering coloured animal shapes around the room and onto Victor. He tried to move, but his bonds held fast; whoever had tied the knots knew what they were doing. Victor found it hard to breathe; a rag had been jammed into his mouth and another had been tied around his face, preventing him from making a sound. He breathed as best he could and looked around the room, searching for some means of escape.

As his eyes adjusted to the dark, Lucy entered the room, carrying a large teapot. She approached Victor, pulled down his gag, grabbed him by the nose and yanked his head back, emptying the entire pot of boiling tea down his throat. Victor struggled and screamed, but Lucy held him fast, and his screams came out as a gurgling sound – hardly loud enough to attract any attention from the street outside. The scalding pain in his throat was unbearable and Victor passed out.

The next time he regained consciousness, the gag was back in Victor's mouth, and the tea that had spilt down the front of his chest felt cold and wet. His throat felt as though someone had filled it with razor blades, and he was having terrible trouble breathing. As Victor struggled to get air in through his nose and down his swollen, blistered throat to his lungs, he spotted Lucy sitting on the bed, watching him. She held a worn cuddly toy with long floppy ears in one hand and an old-fashioned men's razor in the other. When she saw that Victor was conscious, she sat the toy rabbit down carefully on the bed and approached Victor with the razor.

Victor tried to scream, but succeeded only in making a small mumbling sound. As Lucy neared Victor, light from the lantern momentarily reflected in her eyes. They had a glazed, trancelike expression. Victor threw his weight around in the armchair and managed to rock it slightly from side to side, but it was a heavy old oak chair, specially chosen for its solidity, and it held firm. As Lucy reached him, Victor froze. The woman's eyes had come alive; they burned with a fathomless hatred, hunger and rage. They burned like Victor imagined the bottomless pit of hell to burn, and Victor recognised that fire. He gazed in awe as Lucy leaned over him. She looked him straight in the eye and told him, "Daddy, you've been naughty".

The last thing Victor saw was the flash of the blade, how red his blood looked on Lucy's pale, milky flesh, and a large horse made of red light galloping over his genitals as Lucy held them aloft, a look of crazed triumph distorting her delicate face.

She stood there, gazing down at the mutilated man until his body stopped twitching. Then she walked quietly out of the room and fetched a glass jar into which she placed her grisly trophy. She filled the jar to the brim with formaldehyde and screwed on the lid. She took the jar to a large cupboard and placed it among all the other jars. She studied her collection – several dozen in all – simultaneously repelled and fascinated by the withered chunks of flesh that gave so much pleasure to men and so much pain to little girls. She locked the cupboard, mopped up the blood and spilt tea, and went downstairs to watch television. She would dispose of the body after dark.

THE HAGGIS QUEEN

THE HAGGIS QUEEN

I WOKE WITH a start, instantly aware that I was no longer alone in the flat. The jarring sound of crockery being knocked together emanated from the next room.

I was about to call the police when I remembered the stray cat that had decided to move in with me the other day – wandering in through an open window and making itself at home without so much as a by-your-leave. The animal was innocuous enough and, apart from demanding food from time to time, it kept itself pretty much to itself – sleeping mostly. It was, however, I quickly found, actually a fairly welcome presence when I came home from work in the evening – greeting me by purring and patiently tolerating being stroked once I realised that doing so seemed to bring me some relief after a stressful day at the agency. But being woken up at five a.m. by it messing with my designer plates was definitely not soothing.

My fear turned to annoyance. I put down the phone and headed to the living room. The sounds stopped when I entered. I stopped too, peering into the pre-dawn gloom. My trendy apartment – in a recently regenerated part of Glasgow's old factory district – may have only had one bedroom, but made up for it with the vast, high-ceilinged space that was the reception room and dining room in one, with a sink and kitchen units at the far end.

There was a dark figure by the kitchen sink, its back to me. I honestly thought I was going to drop dead on the spot. *Thirty-three-year-old advertising executive found dead in Glasgow apartment. Suspected heart attack. Badly decomposed body lay undiscovered for months.* I cursed myself for having left my phone by the side of the bed. The figure had frozen too, apart from incessant jerky movements of its hands. What was it doing? My biggest fear was that it would turn around and see me. The living room was large, the sink was on the far side; I had time to flee to the bedroom, block the door and call the police. But I couldn't move.

I watched the figure. It was wringing its hands together – over and over – washing them, I finally realised, but the tap was off. As my eyes adjusted to the gloom, I saw that it was smaller than I'd previously thought – it was female. Not young, I thought, but not terribly old either. She was wearing a dark dress; a black shawl covering her head and shoulders. Not very fashionable – not the kind of gear we'd ever create an advertising campaign for. And what was she doing in my kitchen anyway? So I couldn't move, but I could certainly tell her to get out of my flat. How the hell had she got in in the first place? If she'd broken in, she sure as hell was going to pay for any damage.

"Hey!" my voice sounded steady and authoritative enough. "Hey you, what are you doing in my flat?" The woman stopped wringing her hands. *Oh no, she's going to turn around and look at me. What have I done?* But she didn't turn around.

"I hate haggis," she finally said. "Ye cannae get the reek off ye."

The reek – that's when I noticed it. A sickly-sweet, cloying, choking, acrid smell. I was no fan of haggis, or the odour of it, but the overpowering stench of burning flesh in my kitchen wasn't it. The reek shocked my body back into life. I ran for the bedroom and dialled 999.

By the time the two police officers arrived, the smell was gone, the woman was gone, and there was no sign of a break-in. By the time they'd finished taking the piss out of the "English poofter" who'd damn near pissed himself at the thought of a woman in his flat, I was wishing they'd just charge me for wasting police time and get out. As they were heading out the door, the older officer took pity on me and decided to give me a break.

"Dinna you worry, laddie," he said, "it wis jist the Haggis Queen." I stared at him, emotionally exhausted and ready to break down at the slightest provocation. "Ye ken, there wis a meat factory here before, mostly women workers. There wis a fire an' there wis some deaths. Ye're no the first to see her and I daresay ye winna be the last."

He wasn't joking. I made enquiries, and there had indeed been a meat factory and a fire – a horrific, uncontrollable inferno. Nearly every family in the surrounding area lost a mother or a daughter or friend. Not all the workers were registered so not all of the victims could be identified.

Luckily I didn't see the Haggis Queen again. For several months.

But now it's five a.m. and I'm wide awake. I can hear cups and plates being knocked about in the sink, though I know I put them away last night. The cat is hissing beside me, sharp little teeth bared, tail twitching from side to side. I could put on my headphones, lie back down and listen to my iPod. Or I can go in there and try to see her face...

THE CAT SITTER

THE CAT SITTER

A T FIFTEEN ACRES, the wood wasn't particularly large, but the brooding, oppressive atmosphere, which so belied the usual beauty of ancient English woodland, gave it an air of menace infinitely vaster than its physical area. If an unwary rambler, caught up amongst what should have been a splendid array of native trees, were to analyse why he or she felt unease rather than tranquillity amongst the leafy bowers of Ash Wood, here's what they might conclude...

The wood was darker than it should have been. True, the centuries-old trees that formed it grew tall and dense, but the permanent gloom that appeared to rest upon Ash Wood contravened the laws of light and shadow. The twigs and branches of its trees creaked and rattled like dry bones. Leaves were parched brown. Flowers, on the rare occasions that they bloomed, grew dried and shrivelled on their desiccated stalks. It defied logic how, even when the surrounding area became waterlogged after heavy rains, the soil in the wood remained dry and cracked. The more imaginative visitor might surmise that it was as if the very earth of the wood smouldered with an insatiable ire that sucked the nurturing moisture out of anything that tried to flourish within it.

Shadows flitted uneasily amongst the trees, and the undergrowth rustled with a wrathful air of impatience. And yet no animals ventured into the wood to account for these phenomena. There was no birdsong either, as living things seemed to shun Ash Wood and skirted fearfully around its perimeter, preferring instead to purloin a bit of greenery, an earthworm or a sip of water from the cottage garden that backed onto the wood.

Thursday 27th April

Jane was excited at the prospect of seeing Isabelle's new house, and of seeing her old friend again. The last time they'd met was at a friend's wedding in Denmark, and that was well over a year ago. Even the long drive to Sussex, the surprisingly heavy traffic and the frustration of getting lost a couple of times on ridiculously narrow country lanes didn't dampen Jane's enthusiasm.

Jane and Isabelle had both studied at St Hilda's College, Oxford. Isabelle had finished her English studies after three years and moved to London, where she'd worked in retail for eight years before meeting and marrying Jonathan. Jane's degree in Human Sciences had stretched to four years – the result of her third year consisting of a ten-month placement at a prestigious American university. After finishing her degree Jane had moved back to Manchester and the two girls had lost touch, only reconnecting via social media years later.

The houses along the country lanes became fewer and fewer, and finally dwindled away to the odd farmhouse. Soon these too disappeared, leaving only vast stretches of farmland, punctuated by the occasional derelict outbuilding or disused barn.

Isabelle had explained that she'd had enough of London, and couldn't wait to buy a house with Jonathan in the countryside and take her fledgling internet retail business to 'the next level'. Her dream had finally come true when the estate agent managed to procure a cottage on the outskirts of Wraithsfield – a small village in East Sussex. Jonathan could still commute into London three times a week, Isabelle could travel into the capital too when absolutely necessary, but other than that they could live the country idyll – along with Milly the cat.

Jonathan hadn't wanted a cat. He was sure that it would wreak havoc with the rabbits, squirrels, birds and other gentle wildlife that frequented the back garden of Ash Wood Cottage, and he was right. But Isabelle – a robust and unsentimental lass if ever there was one – had little sympathy for anything that couldn't cope with a bit of Darwinian selection (albeit not of a very natural origin), and insisted that she wanted an animal to keep her company inside the house – not just ones that gate-crashed her garden and fled as soon as they caught wind of her. And Jonathan certainly wasn't going to let a few dead bunnies stand between his beloved and her happiness. So Milly the cat was promptly purchased and named, and now constituted the perfect excuse for Jane to come and visit her old friend's new house.

More country lanes, fringed on either side with claustrophobic, impenetrable hedges. Then these too gave way to an open vista of sizeable fields, empty save for the odd cow, and finally Jane passed a small lane leading off the road to a white-walled two-storey cottage. She brought the car to a halt, made sure the deserted road was still deserted, executed a somewhat clumsy three-point turn and doubled back, turning up the lane leading to the cottage. She parked alongside her hosts' gleaming SUV and got out of her battered old Peugeot, relieved to be out in the fresh air and stretching her legs and back. She took her small suitcase out of the boot, locked the car, and headed for the house.

"Jane!" Isabelle had spotted her through the window and was beaming at her from the doorstep. "You're here!"

"No thanks to the traffic." Jane put down her suitcase and embraced her friend.

"Let me take that!" Jonathan appeared from behind Isabelle, gave Jane a hug and carried her suitcase into the house.

Ash Wood Cottage was a curious mixture of the very old and the very new. The estate agent had told Jonathan and Isabelle that some parts of the cottage originally dated back to the seventeenth century, but even those parts had been obscured by centuries of renovations and 'improvements'. Now the cottage boasted a fitted kitchen with fully integrated appliances, two double bedrooms, a bathroom with a power shower, and a spacious sitting room. On one side the sitting room opened onto a dining room; on the opposite side and in the far wall it had two large double-glazed windows that met at right angles to form a vast frameless corner window, overlooking the pretty garden and the wood beyond. The entrance to the cottage was at the side of the building, leading directly into the kitchen.

Jonathan carried Jane's bag up to the spare bedroom, while Isabelle took her on a tour of the cottage and showed her where she could find kitchen utensils, Milly's cat food, replacement cat litter and anything else she might need during Jonathan and Isabelle's long weekend in Spain.

"I guess it's time you met Milly," said Isabelle. "I expect she's in the garden as usual. Shall we have a quick look?" Jane nodded enthusiastically and they went outdoors.

Isabelle was somewhat miffed by the fact that Milly spent such a great deal of time in the garden. What was the point of having a pet that was meant to keep her company indoors when said pet spent much of the day outdoors, staring into the wood at the back of the house, only to come fearfully inside at night when the shadows among the trees got too much for her? Isabelle had all the downsides of owning a pet – scratched furniture, decapitated bunnies, dead birds and bleeding field mice – without the companionship that she'd anticipated when Jonathan was away and she sat at her computer alone. But still, when Milly did venture in, she followed Isabelle around, purring at her, rubbing up against her legs, allowing herself to be stroked and obligingly chasing the piece of string that her mistress sometimes dangled in front of her. *No such thing as the perfect pet*, thought Isabelle, as she led her friend across the small patio and up three stone steps to the overgrown lawn.

"Milly!" The cat had been standing at the far end of the lawn, gazing into the woods, and now turned to look in the direction of the two women. "Come and meet Jane!" Milly trotted over to Isabelle and allowed herself to be picked up and stroked. "This is Jane." Isabelle turned the cat to face her friend. "She's going to look after you."

"She's beautiful." Jane reached out to stroke Milly, but the cat meowed loudly in protest, wriggled out of Isabelle's grasp and ran off.

"Oh, sorry about that," said Isabelle. "It takes her a little while to get used to people she doesn't know. She'll be fine in an hour or so."

"It's all right." Jane smiled shyly, doing her best to hide her disappointment at the rejection by her furry charge.

Dear Jane – thought Isabelle – *sweet, sensitive, chubby Jane, with her little round spectacles and her mild manners. Even the cat has a stronger personality than she does.*

"Come on, let's go have some tea," suggested Isabelle, and headed back towards the house. As Jane turned to follow, she thought she heard someone whisper her name. She glanced back at the woods, startled and a little afraid, but it was only the wind sighing in the dry branches.

Jane never slept well in an unfamiliar place, and that night was no exception. She, Jonathan and Isabelle had stayed up chatting for a while after dinner, but her hosts had an early start the following day, so the three of them retired early. The spare bedroom had been turned into a study for Isabelle, but it doubled as a guestroom and contained a single bed. As Jane draped her clothes over the armchair in the corner, she caught a whiff of a strange smell – faint, but unpleasant nonetheless. Then it was gone.

Jane read for a little while, then tossed and turned for a long while, then fell asleep, only to dream about the dark expanse of wood behind the cottage. She was standing on the lawn, peering into the trees in a vain attempt to see who it was that had called her name. Her unease grew as she noticed shadows moving among the trees, and she decided to return to the cottage. She tried to move, but found herself rooted to the spot. She was forced to watch as the shadows danced and swayed, merging with each other and congealing into a single vast darkness. As tendrils of black mist spilled forward, reaching for Jane, the anxiety levels in her sleeping body soared enough to wake her up.

The particulars of her dream faded quickly, but a sense of disquiet lingered long enough for her to switch on the bedside lamp and read some more before attempting to go back to sleep.

Friday 28th April

In the morning Jane got up early to wave her friends goodbye and feed the cat. Milly purred while Jane opened a tin of cat food and scooped it out into a plastic bowl, but shied away the moment Jane tried to stroke her. She wolfed down her food and immediately demanded to be let out. Jane obliged, then went back to bed to try to make up for her poor night's sleep. There was definitely a stale smell in her room, and Jane wondered absentmindedly whether her friends' dream house had damp, before dozing off for a couple of hours.

After a late breakfast – brunch really – Jane decided to check on the cat and go for a walk. It was a sunny day and Milly was lying in the long grass in the garden, eyes fixed on the wood beyond the lawn. Jane admired the cat's unusual calico colouring – black and ginger patches all over, with a white belly, collar and socks. But strangest of all was Milly's face – half of it black with black whiskers and a yellow eye, the other half ginger with white whiskers and a blue eye. If that wasn't quirky enough, the rim of Milly's black ear was tinged with ginger, while her ginger ear was similarly tinged with black. And the cat's ears were pointed and tufty, giving her an altogether somewhat demonic appearance.

Milly didn't move as Jane walked past her, neither did she follow as Jane stepped over the fallen single-wire fence and headed off into the woods. She stared after the departing woman, still as a sphinx, and only her twitching tail gave away her agitation at the cat sitter's disappearance into the wilderness that fascinated and frightened her at the same time.

Ash Wood would have been beautiful, thought Jane, if only the trees and bushes didn't look so unhealthy. There was nothing wrong with them really, apart from the fact that they seemed dehydrated. Odd, considering that it had been a rather wet April. But even in its current state, the wood impressed with its wide variety of deciduous trees and a few evergreens to boot. Jane knew a little about trees – she made a point of knowing a little about everything – and there was one thing that puzzled her. She had spied alder, willow, oak, yew, aspen, hawthorn, birch, holly and hornbeam, but there was not an ash tree in sight. And yet the wood was named Ash Wood.

As she headed further into the wilderness, Jane kept her eyes peeled for the eponymous ash trees, and in the end spotted three – in a wood of thousands of trees. She knew that place names often made little sense, but for some reason the discrepancy bothered her. She sat down for a while on the trunk of a fallen oak and listened to the profound silence around her. The absence of birdsong was strange, the lack of any evidence of wildlife surprising, and Jane wondered whether a harmful chemical had been dumped or buried in the soil.

As she sat and pondered, Jane's mind unexpectedly went blank, as if her train of thought had been cut off abruptly. As she struggled with the sudden disorientation, her ears started to ring – a low, hollow sound. Then something seemed to be pushing at the edges of Jane's consciousness, like an icy tentacle reaching its way inside her head, probing her mind, displacing her thoughts. Jane tried to pull herself together, she tried to focus on something – anything – but she couldn't get a mental foothold and she started to lose her sense of where she ended and the wood began. She battled to get a grip on herself, but the ringing in her ears had become a sickening rhythmic chanting, and it was intensifying, preventing her from hearing her own thoughts.

"No!" With a supreme effort Jane regained control and snapped out of the disembodying, trancelike state. The ringing in her ears was gone. She leapt up and ran through the woods back to the cottage.

Milly, who was still lying in the same spot on the lawn, started as Jane ran past her.

As Jane opened the front door, she noticed that the telephone was ringing. She had no strength left to run, but moved as swiftly as she could to the sitting room and picked up the receiver.

"Hello?"

"Jane?" It was Isabelle. "Are you okay?"

"I was outside."

"Oh, sorry I dragged you in." Isabelle relaxed a little, putting Jane's strained panting down to having run for the phone. "You better get your breath back."

"I'm okay."

"Good. How's Milly?"

"She's fine. She's in the garden. I'm going to give her some biscuits soon."

"Thanks a lot, Jane. I really appreciate your help. Jonathan and I really need this."

Jane spent the rest of the day indoors. She couldn't understand what had happened in the woods. Could it have been a psychotic episode? An indicator of the early onset of some kind of dissociative disorder? Schizophrenia perhaps? But there was no mental illness in her family, and an attack like this, with no previous hint of disease, made little sense. She'd been looking forward to spending the bank holiday enjoying the sunshine, but now she felt reluctant to leave the house. Confinement within the four walls of the cottage made her feel less vulnerable. Besides, it would be getting dark soon, and she certainly had no wish to go out after dark. But she didn't want Milly to stay out after nightfall either. Isabelle would never forgive her, and she'd never forgive herself, if something happened to Milly on her watch. She'd have to bring the cat back in and she'd have to do it soon.

When Jane finally plucked up the courage to go out, she skirted along the wall of the house until she reached the corner, where the patio began. She craned her neck, but couldn't see the cat, so she eventually scaled the steps that led up to the lawn and peered reluctantly in the direction of the wood. Sure enough, Milly was there – sitting at the far end of the lawn and gaping into the wood as though she was drawn to it, yet feared to set paw in it at the same time.

"Milly!" The cat turned her head to look at Jane, but didn't move. "Milly, come on! Come here! Good kitty!" Nothing. After a while Milly turned her head back towards the trees and ignored Jane's further entreaties altogether. Jane couldn't bear to cross the lawn. She thought for a minute, then headed back to the house, emerging moments later with a box of cat biscuits, which she rattled enticingly. Milly perked up.

"Come on, Milly! Biscuit time! Here, kitty, kitty!" Jane shook the box once more and this time it did the trick. Milly stood up slowly, stretched, then walked in a slow and dignified manner towards Jane, finally following her into the house.

Jane locked the door behind them. She was grateful to have Milly's company and found the crunching sound of her devouring the dry cat food somehow soothing. She ventured to stroke Milly again and this time the cat didn't flinch. Jane smiled as Milly purred and arched her back beneath Jane's hand. She made sure that the doors and windows were locked, and the two of them watched television together – Milly in Jonathan's chair and Jane on the sofa.

There were no curtains or blinds in the sitting room – either because Jonathan and Isabelle didn't feel the need for them (there were no neighbours to look in from the back of the house) or because they simply hadn't got round to putting any up. Either way, Jane consciously avoided looking out of the window as the woods beyond the lawn darkened and shadows moved among the trees. When night fell fully, Jane couldn't shake the feeling that she was being watched, so she switched everything off and went upstairs to bed. There was that faint, irritating smell in her room again, but she felt mentally and physically drained, and soon fell asleep.

A sharp meow woke her up. She was standing at the front door, hand on the door handle, Milly gazing up at her and meowing in alarm. Jane cried out in distress, and Milly ran out of the kitchen. As the shock wore off and Jane's heartbeat returned to normal, she noticed how cold her feet were on the stone-flagged kitchen floor. She made sure the entrance door was still locked, put on the kettle, and went upstairs to don her slippers and a dressing-gown.

Back in the kitchen, Jane tried to analyse the day's events rationally. She had never sleepwalked before and she'd never had a dissociative episode. Then again, she'd never been on her own in such an isolated place. There was something eldritch about the secluded cottage and the strange, withered wood that all but surrounded it. And it was in the wood that Jane believed the key to the mystery of her unprecedented episodes lay. She thought back to the dry, parched earth, the desiccated plant life and lack of animal life, and the disturbing notion that the land might be chemically poisoned or otherwise toxic resurfaced in her mind. That would explain her auditory hallucination and her sudden disorientation; perhaps the sleepwalking as well.

But if there was something toxic in the ground, then how come nobody seemed to know about it? She'd have to tell Isabelle and Jonathan. She didn't want to spoil their pastoral idyll, but she'd have to share her suspicions with them. Isabelle would be gutted. The thought of being the harbinger of bad news upset Jane.

Milly wandered back into the kitchen, and Jane decided to spoil her by topping up her cat biscuits. She watched as the cat crunched voraciously, and drank her own hot chocolate slowly, returning to bed only when the dawn chorus started up outside.

Saturday 29th April

Jane woke to the sound of meowing outside her bedroom door. She fed Milly and hesitantly let her out into the garden, leaving the front door open for her. As she returned to her room to dress, she got a strong waft of the unpleasant smell. It was pungent and rather nasty. Jane had a quick look around the room, but didn't see anything untoward. She opened the window before going back to the kitchen to make her breakfast. To her surprise, Milly was sitting on the floor by the sofa, looking up at her expectantly as Jane walked in with a cup of tea.

"Hello, Milly," said Jane, settling down on the sofa. As soon as she sat down, Jane jumped up again in surprise, spilling her tea on the cream-colored rug. "Oh my God!"

She stared down at the soft, sticky thing she'd squashed when she sat down. It was a dead field mouse, blood still oozing from it onto the sofa. "Oh, Milly... you got me a present." Jane looked down at the cat in exasperation. Milly was purring loudly, tail weaving slowly from side to side on the rug, waiting to see whether the gift she'd procured for her new friend and placed on her spot on the sofa would be appreciated.

"You shouldn't have," Jane told the cat. "I mean, you *really* shouldn't have." Milly came over and rubbed herself against Jane's leg. Jane stroked her briefly before setting about removing the little corpse, cleaning the tea off the rug and washing the blood off the leather sofa and the seat of her trousers.

The rest of the day passed uneventfully. Milly was back outside, staring at the woods. The weather was good and for a moment Jane felt relaxed enough to contemplate going for a walk, but the incident in the woods still haunted her and she decided to remain indoors. She remembered the horrible ringing in her ears – the pulsing, stupor-inducing humming, like the chanting of people in some kind of trance – and the lower-pitched, darker, unfamiliar and altogether more menacing sound behind it. An image insinuated itself into Jane's mind – a horrible half-glimpsed image from the past that she'd tried hard to forget.

During her third year at Oxford, Jane had travelled to the United States as an exchange student. Her tutor, Dr Cornelius Bainbridge, had a fascination with books of ancient lore – a fact he kept quiet from the rest of the Human Sciences Department, as such things were frowned upon among the dreaming spires. Bainbridge had always wanted to spend some time studying the rarer occult tomes housed in the famed library at the Miskatonic University in Arkham, Massachusetts, but he'd already spent his sabbatical perusing archaic Sumerian texts in the Middle East, so he devised the cunning plan of arranging an exchange between some of the most gifted students from his department and students from the Miskatonic's Anthropology Department. Fortuitously for Bainbridge, the Department Head at the Miskatonic, Professor William Freeborn (great nephew, as it happened, of the late Tyler M. Freeborn – valued Professor at the same Department in the 1930s), harboured an almost obsessive desire to get his hands on the notorious *Liber Tenebrarum*, the original and last surviving copy of which was purported to be held in the vast labyrinthine stacks of the Bodleian Library in Oxford. The two academics managed to persuade their respective universities to agree to the exchange, which Bainbridge and Freeborn of course insisted on overseeing personally.

Jane was one of only five students from Oxford to have been selected. Dr Bainbridge had a lot of time for the ungainly, introverted girl because of her higher than average intelligence, superior reasoning skills, tenacious mind and protestant work ethic. And so, when Jane expressed an interest in his work, Bainbridge arranged permission for her to accompany him on one of his research days. Staff at the Miskatonic objected on the grounds that their own undergraduates were not permitted to access the most famous artefacts in the library's occult collection – not just on account of their age and concomitant fragility, but also due to the effect that studying their contents might have on young and impressionable minds prone to flights of fancy. Bainbridge had vouched for Jane's good sense in handling precious and delicate documents, and for her sensible and healthily sceptical attitude towards any reading matter she might encounter. And so Jane was allowed to view the Miskatonic's most treasured volumes of arcane literature under the supervision of her tutor.

The two of them were ushered to a restricted room within the library, where Bainbridge had free access to such dread marvels as von Junzt's *Unaussprechlichen Kulten*, the mysterious and fragmentary *Book of Eibon*, and perhaps the most infamous of the library's collection – Abdul Alhazred's *Al Azif*, better known by its Greek name: *Necronomicon*. It was in the *Necronomicon* that Jane had caught a fleeting glimpse of an illustration depicting shadowy figures performing an ancient rite; a fleeting glimpse because at that moment Jane's vision blurred, her ears started to ring and a sharp, thumping pain erupted inside her head, resulting in her first ever migraine. Dr Bainbridge commented that it must have been the culmination of hours spent pouring over musty books in a dusty, ill-ventilated room, and he was probably right, as, after a drink of water, plenty of fresh air and a good night's sleep, Jane felt considerably better.

Funny that she'd forgotten all about the ringing in her ears that had preceded the migraine – the ringing she'd heard again in the forest before her episode. She hoped she wasn't going to have another migraine, although in a way that might be preferable to the terrifying blackout or panic attack she'd experienced yesterday. She hadn't seen the horrid illustration clearly – that day in the Miskatonic library – and, even now, it was more a feeling of cosmic dread that suffused her memory than a clear recollection of anything she might have seen.

Jane distracted herself by watching daytime TV and reading. Once or twice she peered outside to see if she could spy Milly in the long grass, but the cat was probably on the far side of the lawn, which wasn't visible from the sitting room window. In the end she'd deemed it best to keep the front door locked, and opened it only occasionally to check if Milly were sitting there, waiting to be let in. She wasn't. When the sun started to set, Jane took the box of cat biscuits and braved the outside world.

"Milly! Here, kitty! Biscuit time!" But there was no response.

Jane climbed the steps from the patio to the lawn, but there was no sign of Milly. She rattled the dry cat food once more.

"Milly! Here, kitty, kitty!" Silence. Then a troubled meow from somewhere up ahead. "Milly!" Jane hesitated for a moment longer, then headed off across the lawn, alternately shaking the cat biscuit box and calling out. But there was no further response.

Jane slowed as she neared the end of the garden. She called out again, and this time was rewarded with a small, plaintive mew just ahead of her, in the unmown grass by the fallen wire fence demarcating the boundary between the garden and Ash Wood beyond. Then cat biscuits were spilling on the lawn as the box slipped from her grasp. Her ears rang with the stupefying, ominous, primal chant – like the rhythmic pounding of a giant black heart or the pulsing of a dark star on the far side of the cosmos. She was paralysed with fear, unable to scream as a will stronger than her own forced its way into her mind. Her thoughts were fragmenting, dissipating; her very essence was being forced from her body into the chill evening air. Then something bumped against her leg, and an urgent feline yowl burst through the veil that was descending upon

Jane, breaking the spell, bringing her back. She was Jane once more and she was screaming. She scooped Milly up in her arms and ran back to the cottage.

Once they were through the front door, Milly tore herself from Jane's grasp and fled into the house. As Jane locked the door and turned to follow the cat, she caught sight of the calendar hanging on the wall. 29th April. 30th tomorrow – May Eve. Walpurgis Night. One of the four major feast days celebrated by witches, second only to Hallowe'en. An ancient day of power when magic and dark ritual were at their most potent. Jane chastised herself for these silly associations, but then the hazy image from the *Necronomicon* flared in her mind once more. Obscure, silhouetted figures enacting something pre-Christian, pre-pagan; some ageless ritual pre-anything known to modern man... but to what purpose? And what did this have to do with her current situation?

Jane went around the house making sure all the windows were closed, although she hesitated before shutting the one in her bedroom. It had been a warm day and, despite the open window, the foul smell in Jane's room persisted. But she felt safer with the window closed.

Jane wanted to phone Isabelle and tell her that she couldn't stay any longer. She brought up Isabelle's mobile number, but couldn't face the conversation that would doubtless follow – the concern in her friend's voice, the questions. She'd leave food and water for Milly and lock her in the house. Isabelle and Jonathan would be back the day after tomorrow. She'd leave them a note, apologising; she'd try to explain. But what exactly would she say? And how could she leave Milly? As if by some feline sixth sense, Milly, who'd been hiding in a secret place unbeknown to anyone but her, appeared by Jane and placed her head under Jane's hand, looking up at the woman and meowing.

"Oh, Milly," said Jane, stroking the cat's head. "I messed up with your biscuits, but you can have some *Whiskas* tonight by way of an exception. Okay?" Jane fed the cat and they watched television together. This time Milly sat on the sofa next to Jane, watching her intently with, it seemed to Jane, a concerned expression in her yellow and blue eyes. The result of such close heterochromic scrutiny was a little disconcerting, but Jane gleaned some comfort from Milly's presence, and was grateful for their developing friendship. One more night after this one, and then Isabelle and Jonathan would be back and she'd be out of there.

Jane was gradually drifting off, despite the foetid odour she'd been forced to seal in with herself due to her unwillingness to sleep with the window open – not least because of yesterday's sleepwalking episode. After another sunny day, the smell was definitely worse, suggesting that it probably wasn't damp. It was probably food that had been allowed to rot – but where was it? Jane would have to look for it in the morning. Now all she wanted to do was sleep.

She woke up on the lawn. She'd been headed for the woods, but in her stupor she'd walked right into the pile of spilt cat biscuits, and the sharp unnatural scratch of the things against her bare feet had brought her out of her trance. She stood for a moment, not knowing where or who she was. Someone in the woods was whispering her name. A wind whipped up from nowhere, and with it came the ringing, the otherworldly chanting, and Jane started to move forward again – the pull of a powerful alien will forcing her on. But Jane was wide awake now, and fighting with all her might. Milly was behind her, crying in the long grass – a plaintive howl of feline protest and fear like nothing Jane had heard before. She focused all of her dissipating being on that cry of distress behind her, and, with a supreme effort that felt like moving through quicksand, she turned and ran back towards the house. She was vaguely aware of Milly leaping through the grass ahead of her, and of the rush of cold, biting, hissing air that followed her. Then she and Milly were in the cottage, and Jane was locking the door once more.

Jane was shaking as she made herself a strong cup of coffee. She wasn't going to sleep again as long as she was in the cottage. Milly wouldn't leave her side and followed her everywhere, finally settling down on the sofa right by her sitter. Jane flicked through the channels until she found a romantic comedy. She normally hated those things, but tonight the inane, trite stupidity would hopefully wind her up enough to keep her awake. Milly pressed herself against Jane's thigh, her little heart beating rapidly. When Jane went to the bathroom, or to the kitchen to make another cup of coffee, Milly went with her, disparate eyes following every move that Jane made. Each time she caught herself drifting off, Jane would pinch herself or bite her own hand or go for a walk around the house. She had put chairs in front of the windows in the sitting room and piled them up high enough with blankets to block out the view of the garden and the wood. By morning, Jane was exhausted, bewildered, shaky, but still awake.

Sunday 30th April (May Eve – Walpurgis Night)

Jittery and fragile, Jane went to her room for a fresh change of clothes. It had been a warm night, and the stench hit her full force. She ran to the bathroom and threw up all the coffee she'd spent the night drinking. When she had nothing left in her stomach, she returned to her room and searched it top to bottom. From time to time she paused, the reek of what she was now convinced was decomposing organic matter threatening to make her sick once more. Milly joined her, watching from the doorway as Jane searched in the bin, looked under the bed, opened drawers and cupboards. Her nose kept leading her to a corner of the room, but there was nothing there except the armchair. Jane grabbed the armchair by the arms and yanked it away from the wall. The sight that greeted her made her grateful that she had nothing left to throw up.

"Oh, Milly." The cat had obviously crawled right under the armchair with the decapitated rabbit and stuffed it in at the far end, against the wall, a day or two before Jane's arrival. It was well concealed – no wonder Isabelle hadn't spotted it and Jane hadn't found it before.

Jane was weak and disorientated. She had to remove the festering headless bunny, but she wasn't going outside. Milly watched with some interest as Jane opened the window, picked up the rabbit by its back paws and threw it out, trying not to hear the sound it made as it connected with the paving stones beneath. Then she closed the window again and changed her clothes.

Jane was amazed at how just one partial night's worth of sleep deprivation could have such a major effect. She found she had to concentrate on every little thing she did, and pay extra attention when doing things such as making tea, as objects seemed to slip through her fingers if she didn't take the utmost care with them. She kept glancing back at the calendar in the kitchen. It was Walpurgis Night. Witches, Satanists and other cultists would be performing all kinds of bizarre rituals tonight and, although she didn't believe in the magical effects of such things, it did mean that there might be some unsavoury people out and about tonight, intent on making mischief. The kind of people who occasionally amused themselves by torturing and killing domestic pets. Milly meowed and scratched at the front door, but Jane wasn't going to let her out today.

At lunchtime Isabelle phoned. The exhaustion and wariness in Jane's voice caught her by surprise.

"Jane? Are you okay?"

"Why is it called Ash Wood?"

"Excuse me?"

"There are practically no ash trees in it. So why is it called Ash Wood?" The bizarre question and the distracted, haunted quality of Jane's voice alarmed Isabelle.

"A witch's ashes were scattered in it... Jane...? You still there?"

"I'm here. What do you mean, a witch's ashes were scattered in it?"

"Look, now's not the best time. I'll tell you the whole story when we get home."

"Tell me now. Please."

"It's just a stupid story. I don't know all the details."

"Please, Isabelle."

"All I know is that in the seventeenth century a woman who lived in the cottage was accused of bewitching a couple of men in the village, including the priest. And the villagers blamed her for the disappearances of several children. She was burnt at the stake and her ashes were scattered in the wood."

"Where in the wood?"

"I don't know. All over, I guess. Anyway, it's probably not even true. It's just a story an old man told me in the pub... Why is this so important to you?"

"You should have told me."

"Jane, don't be silly. Look, we're back tomorrow. We'll talk then. Okay?"

By teatime Jane was suffering from microsleeps. She'd catch herself nodding off for a moment, and each time it happened she came to in a state of abject fear. Sometimes, for the second that she was asleep, she thought she could hear the eerie chanting. She hated herself for ignoring Milly's begging and crying to be let out of the house. When the sun set and the shadows lengthened, Milly stopped her entreaties and peered fearfully out of the sitting room window, over the blanket that had partially slipped to reveal the woods outside.

Jane was finding the urge to sleep increasingly difficult to combat. At one point she dozed off on the sofa and only woke up when Milly placed her black and pink nose up against Jane's nose. Jane got up, disturbed by a momentary, but frightening dream that she couldn't remember. She tried pacing around the house, but soon got bored and tired, and sat back down on the sofa. She spun round when she thought she heard someone behind her whispering her name. She tried to console herself that it was just an auditory hallucination. She readjusted the blanket that was covering the window so as not to see the shadows crowding in the dusky wood. Then she was dozing off again, and Milly was meowing. The ringing started in her head, and she was dozing off, and Milly was pawing at her leg. But she was too exhausted to react, and Milly was yowling, and her limbs were too heavy to lift, and she was falling asleep. Then she was in the woods.

Jane was wide awake, shivering with cold. It took her a moment to realise where she was, and then her fear nearly drove her out of her wits. She was in almost pitch blackness, the dry trees around her creaking and rattling despite the absence of wind. For a moment she had no idea which way to go, but then in the distance she saw the dim lights of Ash Wood Cottage. She took a tentative step in their direction, and then she heard someone whisper her name. Jane froze, but didn't turn around.

"Jane." The whisper came again – this time from a different direction. "Jane." Then another and another – encircling her – as though the wood itself were whispering her name from under every bush and behind every tree. Jane was sure now that she was losing her mind. Despite the dark and the uneven terrain, she tried to run, but from all around her came the sound that she had come to dread. Her ears rang from the horrendous humming, which became a chanting – frightening, lulling, overpowering, mesmerising, rising in pitch and volume until it became like the scream of a million damned souls in hell, and coupling with the infernal drone of a boundless darkness that was reaching for her.

Visions of a terrifying nature swam before Jane – glimpses of things that no mortal should ever see. Shadowy, silhouetted figures swaying around a fire – some human, but others... others were horned, winged, animal-headed – ancient, horrifying creatures that had no right to walk among men. As the flames of the fire grew, the vision shifted, metamorphosed into a huge fiery pit in which burning souls screamed in perpetuity. And behind the torture and the carnage Jane could sense the hideous pulsing of the eternal abyss.

The sound in her head was unbearable. Jane was losing all sense of where she was, of who she was. The rhythmic pounding of the chanting and the fathomless darkness of the infinite void were all she could see and hear. A preternatural wind whipped up around her, trapping her in its vortex. Then the ice-cold tentacle was entering her head, her mind; probing like a violator inside her skull, her thoughts; its chill spreading through her very core. She battled it with all of her being. She tried to remember where she was, who she was – *I am Jane!* – but all she could feel was the numbing cold creeping inside her skull, exploring, expanding. *I am Jane.* All she could hear was the terrible din of the chanting and the sombre pulsating of the dark eons engulfing her. *I am...* And she was forgetting where she was and who she was, and the thing in her head was pushing and pushing. *I...*

And all that was left was a silent scream, and Jane was out of her body, and the wind was scattering her, and she was in the leaves, in the parched earth, in the gnarled blackened roots of the dark wood. She was festering in the dust and the dirt, and bugs were crawling over her and burrowing through her. She was in every rotted leaf and every dry twig and every wizened branch and every parched bit of dust, and small crawling things were devouring her and dying in her and rotting inside her. And she had no body, yet she could feel the things crawling and burrowing and eating and dying and rotting. She was nowhere. She was everywhere. On the ground, in the ground, in the putrefaction.

Monday 1st May (May Day)

She lay unconscious for hours on the forest floor. When her body finally twitched into life, she opened her eyes to the dawning of a fine May morning. She sat up slowly, looked at her unfamiliar hands, her feet, her legs, her body. She was cold and streaked with dirt, but otherwise unharmed. She smiled as she got up calmly and started to make her way through the woods towards the cottage. As she crossed the fallen wire fence, she spotted Milly waiting on the lawn.

As she approached, the cat's fur bristled, tail several times its normal size, ears laid flat against her head in fear. Milly hissed and started backing away.

"You dare hiss at me?" she demanded of the petrified feline. "You will come here, like a good cat."

Milly dropped to her haunches and, quaking from nose to tail, crawled on her belly towards the cat sitter.

Isabelle and Jonathan got home tired. They'd left their car in one of Gatwick's long-stay car parks, and the drive from the airport wasn't particularly lengthy or strenuous, but the flight had been an early morning one and they hadn't had much sleep. By the time they walked through the front door it was gone midday.

"Hello!" Isabelle called out, setting down her suitcase at the bottom of the stairs. "We're home! Jane? Milly!" But the house was silent, and neither Jane nor Milly, who usually greeted her mistress with a castigating meow, were anywhere to be seen. "Milly! Here, Milly!"

Jonathan set the rest of the luggage down next to Isabelle's suitcase, and followed his wife into the sitting room. The sight that greeted them stopped them in their tracks. Jane was sitting in Jonathan's favourite armchair, stroking Milly. The cat sat calmly and quietly on Jane's lap. Milly was a friendly cat, but she was no lap cat, and would meow loudly and wriggle free if ever Isabelle or Jonathan tried to hold her for any length of time or sit her on their laps.

"Wow!" Isabelle smiled at her friend in amazement, quickly dismissing the little stab of jealousy she suddenly felt over her cat's affections. "Look at the two of you! Best of friends!"

The creature that wore Jane's body smiled coldly back at Isabelle.

"Hello, Isabelle," she said. Her smile broadened visibly, transforming into a look that could only be described as lascivious as she turned her attention to Isabelle's husband. "Hello, Jonathan."

"Hi, Jane," Jonathan replied, a little puzzled, but not in a bad way. Jane usually looked at her feet when Jonathan addressed her – something he put down to her shyness and awkwardness around men. Isabelle threw her husband a disapproving look and he shrugged back.

"So, was everything okay when we were away?" Isabelle asked.

"Why wouldn't it be?" responded Jane, never taking her eyes off Jonathan. Isabelle studied her friend's leering face. Jane looked different somehow. She was wearing make-up. That was it: not only was she wearing make-up, but the shade of lipstick she'd applied thickly to her lips was identical to Isabelle's. Jane had been using

Isabelle's make-up. Not just that, but she'd somehow squeezed into Isabelle's low-cut blue top and her short, stretchy black skirt.

"Uh, you're wearing my clothes," Isabelle finally said. Jonathan, who wasn't very observant when it came to ladies' fashion, looked at Isabelle in surprise, then back to Jane. There was indeed something familiar about the clothes that Jane was wearing, but they looked totally different on the larger girl, who was spilling out of them in a rather alluring way. Jonathan was nonplussed to find himself feeling rather aroused. Jane finally turned her attention back to Isabelle.

"Oh yeah," she said. "I ran out of clean clothes and I didn't know how to use the washing-machine. I'll give them back before I leave."

"No problem," said Isabelle. But she wasn't buying the washing-machine story. Jane might be shy and frumpy and awkward, she might even sometimes give the impression of being a little slow, but she was sharp as anything when it came to figuring out how things worked. It was no coincidence that she'd been selected by her tutor at Oxford as the only girl to be part of the exchange with the American university. So no – Isabelle wasn't buying the washing-machine story, but she would let it slide. "You hungry, Jane?" she asked.

"Sure," Jane replied, all the while continuing to stroke Milly impassively. Milly didn't so much as twitch a muscle. She seemed completely mesmerised, her eyes staring into space like different coloured marbles. But she wasn't purring. And Isabelle suddenly had the bizarre notion that the cat was terrified into utter submission. She dismissed the idea immediately. She was tired, and seeing Jane all dolled-up like that, and in her clothes as well, had caught her off guard, but there was no need to start freaking out.

"Well, why don't you just relax," said Isabelle, heading out of the sitting room. "I'll have a quick shower and then I'll sort us out some lunch."

"Sure."

Isabelle paused in the doorway when she realised that Jonathan wasn't following her.

"Honey?" She stared pointedly at her husband.

"What?" Jonathan tore his eyes away from Jane. "Oh, okay. I'm coming."

Jonathan reluctantly followed his wife upstairs and half-heartedly unpacked his suitcase while she showered.

"I doubt there's any food left," said Isabelle, rubbing her hair with a towel as she entered their bedroom. "What do you want to do?"

"I'm shattered, baby," said Jonathan. "I can't face getting back in the car. You wouldn't be able to pick up a few things while I shower and make a quick work call, would you?" There was a pause as Isabelle contemplated her husband's suggestion. A nasty paranoid thought about Jane and Jonathan reared its ugly head in Isabelle's mind, but she dismissed it before it could fully form and take root. How could she even think such a thing for a moment? Jonathan had been nothing but loving and loyal to her ever since they'd met, and she hated herself for thinking ill of him even for a second.

"Sure, hon," she finally replied. "I'll be back soon."

Isabelle carefully backed the Land Rover out onto the road and headed for the village. She couldn't fathom what had happened to Jane. Jealousy – that was it. Isabelle had a home, a husband, a career, even a pet. Poor Jane had nothing. It was obvious that Jane's envy of everything that Isabelle had, and she didn't, had got the better of her. She'd somehow won over Milly by feeding her treats and spoiling her, and she'd thought she'd make a play for Jonathan too. Well, that was too much. Isabelle was sorry for her, but she was going to make damn sure that Jane never set foot in Ash Wood Cottage again. From now on, they'd use a local cat sitter.

Isabelle picked up four salmon fillets and some fresh fruit and veg from the village supermarket. By the time she was on her way home again, her anger had subsided and she even felt a little guilty about how glad she'd be to see the back of Jane. After all, Jane had come a long way and given up her bank holiday weekend to look after Milly. By the time she turned into the driveway, Isabelle had almost forgiven Jane. And then she felt even guiltier when she saw that Jane's car was gone. She walked into the kitchen and put down the groceries.

"Hello! Anybody home?" But there was no reply.

Friday 1st September

The paint had already started to flake on the FOR SALE sign outside Ash Wood Cottage. Had Isabelle decided to stay following Jonathan and Milly's disappearance, she might have noticed the change in the wood behind her house.

The trees were verdant, their leaves a lush and vibrant green in spite of autumn's rapid approach. Some of them still flowered despite the time of year, and sunlight streamed in through their mighty boughs. If a walker were to find themselves among the beauty of this ancient place, he or she might wonder at the moistness of the earth following such a dry summer. The ground was damp, muddy almost, as water seeped from the soil like tears.

Animals had moved into Ash Wood; from the undergrowth to the crowns of the tallest trees, the wood teemed with life. And yet for all its beauty, anyone who wandered into the wood emerged feeling pensive and a little sad. Even the birds that thrived in this quiet place sang a melancholy song.

THE LEMMY/TRUMP TEST

THE LEMMY/TRUMP TEST

> "It is difficult to know which came first, the supply or the demand. ... food from a food bank – the supply – is a free good, and by definition there is an almost infinite demand for a free good."

> Lord David Freud,
> House of Lords debate, 2nd July 2013

AIM FOR THE head – that's the only way to make sure they stay down. Don't get their blood on you and, whatever you do, don't let them bite you!

Oh, for Christ's sake, man, don't look so worried. We're not going anywhere near them. Why d'ya think I brought *this*? ... Pretty, isn't it? Nothing like a family heirloom. My great grandfather used it to hunt elephant in India. Just imagine what it'll do to those stinking bastards.

They hang around the food bank during the day. Food bank's been closed for weeks, but the dumb fucks just won't leave. It's like they're totally brain dead – just keep repeating what they used to do before. Shuffling around, going through the motions. ... It's not need; it's greed! ... LOL! ... At night they scavenge around the bins. Look – over there! Here they come.

Stacey follows the others round the back of the row of restaurants, one hand clutching her daughter's little hand, the other resting on her own swollen belly. She still can't fathom how quickly her life has turned to hell.

A tear rolls down Stacey's cheek as she recalls coming home to find police on her doorstep, waiting to give her the devastating news that the man she'd shared her life with since university had jumped off the balcony of their fifth floor council flat. The council flat they were being evicted from after losing their benefits. The note said that he was sorry, that there was nothing else he could do to keep them off the streets, and he couldn't live with that; that he loved them. Stacey had considered taking her daughter in her arms and following her husband – like the young woman she'd read about in the papers, but she didn't.

Stacey and Phoebe now lived under Hammersmith Bridge, part of a small community of homeless people who had taken in the heavily pregnant woman and her daughter. They'd lived on the one meal a day they'd been getting from the over-stretched food bank, but when that was forced to close, the hunger became unbearable.

Stacey begged outside the Riverside Studios or Hammersmith Mall during the day. Some people spat at her, accused her of having 'borrowed a child' to gain sympathy, and lectured her to get a job. Others looked at her with pity and threw her a few pence, sometimes a pound coin. One elderly gent had taken her and Phoebe to McDonald's, but the manager had soon thrown them out – their smell and general appearance was putting the other customers off their food.

On days when she didn't get enough from begging to buy food, she'd wait till dark and go through the bins, hoping that no one would see her. It seemed that many people had the same idea. They were a motley crew: many of them elderly, some disabled, some mentally ill, and some like Stacey: middle class, well educated, well adjusted, for whom what should have been a temporary setback – her husband's redundancy – had turned into a life-altering tragedy as societal safety nets had ripped open and Stacey and her family had fallen through.

Stacey tells Phoebe to wait quietly while she lifts a dustbin lid. That's when the shots ring out. Not far from Stacey an elderly man collapses, crying out in pain. Then people are screaming and running all around her. Stacey grabs her daughter by the hand, and they run too.

The hissing sound of compressed air behind her, and something strikes the back of Stacey's head. She is thrown forward onto her belly, pulling her daughter over with her. The last thing Stacey sees is her child wailing in terror and pain.

What's wrong? You're not upset, are you? They're only bloody Scroungers. You heard what the Welfare Minister said: in order to save the economy, we must get rid of 4 million useless mouths. Well, you didn't think he meant: buy them plane tickets to Timbuktu, did you? ... Come on, let's get to Rupert's. His soiree must be in full swing by now.

They're easy to pick off – Scroungers. And you're doing the country a favour. But you can't really have much fun with them. You never know what disease they might be carrying – most of them living rough now, like animals. It's best just to get a clean kill and get out. If you want to have some fun first, you should keep your old man covered, if you know what I mean. Best to sow your wild oats in the slightly 'better' areas.

We'll be sporting in Notting Hill tomorrow; if Rupert and the chaps like you, you can tag along. An initiation, if you like. We'll all be doing it together. The trick is to get a girl alone, maybe two girls. You can even do a couple – shag the girl and make the guy watch. Or shag them both. It's best not to leave any witnesses.

The Club awards points for a kill – the better the kill, the more points. And the more points, the higher you advance in the Club. Imagination is rewarded, but we value tradition above all. If you have to go in for a quick kill, try to crush the nose and gouge out the eyes at the same time – it takes some skill, but manage that and you'll get automatic membership. 'Tipping the lion', it used to be called; we just call it 'Fuckface'. But if you manage a Blood Eagle, you'll automatically advance to the level of Adept. It takes time so you can only do it in a secluded place. You get the prey on its front and cut the ribs by the backbone, breaking them outwards and spreading them, and pull out the lungs, one to each side. None of the other Clubs do it – it's our trademark. It has a demoralising effect on the natives, and warns other Clubs to stay off our sports ground. And it has a grand sense of the theatrical, which I must confess rather appeals to me. Have you ever thought of treading the boards?

Here we are. Rupert's is the last house on the left. Go ahead, don't be shy. I'm sure the chaps will like you.

Emily's eyes widen as the blade opens her vein. Wagner's 'The Valkyrie' blares from the sound system in the corner. The girl tries to scream, but succeeds only in choking on the gag that's been shoved into her mouth. Blood pours out of her lacerated wrist, almost missing the silver cocktail shaker that's waiting to collect it. The tall young man with blond hair and chiselled features – the one who'd offered Emily a hundred pounds to help serve drinks and canapés at his friend's party – giggles as he catches the blood. He holds down the lid on the metal container, doing a little dance as he shakes up the contents. "Shaken, not stirred!" he shouts over the opera. "Who's got the glasses?" Someone holds out a tray with tall glasses; each one has a piece of celery sticking out of it. The blond 007 wannabe opens the cocktail shaker and distributes the contents.

I love the smell of vodka in the morning! Well, it's gone midnight – that technically makes it morning, does it not? What's wrong? Never had a proper Bloody Mary? ... Who *is* she? What do *you* care? She's a student Matthew picked up. They'll do anything now that their loans have been called in. Don't worry about it. Drink up, man! To the Club!

You know, you're pretty lucky to be here. We don't usually allow non-members. But I knew from the moment I saw you that I was going to like you. You know how I knew? I call it the Lemmy/Trump test. You look puzzled. Well, when I meet someone for the first time, I try to work out whether, given the choice, they'd rather hang out with Lemmy or with Donald Trump. If I figure they'd rather hang out with Donald, then I know I'm going to like them. Don't get me wrong, I don't like new money; I wouldn't hang out with Trump myself, but I like the sensibilities of the self-made men and the city wide-boys. Ruthless, like sharks. I have a certain sentiment for predators. They have a healthy attitude to life. It's the hippies I can't stand. The hippies and the rock'n'rollers, the wasters, the johnny-do-rights, the tree-huggers, the lefties, the whiners, the darkies, the single mothers and all the other scum. Too old, too sick or too lazy to be of any use to anyone. The Benefits Brigade. The Scroungers. Whether they're bleeding the country dry or helping others do so, they all have the same mentality. They're weak. They're victims. And there's nothing I hate more than a victim. Give me the Donald Trumps every time. Now *you* – as soon as I saw you, I knew you were a Donald Trump type.

But look at me, rambling on, while the chaps have got some entertainment lined up at the pool.

Marie whimpers as her chair is jolted roughly from behind. The wooden plank looms closer as Marie is pushed towards the deep end of the swimming-pool. She tries to cry out for help, but the multiple sclerosis took her voice a long time ago. She tries to struggle, but her muscles are no longer hers to control. The only thing she can do is grab hold of the wheels of her chair and try to block the forward motion generated by whoever is pushing it. The unseen assailant behind her back shoves the chair harder, and Marie flinches as the rubber of the wheels burns her palms and fingers.

When the doorbell rang, Marie figured that her daughter must have forgotten her keys when she went to the supermarket. She'd wheeled herself to the front door and opened the latch that had been lowered specially to be within her reach. But it hadn't been Sylvie at the door; it had been two smartly dressed youths, who'd taken hold of her chair and wheeled her out into the street.

Marie tries to push the youths off as they strap her to her wheelchair, and the chair to the large plank of wood. Fear constricts her throat; she gasps like a beached fish, trying to get air into her lungs. Another youth joins the group and, as they push her end of the plank over the pool, Marie urinates on herself. Then the wheelchair is over the water, the weight of it bending the plank so that Marie is in the pool. She tries to scream as the water closes over her head.

The youths attempt to pull the plank up and away from the pool, planning to emulate the trial by water used in medieval witchcraft trials. For a moment Marie's head is above water again, and she pants desperately for air. But the weight of the wheelchair is too great, and the plank snaps, the metal of the chair dragging the terrified woman to the bottom of the pool.

Oh dear, she drowned. I guess she wasn't a benefit cheat after all! ... Didn't you see that cartoon on Facebook? Assessing disability benefit claimants by ducking? If they drown, they're eligible for benefits? Hilarious! When Rupert saw it, he suggested it to the bird from Assessment Services that he's been shagging. He said she paused way too long before laughing it off. Can you imagine? Natural selection through benefits assessment. ... LOL! ... We'd soon have the country back on its feet! ... Anyway, Rupert's bit of fluff has proved a gem. She has files full of info on Scroungers – home addresses and all. Sometimes it's fun to choose your quarry to order. See the look of surprise on their little faces when you ring their doorbell and address them by name.

But there I go, rambling again. ... Let's go back inside. I think Rupert likes you. That's a good sign. If you fare well at the sports tomorrow, you could be in.

THE GATEHOUSE

THE GATEHOUSE

RACHAEL STOPPED HER little car at the side of the road and stared up at the crooked, dark building. She shivered, but not with dread; rather with anticipation and a feeling of unexplained familiarity. She took out the set of keys that the solicitor had given her, along with her late uncle's will. As she walked up to the gate, she glanced up and thought she caught sight of a shadow moving across the window of the room above it. A longer look led her to dismiss this notion. She braced herself against the sudden cold, opened the gate and drove into the courtyard that had been created when a small plot of land behind the Gatehouse was fenced off in the early twentieth century.

As Rachael unlocked the entrance door to the Gatehouse itself, she noticed that the building was charred in places. A torrent of heart-breaking memories overwhelmed her, and she grabbed onto the wall of the Gatehouse to steady herself. She noticed to her surprise how comforting the dark stone felt beneath her palm – almost warm... no, that couldn't be right – the stone could not be warm. She withdrew her hand and hurried into the house.

There was a small parlour downstairs and an ample kitchen. Upstairs was a bedroom, a bathroom and a study of sorts – filled with dusty old books and cobwebs. A simple enough arrangement, but Rachael couldn't help feeling that there was more to the Gatehouse than met the eye. The sad, brooding building seemed to sense her presence. Somehow it knew that she had suffered loss, and empathised with her, thought Rachael, then chided herself for being silly.

She made a mental note to look through the books and papers in the study, curious about the uncle who'd wanted her to live in his strange, melancholy house. Her curiosity surprised her – it was the first time since leaving the hospital that something had taken her mind off her husband and little girl. As soon as she thought this, the memories flooded back, and with them the pain. The Gatehouse darkened around Rachael, sensing her sudden change of mood. Or perhaps a cloud passed in front of the autumn sun.

Rachael wondered vainly whether she could get all her shopping delivered and avoid dealing with the outside world, but the village she had driven through didn't have so much as a supermarket. Reluctantly she picked up her coat and handbag, and headed out to the shops.

At the grocery store Rachael ran headfirst into a dark-haired, athletic man in his thirties. He apologised for having startled her, and picked up her car key from the floor. The store's proprietress looked on with mild disapproval from behind the counter as the man introduced himself. His name was John Fielding and he was the local police Sergeant.

"You're not wearing a uniform," Rachael responded after a brief, but awkward silence.

"It's my day off." He smiled.

Rachael tried to move past the man, but he wouldn't let her go until he'd ascertained that she had just moved into the Gatehouse.

"Spooky old house," he commented. "Will you be living there alone?" Rachael didn't want any friends.

"I like the house," she said a little too defensively. John put up his hands in a placatory gesture.

"Hey, there's no accounting for taste... Why don't I drop by later and see how you're settling in?"

"I'm not ready for visitors yet," Rachael squirmed. "I mean, I haven't unpacked yet or anything."

"Just a quick, neighbourly visit," continued John, "check that your security is okay, that sort of thing". He noticed Rachael's worried expression and added, "Not that we have much trouble around here... Anyway, welcome to the neighbourhood... and see you later." He smiled disarmingly and ducked out of the shop before Rachael had a chance to protest.

Rachael was in the kitchen when she heard John's car pull up outside. She stiffened, nervous and unsure of herself. Around her the Gatehouse creaked disapprovingly and somewhere upstairs a door slammed. The doorbell rang and Rachael went to open it. To her surprise the door stuck and she struggled with it for a moment before getting it open. Any doubts she might have had about letting John in dissipated when he smiled at her. Not so the Gatehouse. As Rachael returned his smile and stood aside to let him in, John touched the doorpost and winced, drawing back his hand.

"What's the matter?" asked Rachael.

"Nothing, nothing... just something sharp on the doorframe there." John sucked his finger and inspected the doorframe, but saw nothing that might have been responsible for the scratch he'd sustained. As Rachael shut the door behind him, he produced a small bunch of flowers that he'd been holding behind his back. He noticed Rachael's hesitation and said, "Welcome."

"Thank you." Rachael found a tall glass to put the flowers in. She turned on the tap, but nothing happened. Perplexed, she turned the tap some more. Nothing, and then a considerable amount of cold water under pressure shot out, bounced off the bottom of the sink and splattered on Rachael's face and clothes. She jumped back, startled.

"Looks like the plumbing needs fixing."

"It was fine before," mused Rachael, filling the glass and then putting on the kettle.

Rachael and John drank tea and chatted – that is, John chatted and Rachael listened. He'd always wanted to be a police officer and he loved his job, but the village was rather dull and the closest thing to a crime hotspot was the church hall on ladies' bingo night. Rachael's mind had started to drift when she noticed a foetid odour in the room. John noticed it too.

"Your pipes are really gonna need sorting. Would you like me to take a look?"

"No, no. Thank you. I'm sure it will be fine."

"Well, I guess I'd better get going. Promise me you'll call if you need anything. Anything at all."

"I will." The light over the kitchen table flickered and John shook his head at it.

"Are you sure you'll be all right here?"

"I'm sure... Thank you."

"Can I pop in and see you again sometime?"

Rachael nodded absentmindedly, wondering where the horrible smell was coming from. The light flickered again and dimmed visibly.

"Right, then. Well, see you soon."

Rachael walked John to the door. It opened easily and the policeman left reluctantly, looking back over his shoulder and waving. Rachael locked the door behind him and determined to seek out the source of the bad smell, but it was gone. As she went to wash the mugs, the lamp shone steady and bright over the kitchen table.

Rachael's first night in the Gatehouse was a sleepless one. Something kept scratching behind the wall of her room. Each time she put on the light, the noise stopped. When she switched the light off again, the scratching resumed – sometimes weak and distant, sometimes loud and persistent as though a cat were sharpening its claws on the side of her bed. A perfunctory search revealed nothing, and Rachael returned to bed. After a while the scratching resumed, briefly this time, giving way to whispering and murmurs. Then Rachael heard distinct footsteps running through the house. The mysterious sounds got the better of her and she put on the light again, curious but unafraid. She investigated more thoroughly, but found nothing. She couldn't understand why she wasn't terrified of the eerie house with its strange noises. She lay in the dark, listening. As the first glimmer of dawn flickered in the window, the noises subsided and Rachael finally fell asleep, waking up late and feeling less tired than she might have expected.

Rachael spent the following days unpacking her few belongings, cleaning, and looking through her uncle's papers and books. Some referred to the history of the Gatehouse. Others dealt with subjects like philosophy and theology, and were harder to follow. A few showed a frightening-looking winged creature: half human, half goat. Although Rachael associated the image with the devil, it seemed that this was a positive being, representing the universal life-force and the perfect synthesis of the earthly and the divine – a state that human beings should aspire to. Rachael poured over these texts, while the Gatehouse walls leaned gently down towards her, cradling her and hiding her away from the world that had taken her husband and child.

The growing harmony between woman and house was disturbed only by visits from John, who never managed to stay long, as the Gatehouse would assail his nostrils with foul smells, bristle with splinters that scratched his fingers, and spit water at him whenever he went near a tap. He would make his excuses politely and leave. Rachael couldn't deny her physical attraction to him, but life was so much less complicated when it was just her and the Gatehouse. The only problem was that her sleep was increasingly disturbed by vivid nightmares: flashbacks of the firemen dragging her from her burning house as she reached back towards her husband and daughter mingled with the fire and screaming and slaughter of a previous age. And the night-time noises grew more insistent. Sometimes Rachael could hear crying, sometimes laughter. The scratching often turned into a pounding that reverberated throughout the house. She would lie awake, listening to the different sounds, strangely unafraid, knowing that a further search for their source was futile, but curious about it nonetheless.

One evening John had been over for dinner. He had stuck around after the meal and tried to kiss Rachael as she washed the dishes. The house came to the rescue as a picture fell off the wall behind them.

"I guess that's my cue," quipped John, awareness that his love interest's house was not overly fond of him beginning to register. "Thanks for dinner. See you tomorrow?"

Rachael smiled and walked him to the door. He managed to kiss her goodbye on the doorstep. She pulled away eventually, but John seemed satisfied as he strode off to his car.

As Rachael was hanging the picture back up, the doorbell rang, startling her. John must have forgotten something. She opened the door with the words "Back so soon?", but stopped mid-sentence at the sight of a strange couple on her doorstep.

"We're sorry to disturb you," said the tall, slim man with piercing blue eyes. "Your uncle was a close friend. There are things he wanted us to tell you about the Gatehouse. Please, could we come in for a while?"

Rachael estimated the man's age to be about forty. His voice was soft and he had an air of calm about him. Rachael started to move aside to let him in, but then she glanced at the fiery-haired, wild-eyed young woman next to him and changed her mind. There was something feral about the redhead that Rachael didn't like.

"I don't think so," she said, turning back to the man. But he wasn't giving up easily.

"Please, Rachael, this really won't take long. It's what your uncle wanted."

"He was a wonderful man," interjected the woman, with a touch of Irish lilt. She smiled at Rachael, but Rachael still didn't like the look of her.

"How do you know my name?" she demanded of the man. The man and woman glanced at each other, then the man turned back to Rachael.

"Your uncle was a very dear friend of ours. When he was coming to the end of his earthly life, he often spoke of you. You were his only living relative. He had high hopes for you."

"He never even knew me." Rachael decided to let the 'earthly life' bit slide. Her curiosity about these people was growing. What could her uncle, a notorious recluse who shunned the villagers and the world at large – according to his solicitor, at any rate – have had to do with these hippy weirdoes? Perhaps they were making everything up – but why?

The man's eyes were boring into her and Rachael couldn't think straight. She turned away for a moment and glanced over her shoulder, into the depths of the Gatehouse. She didn't notice the couple exchange glances again, or the dark, troubled look that momentarily crossed the man's features. By the time Rachael turned back, the man was regarding her amiably once more.

"He never met you, that's true," the man said calmly, "but he followed your life at a distance; he... knew of the terrible ordeal you suffered." Rachael frowned. "Your uncle truly believed that the Gatehouse would help you heal. He made it his mission to have you brought here once he passed on."

"I like the house," admitted Rachael. The strangers grasped at her unintentional offering.

"Good," said the man, while the woman watched Rachael intently. "We have so much to tell you about it. The Gatehouse is a special place."

Rachael studied the couple closely. Did they really know things about her mysterious, magical house?

"I'm Nick," the man said suddenly, as though sensing Rachael's weakening resolve, "and this is Cat". The woman nodded at Rachael and braced herself against the cold wind that had started to blow.

"Okay, come in for a bit."

Cat smiled triumphantly and brushed past Rachael into the house. Nick looked up at the house in awe and touched the doorpost before entering. Rachael noticed that the Gatehouse didn't harm him. She closed the front door and followed her guests. Their confidence in moving through her home was rather irritating. They'd obviously been here before, and the house seemed to accept them. Annoyed at herself for feeling jealous about a building, Rachael went into the parlour, where her guests were already seated. At least neither of them was sitting in her favourite armchair.

"Would you like a drink?" Now that she'd let them in, she'd have to play the hostess.

"No thanks," said Nick, "we have a lot to tell you and we don't want to take up too much of your time."

Rachael looked at Cat, who shook her head.

"So, how did you know my uncle?" Rachael asked, gazing into Nick's striking eyes.

"Your uncle was a great man, a visionary. We showed him the potential of the Gatehouse, but it was he who took the lead and set world-altering events in motion. Unfortunately illness overtook him before he was able to complete his work."

Rachael sighed. Perhaps they were just loonies after all.

"Look, I'm afraid I have no idea what you're talking about."

"I'll try to explain everything from the beginning," said Nick. "Please, bear with me. You might find what I have to tell you difficult to believe and even frightening, but it's all true and there's nothing to be afraid of." Rachael opened her mouth to protest, but Nick held up his hand. "Please, hear me out, and then, if you still want us to go, we'll go."

"During the Middle Ages, the Gatehouse was the entrance to a Templar stronghold. The Catholic Church turned on the Knights and murdered them all except for one. The Last Knight hid in the catacombs beneath the Gatehouse and vowed to bring back his dead brothers." Nick ignored Rachael's incredulous expression. "As you know, there are places in the world that are believed to have special powers. For example, holy places where people go on pilgrimages, to be healed, and haunted places, which always feel cold and sad, where some people claim to see or hear ghosts." Rachael thought about the noises in her own house. "Such places of power are created in a number of different ways, but they always involve human activity and powerful emotions, be they positive or negative. For example, if someone dies in violent or tragic circumstances, their emotional energy stays in that place. Other people who go there pick up on the melancholy or fear that remains, themselves feeling fear or sadness, which adds to the original energy and strengthens it. And so the negative emotions in a place grow, feeding on visitors' feelings and perpetuating. The same happens in a holy place, where the prayers of thousands of people linger and add to the positive atmosphere."

"So you're telling me that the Gatehouse is a place of power?" Rachael decided to play along for the time being.

"Yes, but the Gatehouse is much more than just an ordinary place of power. It has the potential to become – quite literally – a gateway."

"A gateway to what?"

"A gateway between this world and the next."

"And what's that supposed to mean?" Rachael was struggling not to sound sarcastic.

"It means that if the gateway is opened, there will be no more death."

"Oh, come on! You must think I'm really stupid."

"No, not at all. Far from it." Nick held Rachael's gaze. "You're the one who can open the gateway."

Rachael stood up, annoyed.

"Look, I think it's time you left."

The strangers stayed in their seats. Cat looked at Nick with an 'I told you so' expression.

"Rachael, please, you promised to hear us out."

"I did hear you out, and you promised to go."

"I haven't finished yet. I promised we'd go once you hear us out, and we will. You have my word on that. But please, let me finish what I have to say. It's the least you can do for your uncle who was my friend and who gave you this incredible house."

Rachael became aware of her house. It hadn't played up since the arrival of the strangers. The lights were burning brightly; no window had slammed or door creaked. The guests hadn't cut themselves or picked up any splinters, and the whole house seemed to be still, as if listening to Nick expounding its history. Now, with her attention focused on the house, Rachael noticed the curtains rustle gently, reassuringly.

"Yes, okay." She sat back down. "I did promise to hear you out, and if you're really my uncle's friends, as you say you are, then I want to hear what you have to say. Please go on."

The atmosphere in the room relaxed, the curtains fell still and all attention focussed on Nick.

"For over seven hundred years, a succession of gatekeepers has lived in the Gatehouse, guarding it and waiting for the right time to open the gateway."

"The right time?"

"The opening ritual described in the Book of the Gate can only be performed when the major planets of our solar system are in specific positions in the sky. The correct alignment only occurs once every two hundred years. The next time this happens will be at the end of the month, on October 31st."

"Halloween?" said Rachael, barely suppressing a smirk. She couldn't believe how corny this was all beginning to sound – like something out of the Dennis Wheatley novels she enjoyed reading as a teenager.

"Yes." Nick nodded. "This time the alignment is on Halloween. Many people meditate or perform rituals on Halloween, which makes it a day of power. And that means we have even more chance of success."

"What's all this got to do with me?" asked Rachael.

"Since the death of your uncle, you are the new gatekeeper."

"I don't think so!" scoffed Rachael. Nick carried on, undeterred.

"When your uncle was diagnosed with terminal cancer, he despaired that he wouldn't live long enough to open the gateway. He fought for his life with great courage, he meditated, he tried alternative medicines, he prayed to our god. When there was no more hope, he started looking for a successor."

"*Your* god?"

"Baphomet, the perfect union of the physical and the spiritual."

"You're Satanists?" Rachael was feeling increasingly uncomfortable.

"No." Nick shook his head.

"You worship some god with a goat's head – yes I *have* seen pictures of him in my uncle's books in case you're wondering – but you say you're not Satanists. So what the hell are you?"

Nick and Cat looked at each other, unsure. Nick decided to tell

Rachael the truth.

"We belong to the Order of the Temple of the West. We've been keeping alive the legacy of the British Templars, and trying to complete the work of the Last Knight. Your uncle was one of us."

"I didn't know my uncle. I don't have a problem with the fact that he was a member of your... Order, but I really don't see what any of this has to do with me."

"Your uncle chose *you* as his successor."

"That's ridiculous! I don't believe in any of the stuff he believed in; I'm not interested in any of it. Why didn't he choose one of you?" Rachael looked Nick in the eye. "Why didn't he choose *you*?"

"I didn't have the right background. None of us did. Sure, we could have a go at the ritual, we might even succeed, but we might not – and that was a chance your uncle wasn't willing to take."

"I don't understand what makes me so special."

"There are certain prerequisites of a Gatekeeper. An auspicious alignment of planets at the time of birth that predisposes a person to great things. Usually these people have terrible tragedy written into their lives, they are put on trial and suffer greatly, their life path eventually leading them towards the possibility of remarkable achievement. Your uncle set about finding a relative who would inherit his house, but who would also have what it takes to be a Gatekeeper. His search led him to you. You had the right kind of birth chart, you'd been through a terrible life-changing tragedy. And... trial by fire..." Nick's voice trailed off and for a moment he looked upset. Cat shot him a worried glance and he quickly carried on. "Your uncle wanted you to take his place, to carry on his work. You have everything it takes to be the next Gatekeeper; to open the gateway."

"I'm no Gatekeeper. I'm just a normal person trying to get over something horrible, and I really need to be left alone."

"Rachael, destiny has led you to where you are today. Like the Gatekeepers before you, your courage has been tested, and your will to live, and you've come through it – to where you are now."

"You're wrong. I have no will to live and no courage. I fail on all the counts you've mentioned. I don't want to be the Gatekeeper and I don't want to live without my husband and daughter. The only reason I haven't killed myself yet is because I still believe that one day the door will open and they'll come walking in."

"Don't you see, Rachael? That's exactly what will happen – if you want it to."

"Don't…" Rachael's anger choked her and she could hardly speak.

"You can bring them back, Rachael. If you only…"

"Enough!" Rachael stood up. "You have to go now. I mean it. I want you out."

"Look…" Cat started to argue, but Nick stayed her with a hand gesture.

"Okay, Rachael. We're leaving." He got up and Cat followed suit. "You've had a lot to take in, and I'm sorry I've upset you. We're going, but please just let us have the book. I promise we won't bother you again."

"What book?"

"*Liber Portae* – the Book of the Gate."

"I don't know what you're talking about."

"It's an old leather-bound book. It's in your uncle's library. You must have seen it."

"There's no such book." Rachael tried to usher Cat and Nick out of the door.

"There is. Please, if you just let us have a quick look in the library…"

"No way. I want you out of my house. Right now!"

"Please, just let us take the book and we'll never bother you again." The urgency in Nick's voice unnerved Rachael.

"Please go or I'll be forced to call the police."

Nick's calm demeanour returned instantly. He waved Cat towards the front door and backed slowly away from Rachael like from a stray dog that has suddenly bared its teeth.

"It's okay, Rachael," he soothed. "I'm so sorry we upset you. We won't bother you again."

Rachael locked the door behind them and watched them through the window, making sure they left. Nick glanced back once, then led Cat away from the house.

Rachael determined not to give up until she found the book. It took her over an hour, but her persistence was doubly rewarded when, at the very back of the lowest bookshelf, hidden behind other books, she found the ancient leather-bound volume and what turned out to be her uncle's diary with copious notes he had made to accompany the *Liber Portae.*

Rachael took the two books through to her bedroom and tucked herself up in bed before opening her uncle's diary. She was surprised to find a letter inside it addressed to her. It read:

Dear Rachael,

If you are reading this letter, then you have probably made a new home for yourself in the Gatehouse. I hope you are happy here; the house is truly remarkable and if you take care of it, it will take care of you.

You may already have met Nick and the others. If so, I hope they did not alarm you unduly. I asked Nick to explain my work to you, and to beseech you to join him and the other members of the Temple in finishing what I started. I know what he told you sounds incredible, but every word of it is true. Once you have read the Book of the Gate, you will realise how great an opportunity has been given us: to defeat death forever, to obliterate the pain of having our loved ones taken from us, and crush the mortal fear that each one of us faces as we wait for our own demise. If Nick has not come to see you yet, then please receive him in your home and hear him out.

I beg you, Rachael, accept the great task that is

your destiny. You are my only hope and the hope
of all mankind. Please, don't let me down. Don't let
your husband and daughter down.

Until we meet,
Your uncle, William Algernon Varney

Angry and confused, Rachael threw the letter on the floor and cried herself to sleep.

She dreamt that the world was on fire; men on horseback had set it alight, and now they rode hither and thither, shouting and swinging their swords. On the ground around Rachael lay bleeding, dying monks. Some prayed, others screamed as the flames engulfed them. Then, through the flames, beyond the scene of murder, Rachael thought she could see two figures – one big, one small – watching her. She tried to move towards them, to get a better look, but the fire was too hot. She tried to call to them, but the crackling of the flames drowned out her voice. All she could do was reach out in their direction, but then fire flared up in front of them and they were lost from sight. Rachael woke abruptly and lay awake in the dark.

She realised that she could hear someone moving around in the study. This was not like before. These were not the ethereal murmurs, sighs and footsteps that Rachael had got used to. These were real people and they were in the next room. Rachael felt afraid. She put on her bedside lamp and got out of bed, pulling on a dressing-gown. She hid the Book of the Gate and her uncle's diary under her pillow, picked up the empty bottle of wine she'd left by her bed the other night, brandishing it in place of a weapon, and headed for the study. As she walked out into the corridor, she caught a glimpse of someone ducking down the stairs.

"Hey!" But it was too late. She ran downstairs, but when she reached the bottom of the staircase the intruders were gone. Literally – gone. Still gripping the wine bottle, Rachael went to the front door – it was locked on the inside. She checked the windows – all locked. She searched the kitchen and the parlour – nobody there. In any case, Rachael could sense that there was no longer anyone in her house.

Upstairs once more, she placed the bottle back by the side of her bed in case of another intrusion, then went into the study. The room was a mess. Books had been pulled off shelves and left lying around. It was Nick and his cronies – Rachael was sure of it. They had turned the study upside-down, but they hadn't found what they'd been looking for. Her fear and anger turned to perverse satisfaction. She replaced the scattered volumes and returned to her bedroom to look at her prized books. She retrieved her uncle's letter from the floor and put it away carefully. Then she opened the diary and spent the rest of the night finding out about her uncle and the Gatehouse.

> *July 1st*
> *I buried my beloved Emma today. My life is over. I would give my immortal soul for just one more day with her [...]*
>
> *July 10th*
> *The voices under the floor again. I'm sure there is someone in my house – under my house [...]*
>
> *July 29th*
> *I have traced the source of the voices. I am sure it is behind the fireplace [...]*
>
> *August 2nd*
> *What a night! I have finally met the people under my house. I explored and poked every inch of the fireplace and was rewarded with finding a door handle. It turns out that there is a door in the back of the fireplace, which opens onto a staircase leading down into catacombs beneath the Gatehouse. I went down and met Nick, Cat and their friends. What amazing people! They have*

told me the secrets of the Gatehouse and of the gateway to the next world. They say they can bring back the dead and they want my help. Sounds crazy, but I believe them! Perhaps I can get my beloved Emma back! [...]

'... a door in the back of the fireplace, which opens onto a staircase leading down into catacombs beneath the Gatehouse.' Rachael re-read the sentence twice before rushing downstairs to the parlour.

She lit a candle and went to inspect the fireplace. She crouched down and started to feel around the back. Sure enough, there was a small handle, which opened a door when she pushed it down. A moment later and Rachael was crawling through to the other side.

Rachael quietly pulled the door to behind her, but not all the way, making sure she could open it quickly if she needed to. She moved cautiously into the darkness beyond, the light from her candle picking out a narrow stone staircase spiralling down into the shadows. Her candle flickered and she slowed down, worried that it might go out and plunge her into absolute blackness. She looked at the damp, moss-covered walls around her, expecting to feel claustrophobic, thinking that perhaps she should go back up and continue this tomorrow. But she sensed the house around her, watching and protecting. In the flickering candlelight, the walls seemed to breathe gently and the light from her candle grew stronger until it burned with a steady golden glow. The house guided Rachael down, keen to share its secrets.

Finally Rachael reached the bottom of the staircase. Here the walls widened away from her. She knew she was in a large space, but her candle was not powerful enough to show her just how large. She figured from her uncle's diary that this was the chamber in which he'd hoped to carry out the ritual of the opening of the Gate. There must be some illumination on the walls; there was no way the cultists could operate in here at night without some kind of light. Rachael skirted slowly along the perimeter of the chamber. This soon paid off and she lit a couple of wax-soaked hessian torches that she found fixed to the walls.

The chamber seemed beautiful to Rachael. A vast underground cavern, the damp walls gleaming like jewels in the restless light of the torches. Big wooden beams held up the high ceiling, and wooden cladding both decorated and supported the walls in places. Large velvet drapes had been hung up, adding warmth and an air of grandeur to the place. A feeling of excitement and hope for the future surged through Rachael. The torches on the walls burned brighter and she imagined the Gatehouse sharing her unexpected moment of happiness.

Rachael searched the walls of the chamber until she found the exit the cultists had been using to get in and out of her house. It was a small door behind one of the drapes. She pulled it open; the air beyond smelled of earth. It probably led out into the ruins behind the Gatehouse – that was a matter for investigation by daylight. She would find a way to lock or block the door in the morning so that Nick and his little red-haired friend couldn't break into her house again; hopefully the elaborate old key that hadn't fit any of the locks in the Gatehouse would be good for the job. Right now she still had some exploring to do.

Rachael let the heavy drape drop back down over the door, and made her way to the centre of the chamber. She looked around, gasping when she noticed a figure watching her. She stood very still and realised that the figure wasn't moving either. It wasn't even breathing. She sighed with relief as she worked out that it was a statue, and moved cautiously towards it. It was life-size – a little larger than life. Sitting on an elevated stone throne was a hermaphrodite human form, with a goat's head and a goat's hind legs. Its vast wings were folded behind it; two fingers on its right hand pointed upwards and two on its left hand pointed down, expressing the perfect harmony of light and dark, of mercy and justice. The statue had once been painted; the paint had almost totally faded, but the yellow glass in the creature's slanted eye sockets sparkled brightly. For a moment the creature seemed alive, the look in its eyes infinitely knowing and malevolent; the horror, despair, suffering and hatred of aeons peering out into the modern age, scrutinising the small figure that stood before it, candle raised in one shaking hand.

Rachael lowered the candle and the infernal light left the deity's eyes; it was only the tiny flame reflecting in the yellow glass that had animated the statue, she told herself. But still she couldn't shake the disquiet that had lodged inside her. The statue was splendid and awe-inspiring. Rachael remembered being taken to a church in Paris as a child. She had gazed up at a statue of the crucified Christian Messiah. She had felt some sort of awe, but it was nothing compared to what she felt now. The Christ's eyes had been vacant, whatever they had experienced of human pain was long gone; his eyes spoke of nothing, knew nothing – they were the blank eyes of a dead man. Baphomet, on the other hand, seemed very much alive.

A perfect being, Baphomet had spent centuries watching and waiting. It had experienced God and beast, and all the men and angels in between. The Templars had recognised its uniqueness – its power both human and divine, animal and angelic. They had elevated Baphomet to the status of a god, and it was a good god – it did not judge or punish, and it let its followers share of its power.

But hate is stronger than love, and a broken, blackened human heart has the power to bend even a divine will. As the Last Knight hid in the catacombs beneath the Gatehouse, he lamented his slaughtered brothers and prayed to Baphomet. His prayers were ones of hatred, of bloody vengeance and of death.

Through years of the Knight's dark worship, the deity itself started to lose the power of the Light. It became a god of darkness and death, of human sacrifice and cruel justice dispensed without mercy on all those that the Knight saw as his persecutors – and that was the whole world. So strong was the Knight's hatred, that it turned his own god into a demon.

The Knight's despair and rage grew. He came to believe that the only way he could expiate his pain was to open the gates of hell itself and release all the damned creatures that dwelled within it – among them his fallen brothers, who had died unprepared for heaven, their unconfessed sins lying heavily upon their souls. He would be re-united with his brother Templars and together they would wreak vengeance on the surrounding land and people. The Gatehouse would become a gateway to hell.

As the Knight cursed the earth, prayed to Baphomet and waited for the right alignment of stars in the heavens to bring about his hellish plan, a pestilence crept across the land. Cattle fell sick and crops died, people went hungry and suffered. But old age caught up with the Knight. His hatred kept him alive for over a hundred years, but finally he fell into eternal sleep in the bowels of the Gatehouse, the gateway not yet open.

Rachael reached up a trembling hand and touched a stone hoof. The flame of her candle flared unexpectedly and the eyes of the great god shone like yellow diamonds. The wooden beams of the chamber creaked as a shudder of anticipation passed through the house. Rachael gazed into the eyes of the Beast and resolved to complete the work of the Last Knight. She prayed until exhaustion overcame her, then allowed the house to guide her back to her bed and another half-night of fitful sleep.

Fire. The world burned and the dying monks' screams merged with the sound of the flames. The horsemen were gone and two figures emerged from the depths of the carnage. Rachael struggled to reach them. Then the drifting smoke parted and she saw them clearly – her husband and child. They were smiling – smiling! – as they walked unharmed from the fire and blood and death.

The next day Rachael woke up even later than usual. It was afternoon and there were few hours of daylight left. She washed and ate, and went back to reading her uncle's diary.

> *September 12th*
> *Deciphered a very important passage of the book*
> *today. I have no doubt that the next alignment will*

be next year on 31st October. Just one year and forty-nine days until I am re-united with my beloved Emma [...]

February 5th
The cancer is eating its way through my liver. I don't have much time left. I am so afraid that I will go alone into the darkness of my own solitary afterlife and never see my Emma again. I cannot bear to let her down again. I must live long enough to open the gate. I must live [...]

Her uncle's despair as his hope slipped away like his life – relentlessly, one pain-filled day after another – was too much for Rachael and she turned her attention to the Book of the Gate. The leather binding was cracked and sticky with dirt, the pages yellowed with age, but the ritual passages contained within had lost none of their power. Rachael had learnt Latin at school, she had even taken it as far as A-level, but her residual knowledge was nowhere near good enough to follow the complicated text. She was grateful to her uncle for including in his diary a translation of the most important passages. How long it must have taken him! She could picture him sitting for hours at his desk in the study, piles of Latin dictionaries and reference books by his side, pouring over the ancient manuscript in a desperate bid to bring back his beloved Emma. Rachael wondered if her husband had ever loved her that much. Would he have been willing to do what she was now contemplating, to free *her* from the grave?

And what of the Last Knight, the one who had written the book, who'd taught others the secret of life and death, but had died before he was able to use his knowledge to bring back his brothers?

I, the Last of the Templars of the West, write this,
The Book of the Gate, in the name of the great god
Baphomet, for my brothers, that they might rise

again and destroy our common enemies [...]

What would he have thought had he known that his great work would fall into the hands of a twenty-first century housewife? How ludicrous was *that*? And how she wished she could concentrate on the Latin rather than getting sleepy again only a few hours after getting up.

The doorbell rang, startling Rachael. She remembered the break-in the night before and stormed downstairs, ready to confront Nick and his creepy friends. She opened the door aggressively and stopped in her tracks, seeing John smiling at her from the doorstep and holding out a bottle of wine.

"Oh, it's you," she exclaimed before she could stop herself.

"Why? Who were you expecting?" John's smile took on a slightly strained air.

"Oh no, no-one," Rachael stammered. "I just wasn't expecting you, that's all."

"We did say today, didn't we?"

"Did we? Oh, maybe we did. I'm sorry."

"Well, aren't you going to invite me in?" asked John, attempting to move forward into the house, but Rachael blocked his way.

"Look, John, you're a nice man and you've been very kind to me, but I'm afraid I won't be able to see you anymore."

"What?"

"I'm really sorry. I'm afraid you can't come round anymore."

"Why?"

"Well, the fact is... my husband and daughter are coming home."

"What? What husband and daughter?"

"*My* husband and daughter."

John looked like he'd been slapped in the face. Rachael felt sorry for him, but she could do nothing to change the fact that there was simply no room in her life for him.

"You never told me you were married. Or that you had a daughter. How could you do that? How could you not tell me something like that?"

"I'm sorry, John. I didn't tell you because I didn't think I'd ever see them again."

"I don't believe this." John backed away from Rachael. He wanted to get as far away as possible before these horrible feelings of anger and betrayal overwhelmed him. As though from far away, he could hear her apologising. The blood was pumping in his ears. He turned away and headed back to his car.

Rachael watched him drive away. Perhaps under different circumstances they might have had a chance together, but she was not a free woman. She had a husband and daughter, and she had things to do.

The next couple of weeks went by quickly. Rachael spent her days reading and her nights praying to the monstrous divinity in the bowels of the Gatehouse. One time she thought she heard the cultists trying to get into the chamber through the door she'd locked. It held fast and they gave up and did not return. She had the feeling that they were waiting outside the Gatehouse and watching. She thought she'd caught a glimpse of Cat's fiery hair in the moonlight one night, but that didn't bother her. They could wait and watch as much as they liked – it made no difference to her, not now that they had no way of getting in.

It seemed John had forgiven her and had taken to driving by her house regularly and even sitting in his car across the road and watching for any sign of her in the windows. He could wait and watch as much as he liked – it made no difference to her, as long as he stayed beyond the Gatehouse walls.

One day Rachael went to the fridge and found it empty. The freezer and cupboards were not much better. She was annoyed at the thought of wasting time on going to the store. But there were still ten days left and she would have to eat. She put on a coat with a hood and a pair of sunglasses. She'd take her car and fill it with supplies. She'd stack up the freezer with perishable goods and the cupboards with canned goods so that she wouldn't have to leave the Gatehouse again. She prayed that no-one would recognise her in the village. Actually the only person who knew her was John, and it was him that she wished to avoid at all costs. But prayers are rarely answered, and John cornered her as she was loading up her car.

"Rachael!"

"John."

"I've rung your doorbell a few times."

"I know."

"You didn't open the door."

"I know."

"I've been worried about you."

"I'm fine. I'm very well, in fact."

"Why are you being like this? I thought you liked me."

"I do like you."

"Then why have you shut me out?"

"I told you. My husband and daughter are coming back."

Rachael finished loading up the car boot and went to leave, but John grabbed her arm. She threw him a resentful glance and he let go.

"I bumped into Smithson, you know." Rachael looked at him blankly. "Smithson. The solicitor who handled your uncle's will." Rachael frowned. "He told me what happened. About the fire." Rachael turned away from John, towards the car door. "About how your husband and daughter died in the fire." Rachael got into the car. "Why did you lie to me?" Rachael started the engine. She rolled down the window and, taking off her sunglasses, looked John straight in the eye.

"John, if you ever had any feelings for me, any feelings at all, then please... please respect my wish to be alone right now."

She drove away, leaving John more determined than ever to keep an eye on her.

Rachael read the Gate opening ritual over and over. She wanted to know it by heart so that she could perform it without hesitation when the time came. The Gatehouse hummed with anticipation.

Rachael's mood lifted with each passing day and, by the time Halloween arrived, her heart was soaring. As darkness approached, she put on her best dress, picked up the Book of the Gate, lit a candle and headed through the fireplace to the chamber below.

John sat in his car, watching Rachael's house. The Gatehouse had always been a popular place with local youths, who dared each other to break into the catacombs at night or bring some charred piece of stone out of the ruins behind the house, and Halloween was a particularly bad time for these sorts of activities. He wanted to be there for Rachael if there was any trouble.

Children and teenagers were running around in grotesque costumes. Some of them wore rubber masks emulating their favourite horror movie characters. John didn't like horror movies and he didn't like Halloween. Life was violent enough without watching bloodshed and mutilation on TV or in the cinema. John jumped in his seat as an excited teenager ran into his wing mirror and snapped it back. He cursed and rolled down his window. As he clicked the mirror back into place, he caught sight of a large group of people in brightly coloured costumes. These were no children.

John slumped down in his seat and turned to watch. The group hung around in the bushes near the Gatehouse, while one of them – a tall, slim man in a purple robe – went to ring the doorbell.

John was ready to spring into action at the first sign of trouble, but Rachael didn't come to the door. No surprise there, he thought. He'd been a reasonably happy, easy-going kind of person until Rachael had moved into the Gatehouse. He'd been instantly smitten by her dark silky hair, delicate pale face and fine figure – that first time he'd seen her in Mrs. Malina's store – and his feelings had grown steadily since. He'd been devastated when she told him that she was married, with a child, and disturbed to hear that her family had actually died in a fire. Why on earth would she have lied about something like that? Was she that desperate to get rid of him or was she going through some kind of emotional breakdown? John's manly pride steered him to the latter explanation; he resolved to be there for Rachael when she came out of whatever it was she was going through or, if necessary, to drag her out of it kicking and screaming.

John was about to get out of the car and ask the tall man what he wanted at Rachael's, but the man gave up on the doorbell and re-joined his companions. John figured they were probably hippy freaks with some small knowledge of local history, drawn to the Gatehouse on Halloween because of its alleged connection to the Templars. Hopefully they'd go back to where they came from and spend the night smoking dope. But, as John watched, the whole group moved silently round to the back of Rachael's house. John waited a few minutes for them to reappear, but they did not. Concerned, he got out and went round to the back, but saw no sign of the group anywhere. They'd vanished into thin air.

John rang Rachael's doorbell, then banged on the door. He really had to let her know that there were strange people loitering around. Perhaps they'd somehow found a way in. There was no telling what they wanted, and he should be there to protect Rachael. Surely, she must have heard him. She wasn't answering her phone as usual, but she was definitely in the house because he hadn't seen her come out and he'd been in the area for most of the day.

"Rachael!" he shouted. "Rachael, open up!" No response. The Gatehouse stood silently, glaring down at him through its upstairs windows. God, how he hated that house! Just living in it would be enough to drive a person crazy. Maybe that's exactly what had happened to Rachael.

John couldn't see in through the ground floor windows because of the bushes and vines. He looked around for something he could stand on and spotted a large bin. He dragged it over and clambered on. If he stretched himself out just a little more he would have a good view of the downstairs. As John stood on tiptoes, an upstairs window opened suddenly, then slammed shut, the unexpected noise sending the policeman toppling over together with the bin.

Moving confidently around the chamber, Rachael lit the torches on the walls and walked over to the statue of Baphomet, awed as ever by the dark knowledge glowing in its malevolent eyes. She closed her eyes for a moment in an attempt to slow down her breathing and the rapid beating of her heart. At that moment she heard a rattling sound at the locked door to her left. Someone was trying to open the door from the outside. The lock held firm. Rachael had no doubt that it was Nick and the other cultists. The rattling stopped and Rachael heard a knocking on the door. She considered her options carefully. Her confidence and faith were strong – strong enough to admit those who wanted to share in the great event that was about to unfold through her actions.

Rachael made up her mind. She unlocked the door and stood aside for Nick and the others.

Nick gazed at Rachael in wonder before entering the chamber. She had transformed from a frightened, broken woman into a strong, radiant priestess. He knew now that he'd been right all along – she'd been studying the Book and preparing for tonight. His faith in her had been justified, and he would be rewarded by being allowed to witness the start of a new age, which he was confident she would succeed in bringing about.

A burden he'd been carrying for a long time was lifted from Nick's shoulders. The fire he'd started at Rachael's home at her uncle's behest – the fire that had killed Rachael's husband and child, and fulfilled the trial by fire prerequisite of Rachael's ascendancy to potential Gatekeeper status in the face of her uncle's impending demise – would be nullified. Rachael would have her family back, there would be no more death, and Nick's soul would be purged of the stain his barbaric act had engendered. It would be as if it had never happened. The greater good would be served, and the sacrifice would be vindicated and reversed.

They filed past Rachael into the chamber – twelve of them in all. Cat had lost her annoying air of superiority and looked at Rachael with respect, quickly dropping her gaze when their eyes met. The others were a mixture of ages, races and class – hardly what you would expect in a tediously homogenous village like this one. Rachael figured that they were what the proprietress of the grocery store liked to refer to as 'out-of-towners'; some, Rachael suspected, may even have come from abroad to see the end of the world as it had been until now – flawed, painful, redundant.

Rachael watched her visitors arrive. There was a man in his late forties with a small black moustache; a woman of around sixty with a purple hair rinse and large rings on her fingers; a beautiful young oriental-looking woman with almond-shaped green eyes rather like a cat's – she was Rachael's favourite; a young Chinese man; a middle-aged Japanese man; an elegant black couple in their thirties; a small, frail and very old lady; a fat bald man and a tall albino man with pink eyes and translucent skin. Under different circumstances, Rachael might have noticed that her guests would not have looked out of place on the set of an early Roman Polanski movie. She simply smiled at them magnanimously; she was enjoying her role as hostess.

It dawned on Rachael that all of the new arrivals were wearing colourful robes – the robes of Catholic priests. Nick came up to Rachael and held out a splendidly embroidered red robe to her.

"Are these from a church?" she asked.

"I'm afraid so," said Nick, smiling sheepishly. "We've also brought these..."

Rachael peered into the box he had opened for her to inspect. There were chalices in it: one with wine and one with perfectly round communion hosts.

"Why?" asked Rachael. "It's not written anywhere in the ritual".

"No," answered Nick, "but the Christian sacrament is powerful because of its symbolism and centuries of ritualistic use. The notion of sacrifice, of eating flesh and drinking blood, the idea of the dead rising and walking – all this is conjured up in the Church rites, and we can turn that power to our advantage. Even the robes themselves are powerful because of their ritualistic use and the symbolic meanings of their colours... Here..." He placed the red robe on Rachael's shoulders; she didn't protest. "The colour of fire and blood

– of purification and birth." Rachael pulled the robe firmly around herself and smiled at Nick, glad to have his support after all. Nick smiled back and gave Rachael a communion host to eat and the wine chalice to sip from. Once he and Cat had gone round all the other cultists with the two chalices, Nick gestured for Rachael to begin.

"It's time," he said. "We are here for you and we will be right behind you."

John was furious. He wasn't hurt in his fall from the bin, but it took him a while to wipe off the dirt. He went around the house, trying the downstairs windows to see if he could get in. The upstairs windows were opening and slamming shut again.

"Shut up!" he yelled, glaring up at the house.

In the catacombs beneath the house, the torches were burning brightly.

Rachael stood in the centre of the chamber, facing the statue of Baphomet. Nick and the others were positioned around the walls behind Rachael, watching her. Rachael whispered the opening lines of the ritual she knew so well. Turning to face the four corners of the earth, she welcomed the spirits of the air, earth, water and fire. She addressed the denizens of the heavenly and infernal spheres; she called upon the old gods, the ancient watchers, and the souls of those departed and those not yet born. She welcomed them all in the name of Baphomet.

The torches flickered and dimmed; a cold wind stirred in the chamber, rustling the velvet drapes and the robes of the witnesses. Baphomet's eyes glowed with a cold inner light that grew even as the torches dulled. The ritual had begun.

In the sky outside, the stars shifted and the planets aligned fortuitously for the opening of the Gate.

John stopped for a moment, a cold tingling in his spine compounding the unnerving feeling that something important was happening – something he didn't understand, but which he needed to stop at all costs. He took out and extended his truncheon, smashed a downstairs window, eliciting a low hiss from the house, reached in and raised the latch. He scrambled up on the sill and squeezed in through the window.

The wind whined with a low, hollow sound, and Rachael raised her voice to make herself heard. The flickering torches cast vast seething shadows across the chamber. In the darkness beyond the statue of Baphomet, intangible shapes, blacker than the shadows, seemed to rise up and writhe in the thick air. Rachael trembled with excitement, but her voice remained steady as she recited the magical passages. She gazed at Baphomet, who seemed to move as the shadows whirled around him.

John had been searching the house for any sign of Rachael and the intruders. He'd come back downstairs and, after inspecting the kitchen, entered the parlour. He scrutinised every inch of the room until finally his eyes fell upon the fireplace. The small door in the back had been left open and John thought he could hear Rachael's voice and another, louder sound emanating from it. He rushed towards the door, which slammed before he could reach it, but he prised it open and pushed his way through.

The cultists looked on in awe as Rachael shouted the last passages of the ritual over the howling wind. Baphomet's eyes burned fiercely and the statue seemed to catch fire. But the blinding light was coming from behind the effigy, where the teeming shadows now contended with flames of pure white light. The wind grew to a piercing high-pitched scream. Rachael and the others were forced to cover their ears as the scream reached an unbearable volume and splintered into a myriad voices as all the demons in hell, the angelic hosts and the human souls in the afterlife cried out, the planets moved into perfect alignment, the world trembled and the gateway between earth and heaven, heaven and hell, life and death began to open.

A flash of white light and a piercing howl caused John to stumble on the spiral staircase leading down to the catacombs. He righted himself, holding onto the cold stone walls for a moment, then carried on, reaching the bottom and crouching out of sight. Seconds passed before he was able to make some sense of the scene in front of him. He saw Rachael with her hands outstretched towards a grotesque statue, behind which a scene of insanity was unfolding. He saw the strangers watching, some laughing, others crying; all of them in some kind of bizarre trance.

John watched in horror as black shadows coalesced among the white flames and started to move towards the waiting people. Something stirred in the earth of the catacombs. The shadows became substantial, taking on humanoid forms. Hands reached out and figures started to emerge from the other side.

Burnt, scarred monks who had died near the Gatehouse came out first, walking slowly towards the living. They were led by their Master, the Last Knight.

The cultists' awe turned to elation as they recognised their friend and former Gatekeeper amongst the emerging figures.

"Uncle?" Rachael whispered her amazement and wonder.

Then, beyond her uncle and the Knights, Rachael caught sight of her husband and daughter. She let out a cry of joy and ran towards them.

John couldn't watch this obscene travesty any longer. He shouted Rachael's name and threw himself towards her.

Nick, Cat and the fat man were the first to react, blocking John's path and trying to bring him down. John struggled with them and managed to break loose, but now the other cultists were heading in his direction. He managed to grab a torch from the wall and brandished it at anyone who came near him. He could see over their shoulders Rachael making her way past the shuffling corpses of the monks towards the figures of a man and a little girl.

The fat man ran at John and tried to wrestle the burning torch from his hand. The two of them toppled over, pulling down one of the velvet drapes on top of themselves. The curtain caught fire and burned quickly. John crawled out, but the fat man was trapped under the heavy drape.

As the black couple tried to put out the burning, screaming man, Cat, Nick and the Japanese man tried to stop John. Around them the flames spread with lightning speed. John pushed Cat away and struggled with the two men, the remaining drapes catching fire around them. The Japanese man hurled himself at John, but the policeman was quicker, knocking his assailant off balance and sending him sprawling. Nick threw himself at John, while Cat leapt on the policeman's back. John spun round and managed to dislodge the woman. She fell onto Nick and the two of them went down, the flames engulfing them as they hit the floor. John ran towards Rachael. The wooden beams and cladding were burning, and soon the whole chamber was alight.

The fire devoured mercilessly everything in its path, and soon both the living and the dead were burning and screaming.

Rachael saw her husband and child catch fire, and cried out in anguish. They reached out to her and she fought desperately to get to them, but John grabbed her, lifting her off her feet, and carried her kicking and screaming to the stairs leading back to the house.

Struggling against John, Rachael saw a sheet of flame engulf her family. She screamed, madness in her eyes, then passed out. John carried her up the narrow staircase, flames licking at his heels. The Gatehouse was filling with smoke, and Rachael was getting heavy, but he managed to get her out of the Dantean chaos and away from the burning building, dropping her onto the cool ground outside.

Rachael regained consciousness and started screaming again. She began to crawl back towards the inferno, back towards her family. This time they weren't going to die without her. John grabbed her by the ankle, dragging her away. Rachael fought him off, hitting, clawing, biting. He managed to pin down her arms and hold her fast, but one look into her unseeing eyes told him that the woman he had briefly known and loved had died with her family in the underbelly of the house that he hated.

Rachael continued to scream as the fire raged; the vision of her burning husband and child seared onto her retinae forever. The Gatehouse screamed with her, agony in every piece of wood that burned and every stone that fell. Windows gaped like flame-filled mouths. The house that had stood for hundreds of years burned to the ground and sank, howling, into the catacombs.

A WALK IN THE PARK

A WALK IN THE PARK

I WAS GOING into the supermarket last week. Second time that day.

"You got the wrong tin! How many times do I have to tell you: it's the green tin, not the blue tin!"

I honestly thought my mother-in-law was going to have a fatal fit of some kind when I'd bought the wrong type of tuna on my first supermarket trip, which perhaps wouldn't have been altogether a bad thing. But she didn't. Instead she continued to inform me at length how stupid I was, how I couldn't get even the simplest thing right, how she didn't know why her son had married me.

"He could have done so much better!" she hissed, spittle from her sneering mouth spraying over the sheets I'd just changed. "He could have had any girl he wanted. I'll never understand why he wasted his life on a mousey good-for-nothing like you."

I'd heard it all before, of course, and I was furious with myself for letting it get to me. I left the room before she could see the tears welling up in my eyes. And I went back to the supermarket to get the green tin.

So I was going into the supermarket when I saw a grey toy poodle tied up outside, evidently waiting for its owner to re-emerge. The sight of the little dog unsettled me – it brought back an old memory from that deeply buried past that was my former, happier life.

In the mid-nineties, my husband and I had moved to the little village of Wraithsfield in East Sussex. We had a dog then – a Chihuahua called Amber. There was a lot of beautiful woodland around Wraithsfield, but Amber got tired quickly – on account of her little legs – so I usually took her for walks on the village green or in the smaller, more cultivated parks in the neighbourhood. We hadn't been living in the area long, and I was still exploring the village and its immediate surroundings, taking Amber with me, walking her some of the time, carrying her when her diminutive paws grew tired. That's how we ended up in the old park on the outskirts of the village.

It appeared there'd once been an entrance gate, but it was gone now. The wire fencing had seen better days too. As soon as we went in, Amber stopped in her tracks and whimpered, looking around nervously and shaking a little. I figured she was tired and wanting to be carried so I picked her up and walked on with her in my arms. I hadn't planned on finding this hidden, tranquil gem of a park, so I hadn't brought along the pet carrier handbag I normally transported Amber in, but she was so light, and when she got tired she hardly wriggled at all, so carrying her in my arms was not a problem. Besides, I loved exploring – particularly quiet, green spaces such as this – and I was determined not to put off this adventure for a later day.

The park must have been beautiful once. It was dotted with ancient trees and crossed by narrow pathways, now overgrown. There were wild flowers, but also cultivated flowering plants that fought for sunlight amongst the unkempt bushes and weeds. As I walked with Amber in my arms, I wondered at how deserted and derelict this scenic place was. Whether it was the silence or the complete lack of any other people or animals, the park had a melancholy, eerie feel to it – almost creepy. As I walked on, I suddenly felt Amber go tense in my arms.

"What's up, baby?" I asked. Amber was quite still – frozen, her little heart beating rapidly beneath my hand. That's when I saw it – a grey toy poodle, watching us from a few metres away.

"Hello, lovely!" I addressed the little dog. "Where did you spring from?" The poodle wagged its tail and came running up, then shot off ahead, returning to follow alongside Amber and me, milling around us, but never quite close enough for me to stroke it.

"Look, Amber," I said to my dog, "a little friend for you to play with." But when I tried to put her down she whined and pressed against me so I just carried her while the other dog ran beside us. As we passed the halfway point in my circuit of the park, a slight movement in the bushes off to the side caught my eye. Startled, I stopped, then smiled in surprise as a Jack Russell came running towards us and joined the grey poodle in flitting around my legs and running circles about me as I completed this strange walk, carrying my shaking Chihuahua; two dogs happy, one dog apparently petrified, all three bizarrely silent.

As we finished walking around the perimeter and approached the exit gate again, the two canine interlopers were just a few feet away from Amber and me. Amber was shaking like the proverbial leaf and I reached into my pocket to pull out a treat for her. After a moment's hesitation, she accepted the tiny bone-shaped biscuit. When I took my eyes off her again and turned back to the other two dogs, they were gone. I looked around, but there was no sign of them – not even a blade of grass stirred nearby. Confused, I carried Amber out of the park. She was no longer shaking, but wriggling about feistily, demanding to be set down on the ground. I attached her leash and turned to head for home. As I did so, a sign caught my eye. No wonder I hadn't seen it before – it was old and worn, and hardly visible under the trailing vine that had grown over it. I pulled aside the greenery and studied the writing:

> *Former site of Wraithsfield Pet Cemetery. Construction of apartment block scheduled for commencement on 20th September 1982.*

Now it was my turn for a shiver to run down my spine.

I took Amber home, but couldn't stop thinking about our peculiar walk in the dismantled animal graveyard. I was glad the block of flats had never been built on the picturesque, isolated spot – I would have liked to have seen it with the miniature headstones and monuments that must once have been there still in place. When my husband asked where we'd gone for our afternoon walk, I told him we'd walked around the backstreets and the village green. I don't know why I lied. I guess the whole experience had left me unnerved and a little sad. In any case, Amber and I never went there again, and eventually my husband and I moved back to London, to care for his sick mother.

It's been ten years now. Amber's long gone. My husband's never around.

"You have to work hard if you want to get ahead," he says.

And all day, every day, his bedridden mother thumping, banging on the wall.

"Doreen, get me this!" and "Doreen, get me that!" Never satisfied, always criticising.

But since that day outside the supermarket, I know what I have to do. And I wonder... will she come back? Like the strangely silent dogs in the verdant wasteland that was once the site of Wraithsfield Pet Cemetery? When I wring her flabby neck. When I push the pillow down on her grimacing wrinkled face until her limbs stop twitching... Will she come back?

OUT OF THE LIGHT

OUT OF THE LIGHT

"**Y**OU HAVE TO read it with a bishop standing at each shoulder..." Charles tore his eyes from the young man who was wearing nothing but a rubber glove, and looked around for the one who'd uttered those riveting words, "... to stop your soul from flying out of your body in fright." Rupert finished his explanation and, seeing as nobody seemed to be paying him any attention, fell silent.

"Excuse me," said Charles, overcoming his customary shyness. "What are you talking about?"

"*Liber Tenebrarum*," Rupert turned around, spotted the enquirer and positively beamed. "*The Book of Darkness*."

"What is it?" Whether it was the vodka jelly enhancing his enthusiasm or just his innate curiosity, Charles was completely captivated by the idea of such a book.

"I don't know," responded Rupert. "I've never tried to order it up."

"Where from? The Bod?"

"Yeah." The conversation broke up as someone passed Rupert the homemade bong that was going around the room.

The Garden of Eden party was getting pretty wild – even for Brasenose College, formerly host to a branch of the infamous Hellfire Club. A couple of tipsy girls from St. Hilda's had worked out how it was exactly that the bright yellow *Marigold* was staying on the manhood of the Brasenose student, and were now attempting to deglove him. The host of the party evidently felt it his duty to liven up the proceedings, and organised a competition to see who could hang from a wooden beam without letting go for the entire duration of the Soviet national anthem. Male students lined up for their turn, but none of them, it seemed, could beat the scratchy tones of *Gimn Sovetskogo Soyuza*, which now blared from an old record player in the corner of the room. A Physics and Philosophy student shouted over the Red Army Choir in an attempt to impress a female colleague with his explanation of Schrödinger's Cat. And the extremely strong hash in the bong was beginning to claim its first victims.

But Charles wasn't really noticing any of it. All he could think about was the mysterious book and how he was going to order it up from the Bodleian Library stacks on Monday morning. The bong reached him and he inhaled deeply, then coughed up the thick bittersweet smoke. After just one drag his head began to reel and he passed the improvised pipe to the girl on his left. The room shifted and time seemed to split into disjointed shards. The lights fragmented into rainbows, and Charles's last coherent thought was that he was tripping, and what on earth kind of hash was it anyway? He struggled to keep his head together, but eventually gave up and lay on the floor – his upper torso on the edge of a bean bag.

As the bong continued making its rounds, the beam-hanging competition was abandoned – no one even seemed to know who'd won – and the eulogy to the *unbreakable union of free nations* gave way to The Moving Sidewalks' cover of *I Want to Hold Your Hand*. It seemed to Charles that the music intermittently slowed almost to a standstill, then speeded up again, but he figured it was probably his fried brain playing tricks on him. He watched fellow students wandering in and out of the room – those who'd stuck to alcohol and were still able to wander. Some of them had paid attention to the theme for the evening and were dressed as Adam or Eve, or as strange, exotic creatures; most just wore the usual student uniform of the time – jeans and jackets for the boys; short skirts, hot pants or jeans for the girls. Rubber glove man had disappeared somewhere – possibly with the girls from St Hilda's.

After half an hour or so Charles's head began to clear, and he struggled to remember the name of the book. He looked around for Rupert, but couldn't see him anywhere. He panicked as his memory failed, but then it came back to him: something about darkness... *The Book of Darkness*. That was it! *Liber Tenebrarum*. He staggered out of the party and made his way back to University College.

It wasn't far from Brasenose to Univ. Then again, nowhere was particularly far from anywhere in Oxford. Charles passed the porters' lodge and headed through the main quadrangle to his building. On his way up to his room he passed a gated alcove with a small dome, under which reposed a marble statue of the naked, drowned Percy Bysshe Shelley. The poet had briefly attended University College before being unceremoniously kicked out for publishing a pamphlet on atheism, but, as is so often the case, became a revered alumnus as soon as he became famous. Had Shelley lived long enough to witness this turn of events, he may well have told his former college where to put their effigy of him, but he hadn't – and he didn't.

Charles saluted the poet and climbed up the creaking wooden staircase to the rooms he shared with Algernon Pyke. Algy, as he preferred to be known, was having a little party of his own in the joint sitting room. There was a lively discussion going on as to whether the centuries-old oak mantelpiece could be cut from the wall, taken out of college and sold as an antique without anyone noticing. Charles tried to tell Algy about the book, but his friend was too drunk to take in what he was saying.

"Here, old man," he said, thrusting a glass of effervescing liquid into Charles's hand, "have a G&T!" Charles downed the offering, made his excuses and retired to his bedroom, head spinning with more than just the gin.

Sunday passed uneventfully, apart from Algy's essay crisis – the result of a tutorial first thing on Monday. Charles wasn't due to produce an essay until Friday, so he spent Sunday mentally preparing for his trip to the Bod.

On Monday morning Charles was up and out before Algy had even woken up. He was outside the Bodleian at nine o'clock sharp and was the first one in. He sat at one of the computer terminals and typed *Liber Tenebrarum* into the library catalogue search engine. Nothing. His heart skipped a beat. *Book of Darkness.* Nothing. Charles started to feel nauseous. He had skipped breakfast and now his gastric juices were trying to digest his own stomach lining.

Perhaps he'd made a spelling mistake; he tried again: *Liber Tenebrarum*. Nothing. Could it all have been a hoax? A joke at his expense? Rupert had seemed sincere, but perhaps he was just repeating some rubbish that someone else had told him. Charles hurried over to the librarian.

"Excuse me. I'm trying to order a book, but it's not in the catalogue..."

"The electronic catalogue?"

"Yes."

"Try the manual catalogue... Over there."

Charles thanked the man and hurried over to the vast row of wooden filing cabinets that housed the manual catalogue. It was arranged by author. "Shit!" But then a thought struck him: he went to the *A's* and searched under *Anonymous*. He was amazed at how many books there were with no known author. *L-A*, *L-E*, and then there it was: *Liber Tenebrarum*. Charles's head felt a little light as he read the faded entry: *Anonymous. Liber Tenebrarum (The Book of Darkness)*. And nothing more. He filled out a request slip carefully, pausing to wonder how the librarian would find the book among 120 miles of underground passageways with no shelf reference. It was the librarian's problem, not his – he told himself – and placed the slip in the request tray on the counter. The librarian had disappeared, and Charles knew that it would take a couple of hours for his book order to be processed, so, lost in thought, he headed out for breakfast.

"Excuse me..." It was lunchtime, and the *Liber Tenebrarum* still hadn't been delivered. "I ordered a book first thing this morning, and I was wondering when I'll get it."

"Did you put your request slip in the tray?" asked the man behind the counter.

"Yes, I did."

"Before ten?"

"Yes."

"I'm sorry, but all the book orders from this morning have been processed. It must have gone missing somewhere. I'm afraid you'll have to fill out another request slip."

Crestfallen, Charles filled out another form, submitted it and went across the road to the King's Arms for a bowl of soup and a pint.

There was a female librarian on front desk duty when Charles got back. And still no book. After making enquiries, he was told to wait – that his order was probably being processed and would arrive soon. A couple of hours later he was told to fill out another request slip. When it came to dinner time, Charles made a fuss, which only served to make the woman behind the counter defensive – even a little hostile. He put in another request form and headed back to college, arriving late for dinner, having missed all his Monday lectures.

"Where have you been, old man?" Algy greeted him with a booming voice and a Pimm's and lemonade.

"I..."

"Have a Pimm's!" Charles took the glass and perched for a moment on a chair – the sofa being crammed full of Algy's friends from the English Department.

"How was your tutorial?" he asked Algy.

"Oh, you know, old man..." Algy gesticulated theatrically, "I managed to throw something down on paper in the nick of time."

"Good, good." Charles downed the pinkish brown liquid, nearly choking on a piece of cucumber, made his excuses and retired to his bedroom. Algy watched Charles go, a concerned look on his face, then forgot all about it and turned back to a heated debate on whether Alejandro Jodorowsky really gave his teenage Down's syndrome actors cocaine during the filming of *Santa Sangre*.

The rest of the week turned into an Oxford version of *Groundhog Day*. Every morning Charles went to the Bodleian Library and ordered *The Book of Darkness*. Every day the book failed to arrive from the archives. Charles made enquiries, complaints and more enquiries, but none of them ever got resolved. He missed lectures, and took to writing all his essays in the Bod, so as to waste no time in filling out a new request form each time a book delivery failed to deliver. He stopped going to tutorials for fear of missing the book should it arrive, but as he still handed in first-class essays and wrote very polite letters to his tutors, giving a variety of plausible excuses for his absence, there were no repercussions. Algy expressed concern at Charles's long absences and his increasing unwillingness to socialise. Charles tried to explain about the book, but his roommate seemed unable to understand, and merely tried to talk him out of his daily trips to the Bodleian. This state of affairs continued for a month.

Then it was Fifth Week, and Charles sat at his usual spot in Duke Humfrey's Reading Room, staring at the wall and waiting for the next book order to be brought up so that he could confirm the absence of the *Liber Tenebrarum* and fill out another request slip.

Darkness had fallen outside. Shadows started to gather in the corners and around the wooden bookcases. Charles's eyelids grew heavy from the fatigue of endless waiting in the airless room, and he caught himself dozing off. He shook himself awake and decided that leaving his post for a bit of fresh air and a quick cup of coffee wouldn't make much difference in the grand scale of things. He pulled himself up and strode along the shelves of ancient tomes to the exit. A female student smiled up at him as he passed her desk, but Charles didn't even notice. He hurried out of the building and across Broad Street to the café in Blackwell's Bookshop. There was only one person ahead of him in the queue, but even the three-minute wait was too much for Charles. He burned his tongue on the takeaway coffee and, forcing the plastic lid down as best he could, rushed back to the Bod. He stood outside and tried to wait for his drink to cool enough to be potable, but his anxiety became insufferable, so he discarded the coffee and ran up the stairs back to Duke Humfrey's.

As he entered the reading room, Charles suddenly felt cold. He stopped for a moment and hugged himself. The silence in the room was profound, and Charles noticed to his surprise that the handful of other readers who'd been in the room twenty minutes ago had all left. As he took a step forward, the lamps in the library flickered. The late medieval reading room was perpetually gloomy, but now it seemed to darken even more.

Charles hastened towards his desk with a growing sense of unease. As he approached, he could feel that something about his work station wasn't right – something was different. A tangible darkness appeared to have congealed in a rectangular shape on his table and, as he reached his seat, he realised what that darkness was. A shiver passed through his body. He slid onto his chair and sat motionless.

Now that he had what he'd wished for, Charles felt bewildered, exhausted and more than a little apprehensive. He stared at the book and had the ludicrous feeling that the book was staring back at him. It was a fair-sized volume, but not quite as big as he had imagined. There was a musty smell about it, and the binding – in some kind of vellum or hide – appeared to be rough-textured and a grubby greyish brown in colour. On closer inspection, Charles realised that the tome was covered in dust. He leaned over the book and blew on it. Dust particles rose in the air, making him cough, but the book remained filthy. There was something repulsive about it – something that sent a shiver down the young man's spine, bringing to mind the expression that 'someone had walked over his grave'; something that made him want to get up and run from the library without looking back. Instead he reached out his hand.

As his fingertips touched the cover, Charles winced and pulled back in surprise. The book was burning hot. Ridiculous! He touched it again, and of course it wasn't hot – it was cold – ice-cold, but that was no doubt to be expected of a leather-bound volume that had been sitting for years in an underground tunnel somewhere. Charles took out his handkerchief and tried to wipe off the grime. As he did so, he noticed a small round protuberance on the front cover. He turned the book over and found a similar bump on the back. For some reason he remembered the time when Lucy from Staircase III had got drunk and let him fondle her breasts before changing her mind and throwing him out of her room. He could clearly remember the firm, soft, rough feel of her nipples... A dire thought began to stir in his mind, but he pushed it away before it could fully form. The bumps on the covers were just imperfections in the leather, or perhaps the binding had warped lying there in the cold, damp catacomb from which it had come.

Charles continued to rub the cover. He took a quick look around, checking that nobody had entered the reading room in the last few minutes, and spat onto his handkerchief. It was easier to wipe the dirt away when the material was moistened, and the book itself seemed to relish the fluid, and scrubbed up a glowing golden brown. The texture left a little to be desired; unlike other leather-bound volumes that Charles had seen, there were pores clearly visible in the leather – tiny follicles that brought to mind the hairs that had doubtless once grown from them. But apart from the consistency of the hide, and the pair of hardened protrusions, the book was really quite handsome. Charles wondered why he'd been so repelled by it at first. He ran his hand lovingly over the front cover, stopping only when his index finger touched the bump. Then he opened it. As he did so, the temperature dropped by another couple of degrees, the lamp on his table dimmed a little, and a sigh seemed to echo around the room. Charles felt an inexplicable stab of fear in the pit of his stomach and threw a quick glance over his shoulder, but there was nobody there.

The *Liber Tenebrarum* was a volume of about two hundred pages – some of papyrus, some of coarse parchment, most of the finest vellum. It contained no introduction or contents list, but launched straight into text. As Charles tapped his desk lamp to stop it flickering, and leafed through the pages, he saw that the book was an anthology of sorts. It was full of what looked like anonymous stories, some of which contained geometrical shapes and drawings. The handwriting was diverse; the texts were written in different inks and in various languages. With some of the languages Charles was familiar; others he could only guess at. But he had always been an exceptionally talented linguist, and felt confident that the first three years of his degree in Classics and Modern Languages had prepared him for the challenge. There was no contents list or index at the back of the book either, but Charles did find something that might be useful in making sense of the book as a whole – an Afterword from the editor:

Editoris humilis post scriptum

Vobis qui fatum vestrum perfecistis scribam ego iste, qui sum in tenebras e luce egressus, lingua Creationis angelica ut anima vestra quid lateat in insidiis cognoscat.

Latin was second nature to Charles and he could read the words without effort, but comprehending exactly what the editor had in mind was a different matter. Charles could sense a veiled threat in there somewhere, and smirked at the tacit scaremongering underlying the editor's pompous message.

Directly beneath the Latin was a drawing consisting of two signs, almost touching. On the left hand side of the first sign was a shape resembling a tick, immediately followed by an upright cross that stood on a horizontal line, which led to a vertical line. At the top of the vertical line was a tiny loop and a small uneven horizontal line, ending with an equally small and uneven line that sloped downwards at a shallow angle. The second sign started with a short horizontal line, which led to an uneven V-shape. The left wing of the V was crossed by a line that ended in a small circle; the right wing of the V extended a little higher than the left wing and ended in a tiny rectangle.

The diagram perplexed Charles, but he guessed that it must be a signature of some kind. He read the Latin one more time.

An afterword from your humble editor

To you who have sealed your fate from one who went out of the light into the darkness. I shall

write in the angelic language of Creation that
your soul might learn what lies in wait.

Charles wondered what the angelic language of Creation might be –
presumably, the beautifully presented, perfectly geometrically
arranged collection of unfamiliar characters that followed on from
the Latin, below the signature. If it really was a language, then
Charles would crack it soon enough. After all, he had every book ever
written in English at his disposal, and a good many others besides.
But he was going to read the *Liber Tenebrarum* in the order in which
it was written – or at least put together – and that meant that he
would need a Sumerian-English dictionary to tackle story number
one. For that's what Charles instinctively felt the cuneiform writing
to be: Sumerian.

For a moment Charles's confidence wavered, and he wondered
whether the whole endeavour was beyond his capabilities. He
glanced at his watch and realised that the library would be closing
soon. He had to hurry if he wanted to put in a request for anything
that might help him decipher the first story. He ran his hand over
the book one last time and turned to leave. As he did so, he thought
he detected movement out of the corner of his eye. He peered into
the shadows between the bookcases, but saw nothing. He cast a final
look at the *Liber Tenebrarum* and headed towards the exit. As he
turned right towards the door, something rattled in the half-light
behind him. Charles froze. The noise came again – the discordant
metallic sound of a chain being shaken. Charles turned around
slowly and looked towards the bookcases in the far corner. There was
a chained book on one of them – a gimmick for visitors on guided
tours of the library to see how books were originally stored. When
the library was first opened, each volume was attached to its
bookcase by a chain long enough for the book to be placed on a
lectern and read standing-up. Not the most comfortable way to
study, but that wasn't Charles's concern right now. He looked
fearfully in the direction of the chained book, but the sound had
stopped and there was nobody there. He hurried out of the reading

room, made a quick search of the catalogue, ordered up a couple of dictionaries and a battalion of text books on transliterating and understanding Sumerian, and left the library. It was dark outside and, as he hurried back to Univ, he couldn't quite shake the feeling that he was being followed.

"Back from the Bod, old man?" Algy got up and poured Charles a vodka martini, complete with stuffed olive on a cocktail stick.

"Indeed," Charles accepted the drink gratefully and smiled at his roommate.

"A smile!" Algy was pleasantly surprised. "The first one I've seen since you embarked on your quest for the Holy Grail."

"Hardly." Charles downed the drink in one, grimaced, then smiled at Algy again. "But the book finally arrived."

"The book arrived?" Algy was thrown for a moment. Charles nodded. "Oh... the book arrived! That's fantastic news... Was it worth the wait?"

"I'm not sure... I think so. I haven't read it yet."

"Why not?"

"Well, it starts off in Sumerian." Algy stared at his friend in stunned silence, then poured them both another drink.

Charles slept badly that night. Shadows flitted about his room, the tree outside scratched unsettlingly at the windowpane, and Charles imagined that he heard something whispering incoherently in the far corner. He tossed and turned, and when he finally fell asleep a little before dawn, he dreamt about a darkness that was gathering around him: a shapeless, nameless darkness that brought with it madness, terror and a paralysing feeling of helplessness and despair. When his alarm clock went off at seven-thirty he woke with a start, his heart pounding. He got dressed, forced himself to eat a hurried breakfast, and raced to the Bodleian for opening time. His anxiety only subsided once he saw that the book hadn't vanished. Indeed, it was waiting for him on his desk, along with his Sumerian dictionaries and textbooks.

In the light of day, the small round bump on the front cover looked more disturbing than ever. Charles opened the book quickly and prepared to tackle the title of the first story. Cuneiform, it seemed, was a polyvalent script, and a single sign could represent a syllable, a word or even part of a phrase – not to mention that it could mean a number of different things. Charles knew that at the time the story was conceived, people wrote on clay tablets, and he hoped that whoever had taken the trouble to copy the whole text onto the papyrus had done so without any mistakes. He took a deep breath and started with the first sign. He looked it up in one of the dictionaries and proceeded to jot down all its combinations and permutations in a notebook he'd brought with him. Once he had transliterated all the signs in the title, he puzzled over which meanings were the correct ones. The process took him all morning. By lunchtime he believed that he had the title of the first story.

A cloud passed over the sun beyond the vast stained glass window at the far end of the reading-room, and the soft golden light was replaced by shadow. Charles shivered and stared at the title. He looked over his notes once more, but came to the same conclusion.

How the Great God Namtar was Summoned for the Purpose of Punishing a Woman.

Tired and hungry, Charles decided to have a quick lunch. He left his notes in the library and went across the road to the King's Arms. The sandwich he ordered took far too long to arrive and, when it finally did, he wolfed it down and ran back to the Bodleian. Despite the insanity of deciphering the Sumerian, Charles was desperate to carry on. His only worry was that, at the rate he was going, it would take him weeks just to read the first story. But he was wrong. Any self-doubt he might have had regarding his ability to tackle the task at hand effectively was dispelled as soon as he immersed himself in the text. He'd look up signs, work out a few words, and the meaning of a sentence would come to him instinctively – almost as if the book itself were his guide. In fact, with each passing hour that Charles spent with the book, the faster and easier reading it became. But also with each passing hour, the heavier a weight seemed to oppress his soul.

By the end of the day, Charles had deciphered an impressive three pages of Sumerian, and was about a fifth of the way through the first story. But as he closed the book for the night and packed up his notes, any satisfaction he should have felt at a job well done was crushed by the nature of what he had been reading. The story was a sickening one that might flippantly be described as a 'failed-rape revenge' tale. Narrated in the first person, it related with obscene relish the actions of a man living in the city of Uruk in – Charles calculated – roughly the middle of the third millennium BC. Having failed in his attempt to rape a young woman, the narrator decided to summon Namtar – the demon deity of death and pestilence – in order to avenge himself. Charles had reached the part in which the man decided to procure several children and offer them up as a sacrifice to his chosen god. The brutal images of the attempted rape at the beginning of the story refused to depart Charles's tired brain. As usual, he was the last student to leave the library. He was making his way through the reading room, lost in dark thoughts, when the rattle of chains behind him made him jump. He spun round, but, as on the previous night, there was no one there. The clanking metallic sound came again – this time off to his left. Charles ran out of the room and bounded down the stairs to the exit. He hurried back to college, all the time glancing over his shoulder in a fruitless effort to spy whatever it was he thought pursued him through the night.

"How was the book?" Algy held out a margarita and frowned, disturbed by the return of the morose look in Charles's eyes.

"Fine." Charles downed the sour liquid gratefully. "Thanks, Algy." He threw Algy a wan grimace masquerading as a smile and retired to his bedroom, leaving his roommate perplexed and worried.

From that day on, Charles was in the Bodleian every hour it was open. By the end of his first week's reading, he'd finished the first story. The narrator, whom Charles had come to hate – even across millennia – described in depth the ritual that he'd used to call up Namtar from the depths of the Sumerian underworld. Namtar, it seemed, had under his command sixty demons that could enter the human body in the form of incapacitating diseases. Bribed by the unscrupulous narrator with the burning alive of three kidnapped babies, the hellish deity sent his minions to accost the man's love interest with mortifying sickness of the eyes, heart, feet, stomach, head, back and just about every other part of her young body. As the poor girl writhed in agony, then slipped to the floor, weak and exhausted, the triumphant narrator was able to force his way into her home and into her devastated body. All this described in minute detail and with a sadistic enjoyment that, even in cuneiform, made Charles sick to the stomach.

The second story was written in Aramaic – 'the language of Christ' as Algy aptly put it on the one occasion that he actually managed to wrest some information from Charles with regards to what he was reading. As with the Sumerian, the title took the longest to decipher.

The Art of Death by Crucifixion.

After that, each sentence started to come together faster than the last. Charles read with a growing sense of dismay what purported to be the adventures of one Gaius Cassius Longinus as he traversed the easternmost reaches of the Roman Empire. In actual fact, the story was little more than an instruction manual on how to crucify someone with the maximum amount of pain over the longest period of time. Longinus, according to the writer of the piece, travelled much during his service in the Roman Army, and took a particular interest in observing local variations on methods of public execution, finding crucifixion to be by far the most diverse.

The author briefly digressed into a discussion about building materials – the best wood to use and the best metal for nails – before listing all the different types of crosses and the various ways of attaching victims to them. These ranged from a single upright pole to which a person could be nailed by one nail through the hands and one nail through the feet, to the two-beamed X-shaped cross to which one was nailed through each hand and foot, and the popular double-beamed cross which consisted of an upright pole and a cross-beam. The latter had a number of its own variations, not least the possibility of nailing a person's feet to it with just one nail or two separate ones. And that was where, according to the unknown writer, "the student of this profound science will find much that is of interest and value." For victims could also be nailed to the two-beamed cross upside down, with either their feet together or spread apart, depending on whether the cross-beam was placed closer to the top or the bottom of the upright pole. And the process could be livened up further by lighting a fire at the base of the cross or by enticing wild animals to attack the hanging victim. Such was the author's excitement at this point in the story that he (for Charles assumed the writer to be male) recommended certain embellishments to the practice under discussion. He suggested the possibility of hammering nails into body parts that weren't essential to the traditional process – such as eyes, breasts and genitalia.

After a page of wild and wanton speculation, the writer finally remembered the protagonist of his tale, and returned to Gaius Longinus, stating that the centurion's career came to a very unsatisfactory end. For, after witnessing the crucifying of a Nazarene preacher, Longinus broke a cardinal rule of any successful crucifixion (successful, according to the author of the piece): rather than prolonging the man's suffering, Longinus ended it – by running a spear through the preacher's side – a spear that would become a weapon of power, coveted by warlords in years to come.

Charles had a throbbing headache. He buried his head in his hands and sat in silence until a librarian came and informed him and other stragglers that it was closing time. This time he rushed out before the other readers to spare himself the rattle of chains that so often escorted him out of the reading room. But as the other students scattered in different directions along Broad Street, and Charles was left on his own, he sensed somewhere behind him the oppressive presence that had never quite left him since he'd first opened the book.

Every day that he spent in the reading room, the hallucinations – as Charles tried to think of them – persisted. He heard whispers and moans that none of the other readers seemed to notice; shadows with no discernible source moved around him, and the rattling of chains unnerved him when he was alone. But worse than the spectral sounds and shades was the feeling that there was always someone watching him – someone or something that he felt, but couldn't see.

The third story was Egyptian. It told of a high priest of the Temple of Seth who invoked the object of his worship by re-enacting the culmination of the story of Seth and Osiris using his own younger brother. The unfortunate fourteen-year-old was lured to the temple and precisely dismembered over a period of hours, starting with that part of Osiris that was never found. Charles's sensitive mind, which was taking in these unthinkable acts one hieroglyph at a time, struggled to retain that orderly functioning that we know as sanity. During the day, his head was full of the vile images transcribed by the authors of *The Book of Darkness*, and at night his dreams were a chaos of torture, rape and mutilation; or worse still – he dreamed of the darkness that was coming for him – a little closer night by night.

Charles became increasingly withdrawn. He skipped meals and started to look positively gaunt. He scuttled about college like a beetle that's just had the rock it was hiding under removed, unexpectedly finding itself exposed to the discomfort of bright sunlight. He would scurry back to the Bodleian at every opportunity, and was always glancing nervously over his shoulder and jumping at his own shadow. Charles's anxiety edged its way toward depression. Algy worried about Charles, but couldn't quite commit himself to the serious business of helping him. In any case, he wouldn't have known what to do. So he looked on in a concerned, but increasingly distant manner.

Eventually Charles stopped attending lectures and tutorials altogether. He didn't pick up work assignments and failed to hand in essays. His college tutor summoned him and tried to ascertain what was going on. Charles said that he hadn't been feeling well. He negotiated to be allowed to stay in college over the vacation, to make up for what he'd missed. If he passed a penal examination at the beginning of the following term, no disciplinary action would be taken against him. Charles promised to work hard over the break and to pull his socks up next term. Whether he believed in any part of the promises he made to his tutor was dubious. His intention was not to work on his degree subjects; he merely needed a place to stay so that he could finish reading the book.

Charles explained to his parents that he had to stay up at college over Easter to study. They were disappointed, of course, but they thought they understood. Their son had always been an outstanding student, and they were very proud of him. Ever since he was little, he'd amazed everyone with his ability to learn languages. Wherever the family holidayed with little Charlie, he became fluent in the local lingo within a week. Back home he would insist on giving directions to lost tourists in their own language, he would point out mistakes in inscription translations at the British Museum, and was able to read the Latin on gravestones long before he started learning the dead language at school. So although they'd miss him terribly, they believed that he was destined for greater things, and left him to do what he had to do.

"You're mad!" Algy hauled the last of his suitcases into the corridor, and came back in to say goodbye. It was the last day of term, and Charles looked pale and listless. "It's that book, isn't it?" But Charles shook his head firmly.

"I just need some time to think."

"Well, don't think too hard – it's not good for you."

"Okay," responded Charles.

"And don't sell the mantelpiece without me!" Charles's attempt at a smile reassured Algy a little. "See you in six weeks, old man," he added, shaking his roommate's hand warmly. But as he turned to leave, Algy felt an inexplicable pang of sadness.

Charles was exhausted and traumatised. He no longer wanted to get out of bed. He no longer wanted to live. No longer wanted to read the book. But it was inside him now – in his blood and in his bones. It had crawled into his soul, where it festered. And every day it was there in the library, waiting for Charles patiently – like a faithful lover or an old friend. And when the young man tried to stay away, his body was racked with terrible pain and uncontrollable nausea. Like a sick junkie he dragged himself to the Bodleian every day, wishing with all his might that the book not be there, but desperate to read it to the end.

The fourth story was written in Arabic in the eighth century. It told of the terrible fate that befell a scholarly man named Abdul who accidentally found artefacts of power that allowed the opening of a gate into a world of ancient and evil gods. Abdul tried to warn mankind of "the Terror that walks Outside and crouches at the threshold of every man." His punishment was terrifying. He was torn apart by "jackal-headed demons, Emissaries of the Gods of Prey, that gnaw on the very bones of men", and devoured by the Maskim and the Rabishu. His immortal soul was snatched by "vulture-faced Pazuzu, horned master of all plagues, four-winged lord of the desert wind that brings madness, with rotting genitalia from which he howls in pain through pointed fangs", and condemned to an eternity of torture – unspeakable, but nonetheless described in detail by the story's unnamed author.

Charles was able to read the fifth story without a dictionary, as it was in Latin. It concerned the flaying alive of a child, in order to use its skin to create a homunculus. As the procedure inevitably led to the victim's death, the child had to be raped first in order not to incur the wrath of the goddess Diana, who was known to inflict severe punishment on those who murdered virgins. Charles couldn't eat after reading this particular story and, when he finally got to his bed that night, he couldn't sleep either. He anaesthetised himself as best he could with the aid of the alcohol that Algy had kindly left him, and lay awake – his eyes tightly shut lest he catch a glimpse of whatever it was that crouched, whispering, beside his bed.

The sixth story, written in Hebrew, was entitled: *How to Reincarnate by Force the Soul of a Murderer for the Purpose of Creating a Dark Golem*. The author presented a complicated ritual with a foul necromantic rite at its core, then went on to describe the slow and torturous deaths that the monster which was produced inflicted on the enemies of its creator.

The seventh story was a German language account of the actions of a Prince of Wallachia in the mid fifteenth century. Vlad Tepes needed no introduction as far as Charles was concerned, but the detailed account of the impalings, burnings, skinnings, boilings and drownings perpetrated on the Prince's orders was nonetheless upsetting to him. It seemed that no matter how far Charles delved into the book, reading about the acts of torture, perversion and murder contained within its pages became no easier for him. He took to scrubbing himself raw in the shower every night, but nothing he did could stop him feeling soiled or ease the self-hatred that grew with each passing day. Still he kept going back for more.

A month into the Easter holiday, Charles was over halfway through the book, and yet it seemed like the self-imposed torture of reading it would never end. The extraordinary eighth tale, written in Spanish in the sixteenth century, commenced in Mexico and followed the adventures of one Juan Sánchez el Rojo, a Spanish cleric happily carrying the one true faith to the heathens, and performing all kinds of exciting feats in the service of the Spanish Inquisition. So fascinated did the padre become with the finer points of the human sacrifice practised by the Aztecs, that he decided to dedicate the rest of his days to a search for the most terrifying method of killing he could find.

His new hobby led him to undertake the extremely dangerous self-appointed mission of penetrating the hostile kingdom of England – on an assignment that made every nerve in his body tingle. For he'd heard tell of a strange new instrument housed in the Tower of London that could make a sinner confess to every wrongdoing under the sun, and make him suffer in a hundred different parts of his body at once; killing him only when the interrogator was done. Connoisseurs of such matters said of the device that it was "a companion piece to the rack", and yet worked "in a way that was opposed to it". Try as he might, the curious cleric was unable to glean any further information, so he decided to risk everything to see this fine machine in operation. As fortune would have it, the protagonist of this swashbuckling tale came from a family no less wealthy than it was well-connected. And so contact was established with members of a secret organisation of the one true Church who, despite their Catholicism, had access to the best guarded places in the possession of the English Crown.

And so it came to pass that, with much cloak-and-dagger activity, and a considerable amount of money changing hands, our adventurous friend was smuggled into the Tower of London – there to see with his own eyes the peculiar device known as the Scavenger's Daughter. For it was one Leonard Skeffington – alias Skevington – Lieutenant of the Tower of London during the reign of King Henry VIII, who was the curious thing's father and creator. Quite how his name devolved from Skevington to Scavenger is a question for scholars of greater learning than that of the unknown author of Juan's story – and indeed than that of the priest himself. Not that the brave cleric cared much for philological niceties – he had things of divine importance on his mind. If at first he was a little taken aback by the unglamorous appearance of the object that he'd travelled hundreds of miles to see, his insatiability for observing new modes of torture was amply rewarded when the bribed guard showed and explained to him how the thing worked. This particular rack functioned on the basis of compression rather than stretching. The instrument was made up of a single iron bar that connected iron shackles fastening around the feet, hands and neck. It pushed the head and knees together, crushing victims until they bled from their nose and ears, and their bones snapped. The unnamed writer of the tale described how "the priest's eyes shone with excitement, and he shook the hands of his guides a dozen times, so inspired was he by what he had seen". His expedition had been worth the dangers, even though he narrowly escaped with his life. For the very next day after his momentous trip to the Tower, war broke out between England and Spain, and Juan Sánchez barely made it back across the Channel. Providence had been smiling on him, he thought, as for many years to come no amount of secret societies would be able to smuggle a Spanish Catholic cleric into England, let alone out again.

The ninth story was written in the first person, in an elegant, feminine hand. The author described the difficulties a noblewoman faced in the corrupt, power-crazed Kingdom of Hungary at the turn of the sixteenth and seventeenth centuries. She wrote of the man she'd been forced to marry as part of a loveless political match, and of the hideous men of power who gathered like vultures around her person and her wealth after his death. She wrote of falling in love for the first time as a woman in her maturity, and of her heartbreak when she thought that her young lover had left her on the eve of their planned marriage. Unaware of the conspiracy to kidnap her lover and keep him from her, she became obsessed by the notion that she had been abandoned because she was not in the first blush of youth. The idea so consumed her that she contrived at all costs to regain and retain the supple beauty that her skin had once possessed.

As she watched the young women and girls in her service, the countess realised that their skin was aglow no matter how hard they worked. It was youth that gave their skin that sheen – the youth that flowed in the blood of their veins. From that day on the woman contrived to create an elixir of youth by mixing young blood with herbs and a little goose fat. The ointment worked, but only briefly. The amount of blood she was able to mix and smear on her face was insufficient. She needed more. Her devoted servants brought her girls – fresh-faced maidens whose blood was not only youthful, but pure. Her servants helped her cut the girls and trap the blood, but too much of it was spilt. She used her learning to invent elaborate devices to hold the girls still and cut them slowly, to prolong and maximise the amount of the blood that could be used. But her impatience got the better of her – she wanted more blood. More and more girls were brought to the castle and bled to fill her bath. But blood congealed so fast and in the end the best way was to lie in the bath herself and have a girl trussed up above her. On her signal, the girl's throat would be cut and the countess would revel in the scarlet shower. But still it was not enough.

She dispatched servants to seek out girls, and scouts to look for her young lover. But it was not her lover who burst into the castle in the middle of a moonless night – it was a party of her enemies, using the excuse of missing girls and whispered rumours to violate her sanctuary. And now her haven had become her prison, as a court of men tortured her faithful servants to death and walled her up in her own chamber. And it was there, sealed in her premature grave that she wrote her story, watching her skin age and wither, and waiting for death.

Dear Reader,

the tenth story proclaimed,

> *take heed and steel yourself for the most brutal and lubricious of tales. For depucelation of innocents snatched from their mothers' arms and ignominious acts steeped in bile and blood. The hero – and villain – of our tale is a man of noble birth, who once rode with the Maid of Orléans. But there are no depths to which perverse vanity and profuse lust will not drag even the noblest heart...*

The French story was written in black ink, with a fine quill. *De Sade*, thought Charles, but he felt no satisfaction at the possibility of having found a long-lost story by the notorious author, foreseeing the atrocities that lurked within. The tale concerned a fifteenth century baron who gave up an illustrious military career to pursue artistic endeavours. Like Nero, perhaps, he fancied himself something of a poet, and wrote a play consisting of 20,000 lines of verse about the Siege of Orléans, in which he had taken part alongside Joan of Arc. There were 140 speaking parts, and 500 extras were required. 600 elaborate costumes were made for the occasion, worn for one performance, then discarded – to be replaced by new ones.

The nobleman gathered as big an audience as he could to view his magnum opus, and provided all its members with unlimited quantities of food and drink at his own expense. Having already spent much of his fortune on the creation of an impressive chapel in which he presided in robes he'd designed himself, not to mention a lavish lifestyle, the baron found himself broke, with no friends to turn to. Enter an alchemist, a magician of some power, who befriended the young baron and persuaded him that his wealth could be restored by the sacrifice of children to the powers of darkness. But even the alchemist could not have predicted – or perhaps he could – the enthusiasm and wicked pleasure that the young nobleman would come to take in the rape and slaughter of the innocent. It was only when the baron kidnapped a cleric in an attempt to snatch back one of the castles he had been forced to mortgage, that a formal investigation accidentally uncovered his heinous crimes. The author never said whether the baron's Satanic pursuits restored his squandered riches, but he did describe with clinical precision the hanging and setting alight of the disgraced noble.

Back at college that night, Charles spent an hour under the shower, trying to erase the filth of the day, but – as usual – his cleansing ritual failed to purify. He lay awake with his eyes closed and his hands clapped over his ears to shut out the whispering of whatever was leaning over him.

The eleventh story described the rivalry between two magick lodges. The grand master of one of the lodges held an all-too-realistic ritual reconstructing the rape of a nymph by a group of drunken satyrs. The stated aim was to evoke a physical manifestation of the god Pan, who would then violate the wife of the grand master of the rival lodge. This elaborate plan was outlined with much pompous philosophising by an author writing in English and hinting at his own identity by calling himself the Brother Who Would Endure Until the End.

It took Charles a long time and a great deal of trouble to work out the language of the twelfth and penultimate text, even though it was contemporary. The story was written in the Nilo-Saharan language known as Fur. More of a vision than a story – the vision of a twelve-year old Sudanese boy, noted down by village elders who believed him possessed by a saint. In a childish tongue he spoke of the century past and the century to come: of chimneys that spewed out the smoke of millions in a Europe occupied by men in black uniforms with silver lightning flashes and death's head insignia. Of the House of Karaman in which women were raped and forced to bear the children of their violators. Of burning oilfields and children dying under rubble. Of men tortured for years in secret places with no windows by governments that spoke of freedom, and of earthquakes, giant waves and death-bringing snow that devastated the Land of the Rising Sun. The boy spoke of the militias that raged much closer to home, of the destruction of his village and his own death under the curved knife of a tribesman butcher. Lastly he spoke of the war of the three great religions: of the annihilation of one by two, then the destruction of one of the remaining two by the other, and finally of the end of days in accordance with a hadith interpreted by the captive Ottoman scribe of the Letters of Light – in the year 2129.

The script containing the boy's vision did not burn with his village – even as the boy himself burned – but was taken by a tribal Emir and militia leader as a memento of sorts, probably on account of its pretty animal skin binding. How the editor of *The Book of Darkness* had acquired it for his work remained a mystery.

Charles was at a very low ebb. Term-time would start in a week and he had no energy to face it. There was one piece left to read – the thirteenth text: the afterword by the editor.

Charles's research into what the angelic language might be led him to the work of sixteenth century English mathematician, astronomer and occultist Dr John Dee. It was claimed that the angels spoke to Dee and taught him their language. Armed with a body of work by the magician and his partner Edward Kelley, along with an array of modern dictionaries and textbooks, Charles had a chance of finishing by the beginning of term, but somehow he couldn't see beyond the book. He could no longer remember a time before the book, and he couldn't envisage a time after it. He had come too far to stop now, but he felt as if all the energy had been drawn from him and he wasn't sure if he could muster the strength to carry on. He opened the book and was about to leaf his way to where he'd left off, when the pages started to turn rapidly past his fingers, stopping at his target.

> *To you who have sealed your fate from one who went out of the light into the darkness. I shall write in the angelic language of Creation that your soul might learn what lies in wait.*

It dawned on Charles: the words contained no subtle threat; the editor was merely stating facts.

Having read a number of spirit invocation passages in the previous texts, Charles now knew that the line drawing beneath the Latin was the seal – or sigil – of an angel. He searched through the encyclopaedia of angels at his disposal until he found a sigil with the distinctive tick and cross-shape at the beginning. It was the sigil of Samael. He looked up Samael and frowned. "(Hebrew: סמאל) (also Sammael) Angel of death. One of the seven angels of Creation. Archangel of the planet Mars. Angel of seduction and destruction. Fallen angel, leader of the evil spirits, ruler of the fifth heaven. Also known as Satan."

The library was very quiet. There were no mysterious susurrations tonight, and Charles listened for a while to his own breathing and the steady beat of his heart. He dismissed the angelic signature as cheap theatricality on the part of the editor, and delved into the final piece.

At first glance the text did not appear to be in any 'language' as we understand the term. But the letters that formed it were the most beautiful that Charles had ever seen. They were arranged in 49 tables. Every table was made up of 49 by 49 squares, each containing a letter. Square by square – letter by letter – Charles started to decipher the script. Each element of each table had 49 different meanings, and the ensuing experience was like reading 49 diverse tongues, all of them reverberating in Charles's head at once.

It was like existing concurrently in 49 parallel dimensions, and opening 49 different doors at once. And each door uncovered before the unfortunate young man a deeper circle of hell. For the words that Charles read assaulted him with every suffering, every perversity, every darkest fear; with horror beyond even the most twisted human imagination. It was like looking into the most depraved heart and sensing every perverse, twisted, homicidal sensation at once. Charles saw in an instant the torture, rape, murder, mutilation and genocide of millions. He saw every war crime, every disease, every form of tortured life and painful death. And he not only saw, but smelt, tasted, heard and felt every twinge of every tortured nerve. For the reading was like synaesthesia – Charles's senses intermingled and fused together, so that he smelled simultaneously the fear of the victims and the arousal of the perpetrators, he tasted the screams of the damned, he heard the blood and bile that flowed from a million festering wounds, he saw intolerable pain, and touched the anguish and hopelessness of the human misery that raged before him. All this as plain as a canvass spread before him, behind him and all around.

The perfect letters of the perfect words told of the infinite abyss of fire waiting for his immortal soul; of the darkness that had caught up with him, and of suffering, despair, madness and horror without end. Charles read and understood.

When the librarian made her closing-time rounds of Duke Humfrey's Reading Room, and asked the studious young man in the corner to get ready to leave, he made no response. She thought that he'd fallen asleep at his desk, and touched his arm. He did not move. Bending over him in the half-light, she couldn't see that his eyes were open and staring. She shook his arm gently, crying out in alarm as his body slumped forward and his head hit the table with a lifeless thud. Dictionaries and textbooks fell to the floor, but *The Book of Darkness* was nowhere to be seen.

FORMBY POINT

FORMBY POINT

"THE NORTHWEST IS like the body of a beautiful woman. North of Liverpool lie her breasts. And Formby... Formby is her nipple."

"Which nipple?"

"What do you mean, which nipple?"

"Well, is it the right nipple or the left nipple?"

Irritated, Pete switched off the radio. He was born in Formby, but hadn't been back since he'd left for London University (and stayed) and his parents had moved to Manchester. Twenty-five years ago now. He'd just been visiting them for the long bank holiday, but some twang of nostalgia for his modest, but occasionally magical, childhood spurred him to say his goodbyes early on the Monday morning and head off west down the M602.

He'd told his parents that he had to get back to London early to prepare for a presentation the next day. This tiny lie seemed easier than explaining that he wanted to get to the beach quickly and walk at his own pace, not constrained by anyone's arthritis or rheumatism or dodgy knee, and without the constant worry that one of them might tumble and do themselves an injury. A nagging feeling of guilt accompanied his deception – after all, they'd taken him to the beach on many an occasion when he was little, and now perhaps they'd be grateful for being given the opportunity to revisit the seaside themselves. But as he turned off the M62 onto the M57, the guilty feeling dissipated and he started to look forward to the trek across the sand dunes, rewarded by the stunning view of the sea off Formby Point and the sea breeze as he approached the water. He wondered whether the tide would be in or out.

Serendipitously, there appeared to be a programme on the radio about Formby; or, more accurately, two sports commentators seemed to be engaging in some increasingly annoying banter, but Pete felt like he needed something to occupy his thoughts, so he turned the radio back on.

"Of course, Formby is now best known as the residence of the late Phil Rafferty, the footballer who had his foot cut off by his lover's jealous boyfriend."

"Ex-boyfriend."

"For those of you who haven't been following the story, the ex-boyfriend of Rafferty's girlfriend Linda Frome broke into the footballer's 2.5 million pound Formby home, overpowered him while he slept and cut off his famous left foot."

Pete wasn't much of a football fan, but he'd heard all about Rafferty of course. The mutilation and subsequent suicide of the footballer had caused a media feeding frenzy the world over. The promising young Irishman had been signed by Liverpool only six months earlier.

"The foot was never found."

Pete switched the radio off again.

Eventually the motorway came to an end and Pete continued up Broom's Cross Road, the flat green fields on either side a familiar, welcome, yet disconcertingly desolate sight. Once Broom's Cross Road gave onto the Southport Road, Pete was on the home stretch, yet the feeling of unease persisted. By the time Southport Road became Ince Lane, then Moore Lane, it took all of Pete's willpower not to put his foot down. No matter how many times he drove down this stretch of road, childhood fears surfaced to spook him. To his left, The Round House — an eighteenth century brick building with a conical stone slate roof – marked the approach to the stretch of Ince Woods allegedly haunted by the so-called Grey Lady. To Pete's mother's despair, a helpful aunt had told little Petey about how a mysterious female figure would wander out onto Moore Lane from Cross Barn Lane just beyond and across the road from The Round House, causing vehicles to swerve off the road. Petey had taken the story to heart, and the subsequent designation of the stretch of road running through Ince Woods as an accident black spot, and the discovery one winter of the frozen body of a school friend's grandmother in a ditch at the side of the road where the Grey Lady was said to walk, just served to strengthen little Petey's terror. Fits of hysterical tears from age six to age eight had forced Pete's father to take an inconvenient detour every time the family left Formby for a day out, and even now Pete chastised himself for not having taken an alternative route. But, as usual, there was no Grey Lady (not that he expected one), he managed to avoid any hint of a possible accident, and he was soon quickly and efficiently heading for the Formby Bypass and Liverpool Road beyond, then turning left onto Raven Meols Lane.

Pete drove all the way to the end of Raven Meols Lane, which turned into Queen's Road and then into Bushby Lane, stopping just before Bushby Lane turned into Lifeboat Road, and parking up in a side street. He set off up Lifeboat Road on foot. To his left was a fair-sized fenced-off area of woodland, which housed Shorrocks Hill nightclub and what was once a members' only day spa with indoor and outdoor pools – now turned paintballing headquarters. To his right were a couple of millionaires' houses, one of which had previously belonged to the unfortunate Phil Rafferty. Pete frowned at the FOR SALE sign nailed onto the gate post, and found himself wondering about the last resting place of Rafferty's left foot. He shook off the morbid reflection, annoyed at himself for allowing the imbecilic radio presenters to get under his skin.

Soon the dead footballer's estate gave way to woodland, and Pete wandered off the road into the pine trees that constituted Formby's famous red squirrel reserve. Pete had loved playing in the woods as a kid, and the Scout troop in which he'd been a Cub often went hiking in the picturesque landscape, collecting pine cones to sketch and learning about the glorious variety of fauna and flora. But as Pete now walked deeper into the woodland, orienting himself to stay parallel to Lifeboat Road, there seemed to be something different about the woods. Something Pete couldn't put his finger on. Something not quite right.

Pete slowed his pace, peering into the trees, listening intently for any sound out of the ordinary. He couldn't shake the feeling that he was not alone. Each time he took a few steps, he thought he heard something moving in the undergrowth nearby, but, when he stopped, there was only the sound of distant birdsong and the breeze sighing in the pine tops. Pete listened for a while, distinctly ill at ease in the place that had formerly brought him solace and joy. Then he hatched a plan: he'd walk quickly for a bit, then stop abruptly enough for whoever might be following him to be caught off-guard and take at least one more step so that Pete could ascertain where the footfalls were coming from. But the plan backfired when Pete stopped suddenly and nearly jumped out of his skin as a startled woodpecker which had been keeping pace with him burst from the bushes to his right and flew off into the trees.

Relieved, but irritated with himself for being frightened by something as innocuous as a ten-inch bird, Pete continued through the pinewoods in the general direction of the beach. And yet he still couldn't recapture the carefree, light-hearted feeling he'd always experienced here as a child. He'd only walked a dozen or so metres when he noticed a red squirrel – dead, lying on the ground, its eyes decomposed, flies and bugs swarming all over it. Great. He'd never so much as caught a fleeting glimpse of a red squirrel before, and now here was one oozing putrescence before his very eyes. Disgusted, Pete headed left – back onto Lifeboat Road. Perhaps it would be simpler to stick to the path. But he hadn't got far when he passed a dead baby rabbit on the side of the road. Then another and another. Christ. Where were all these dead rabbits coming from? Perhaps they'd wandered out onto the road and been hit by cars, but the road leading up to the beach was narrow and cars here drove too slowly to hit so many rabbits... surely?

To say that Pete wasn't enjoying the walk to the beach as much as he'd anticipated would be something of an understatement. Eventually the pine trees gave way to grassland and the odd low, squat tree, weirdly misshapen and growing crazily in the direction dictated by the constant battering of the wind. Soon the road became a dirt track, and Pete was walking through another area of special interest: a space fenced off to protect northern dune tiger beetles and Formby's famous natterjack toads. Pete had never seen a natterjack toad. But wait: what was the putrid thing lying at the side of the track, front legs curled over its chest, two disproportionately large hind legs pointing lifelessly at the sky? No... really? Pete wasn't even going to contemplate the bizarre possibility of another dead animal. It was a children's toy – he told himself: a toy dropped, forgotten and trodden into the dirt. He looked pointedly ahead and strode as quickly as the increasingly sandy constituency of the path would allow.

Soon the whole path was covered in sand, and on either side of it rose the famed Formby sand dunes, dotted here and there with spiky marram grass. The path – what there was of it – now wove up and down amongst the dunes. Traipsing through the sand was increasingly heavy-going and Pete had to stop a couple of times to tip thousands of tiny grains out of his shoes. After a while he started to doubt himself: had the path to the beach really been this long? It seemed like he was lumbering through the sand forever, although in actual fact it couldn't have been more than ten minutes or so. He stopped and tried to catch his breath. This next dune was surely the last one, and of course it had to be the biggest. He was glad he'd given up smoking for New Year. If he hadn't, he'd be filling his lungs with tar round about now, and the trudge uphill would probably be even harder. Pete braced himself and climbed the last few epic metres up the final sand dune.

Finally at the very top, Pete was rewarded by a view that took his breath away no matter how many times he saw it: laid out before him, the golden-white sand of Formby Beach and beyond it, in the distance, the steel blue-grey of the Irish Sea. A relatively recent addition to the scene was the Burbo Bank Offshore Wind Farm – a constellation of twenty-five wind turbines on a vast sandbank – straight ahead and to Pete's left, towards Wales and the Mersey estuary. At 300 feet high, each turbine was nearly as tall as the Blackpool Tower, but their distance, at four miles off Formby Point, belied their imposing stature. Pete looked south down the coast, towards Crosby. He knew there was an extraordinary art installation there: one hundred cast-iron, 650 kilogram, life-size figures spread out along three kilometres of the foreshore and stretching almost one kilometre out to sea, made from casts of artist Antony Gormley's own body, embedded in the sand and staring forever seaward. Perhaps another time he'd visit the Gormley statues, but that would have to wait – there were other wonders for Pete to explore today. The unease of all the dead animals lifted slightly and he gazed out to sea.

The tide was out – as far out as Pete had ever seen it – and to his delight the receding sea had uncovered the eerie black skeleton of the *Ionic Star*. Pete knew there'd been a solar eclipse on Friday, and he'd read in the *Liverpool Echo* about how the subsequent gravitational pull of the sun, moon and planets had caused a supertide, the extreme low tide that followed exposing some of the dozens of shipwrecks off the Mersey coast. But the article hadn't prepared Pete for the breathtaking spectacle of actually seeing the desolate remains of the *Ionic Star* embedded in the mudflats off Formby Point. Pete could clearly see the tiny silhouettes of people exploring the unfortunate cargo ship's giant ribs. Enthralled and unnerved in equal measure, he made his way down onto the beach, determined to investigate the vessel from close-up.

The Blue Star Line Company had been building ships since 1891. Throughout the many years of the company's illustrious existence, numerous of its ships met a sticky end – sunk by enemy torpedoes or wrecked on foreign shores. The fate of two of these sister ships springs to mind if only for the reason that they perished within two months of each other. These steamships were the *Ionic Star* and her younger sister the *Doric Star*, but lucky Stars they certainly weren't. The *Doric Star* was sunk by the German Battleship *Admiral Graf Spee* off the West coast of Africa on the 2nd of December 1939. Less than two months earlier, on the 16th of October, the *Ionic Star* had almost made it home and to her Liverpool destination with her cargo of fruit, cotton and meat before running aground on the treacherous sands of Mad Wharf, a mile west of Formby Point. The position of the ship made salvage nigh-on impossible and so, to add insult to injury, she was used for target practice during the Second World War.

As he walked out onto the pale golden expanse of Formby Beach, Pete paused for a moment at the ruins of the old lifeboat station. Built in 1809, the station – now reduced to melancholy grey and terracotta brick foundations – had itself been built on the site of Britain's first lifeboat station dating back to 1776. Depressing and strange, the fractured remains jutted red and orange from the golden-white sand. But Pete had inspected them a hundred times as a boy, and now his heart was set on the vast black ruin that he'd only seen a couple of times before, and never this exposed. The *Ionic Star's* dark carcass was usually completely covered by the sea, and, although Pete had seen parts of the wreck a couple of times before, it still unsettled him.

He started walking out towards the sea and that's when he noticed the dead jellyfish. One, then another, and another – until it seemed that the whole seaward side of the beach was littered with slimy tentacled corpses. Dead jellyfish on the beach were nothing new, of course, but Pete had never seen so many at once. Then something caught his eye. A gelatinous pink-beige blob some half a metre in diameter. Flaccid arms spread out from its centre like a grotesque knobbly star. As Pete stared at the hideous spectacle in fascination, a couple who'd been strolling on the beach behind him noticed the transfixed man and followed his gaze.

"Oh my goodness!" exclaimed the woman. "It's huge."

Pete couldn't help but smile at the woman's words, but quickly composed himself and gave the couple an acknowledging nod.

"Hi there." The couple smiled back at Pete, then proceeded to take photos of the decomposing barrel jellyfish and of each other with it. Pete left them to it and continued towards the *Ionic Star*, careful not to tread on any of the decaying monstrosities. Soon he was out of the 'dead zone' and heading across the wet sand to his goal. For a moment there was total silence – not even seagulls calling overhead. Then the wind blew from the sea – cold, loud, humming and whistling around Pete, until it felt like its persistent eldritch wail was right inside his head. And then a voice rang in Pete's ears – distant and shrill, the desperate cry of someone in mortal peril.

"Help!" the voice came from up ahead and a little to Pete's right. Pete looked back to see if the couple he'd met had heard it too, but they were nowhere to be seen. "Over here!" He looked around in alarm and eventually spotted what looked like a barnacle-covered rock protruding from a pool of water in the sands ahead of him. Pete had never noticed the rock before; then again, he'd never seen so much of the beach exposed before. Alongside the rock curved a row of what looked like rotting grey-black wooden stumps, and Pete realised that he was looking at another wreck – one that he'd never previously seen. The rocklike structure was the sunken vessel's two cylinder vertical engine, completely covered in mussels.

The *Bradda* had come to rest – if that's how the ill-fated steamer's desperate, violent end could be described – about 300 yards north of the *Ionic Star* and three years earlier than the larger vessel. On the 9th of January 1936, the Dutch-built, Isle of Man based steamer set off from Birkenhead with her cargo of coal, bound for Rogerstown in the Irish Free State. It was already dark and the weather was poor when the small coaster headed off down the River Mersey. Within minutes, a terrible gale ensued and hurricane winds of a hundred miles an hour lashed the *Bradda* mercilessly.

Arthur Cregeen had experienced many a storm in his years as master mariner at the Ramsey Steamship Company, but never anything as swift and violent as this. He knew better than anyone how to handle himself and any vessel in his charge, and he recognised that this was a battle they weren't going to win. To make matters even worse, he hadn't been able to keep course along the deep centre of the Crosby channel – two boats had passed the *Bradda*, and the smaller vessel had been forced to keep to the Formby shore side, too close for comfort to the limestone training wall designed to stop shipping from becoming grounded in the shallows. They'd just passed the Great Burbo Bank; the guiding light of the Crosby Lightship, moored off the northeast elbow of the vast sandbank, glowed faintly to their port side. Any further and they'd be blown out into the open sea. It was now or never.

"We're turning back!" the captain shouted to his crew of five. But the storm had the vessel in its deadly grip, and when Cregeen tried to swing her round, the *Bradda* did not respond. "She's refusing to answer the helm! Brace yourselves!"

At sixty-two years of age, Robert Harrison had been an able seaman for more years than he cared to remember. It had been exciting at first, but lately all he could think about was making retirement age so that he could spend more time with his wife and fifteen-year-old daughter. He'd served as helmsman under Cregeen before, but this was the first time he thought he could detect a note of concern underpinning the customary calm of the forty-five year old captain's commands. The other sea veterans – sixty-year-old chief engineer Thomas Tasker and fifty-four-year-old second engineer William Clewis – were also too well aware of how quickly their current predicament could turn lethal. Able seamen Samuel Ball and Isaac Skillen were much younger than the others. Isaac still lived with his parents in Douglas. He'd been looking forward to his twenty-first birthday next month and to spending time with his fiancée.

The wind whistled and screeched, driving waves of stinging rain and icy spray into the lightly-built vessel. The gale raged all around, whipping the dark waters into a frenzy. Then an enormous wave struck. There was a back-wrenching jolt and a shudder as the *Bradda* was blown stern-first into the Mersey training wall designed to keep shipping in the Crosby channel. Now quite out of control, she breached the wall into the shallower Formby channel and ground to a halt on the sandbank beyond.

From his post at the wheel, Cregeen fought valiantly to free the *Bradda* from the sandbank, but the violent, churning sea and the cloying, hard-packed sand pinned her in.

"Get the flares!"

Wrestling not to lose their footing on the slippery deck in the face of the tempest's onslaught, the *Bradda's* crew sent up flare after flare and rocket after rocket, in a desperate attempt to summon help. The Crosby Lightship wasn't far; surely someone would spot them? They must have sent about fifty distress signals, but help did not come. Cregeen was starting to despair for his crew.

"Put on your lifejackets!" he shouted over the maelstrom.

Soaked through and despairing, they continued to send up flares and rockets in the hope of attracting the attention of the lightship, a lifeboat, or any passing vessel. Their signals tore through the miasma of the storm-black sky, scant competition for the thunder and lightning that crashed and streaked overhead. Boats passed no more than half a mile away, and each time a glimmer of hope flickered for Cregeen and his crew.

"Help! Over here!"

But the passing boats took no notice. Perhaps they failed to spot the *Bradda*. Perhaps they knew that following her into the shallow Formby channel would entail meeting the same fate as the doomed vessel.

When the boat's supply of flares and rockets ran out, the men soaked towels and rags in paraffin and fired those instead. After two hours of continuous assault from the elements, the boat began to list very badly and the men used the last of their strength to climb onto the port side of the bridge. Then a great wave struck the *Bradda*, and she went right over. Physically strong and athletic, Samuel Ball managed to climb further up. The next wave washed Harrison, Tasker and Clewis away. Harrison hit his head hard as he went over; for him the fear and pain was over before the swell took him. Another wave struck the vessel, then another, and Ball was ripped right off the bridge to which he was clinging. Out of the corner of his eye he saw Skillen washed overboard as well.

"Isaac...!" the Captain cried out after the last of his men, and then he too was gone, into the black and angry sea.

But the waves parted long enough for Ball and Skillen to swim clear of the stricken vessel and the danger of being battered and crushed against her bulky, wave-swept corpse. Ball, the strongest swimmer of the crew, spotted the younger man.

"Skillen! Over here! Isaac!"

Ball noticed a piece of timber that had broken off the *Bradda* and was being thrown about by the waves nearby. He grabbed it and swam towards Isaac, pushing it out in the young man's direction.

"Grab a hold!" he shouted, planning to pull Isaac to shore.

Isaac reached out – as far as he could. For a moment his fingers almost touched the sodden timber, but then a huge wave parted the two men and Isaac disappeared from view.

"Isaac! Where are you?!" Ball called out over the hurricane. Was that a human voice in the darkness? Isaac's faint cry for help? Or just the wind shrieking? "Isaac!"

Battling the swirling, heaving waves, Ball swam towards what he thought was the spot where he'd last seen the other youth, but there was nothing but wild, inky water all around. Unable to swim any further, he drifted for a while, calling out, listening, trying to keep his head above water. The sea was pitch black. The best thing he could do was bring back help. He scoured the horizon, and oriented himself towards the Formby Lighthouse, and then a smaller, closer light that glowed in a window of the tide gauge attendant's cottage on Lifeboat Road. In the dark sea behind him, unheard by Ball, Isaac surfaced one last time.

"Help! Over here!" Then he was gone for good.

The *Bradda* lay considerably closer to shore than the *Ionic Star*, yet while Pete could distinctly see people walking right up to the *Ionic Star*, much of the closer wreck was submerged in water. Pete figured that the smaller vessel must be in a trough or lake of sorts. The sands off Formby point were anything but flat – their shifting, treacherous surface concealed all manner of gullies and channels. In some places you could walk right out to sea, at others rivulets connected deeper pockets of water, and an unwary rambler, unaware of the tides, could easily become cut off from the shore.

The sound of the wind increased, though not its strength. Pete was perplexed when he realised that the wail of the wind was out of all proportion to the feel of it against his skin. He strained to hear the voice again through the whistling and howling. And it came.

"Help! Over here!" Definitely from the direction of the mysterious wreck.

Pete walked as fast as he could over the wet sand, trying to see who it was that was calling out.

"Hang on!" he shouted, "I'm coming to get you."

But as he neared the wreck, Pete couldn't see anyone in the water.

"Help!" The voice grew weaker as the sound of lashing rain merged with the ululating of the wind, but no raindrops fell on Pete and, as he looked up, he saw that the sky was still clear. Pete cast a glance towards the *Ionic Star* and saw to his dismay that the people who'd been taking photos of it were no longer there. He looked around and saw the last of them disappearing up the beach, way out of earshot.

"Where are you?!" Pete called out as he ran towards the fading voice.

"Over here!"

A thunder clap echoed overhead, but no lightning, as the phantom storm seethed around Pete. And suddenly the wet sand beneath Pete's feet gave way to a sharp drop, and Pete plunged down into icy water. His startled cry was cut short as his head submerged for a moment, then he was partially out of the water again, struggling to stand. He could no longer hear the pleading voice; only the lashing rain and howling wind of the ghostly storm that raged somewhere on another plane of time. And then Pete was screaming, begging for help, as the viscous mud of the gully into which he'd fallen closed around his feet, clutching, pulling, sucking him down into the seabed. And the crabs were scuttling towards him along the hard wet sand above him and the soft silty quicksand beneath him.

"Help!" It was Pete who was crying out now, arms flailing, voice carried away on a non-existent storm. "Over here!" But there was nobody to hear or to help, and Pete sank slowly, helplessly, his terror prolonged and elongated, as if he were trapped in an eternity of fear and despair. As the tide came rolling in and the dark water closed over his head for the second and final time, Pete's mind mercifully took him out and up. In a split second, he was gazing down at the spot where his own body had disappeared from sight beside the dark wreck of the *Bradda*, then standing on the sand dune, looking at his favourite view, then passing the house in which Phil Rafferty's foot had once landed with a thump on the bedroom carpet, in his car listening to the radio, standing with Bridget at the altar, graduating from university, sharing his first kiss, gazing up at the kind, smiling faces of his parents towering above him. Then one final moment of terror, and it was all over.

Pete drowned before the crabs surrounded him and started to feed.

ROCK STAR

ROCK STAR

DAVID WOODROW HAD everything it took to be a rock star: good looks, long hair, charisma, sex appeal, a big ego and a great voice. Everything, that is, except the remotest ability to write songs.

At twenty-two he was fronting Hellgate, a bunch of guys who had everything it took to be a rock band. Everything, that is, except a singer who could write songs. The guys didn't know this yet and David was going to make damn sure they wouldn't find out.

Hellgate toured the local pubs and clubs, playing cover versions of everything from Carcass to Slayer, from Anthrax to Metallica. With David's great voice and the band's cool look, record label executives were jostling for first shot to sign Hellgate up, but there was one major problem: no original songs. David had been with the band for four months and pressure was mounting on him to do what all lead singers are expected to do.

"I'm working on it", "I have some new ideas I'm trying out", "It's bad luck if I show you before I finish" were just some of the excuses that David was forced to come out with every time a band meeting was called.

James the guitarist had never liked David, and needed little reason to start turning the others against the singer. God, how David hated James, but James was the founding member of the band and the others respected him.

Then one day, when it seemed like his career with Hellgate was about to come to an abortive end, David found a letter on his doormat. The letter contained the music and lyrics for the sickest song David had ever read – the sickest and the best. The writer, who left his letter unsigned, promised David a secret and mutually beneficial partnership: David would drop off a hundred pounds under the left foot of the angel with the broken wing at the north end of the old cemetery in Wraithsfield on Friday the 13th at midnight, and would pick up one more song from under the right foot. David would take the credit for the songs and would never tell anyone that he wasn't the songwriter. When David needed more songs, he would receive another letter with further instructions.

David sat on his bed and strummed the notes of the song. He'd been born in the Midlands and wasn't one for mysteries. He still had ten days to go until Friday the 13th; he didn't have to make any decisions just yet. He'd run the song past the rest of the guys and see what they thought. If they liked it, they could play the song at this Friday's gig at the Bad Apple. If the club crowd liked it, he'd consider paying the songwriter and getting another song.

David sang the song out loud. It was about fucking a woman and then strangling her with a piece of electrical cord. David was not the quickest, and only now did it occur to him that it was a bit creepy that someone with such a sick imagination knew where he lived. Still, the song was good and, judging by the look of Hellgate's small fan club, they might just be sick enough to really like it.

James stared at David incredulously. The other band members thought the song was ultra cool, but James had that disapproving look that made David want to punch his lights out (if, that is, David hadn't been too chicken-shit to punch anybody's lights out). David wondered how such a politically correct, right-on, bleeding heart liberal twat as James had ever managed to become a guitarist in a heavy metal band.

"What?" said David, staring back at James.

"It's sick."

"And?"

"And – it's *really* sick."

"And?"

"And the fans will hate it."

"The fans will love it."

Friday night and Hellgate made the big time. 'Strangled Bitch' set the house alight. Hellgate had been supporting. The kids wouldn't let them off the stage. They had three encores, and when the lead act finally came out on stage (fuming), they were booed off.

Hellgate were immediately approached by an executive from Slaughter Records and offered a record deal. The man from Sony hung back, a little unnerved by the band's harsh lyrics; he preferred to wait and see what happened with Hellgate and Slaughter Records. If the band became really big, he could lure them away from the smaller label without even getting out of his leather swivel chair.

Thus Hellgate got themselves a record deal and David got himself a partner.

David drove past Wraithsfield Cemetery twice before finally spotting it. He'd given himself plenty of time and it was now ten to midnight. He parked his car on a dirt track round the corner, made sure there was no-one around and pulled himself over the cemetery wall.

As soon as he was over the wall, the bravado that had brought David this far dissipated like a ray of moonlight in a dark attic. The cemetery looked like the set of an old horror movie. Crooked, windswept trees, branches reaching out like the claws of grotesque creatures to scratch unwary intruders; neglected old graves, headstones protruding like cracked teeth, some with gaping holes where they had caved in – holes leading down to God only knew what. All that was missing was a little dry ice – tentacles of mist curling around ankles would have completed the picture perfectly.

David seriously considered turning back, clambering over the cemetery wall and going home. But he had a record deal now and a greedy record label executive waiting for at least five more songs. But more than that, he remembered the feeling he'd had on stage when the crowd went mad. It was a small crowd, but there were girls in it – girls who'd sat in his lap after the gig; girls who'd given him *very* decent coke to snort; girls who'd fucked him in the toilets and sucked him off in his car. And all this after one song.

The thought of what might happen after an entire album of songs forced David on into the darkness. He'd worked out (with some difficulty) from the roadmap he kept in his car which way was north, and that was where he now headed.

The darkness in the cemetery was profound, and David nearly fell as his foot sank unexpectedly into a fresh grave. Luckily David's imagination was too limited to conjure up images of what putrescence might be lying inches beneath his foot, and his emotional reaction went no further than annoyance at having sullied his snakeskin cowboy boots. In any case, he'd be able to buy lots more of those when the money from the record deal came through.

As David pulled his foot out of the grave, he thought he heard a rustling in the undergrowth off to his left. He froze for a moment, listening. Nothing. He started walking and the noise came again – the noise of something moving stealthily through the bushes. David stopped and peered into the darkness where the noise had now stopped again. He swore under his breath and headed off again, faster than before. The faster he moved, the more he could hear his own footsteps, breathing and heartbeat, which meant that he could no longer hear the noises in the bushes. Like a child who sticks his head under the duvet and thinks no-one can see him, David was happy enough to stumble through the cemetery making as much noise as possible. Nobody would hear him anyway; there was not a soul around – at least not a living one, and now that he'd found a path leading north through the cemetery he could move fast without the danger of ruining his footwear.

Hurrying along, lost in thoughts of women and cowboy boots, David suddenly got the scare of his life. Standing ahead of him, just off the pathway, was a tall sinister-looking figure. It stood stock still, staring at David menacingly.

"Please don't hurt me," whined David. "I have some money back at the car. You can have it."

The figure didn't respond and eventually David realised that it was standing far too still to be human. Actually, it was a statue – a stone statue. David breathed a sigh of relief and moved a little closer. Now he could see it more clearly. Not only was it a statue, it was an angel. In fact, it was *the* angel that he was looking for. David laughed at himself and went to inspect the angel's feet.

Had he inspected more than the feet, David would have noticed that the angel was one of unsurpassed beauty, sculpted by the hand of a true and unrecognised genius. The angel had delicate feminine features and yet a curious androgyny which rendered its sex impossible to determine.

At first glance the angel, with its melancholy eyes, seemed to be crying. A closer inspection revealed that the corners of the mouth were turned upwards just a millimetre so that the angel had an almost imperceptible smile – a smile which spoke of innocence lost eons ago, of knowledge of basest flesh, of mortal sin, of beings of light and spirit coupling with demons of darkness and putrescence, of condemnation of the divine soul – itself a part of God – to eternal fire and an infinity without light, without love, without redemption. A tiny inscription cut into the stone at the base of the angel's feet read 'ANAEL'.

Once upon a time the Catholic Church noted that there was an archangel ascribed to every planet in the solar system. These archangels guided and protected the planets just as the planets shaped the lives of people born under their influence. One day the Church changed its mind and decided to get rid of the guardian angels of the planets. Some, their place on Earth guaranteed by being well known in Judeo-Christian tradition, such as the archangel Michael, were allowed to live on and be fed by people's thoughts and prayers, but even Michael was never again to be referred to as the archangel of the Sun.

The other angels were cast aside, starved of nurture and of life-giving love and prayer. First they had been forced out of Heaven in order to watch over the Earth and her sister planets, where they became tainted by their involvement with the human world so that they could never return to God. Now the very men for whom they had given up their place in Heaven turned away from them and abandoned them to their lonely fate.

Thus it came to pass that Anael, the most beautiful of all the angels, the archangel of the planet Venus, was shunned by men, by angels and by God, and learned to move among the infernal slime and the slithering loathsome things that dwelt within. Anael's influence over all matters pertaining to human love remained, but as the angel was pushed away from the angelic and the divine, and corrupted by demons and darkness and his days in the abyss, and by man himself, love turned to dark carnal knowledge – foetid, forbidden, destructive.

The Church that had praised Anael for his connection with the planet Venus now cursed him for that very same thing. For Venus, the most beautiful planet in the sky, the first to appear at night and the last to disappear in the morning, was also known as the Morning Star. The Romantic poets, who understood things that we have forgotten, associated the Morning Star with Lucifer, the light-bearer, the proudest of all the angels, the first to fall from Heaven and the first to bring light to man. Lucifer's fall into darkness had lit the way for others, but as Lucifer was given dominion over the Earth itself, the Morning Star came under the protection of Anael. So Anael the beautiful, the innocent, the spirit of air and sky and love, was sullied by his association with the very planet he was sent to guard, then by the people of Earth among whom he sought refuge and the creatures of Hell where he sought solace, and was barred from God's light for all eternity.

A wise man once said that a genius is a person through whom works some higher force; a man with the soul of a higher – super-human – spirit, perhaps an angel. And so the unknown sculptor was driven by a higher force as he coaxed his angel from the hard rock. Alone in his small, dark workshop, he breathed life into every slim finger, every perfect toe; stroked life into every delicate hair, every feather of each airy wing.

But the sculptor did not tease out the smile; the smile was already there – under the rock that the sculptor's hands were working on. The sculptor laboured for weeks, for months, for years, and when he had finished his angel, the two of them stood and contemplated each other – the one crying, the other smiling.

The sculptor gazed upon the beauty that had been created through the vessel of his hands; upon the beauty that came from somewhere beyond his small, dark workshop. The sculptor gazed and wept, and the more he gazed, the lonelier he became. He understood now what it was to live away from God's grace, to spend eternity condemned to wandering far, far from home. The sculptor gazed and wept, and hanged himself from a beam in his small, dark workshop, his tears falling on the angel beneath his feet.

But David only inspected the feet. In fact, he only inspected the space beneath the feet, and his inspection was rewarded with another song; another shot at paradise – the semen-stained, lipstick-smeared, coke-fuelled paradise that was already becoming an addiction.

David quickly unfolded the sheet of paper and struggled to read, but it was just too dark. He folded it back up carefully and pushed it into his jeans pocket. Then he pulled out his own envelope and paused a while, loathe to part with the hundred pounds that his desperately overdrawn bank account had grudgingly spat out through the cash machine installed at his local branch of First Best Bank.

An icy breeze stirred in the stillness of the graveyard, speeding up David's decision. He inserted the envelope with the money under Anael's left foot and walked away.

It was midnight by the time the police finally removed the body from the crime scene. The woman had been found by her five-year-old daughter, who'd sat by her body for eight hours before going next door and alerting the neighbour. The dead woman was in her mid-twenties; she'd been sexually assaulted and strangled with an electrical cord – the police on the scene speculated that the cord had been taken from the kettle in the kitchen. The woman's name was Julia Robson.

David sat in his car, his nerves tingling. He switched on the small overhead light and studied his new song. The notes were bold, the tune catchy, dark and original. The lyrics were written with a characteristic lack of punctuation and it took David a while to work out the sentences. When he finally did, he realised that the song would shoot him into rock and roll notoriety. He hummed the words out loud:

she's just
a little miss roadkill
i got my ten tonne truck
coming down the highway
the way the sun hits her hair
i know she's begging to be spreading
and i'm bored

little miss nothing
little miss roadkill

she's just
a little miss nothing
another spring chicken
waiting for a stuffing
the way she's looking where to run
i know she's dying to be done
and i'm bored

little miss nothing
little miss roadkill

well i gave it to her good
in my truck on the highway
i really gave it to her good
you could say i did it my way
the way her broken limbs were sagging
she was gagging to be shagging
now she's gagged
and she's shagged

and she's splattered all over my hood
she's splattered all over my hood.

little miss nothing
little miss roadkill
little miss nothing
little miss roadkill

David was still buzzing when he got home. He sat in the car outside his bedsit and realised that he couldn't go in. He hated being alone – it made him depressed and bored and scared. Ever since he'd moved out of his parents' house in Clent and come to live in London, he'd lived alone. Sure, he'd tried to flat-share with other people, but somehow he'd always been unlucky; he'd always moved in with people who were really tight and anal – they'd resented the fact that he was a rock musician and didn't have the time to cook or clean or do the shopping. When he met Hellgate, David had hoped to move in with the other band members, but they all seemed to be living with girlfriends or fiancées and didn't want another person around. David figured there'd be no point in dropping in on any of them unannounced at two in the morning; he'd tried it before and met with a very frosty reception. He didn't understand what was wrong with people these days. He touched the pocket with the new song inside and headed for the Bad Apple. Surely the girls would recognize him.

When David finally got back home at five in the morning there was another letter waiting for him. This time the writer stipulated a drop-off point two weeks away, in the third cubicle from the left in the ladies' toilets in the tenth floor restaurant of the Western Tower, and demanded a thousand pounds. David wondered for a moment why it had to be the *women's* toilets, but concluded that the songwriter was smart and must have a good reason for his choice of venue.

The time came to work out Hellgate's contracts with Slaughter

Records and with each other.

"It's fairly obvious," said James. "We split the money four ways."

"Yeah," said David, "except that I get seventy percent and the three of you get the rest."

"Huh?" grunted Rick the drummer, while Brian the bassist scratched his head.

"You've got to be kidding!" James did little to disguise his indignation. "This band is a team. Everyone contributes and everyone gets the same money. That's how it's always been – long before you joined."

"Yeah – and that's why you've always played other people's songs in shitty little clubs. Let's face it – before you met me, you were just one step away from playing the ladies' tea dance at the local bingo hall. Now you have a chance to do something real. But, hey, go back to the Bad Apple if you like, but don't expect to get the same reception as last time we were there because I ain't giving you permission to use my songs. Or have you forgotten that that's what they are – *my* songs?'

Hellgate's growing fan base loved 'Little Miss Roadkill'. Slaughter records introduced the band to a manager. The manager set them up with gigs in some decent clubs, arranged for them to support some great bands and fixed them up to headline at the Hammersmith Odeon in six months' time. The only condition was that Hellgate had their first album ready in time for release just before the concert at the Odeon. And for that they needed at least six songs.

David needed a house with a swimming pool. The advance for the album was not enough. It wasn't even enough to cover David's bills at the bedsit and to pay for 'Little Miss Roadkill'. As luck would have it, Sony bought out Slaughter Records, the advance was increased and the manager of David's local branch of First Best Bank was suddenly so happy to have David as a customer that he arranged for a loan big enough to support David's rock and roll lifestyle – at least for the present, and who cared about the future?

Hellgate got a new manager; the manager got a personal assistant called Debbie; James the guitarist fell in love with Debbie, and Debbie fell in love with David.

Debbie was a sweet, shy girl with mousy blonde hair and a pretty smile. Despite choosing a career in the rock and roll business, Debbie wore pink lipstick and dresses with flowers, and her face went bright red whenever anyone asked her a question. To James, Debbie was like a breath of fresh air: a pastel-coloured innocent among the black and red of the shameless, vulgar rock Amazons; a delicate spring flower among the weeds and thorns of the rock jungle. James watched her growing infatuation with David and didn't know whether to feel anger or relief at the fact that the self-obsessed singer didn't even notice her, let alone see in her anything that he might want. No – David liked his groupies and his rock chicks; he couldn't get enough of them, and Debbie simply didn't come onto his radar.

As for Debbie, David was love at first sight: his tight black leather trousers, his ripped T-shirts, his almost feminine features and his beautiful long dark hair. She hardly ever went out with the band in the evenings, but when there was a social event that she was required to attend, she watched sadly from a distance as sexy leather-clad women pawed and clawed their way all over the lead singer.

The large truck hurtled along the sunlit highway, the violent noise of its engine causing the teenage girl to turn and look over her shoulder. As she did so, the sunlight caught in her long straight blonde hair and a look of fear appeared in her eyes. The girl started to run for her life.

As the truck bore down on the girl, she ran off the highway and into the trees by the side of the road. The truck came to an abrupt halt and the driver got out, walking swiftly after the girl.

The man followed the girl into the woods and she ran from him. She ran into an area where the trees were growing slightly thinner and, as she looked back over her shoulder, she tripped over an old fallen-down gravestone and fell. She'd run into a tiny old cemetery, hidden in the woods.

The man grabbed the struggling girl by the hair and pulled her back to his truck, threw her inside and slammed the door shut behind them.

The girl's open palm struck the glass of the truck's cab window in a last ineffectual attempt to reach out for help before the man bore down on her.

A couple of hours later, several police vehicles, a number of uniformed police officers and crime scene investigators surrounded the broken, blood-spattered body of the girl. Her matted hair was the colour of blood and dirt from the road.

The appointed drop-off date was coming up and not a moment too soon – David really needed another song. Although he'd hated the cemetery, he liked the idea of picking up the next song in a women's public lavatory even less. The writer obviously knew his address and David didn't understand why he couldn't just post the songs to him or drop them through the letterbox. David wondered whether to leave his new address together with the money; the writer had found out his address before and probably would again, but David wasn't willing to take that chance – there was too much riding on him being able to produce more songs before the gig at the Odeon.

It was about this time that David decided he needed a stage name. It would obviously need to be the name of a demon or something else appropriately Satanic. Unfortunately, the names 'Cronos', 'Mantas' and 'Abaddon' were already taken by members of Venom, and Satan or Lucifer was a bit too obvious. Fortunately, one of David's lady friends was interested in the occult and came to the rescue, lending him a book about angels. David protested, saying he was interested in demons, not angels, but Melissa explained that demons and devils were actually fallen angels who had rebelled against God and been thrown out of paradise. David was very stoned, but he managed to pick up on Melissa's point that even Lucifer had once been an angel.

David studied the book and finally chose the name 'Anael' – the fallen angel of the planet Venus and of Fridays. David recalled that all his best gigs had been on Fridays and, as Venus was associated with sex appeal, the relevant fallen angel seemed to be the logical choice. Besides, the name sounded very cool. He would try to persuade the other band members to take on the names of fallen angels too. You needed a proper name to be in the rock business. Even the roadies who lugged around their equipment were called 'Mad Dog' and 'Animal'. Besides, anything would be better than 'James', 'Rick' and 'Brian'.

After the cloak and dagger operation of entering the ladies' toilets unseen, David was standing on the toilet lid in the third cubicle from the left, feeling around the top of the cistern for his new song. His fingertips finally detected it and he clasped it greedily, sat on the toilet seat and studied it carefully. It had no punctuation and was written all in lower case – as always. It was about deflowering a virgin, killing her and dumping her body in a canal. David wondered if perhaps the song was a bit too hardcore this time, but then he remembered how much his fans had liked the previous two songs. Besides, the fans would like anything he gave them.

David placed the thousand pounds and his new address where the song had been; what a massive amount of money it was, but he was hardly in a position to argue. Cautiously he left the ladies' and headed home to practise the song on his guitar.

Another great gig and David was flying high at the backstage after-party. The groupies were fighting over which ones got to sit next to him, and David was in seventh heaven. Debbie watched him from the far end of the table, a sad little pout on her face. James watched Debbie and could not understand what she saw in the singer. David was laughing deliriously at some groupie's lewd joke, head thrown back, white powder staining his nose – not exactly a picture of sex appeal. Sure, the groupies went for it, but Debbie was a smart, sensible girl. It just made no sense.

David and the girls on either side of him were whispering and giggling like excited schoolchildren. Debbie's masochistic streak had evidently reached its limits; she got up and bid a general goodnight. David didn't notice Debbie leave, others returned her 'goodnight' and James offered to see her home safely. Debbie thanked him and said she'd be fine.

James sat and watched David and the women. It was astonishing how within such a short time David had transformed from a somewhat self-centred pretty boy into an unadulterated rock god – the chicks, the drugs, the house with the swimming pool. And David behaved like all this was nothing – like he'd always had it coming. Oh sure, everyone benefited. There were enough drugs and enough girls to go around, and Rick and Brian seemed happy enough to get David's rejects. But David was the only one who had become a rock god.

The giggling and whispering grew more excited as the two girls sitting next to David tried to pull him away from the table to somewhere more private. David allowed himself to be dragged off, pausing only long enough to snort one last line of coke. The other girls at the table cast some disappointed glances after the departing trio, then stoically moved on to the other band members. The subtleties of the situation seemed wholly lost on Rick and Brian, who were having a ball. James turned down an invitation to party with them and the girls; he made his excuses and left.

David, James, Rick, Brian and their manager sat in the Sony lobby, waiting to see Bobby Weismeyer, their record executive. The Sony rep was pleased with the way the band was going; the meeting was to discuss progress on the forthcoming album.

A bowl of fruit sat on the coffee table in front of the band; the grapes so perfect they looked plastic. James eyed the fruit suspiciously. A bowl of cocaine would have gone down better and, judging by the usual state of Mr Weismeyer, he probably had one hidden under his desk.

The manager and band members sat chatting happily enough – all except David, who hated meetings and hated waiting for meetings even more. He sat slightly apart from everyone else, the words of 'I'm gonna fuck you, Virgin Bitch' going around in his head. He needed something to do, so he reached over to the coffee table and picked through the various music magazines lying there. His face turned pale as he pulled out a daily newspaper from under the trade magazines and read the front page headline: 'Murdered fifteen-year-old pulled from canal'.

David quickly picked up the paper. He made sure that none of the others were watching, and read on: 'Second schoolgirl in two weeks falls victim to depraved sex killer. Last week Mary-Anne Smith was sexually assaulted and killed in a hit-and-run. Police are not ruling out a link...' David wasn't sure why he felt so upset about these headlines – they weren't much different from the headlines you got once every month or so in a big city. But there was something about the coincidence between the death and his lyrics that made him feel very uncomfortable.

Just then Weismeyer's personal assistant appeared and beckoned Hellgate into the executive's office. David quickly placed the newspaper on the floor and pushed it as far as he could under his chair with his foot.

Next day, and the band was in another meeting. This time it was a band meeting and it was just the four members of Hellgate.

James was sitting quiet and grumpy in a corner. David was trying to persuade the other band members that they should all adopt the names of fallen angels.

"The band's name is Hellgate," he explained enthusiastically, "which makes us guardians of the gateway to hell. And as guardians of the gateway we can't have names like 'Rick' and 'Brian' and 'James'... No offence," he added, throwing James a defiant glance. "I've chosen the name 'Rabacyel' for Rick, 'Dalquiel' for Brian and I think you, James, should be 'Jabniel'."

"And what's your name going to be, David?" asked James with barely disguised sarcasm.

"I am Anael."

The guitarist's laugh was bitter and took the other band members by surprise. "Is that right, Anael? Well, let me tell *you* something now. I'm sick and tired of the way you think you run this band. You can't come in here and tell us what to do."

"If you don't like it, you can always leave."

"That's right, you'd love to see me go, wouldn't you? To leave the band that *I* started. Well I'll tell you something: I'm not going anywhere. No-one is. We're all under contract for one album. We're going to record the album and then you're the one who's leaving."

"We'll see about that," said David calmly. He made up his mind that he would introduce all the band members by their fallen angel names at the next gig.

"And another thing," James was on a roll. "I'm getting sick of your sadistic, twisted lyrics. All they do is give sick fucks ideas. Look – look at this!" James reached down to his jacket lying on the floor beside him and pulled out a newspaper running an article about the girl found in the canal. He threw the paper down in front of the other band members. Rick grunted and Brian scratched his head uncertainly.

"Are you mad?" asked David. "People get murdered all the time. This has got nothing to do with my songs. Besides, my songs have made Hellgate famous. Or have you forgotten again?"

"We would have made it eventually, with or without you."

"Yeah, right. You're just jealous, aren't you? That's what this is about. I have talent, women want me and the fans adore me. You can't handle that, can you?"

"Fuck you!" James grabbed his jacket and stormed out of the room.

David grinned at Rick and Brian, and shrugged, but James's words resonated uncomfortably as David picked up the newspaper from the floor and stuffed it into his own jacket.

David opened the next letter with a mixture of excitement and dread.

'Dear David,' it read, 'I have been most gratified to see that you are enjoying the fruits of my labour. However, I feel that I too am entitled to a little fun. For this reason, you will drive to the Church of the Martyrs at midnight on Sunday two weeks from now. The church is located 4.5 miles northwest of Chelmsford, off the A1060 to Roding. You will leave one of your fans at the altar. The girl is to be young, attractive, blonde, with large breasts. Your payment will be under the candelabrum on the altar.'

The girl was young, attractive, blonde, with large breasts. She was wearing a black leather miniskirt, black suspenders and fishnet stockings, high-heeled black leather boots, elbow-length black lace gloves and an open black leather jacket under which her Hellgate T-shirt could be seen stretched tightly over her bosom. David had found her at the bar in the Bad Apple and asked her if she wanted to go for a ride.

"Are you kidding? I'd love to!" the teenager could hardly contain her delight. 'This is my friend Cindy," she said, indicating the pretty brunette at the bar next to her. "Can she come too?"

"Not this time, baby," said David smoothly and smiled at Cindy, "I'm a little tired tonight."

The disappointment was plain to see in Cindy's face.

"Later," the blonde told her friend, as David ushered her out of the club.

"So where we going?" asked the blonde, whose name turned out to be Jennie, producing a hipflask-sized bottle of vodka which she handed to David. David shook his head and kept his hands on the wheel. He couldn't afford to get drunk and blow this.

"Somewhere special," he told the girl. "You'll like it."

"Cool... I love your music."

"Thanks."

"When are you going to release an album?"

"In about five months."

"Cool."

They drove on for a couple of minutes in silence, then the girl said, "I've been to all your gigs, you know. That is – ever since you've been in the band."

"Thanks." David was starting to feel really uncomfortable about this. The girl was obviously a genuine fan of his. She was quite sweet and, away from the garish light of the Bad Apple, she looked very young. Then again, rock chicks were tougher than they looked and they knew how to take care of themselves. The writer and the girl would have 'a little fun' together and then he'd drive her back into town. David was sure that the writer wouldn't just leave the girl in the middle of nowhere; he drove a hard bargain, but at the end of the day he seemed reasonable enough.

The girl liked the little church. "Wow, this is great!" She wandered around, checking out the stained glass windows and paintings of tortured saints.

David went to the altar and retrieved the latest song from under the candelabrum, stuffing it quickly into his jeans pocket.

"Where you going?" asked the girl as David walked past her, heading for the door.

"I'm just going to take a leak. Stay here."

The girl giggled. "Don't be long," she said, but David was already gone. She continued stumbling around the church, drunk and not a little high. She giggled again, but this time her giggling was cut short.

David didn't look at the song until he got home. He just wanted to get away from the church as fast as possible. That was a mean trick to play on the girl, even if the writer showed her a good time. After all, she was David's fan and perhaps that meant that he was in some way responsible for her. No – that couldn't be right. David had hundreds of fans and there was no way he could be responsible for all of them.

Once home, David hurriedly pulled out the piece of paper with trembling hands, almost tearing it in his rush to get it out of his pocket.

He stared at the unpunctuated lyrics for some time, trying to make sense of the horrible feeling that was growing in his stomach.

The song spoke of crucifying a blonde bitch with big tits above a church altar, so that she could fuck Christ for all eternity.

David sat down on the floor, trying to figure things out. How come the song was about a blonde girl with large breasts in a church? Did that mean the writer was going to kill the girl he had dropped off near Chelmsford? Had he killed the other girls too? David contemplated going back to the church, but what good would that do? If anything was going to happen to the girl, it would have happened already. In any case, he was probably over-reacting. The song was probably just a song. And David needed two more of them.

'She loves Jesus' was a great success. The added touch of blasphemy delighted Hellgate's fans and roped in several hundred new ones.

Christian groups got to hear about the song and took to protesting outside clubs where Hellgate played. Fights broke out between rock fans and Christians, and the band had to be ushered to their limo through the back door. The band loved it – everyone except James, of course – and the fact that 'She loves Jesus' was banned from radio and television sky-rocketed Hellgate to nationwide notoriety. The band's name was on the lips of every priest and every parent across the country.

Detective Chief Inspector Davies had never seen anything like it. It took him and the other policemen on the scene a while to work out exactly what they were looking at.

Hanging above the altar was the naked body of a young woman, her dried blood a stark contrast to the white of her flesh in the cold dawn light. She had been nailed to the large crucifix, her ample breasts morbidly out of place in the house of God.

Outside, a young police officer was throwing up, while the parish priest who'd found the girl stumbled around, crying and praying.

DCI Davies had a gut feeling that this was the work of the same killer who'd murdered the other two girls and possibly also the young mother. His search of the latest victim's ripped, bloodstained clothes was rewarded when in the right pocket of her jacket he found a flyer from the Bad Apple. At last, a badly needed lead. He walked out of the church; the police photographer had also finished his work. Davies signalled to his colleagues to remove the body of the dead girl and headed for his car.

The Bad Apple was a dark, seedy place. Davies couldn't understand what attracted kids to places like this. He'd been back a couple of times with a photo of Jennie. The first time he was here, it had been a quiet night at the club, so he'd come back on a Friday. This strategy had yielded positive results and Davies was now comforting a blubbering Cindy, who told him that Jennie had left with the lead singer of Hellgate.

"Are you sure?"

"Yes, it was definitely him. Jennie had a massive crush on him. She wouldn't have left with just anyone, you know."

David was in bed with a sexy black girl when DCI Davies came a-knocking.

The knocking on the door wouldn't go away, so David threw on his dressing gown (a black silk one depicting Blake's Dragon on the back – a design probably inspired more by the killer's tattoo in the film 'Red Dragon' than by the poet's original drawing) and went to see who it was.

David was horrified to see a police officer on his doorstep. Davies insisted on coming in. He questioned David about his whereabouts on the night that Jennie disappeared.

"He was with me." The black girl appeared behind David, wrapped loosely in a bed sheet.

Davies was taken aback for a moment, but came back fighting.

"Is that so? Well, how come he was seen leaving the Bad Apple with this girl on the night she disappeared?"

Davies produced two pictures of Jennie – one of the teenager smiling and one from the crime scene. The black girl retreated to the bedroom and David winced.

"Look, I did leave with her, but I didn't kill her."

"Then what did you do with her?"

There was a pause as David thought hard and Davies watched him closely.

"I dropped her off near The Marquee."

"Is that right?"

"Yeah."

"A pretty girl like that and you dropped her off?"

"Yeah. She wanted to carry on partying and I wanted an early night."

"*You* wanted an early night?"

"Even rock stars need an early night once in a while."

Davies was unimpressed.

"Look, I didn't kill her. I'm sorry she's dead, but it's got nothing to do with me. Now, if you'll excuse me, I've got a lady waiting." David hardly knew himself how he was managing to act so cool. Surely the pig could hear how loudly his heart was beating.

"Then you won't mind giving us a sample of your DNA."

"Yeah, whatever, officer. As soon as you have a warrant I'll give you all the DNA you want."

Davies got the message. "Don't leave town," he threw over his shoulder as he left.

The band was backstage, preparing for their next gig. David was preoccupied, upset about the cop's visit. It was only a matter of time before the pig came back with a warrant. If he let the pig have his DNA, he'd be exonerated. Or would he? He might have left some DNA at the church or on the girl. Even if he was cleared of the murder, he could still be done for being an accomplice. Besides, if the police caught the writer they might tie him to the other murders as well, and they'd assume that David had known about everything. If only he could spin things out for two more songs. The record company had wanted ten, but they could release an album with six. Once David had six songs he could break off his association with the writer without getting sued by Sony.

David could hear the crowd cheering. The recorded intro music was playing. It was time to go on stage.

The drummer went out first, followed by the bassist and the guitarist. As David headed for the stage, he heard a familiar voice behind him.

"Just a moment!"

David turned around. It was DCI Davies, triumphantly waving a piece of paper.

"I have the warrant you requested."

David couldn't believe the pig's sense of timing. "Not now man, can't you see I'm going on stage?"

"It's *Detective Chief Inspector Davies* and I don't give a shit."

"Look, I said I'll give you all the DNA you want, and I will. But please, let me do the gig first. I'll be done in an hour. Why don't you stay backstage, make yourselves at home. Enjoy the gig."

David ducked out on stage without waiting for a response. The crowd went crazy and Davies fumed in the wings.

Davies decided not to waste his time backstage. He and the other officers started going through the band members' things, and that was when Davies found David's notebook into which the singer had copied the lyrics of all his songs.

"Oh my God! It's him." The other officers turned to look at Davies. "Look at this. These lyrics describe all the recent sex murders. This singer sicko did them all."

"He could have written about the murders after they were reported in the press," offered Detective Sergeant Stern, but Davies was having none of it.

"No, it's him. I'm sure it's him. There's something in his eyes – something evil."

"Oh, come off it, George. Let's just get a DNA sample before we jump to any conclusions."

"It's *Detective Chief Inspector Davies*, Sergeant, and I'm not waiting any longer."

Teenage fans screamed with delight as Hellgate finished playing 'She loves Jesus'. The last lingering guitar sounds died down and James frowned as David cast him a triumphant glance.

DCI Davies seized the moment, ordering his men to move in from backstage and take hold of David.

"David Woodrow! Police! You're coming with us." There was a note of triumph in Davies's voice.

"My name is Anael!" shouted David as officers dragged him backstage.

There was silence as the remaining members of Hellgate stared after their lead singer and the fans stared at the stage. Then someone in the audience shouted 'Fuck the pigs!' and the crowd rushed the stage, fighting with security in a bid to follow the police who'd taken their idol.

It took officers over an hour to disperse the last of the fans and, once they were gone, the club looked like a battlefield awash with broken chair arms and smashed glass.

David was detained overnight. A sample of his DNA was taken and sent to the police lab for processing.

That same night the police lab mysteriously burned to the ground, destroying all the forensic evidence from the various crime scenes.

DCI Davies tried to make a case for detaining David longer based on the fact that he was the last person to be seen with Jennie, based on his lyrics, which gave details of the unsolved sex murders, and based on his rock and roll lifestyle in general. This latter point seemed to be what irked Davies the most. Detective Chief Inspector Davies was a decent, God-fearing man who'd been dating the same girl for the past year and had so far failed to get so much as a blowjob. The Chief Crown Prosecutor felt that none of the evidence against David would stick in a court of law, and Davies was forced to let him go.

The brief time that David spent in prison, although quite terrifying for David himself, served to enhance his cool warped image, and on his release he was hailed as a hero by rock fans the nation over. The kids didn't even care that he'd been in for suspected rape and murder, and at the next concert teenage girls shouted 'Rape me! Rape me!' and threw their underwear at the singer. James was horrified, but David now understood that everything he'd been through in the past few days was worth it. David spent the next week on one long string of coke and booze binges with girls.

When another letter landed on his doormat, David hesitated for half a day before opening it. He hoped against hope that the writer would want money. But no. The writer wanted Debbie, and David had two weeks to deliver her to room 13 of the Turning Point Inn, off the A41, between Aylesbury and Waddesdon.

Two weeks of soul-searching and bingeing, as David alternately tried to decide what to do and tried to forget about having to decide what to do.

When David finally asked Debbie out, she was over the moon. She couldn't believe that he'd finally noticed her. She put on her best dress and fixed a couple of hairclips with little plastic flowers in her hair.

David picked her up at ten p.m. and explained that they'd be taking a little trip. Debbie had wanted to pack an overnight bag, but David explained that it wouldn't be necessary.

The drive was long, but Debbie chatted away happily, telling David all about her family, her childhood pets, how much she'd hated her girls' school and how going to college had been totally different and really great. David tried to listen, but he was becoming more and more agitated the closer they got to the guesthouse.

Debbie asked where they were going. David responded that it was somewhere romantic where they could be alone together without any interruptions. Debbie went as pink as her dress and giggled happily.

By the time they got to the guesthouse, David was practically shaking.

"Are you all right?" asked Debbie as they got out of the car.

"Get in," said David.

"What?"

"Get in!" David grabbed the girl by her arm and forced her back into the car.

"You're hurting me. What's going on?"

"I'm taking you home." David started up the car and slammed his foot on the accelerator.

Debbie burst into tears.

"I'm sorry," she sobbed.

David said nothing.

"Whatever I've done, I'm sorry."

David couldn't speak. Across the road from the guesthouse a dark figure watched impassively as the red sports car sped off. Debbie sobbed quietly all the way home.

For the next three days David didn't leave his house. He was desperate, not knowing what to do, waiting for a letter to drop through the letterbox.

After three days he could stand it no longer and went out on a bender. He got back at four in the morning and found a letter on his doormat. It was only three words long: 'No more songs'. It took David the best part of a bottle of vodka to stop shaking and fall asleep.

The next couple of months were a nightmare. Pressure from the other band members, from his manager and from the Sony man was mounting on David to write more songs. Debbie was avoiding him. He waited in vain for the writer to relent and contact him again, but no such thing happened.

Eventually David despaired enough to try to compose his own songs. He sat in front of a blank sheet of paper with his guitar for hours, for days. It didn't help. He never could write songs and, with all the stress he was under, that was definitely not going to change now. He increased his drug and alcohol intake and found, one night, to his utmost horror, that he was unable to get it up. The girl was very understanding, but that just increased David's horror.

He stopped going out altogether and told everyone who came

round to 'fuck off'. He missed two gigs and started getting nasty letters from his manager and from the record company, threatening to sue him for breach of contract. He ran out of booze and drugs, and his dealer refused to sell him any more coke on credit. He looked like shit.

David took to sitting in the hallway, watching his doormat. He missed his fans desperately, but he was unable to face them. They mustn't see him looking like this. He felt like he was losing his fans, his women. It was just a matter of time before he'd lose his home, his car, his swimming pool. The thought of being rejected by the rock world and losing his rock and roll lifestyle became an obsession, eating away at David until he could stand it no longer.

If there was nothing landing on his doormat, then perhaps the writer had left something at one of the old drop-off points.

David started going out late at night, re-visiting all the places where the writer had left songs for him. He started with the Turning Point Inn – the drop-off point he'd never reached. He turned room 13 inside out and left only when the owner threatened to call the police.

David worked his way backwards, re-visiting the church, the Western Tower and, finally, the last place in the world he had left to go – the stone angel in Wraithsfield Cemetery.

David hurried through the creepy old graveyard and knelt by the angel. Tears rolling down his face, he looked in the spaces between its feet and its pedestal. David realised that he'd reached the end of the line. He cried for a long time and finally fell asleep at the angel's feet.

A cold dawn, and David woke up shivering to see the angel smiling down at him. From his position on the ground, the angel seemed to touch the sky. David gazed up at the wise face for a long time. He knew now what he had to do and he moved swiftly back through the cemetery to his car, the early morning mist bruising and breaking apart before him.

DCI Davies thought it was Christmas when the singer turned himself in and confessed to all the recent murders.

"The truth will out," he told himself happily, "and God will punish the guilty and reward the virtuous". Perhaps now that he would be hailed as a hero for solving the sex murders, Gloria would agree to have sex with him.

David felt calm, as if a massive burden had been lifted from him. He was sentenced to life imprisonment and turned down his lawyer's suggestion to appeal on grounds of insanity. Many of his fans remained loyal and some even held vigils outside the prison. But few within the prison walls shared the fans' admiration for David or his music or his alleged exploits, and soon he was singled out for the kind of violence that only the incarcerated will ever know. He spent much of his time between the infirmary and solitary confinement, in which he was placed for his own protection, but it wasn't long before he found himself lying in a pool of his own blood in a dimly lit corridor near the laundry room.

The knife attack had been swift, but ferocious, and the perpetrators hadn't hung around to get caught. David struggled to get up, but this simply led to more pain and a hideous wave of light-headedness and darkness before his eyes that threatened to spread and engulf him altogether. Eventually he lay quite still, hands clutched to the pumping wounds in his thigh and neck. Then from somewhere far away he heard a voice.

"You all right, mate?" A grey-haired inmate was bending over him, but David couldn't see him. His distant eyes were peering down from the stage into the darkness of the concert hall and the tiny flames of cigarette lighters held aloft by the crowd. "Blimey! Someone done for you right good. Hang on, I'll get help."

"My fans," croaked David.

"What's that?"

"Tell my fans that Anael loves them."

"I don't know what you're saying, mate. Wait here, I'll get help."

The old man hurried off in the direction of the laundry room, shouting for help as he went. David's fleeting, fragmented thoughts turned to his mother. He regretted not having seen more of her since he'd left home. When she'd come to see him in prison, she'd looked very small and grey. Her eyes were narrow red slits swollen with tears, and she kept dabbing at them with a sodden tissue. David's father had died before David's initial arrest, and he was thankful that his dad didn't have to go through what his mum had been going through.

David could feel himself drifting off. He blinked, confused and afraid.

"I am Anael" he rasped to the crowd that was disappearing in the darkness, along with his mother's tear-stained face. He tried hard to keep his mother's face in focus, but she faded away and David panicked as the night enveloped him.

Then a bright speck of light pierced the darkness that surrounded David, scattering the shadows, growing, spreading, radiating. And all David could see was the dazzling white light and – as the last of his blood seeped onto the dingy floor – a tall, beautiful, winged figure reaching out to him through the light and smiling, smiling at *him*. David's last breath left his body and that breath formed the word 'Anael'.

As the rock world – some of it, at any rate – mourned David's passing, a new band was playing a set at The Bad Apple. Their songs sucked, but the lead singer was young and good looking. To the general relief of the audience, they finished with their own songs and were now playing a cover version of The Rolling Stones' 'Sympathy for the Devil'. The singer sang enthusiastically and strutted his stuff around the stage, unaware that in the shadows at the back of the club a dark figure sat watching.

THE COACHMAN'S COTTAGE

THE COACHMAN'S COTTAGE

T HE VAST GUESTHOUSE that had been hired on account of the
matriarch's upcoming birthday had enough bedrooms to house
all of them bar one. Tony didn't mind being the one to leave the
twenty-strong party of cousins, in-laws and other extended family in
the large sitting room – after dinner and the inevitable quiz devised
by his brother – to head alone to the Coachman's Cottage at the end
of the drive. In fact, the prospect of not being woken by hordes of
screaming brats at the crack of dawn rather appealed to him. But
how welcome the screaming brats would have been now.

*The young bride's lot was not a happy one. Her father, desperate to
hang on to his crumbling hall, had given her in marriage to a
brutal and dissolute man almost twenty years her senior. Charlotte
knew neither kindness nor affection in her husband's house, and her
only solace lay in the long walks she took almost daily on his vast,
wooded estate. But today even the beauty and tranquillity of the
ancient trees brought her little comfort.*

*Charlotte had been feeling extremely fatigued of late, and these
past two mornings she had thrown up at the mere smell of
breakfast. A week before her seventeenth birthday, and despite the
night-time abuse suffered at the hands of her husband on a semi-
regular basis, she was naïve in the way of things, and not yet
cognisant of the new life that grew inside her.*

*She was in the farthest part of the grounds – amongst the
ancient oaks, birches and beech trees – when the dizziness struck.
She sat down for a while on a fallen log, and waited until her head
cleared and the nausea subsided before heading back to the house.
But she felt increasingly lightheaded, and had to stop every so often
to lean against a tree for support. It was as if a dark grey fog were
descending before her eyes, and she struggled not to succumb to it
and to the heaviness that was weighing down her limbs and frail*

230

body.

Finally she came out alongside the coachman's cottage – within sight of the main house, but before she could reach the manor, the heaviness and the fog took her. She gave out a cry of distress and sank to the ground outside the cottage.

"Mistress!" Then a kindly face, not much older than her own, was gazing down at her, and firm but gentle arms were lifting her and guiding her to safety. "Sit here and rest a while. I'll make you some sweet tea. It will revive you."

"No!... My husband... I must go!"

But it was too late. Fate – that dark and twisted monster that lies in wait for us all – had ordained that the lord of the manor and two of his companions should be riding by, and the lord remembered that he had business with the coachman.

"Stay here a while," he told his friends. "I'll not be long."

Tony had quite enjoyed the brisk if somewhat fresh walk from the main house to the cottage. The silence on the shore of Lake Windermere in late January was profound. Not a leaf stirred nor a single animal rustled in the bushes. The Coachman's Cottage was a long, low structure of grey stone. Little remained of the eighteenth century original. The now glass-panelled entrance door opened directly onto a kitchen with a stone-flagged floor, with a small utility room housing the boiler, and another glass-panelled door to the right leading up a step to an ample sitting room with dining area. A narrow staircase led from the kitchen to a mezzanine level with a double bed, a dresser and a shower room. The ground floor had vast glass windows all the way around, and Tony toyed with the idea of going round the entire cottage and closing all the curtains, but he was too tired. He went upstairs, brushed his teeth, and was in bed by midnight.

As he was falling asleep, Tony felt pressure just beyond his feet, as though someone had sat down on the end of the bed. He lay very still, not daring to pull up his feet or make the slightest movement. As he got used to the new weight distribution, he managed to convince himself that the change of pressure at the foot of his bed had never really happened. Eventually he started to doze off again, but this time he was roused by a sudden noise.

Tony lay motionless, listening. The noise came again. He was fairly certain it was the window clattering, but he was lying on his good ear, and he wanted to be sure. He propped himself up on an elbow and listened attentively. Sure enough, the window was rattling in its frame. There didn't seem to be any wind outside – there were no trees rustling and no other noise to indicate that the wind was blowing. Eventually the rattling stopped. Tired, Tony sank back down onto his goose down pillows and fell asleep.

Two hours later Tony woke up briefly from a nightmare he couldn't remember clearly, save a ghastly apparition – female, he thought – chasing him down some long, dark corridors. In his dream, he'd made it to his room, slammed the door on the thing, and cowered by the doorway, holding firmly onto the handle. Tiredness overtook him and he fell asleep once more. This time he woke up to a headache and a feeling of pressure on his chest – a strong feeling of discomfort – pain almost – as if something had been sitting on him.

Immediately on getting out of bed the heaviness in his head and chest lifted, but Tony nevertheless decided to go downstairs to the kitchen and drink a *Beechams* powder dissolved in some hot water, after lining his stomach with a round of buttered toast. He untied the fancy strings holding back the flowery drapes, and closed all the curtains in the kitchen. He didn't feel like going into the sitting room, which looked dark and foreboding while at the same time completely exposed – on account of its copious, large windows – to the night and anything that was prowling it. Tomorrow he'd close the curtains in the sitting room before darkness fell.

"What in the devil's name is this?" Lord Silderbury froze in the doorway, anger tingeing his cruel features a deep shade of red. Charlotte pulled herself up from the table and made a supplicating move towards her husband.

"My, lord! I felt poorly and..." She stopped midsentence as her

husband strode up and struck her full force across the face, knocking her down.

"Lord Silderbury!" The young coachman ran to Charlotte's side, comforting her and trying to help her to her feet.

"Get your filthy hands off her!" Silderbury kicked the young man to the floor, then turned his attention back to his wife. "You brazen harlot! So this is what you've been doing on your walks?!"

"No, my lord!" Charlotte sobbed, shielding her belly from another blow.

"You'll pay for this, but not before you see your lover die!"

The aspirin in the *Beechams* soothed his body, but the feeling of unease did not lift. Tony reluctantly made his way back to bed, wondering what else lay in wait for him in Never-never land. Sure enough, as he was falling asleep, the rattling came again. Thankfully it was outside. But then a noise inside. A tapping sound – just one – like a piece of metal – a key perhaps – gently making contact with a ceramic bowl. But there was no ceramic bowl. So what had made the noise? After a few minutes of watchful sitting up in bed, Tony persuaded himself that it was the radiator cooling down. He lay back down in the dark, but couldn't sleep as something moved around on the roof. A bird – Tony told himself, not allowing himself to speculate what bird would move around on a roof at night.

The next time he woke, it was to a tapping sound. Confused, Tony lay still and tried to work out where the sound was coming from. At first he thought it was outside, that perhaps it was starting to rain, but the tapping came again – from one direction only, and not from any of the three windows that were located on different sides of the cottage. Then a loud harsh noise came from Tony's right. He sat bolt upright in bed and turned on the light. When his heart stopped pounding, he realised that the shower was on in the tiny bathroom. He must not have turned it off properly earlier in the day, and the water had taken some hours to collect before running out under pressure. These things happened.

And so it went on for the next hour or so. Tony would start to drift off, only to be woken up by strange noises in the cottage, which, after the initial shock, he would explain away in some fashion or other. There must be wind outside, there was a bird on the roof, the radiator was cooling down, a mouse must have knocked something over downstairs, the house was settling, he'd eaten too much during dinner and the pressure on his chest was indigestion. But when a cold, taloned hand wrapped itself around his throat, Tony up and ran – barefoot, in his pyjamas – down the stairs and out of the cottage, towards the main house where his family slept soundly in their adjacent rooms.

He'd only run a few steps towards the converted manor house when he saw a shadowy figure between him and it. Which family member was it and what were they doing out in the middle of the night? And his family were all rather on the portly side – the adults, at least – so why was the figure that blocked his way rake-thin? And why was it gliding towards him in that twisted, disjointed, unnatural fashion?

When Charlotte regained consciousness, she was in a small damp alcove. She could hear the muffled sound of rain somewhere on the roof above her, and a little water seeped in through a crack in what she worked out was the outside wall. Above her, in the opposite wall, a small opening above her head let in a shaft of light.

"Help!" she cried out, her heart threatening to burst out of her chest with fear.

"Welcome back, my dear," her husband's muted voice drifted in from the other side of the fresh stonework.

"What's happened?! Where am I?!"

"You liked visiting the coachman's cottage, didn't you? Well, now you'll never have to leave!"

"Please, my lord! Let me out!"

"So you need walks like you need bread and water. Isn't that what you told me?"

"My lord, I never did anything to dishonour you," sobbed Charlotte. "Please, let me out!"

"Now you can have as many walks as you have food and water! ... Seal her in!"

Tony turned back and ran – past the cottage, down towards the lake and the white stone house he'd seen on his walk earlier in the day. A dog had barked at him when he'd walked past the house before, so there must be someone staying there.

The darkness was extreme, and Tony based his descent chiefly on his memory of the route acquired on his daytime walk. Nevertheless, he stumbled several times, and it was nothing short of a miracle that he reached the white stone house in one piece. His feet were scratched and bleeding from the stones on the path he'd taken, but he could hardly feel his injuries, so numb was he from the cold and from his abject terror. He opened the gate without looking back and rushed straight to the nearest window, banging on the glass so hard it should have shattered beneath his fists.

"Help!" he shouted, gagging as he gasped for breath at the same time. "Let me in! Please!" But there was no response, and the cottage remained as dark inside at it was out. Tony spotted the front door of the building and rushed over to bash on that instead. "Help! Please!" He noticed the doorbell and pressed it hard. He could hear it ringing inside. "Open the door! Please!" There was still no answer and, as he stopped for a moment, Tony became aware of a presence behind him. He started to sweat, despite the freezing temperature, and his body began to shake uncontrollably. More than anything in the world he didn't want to turn around, but turn around he must.

There, standing about a metre away from him was the most terrifying thing Tony had seen in his entire life. It was spectral, like a shadow or a black mist, and yet corporeal. It had long, wispy hair, from behind which a pair of malevolent red eyes observed him with what could only be described as hunger – the rabid, bestial hunger of something that hadn't eaten for a long time. Dirty, shapeless rags hung off its emaciated, vaguely female form. As Tony and the creature faced each other for long seconds, he could smell the foetid odour of decomposing flesh rising off it, and he noticed that it was salivating. Then it emitted a feral sound somewhere between a hiss and a growl, and raised a bony, taloned hand towards Tony – as if in supplication.

Charlotte cried out in despair as the shaft of light falling into her living tomb was cut off. She begged and pleaded for mercy, only ceasing her entreaties long after the footsteps and voices had receded. Exhaustion overcame her and she sank to the cold stone floor, sobbing in the dark and the damp. At times her tears were for herself; at times for the young man whose moment of kindness towards her had led to his own tortured demise. She'd pleaded for the coachman's life, but fainted when Silderbury and his men held him down and castrated him, before finishing him off.

A small glow of light emanated from the crack through which a little rain water seeped in now and again, but the illumination was sufficient merely to hint at the shadowy forms of bugs and spiders that crawled around the distraught girl. Her head ached, and sharp pangs wracked her stomach. Despite the nausea that came and went, the hunger was unbearable – Charlotte's body demanded food not just for her, but for the foetus that fought to survive within. Occasionally she imagined that she heard people nearby, and she redoubled her cries. Her fingers bled from trying to pry out the vast stones that had been used to seal her in; her fists were bruised and knuckles scraped raw from banging against the walls of her makeshift cell. But no one heard, and no one came.

Charlotte's hair fell from her scalp and her teeth came loose as her body directed any remaining resources to more vital organs. Her muscles started to atrophy as her body digested them to stay alive. Every movement became painful, and eventually Charlotte moved merely to lick at the rainwater that trickled down from the crack in the wall. It was a rainy autumn, but the water that oozed into her prison served only to prolong her suffering. Sometimes her fear swelled as demons grasped from the walls at her tortured mind. Only occasionally would she call out to her mother. Her senses became numbed, and yet, instead of subsiding, the hunger grew – unnatural, rapacious, insatiable, taking on a life of its own even as its host's life slipped away.

Tony risked a fleeting glance towards the gate onto the track leading back up to the guesthouse, but before he managed to move a muscle, the creature had shifted to block his path. It bared its rank, pointy teeth, and extended its other hand to its terrified prey. Tony screamed and bolted for the jetty at the end of the small garden. Without a moment's hesitation he threw himself into the freezing black water and started to swim. Every muscle in his body rebelled against the paralysing cold, and yet Tony propelled himself forward through the inky water, only stopping when complete exhaustion overtook him.

Tony continued to move his arms and legs just enough to keep himself afloat. His body spasmed insufferably in the icy water and he wondered whether hypothermia was a painful way to die. That's when he heard the rhythmic splash of something swimming towards him through the dark.

THE BLOODY TOWER

THE BLOODY TOWER

SHAKIL HAD MORE in common with Jim Morrison than Osama bin Laden, so it came as something of a surprise to his family when the front door splintered with an ear-rending crash at four o'clock one Sunday morning, and a naked Shakil was dragged out of bed, handcuffed and pulled out into the darkness.

It was a year since the Prime Minister had given his speech in Parliament to accompany his new anti-terrorism legislation, and a year since the ravens had flown the Tower.

The birds had been restless all morning. The Raven Master tried in vain to persuade Thor the talking raven to say "good morning". At around midday, about the time that the Prime Minister sat down amidst a deathly silence a little over two miles away, Thor croaked something that might have been construed as sounding rather like "Nevermore!" and took off – half flying, half hopping, taking the other ravens with him.

"Thor! Thor, come back!" The Raven Master ran as far as he could after the departing birds. Another Yeoman Warder joined him, disturbed by the desperation in the older man's voice.

"Don't worry mate, you know they won't get far with their feathers clipped." But the Raven Master wasn't convinced.

A year later and the ravens weren't back, the Crown Jewels had been removed, the tourist attractions ousted, the Yeoman Warders sacked, and the Prime Minister had his own little Guantanamo right here on British soil – in the heart of the capital.

The Tower of London – in reality a collection of twenty-four towers and various other structures – was nothing if not perfect for the job at hand. It was as if the ancient buildings had been waiting for eighty years for blood to flow down their walls once more. The Tower's last victim had been shot on 15th August 1941: a hapless

German spy who broke his right ankle while parachuting into Ramsey Hollow, Huntingdonshire, and was duly court-martialled and executed before he managed to do any spying. Josef Jacobs's executioners had been considerate enough to allow him to sit before the eight-man firing squad – made up of members of the Holding Battalion, Scots Guards – as his injured leg made standing difficult. The coroner noted during the autopsy that Josef had been shot once in the head and seven times around the white lint target that had been pinned over his heart. The poor man was buried in an unmarked grave at St. Mary's Roman Catholic Cemetery in Kensal Green, Northwest London, and, to add insult to injury, earth was later thrown over his grave, allowing for the cadavers of total strangers to be buried on top of him.

Shakil had enjoyed history at school, and under different circumstances would perhaps have been interested to know that he was being driven into the Tower of London complex, but by the time the tear-stained blindfold was removed from the eighteen-year-old's eyes, he was already in a damp, dark cell, and his only thought was one of fear for his life.

He spent his first half hour shouting for help and looking for a way out, then footsteps resounded and three guards appeared.

"Shut up, you piece of shit! And stand up for the Warden."

The Warden was dressed in an Armani suit and very shiny shoes. His accent was an uneasy fusion of public school and East End wideboy, explainable by the fact that his daddy had paid for him to go to public school, but the boy had not been bright enough to get into university, and had instead used his financial leverage to hang out with bankers, gangsters and aspiring politicians. His money and dubious connections had finally landed him his current position, and he intended to abuse every inch of his power.

"Congratulations," the Warden intoned sarcastically to the frightened teenager on the other side of the bars. "It is my duty as Warden to welcome you here. You are officially the first detainee of the Tower of London Detention and Concentration Facility."

"I didn't do nothing!"

"Shut up when the Warden's speaking!"

The Warden continued by assuring Shakil that during his stay he would not only give up his terror cell, but would also help them to fine-tune the system they were creating.

"But I didn't do nothing!"

"I am referring, of course, to the Government's new anti-terror system."

"But I didn't do nothing."

The Warden laughed. "Get him scrubbed up," he told the guards.

Even as Shakil was told where he was, his family had no idea whatsoever. It was seven in the morning and they had already been waiting two hours at the local police station to speak to someone who might know something. The duty officer told them to come back at nine, when the chief superintendent would be in, but they refused to leave. It took all of Mr Malik's diplomatic skills to stop his wife and daughter ending up in the holding cells, as panic for Shakil made it impossible for the women to sit still and wait in silence.

When the chief superintendent finally turned up at half past nine, he tried to go straight into a meeting, and this time it was Mr Malik whose nerves gave way.

"What have you done with my son?" he shouted repeatedly at the top of his voice. The police station was filling up with other distressed members of the public by now, and the chief superintendent decided that in the interests of public relations it would be best to assist the Malik family rather than incarcerate them. He made a couple of phone calls, and finally informed the Maliks that their son was being held on terrorism charges at an undisclosed location.

"Terrorism charges! Shakil? Do you even know what you're talking about?" Shakil's sixteen-year-old sister Adara yelled at the chief superintendent, while Mrs Malik suddenly felt faint and her husband had to hold her up.

"Calm down, Miss Malik." The chief was starting to seriously consider locking up the lot of them – public relations or not. If the son was a terrorist, then there was a good chance that the rest of the family were as well.

"Shakil – a terrorist? Look, my brother's greatest ambition is to strip at hen parties. How on earth could he be a terrorist?" Adara was hysterical, and Mr Malik tried to calm her down, while holding onto her sobbing mother.

"Mr Malik," the chief superintendent put on his most professional smile. "Why don't you all go home and once we know something more about your son, we'll contact you."

Eventually Mr Malik decided to take the remains of his family home, to regroup and think where to appeal for help. On the way home, Adara replayed the events of the previous night in her mind, and tried to think of anything that could have contributed to her brother's abduction by the Met's Anti-Terror Squad.

Shakil and Adara had been invited to a party. There had been a long discussion with their dad, who hadn't wanted Adara to go. Shakil argued that if his father trusted him with the keys to his car and to his explosives warehouse, then surely he could trust him to bring his sister home safely.

"Your sister's not a car." But Mr Malik lost the argument, as his wife joined in on the side of the children, and the siblings went to their friend's party.

After about half an hour of chatting to each other and the hostess, a blonde girl had come up to Shakil and asked him where he was from.

"East End," Shakil gave the girl his sexy smile.

"No, I mean, where's your family from? You're not English."

"I'm Pakistani."

"Oh... Are you a terrorist?"

"Maddy!" Their hostess's embarrassment was painful to see.

"My dad says that all Pakis are terrorists," explained Maddy. Adara and the hostess exchanged glances, wondering which one of them was going to deck her first, but Shakil merely thought hard for a moment, then said, "I don't know about anyone else, but I *am* a terrorist – a terrorist of the heart."

The girl processed the information for a while, then laughed. Adara rolled her eyes, while Shakil explained to Maddy that his name meant 'sexy' in Arabic. Adara caught Shakil's eye and put her finger in her mouth, making like she was about to vomit. Shakil got that mischievous glint in his eye, and added, "Lots of Pakistani names have Arabic origins, and most of them mean something. For example, 'Adara' means 'virgin'." Everyone looked at Adara and laughed.

"Does not!" Adara stuck her middle finger up at Shakil, eliciting more hilarity. The blonde whispered something in Shakil's ear, "Let's see what you got then, Mr Terrorist," and went to kiss him, her hand straying downwards towards the boy's crotch. But just then Shakil's favourite *Doors* song came on the stereo, "I love that song!", and he was off – leaving Maddy to wonder whether her low-cut top was showing enough cleavage.

As Adara recalled her brother dancing to *Light My Fire* in front of a room of admiring girls and jealous boys, his shoulder length black hair glistening under the dim lighting, Shakil was hosed down with freezing water and his fine locks were shaved off by a brute of a guard who doubled as the prison's 'hairdresser'. Shakil had been very proud of his hair, and the sight of it falling on the stone floor, and the bald, bleeding reflection staring out at him from a mirror that was shoved in front of his face with the words "Who's a pretty boy, then?", broke him. What with the fluorescent yellow jumpsuit he'd been forced to don after his 'shower', in place of his customary jeans, Nirvana T-shirt and leather jacket, the old Shakil was no more.

Then Adara remembered that a couple of the boys at the party had started a conversation about making bombs. One of the boys said that it would be easy to make a home-made bomb, while the other disagreed. Shakil had piped up, saying that you could make a detonator really easily out of just about anything – even a mobile phone. Shakil knew a lot about explosives, as his father was an engineer, specialising in demolitions, who was often asked by the council to demolish traditional areas of the East End so that developers could turn them into car parks or high-rise hell holes for the underprivileged.

"You see, son," Adara had heard her father say to Shakil more than once, "You could be blowing things up too, just like your old man, if you just went to college and studied engineering, instead of playing guitar and thinking about girls all day."

Maybe someone had reported Shakil's stupid teenage conversation to the authorities. How sick would that be? What kind of a world were they living in if you couldn't even chat at a party without being kidnapped by the police several hours later?

"Mum, we gotta go back... Dad..."

"What is it, sweetheart?"

"There was some stupid conversation at the party last night about making bombs."

"Oh God." Mrs Malik was starting to feel light-headed again.

"We have to go back and explain that no way would Shakil make a bomb; he just knows about explosives because of Dad's job."

"Okay, sweetheart, we'll go back and tell them," said her father.

"But what if they take your father away as well?" Mrs Malik had aged ten years in the last few hours. "What if they don't give us Shakil back, but take away your father too?"

"We have to try," Mr Malik was adamant.

So Adara and her parents went back to the police station – that day, as they would every day in the weeks that followed.

The interrogation had not lasted long, as after several pelts around the back, chest, face and head, Shakil was already unconscious.

"We'll have to do something about your technique," the Warden told the interrogating officer. "This isn't going to work. I'm seriously thinking we need to look at the equipment we have at our disposal, starting with that weird looking thing in the basement."

The weird looking thing in the basement was a Scavenger's

Daughter – the one claim to fame of one Leonard Skeffington, Lieutenant of the Tower of London during the reign of King Henry VIII. Mr Skeffington must have been either a very bored or a very unpleasant man – perhaps both – for it would have taken him no small amount of time to come up with a device that matched the infamous rack both in terms of the pain and the damage it caused its victims. And having a day job at the Tower of London, Mr Skeffington would have had ample opportunity to observe both instruments in practice. While the rack stretched people until their limbs were dislocated and then torn from their sockets, the Scavenger's Daughter compressed them – in a foetal position – until they bled from their orifices and their bones broke.

Had the Warden displayed any interest in the Tower's rich history, or had he taken the time to speak to the former Chief Yeoman Warder of the Tower or any of his staff before having them thrown out of the complex, he would have known all about the Scavenger's Daughter, but – perhaps luckily for Shakil – he hadn't and he didn't.

Now a breeze with no discernible source stirred in the torture chamber. The ropes on the rack creaked and shadows flitted uneasily around Mr Skeffington's invention. Eddies of dust formed and whirled out into the corridor, swirling around the feet of a guard who'd been trailing slightly behind the Warden's guided tour of the Tower complex. Bob shivered as the temperature suddenly dropped, and hurried to join the others.

It had been a long tour, but the Warden was still going strong and was just now explaining to the Home Secretary and the heads of MI5 and MI6 his plans for the redevelopment of the Tower.

"As you know, the Prime Minister has informed me that the war on terror will require the detention and interrogation of many more suspects than previously thought." The Warden was positively beaming at the attention he was getting from some of the country's most important men. "So I am having plans drawn up for a large number of holding cells with bunks. We are now about to enter phase one of the project, but once all the work is complete, the Tower will hold more inmates per square metre than any other prison in Europe."

"And how much time do you think you'll need to finish the project, Warden?" asked the Home Secretary.

Several hours later, and the cold wind that had started in the torture chamber now stirred the ropes on the row of gallows outside the White Tower, causing them to creak and swing. Had an observer chanced upon the scene, he or she might have had the impression that something heavy, yet unseen, was dangling from them.

Bob was on guard duty, patrolling the southern part of the Tower complex. He was in the basement of the Wakefield Tower, consciously avoiding the torture chamber and trying not to spend too long gazing into any of the dark corners, when he heard a child crying – a boy.

Bob froze, listening intently. "Hello?" The sobbing came again and Bob moved cautiously towards the sound. "Hello?" A second boy called out something – Bob couldn't make out what. "Who's there?" Bob walked towards the voices, but as he did so they seemed to move away. "Wait!" A flurry of footsteps and Bob followed, determined to find the boys. He couldn't understand for the life of him what they were doing in the Tower, and in the middle of the night as well.

Bob followed the crying up the stairs to the ground floor and out of the building. As he stepped outside, he saw two small figures ahead of him. He hurried after them, calling to them. They disappeared into the Bloody Tower, and Bob went in after them. He didn't see them again, but followed their voices up to a room on the first floor, where all trace of them disappeared. Confused and disconcerted, Bob was searching the room when he heard a blood-curdling scream in one of the adjoining chambers. He rushed next door and stopped short as he saw something coming rapidly towards him from the far end of the room. It was like a mist emerging from the darkness – a mist that transformed into solid matter, as a screaming woman, dressed in what to Bob looked like a ball gown, came running in his direction.

Bob shouted at the woman to stop, but she kept running at him and kept screaming. The guard drew his weapon. "Stop or I'll shoot!" The woman kept coming and Bob panicked, shooting at her a couple of times. As she reached him, the woman finally dropped – facedown – right in front of the shaking guard. Bob closed his eyes for a moment and sucked in air through his mouth; in his fear he had forgotten to breathe. He bent down and checked the woman's pulse – nothing. That was when he noticed the gashes on her back; fragments of whitish backbone protruding from all the blood. He'd only had time to discharge two rounds at the woman, so why was her back slashed a dozen times? Bob looked at his gun, puzzled. Perhaps the new ammo they'd been issued splintered inside a person? He felt bad about killing the woman. He put his weapon away and went to report the incident.

Back in the White Tower, Bob was hurrying to see the Warden, when he bumped into the Head Guard.

"What's wrong, mate?" Pete looked concerned. "You look like you've seen a ghost."

"I just killed a woman."

"What?"

"I just shot a woman. She was coming at me. I told her to stop, but she wouldn't listen. I think she was crazy."

"Bob, what the hell are you on about?"

"I killed someone. I have to go report it."

"Whoa, whoa. Hang on a sec there, mate. Look, don't take this the wrong way, but... have you been drinking?"

"No. No, I haven't." Bob tried to get past the older man, but Pete was having none of it.

"Look, if you killed someone, then there's a body, right?"

"Right... Now let me past. I need to see the Warden."

"Let's go and check that there's definitely a body. You don't want to bother the Warden and get yourself sacked if this is all just in your head."

Pete wouldn't let it go and eventually Bob found himself on his way back to the Bloody Tower.

"This is a strange place," Pete was saying. "Sometimes people see things. My brother knew someone who was a Yeoman Warder here when it was still a tourist attraction. And he said that one of the other Warders left after something tried to strangle him in the Salt Tower – something nobody could see."

"Well, I definitely saw someone," Bob was getting upset again, "and I shot her." But when they got back to the Bloody Tower, there was no dead woman anywhere to be found.

A couple of hours later, around two in the morning, Crewes and Hampel were on guard duty in the White Tower. Crewes decided to check out the armoury. It was like Christmas come early. The gun in his holster forgotten, Crewes was soon happily swinging a poleaxe around the chamber.

"What the fuck are you doing, man?" But five minutes later Hampel too had a large grin on his face and a poleaxe in his hands, and the two of them were giggling like schoolboys and re-enacting some light-sabre battle or other from an early episode of *Star Wars*.

Neither of them noticed the shadow that fell across the threshold, nor the huge masked figure that entered the room, nor the massive axe it was holding. Crewes didn't even have time to discharge his gun or swing his poleaxe, but neither did he see what was coming. Hampel was less fortunate for, although he got to fight briefly for his life, he also got to stare death right in the eyes and see the scant light glint for one blinding moment on the axe's head before it came down and sideways.

As the masked figure strode back to the hell from which it had come, axe in one hand and the fruits of the night's labours in the other, Shakil was lying shackled on the floor of his cell. He was running a fever, slipping in and out of consciousness. In one of his lucid moments, he became aware of a delicate scent, quite out of sorts with the damp, musty chamber that was his new home. He shouldn't have smelled anything, as he could hardly breathe through his pulverised, blood-encrusted nostrils, and yet he did. The scent was sweet and floral – like a woman's perfume, but weak and distant.

Shakil's swollen, cracked lips moved incoherently as he found himself trying to hum a tune: "Sweet Jane. Sweet, sweet Jane". Shakil knew the song so well, but in his present delirious state he couldn't remember who it was by. His failure to remember distressed him and he wanted to cry, but then that scent wafted by again, closer this time. *The Velvet Underground*, Shakil remembered and smiled.

Just then the air in his cell stirred slightly and eddies of dust started to rise and twist. Shakil tried to change position, but only succeeded in causing a fresh stab of pain in his head and chest. He lost consciousness for a moment, then regained it as a soft, cool hand tenderly stroked his face.

"Mum?" he whispered before drifting off into a gentle sleep. But the woman who knelt beside him was not his mother.

The boy could not have been much older than her. His skin, dark compared to the pale young men of the court that she had been used to, made a stark and fascinating contrast with the whiteness of her own hand. There were even darker patches on his skin, where they had hit him, and bloody marks on his face and body.

The girl with the heavy embroidered dress and long, reddish-golden hair continued to stroke Shakil's face, gazing at him with sadness and compassion. A tear fell from her eye onto the boy's cheek, and he stirred for a moment, then fell asleep once more.

As the grey light of dawn filtered in through the tiny barred window at the top of the cell, a gaping wound opened up in the girl's neck and started to bleed profusely. She grimaced in pain and put her hand up to her neck. Her already pale complexion turned white as a sheet and she faded away to nothing. A tear rolled down Shakil's cheek, but he slept on.

The following morning Shakil woke up to his cell door slamming open, and freezing cold water under pressure forced him against the wall of his cell. He was thrown a bowl of slop to eat, and he crawled over to it, stiff and feverish.

While Shakil tried to eat, his family were down at the police station again, being told that if they persisted in asking questions about him, they would be arrested as well. They followed their visit to the police with a trip to the offices of *The Guardian*. After a long wait, a sympathetic journalist informed them that if Shakil was being held on terror charges, then it was probably at the new detention centre in the Tower of London. This being the case, there was nothing *The Guardian* or any other newspaper could do, as there was a Government injunction against reporting on the Tower. Any journalist caught investigating issues relating to the complex would be imprisoned, and there would be repercussions against the editor and other staff at his or her newspaper.

"I am very, very sorry for your son and for your family. But the only help I can give you is to tell you to forget about your son, or you will end up in prison yourselves, along with your daughter.

"I will not forget about my son!" raged Mrs Malik as her husband and daughter escorted her out of the building – just as they would escort her out of various newspaper, police, human rights organisation and government buildings every day in the weeks that followed.

Shakil's second interrogation was even shorter than the first. The boy only just managed to reiterate that all he'd done was to take part in a general drunken discussion about explosives at the party, that he wasn't part of a terror cell, and that during his summer trip to Pakistan his uncle had taken him sightseeing with his aunt and cousins and not to a terror training camp, when Pete came in to report that the bodies of two guards who had been on duty late last night had been found in the Armoury.

"What?" For the first time since anyone in the room could remember, the Warden looked shaken.

"Crewes and Hampel, sir. We found their bodies." Pete's face was ashen, and he seemed unsteady on his feet. "At least, we think it's them."

"What do you mean, you think it's them?"

"The heads sir ..."

"What about their heads?"

"They're missing, sir."

"What?"

"I said..."

"I know what you said, man!" The Warden pushed his seat away from the table so violently that it toppled over, and the interrogating officer dived to pick it up. "Take me to the bodies, and organise a search for the heads at once. Use the dogs." As the Warden swept out of the room with Pete in tow, the interrogating officer piped up in a feeble little voice, "Excuse me, sir..." Despite his fear, pain and confusion, Shakil couldn't believe how the interrogator's whole demeanour changed when he spoke to the Warden.

"What is it?"

"What shall I do with *him*?" The interrogator nodded in Shakil's direction.

"Take him back to his cell. We'll continue this later."

Shakil was thrown back in his cell, amidst his usual protestations that he hadn't done anything, that they'd made a mistake and that he wanted to call his parents; and guards with dogs were dispatched to look for the missing heads.

The search came to an abortive end when the dogs were taken to the Salt Tower. As soon as the shadow of the tower fell on the two Alsatians, they started to whimper like puppies. And as their handler dragged them towards the threshold, they bayed and jumped about, trying to pull away from the building.

"Come on, you little bastards, we're going in!" But Jeffries didn't stand a chance. Max dropped into a crouch and started backing away, eyes fixed on the dark entrance to the Salt Tower, while Theo let out a plaintive howl, bit Jeffries on the hand and, when the shocked handler let go of his leash, ran in the opposite direction like the hounds of hell had been loosed on his fine black pedigree tail – now tucked between his legs, right under his belly, and fleeing for its dear fluffy life.

While Jeffries led the disgraced Max back to the kennels, then rounded up Theo and gave him a good hiding, the other guards entered the Salt Tower and searched it top to bottom, but found nothing. By dusk the heads still hadn't turned up. A discussion flared up as to whether police and crime scene investigation teams should be brought in from the outside, but the Warden categorically refused, on the general rule of thumb that "What goes down in the Tower, stays in the Tower." The search for the heads would resume in the morning. For now, all guards were to be extra cautious and patrol only in pairs. The guards grumbled amongst themselves that Crewes and Hampel were in a pair when they were murdered, but nobody dared contradict the Warden. And so night fell.

Bob was patrolling the Wakefield Tower with Pete. There were only ten minutes left until the end of the shift, but Pete couldn't wait that long.

"I need to take a leak, mate. Wait for me, won't you?"

"Sure." But as soon as Pete disappeared around the corner, Bob heard the heart-breaking sobbing of a child – the little boy from the night before. "Pete? Pete!" But Pete couldn't hear him and Bob couldn't wait, as the child's crying receded down the corridor, joined by the voice of the older boy. Bob threw one last glance in the direction of the toilets, then took off after the boys.

Bob followed the voices and footsteps, calling out to the children as he spotted them heading out of the building. He couldn't see them clearly in the darkness, but the little one looked about ten, and the older one couldn't be more than twelve or thirteen. What the hell were they doing here, and where were they hiding during the day? It wasn't that much of a surprise that the dogs hadn't found them – Max and Theo seemed to be about as much use as his late aunt's toy poodle – but the massive hunt for Crewes's and Hampel's heads should have unearthed the boys' hiding place. Then again, the heads hadn't turned up, so perhaps where the heads were so too were the boys... what a horrible thought. And speaking of Crewes's and

Hampel's heads... as Bob followed the boys into the Bloody Tower, he suddenly realised the folly of what he was doing. He stopped for a moment and thought about turning back and re-joining Pete, but then the little boy cried out somewhere in the darkness ahead of him, so he drew his gun and hurried inside.

Pete came out of the toilet and returned to the place where he'd left the younger guard. He called out to his colleague, then glanced at his watch and figured that Bob must have gone back to the guards' quarters. "Thanks for waiting," he muttered under his breath, and followed suit.

The boys were gone. By the time Bob realised that he was in the same chamber as he'd shot the woman in, it was too late – the woman was running at him from the far end of the room, shrieking. Bob's brain stalled, but his automatic pilot engaged and he pointed his weapon at the woman, shouting for her to stop. This time he did not fire and, as the woman drew closer to him, Bob noticed that she was not looking at him – she was running in his direction, but not actually at him. Now she was close enough for Bob to see the terror and madness in her eyes. As the screaming woman reached Bob, he jumped back, weapon raised, ready to let her pass, but she fell bleeding to the floor, exactly as she had the other night when he'd thought he'd shot her.

When Bob recovered enough to lower his weapon and think rationally, he bent down and studied the gashes in the woman's back. It was obvious now that he wasn't responsible for them. It was as if someone had hacked into her from behind, over and over, while she was running away. Bob looked in the direction from which the woman had come, and that was when he heard the footsteps – heavy and getting closer. Then a sight more monstrous than anything he could have imagined appeared at the far end of the chamber. Striding rapidly towards the guard, giant axe in hand, was a mountain of a man, with a black hood-like mask over his head, holes cut out for the eyes – and the eyes unblinking, deathlike, yet burning with a malevolence that could only have come from Hell itself.

Bob fought to keep a hold of himself. "Stop or I'll shoot!" The monster paused for the briefest moment, looking directly at the guard. Bob could have sworn that the fiend smiled beneath his mask, before moving forward again with added determination. As he approached Bob, he raised his axe. "Stay back!" Bob took aim and squeezed the trigger, but his gun jammed. He tried not to panic; he managed to unblock the gun, and discharged several shots at the approaching giant. He kept shooting, but the monster kept coming. Bob was still shooting as the axe came down. The last thing he saw was the room spinning over and over, and then his own headless body slumping to the ground, then receding in the distance, as his head was picked up and carried off into the darkness.

Shakil had fallen into a restless sleep. He dreamed that he was in a different cell. There was a window at eye level and he looked out of it onto the patch of land known as Tower Green. A scaffold had been erected there and Shakil could see a small crowd gathering. Then he saw a procession of people walking from the White Tower in the direction of the scaffold. Among them was an elderly man, leading the most gorgeous girl Shakil had ever seen. She was slim and petite, with a beautiful face, rendered very pale against her jet black dress. Her hair was hidden by a silk scarf, but a lock of it had escaped, and shone once reddish, once golden in the cold February sun. She held a small book in her hand, and walked like a goddess or a queen might walk.

As Shakil watched, the girl was led towards the scaffold. Shakil expected her to take a place among the crowd, but the elderly man led her up the steps, onto the wooden structure itself. That's when Shakil noticed the large block of wood, and the huge, monstrous-looking, hooded man who stood in the shadows at the side of the scaffold, holding a massive axe. Shakil looked at the girl, who addressed the crowd and read something out of her book, and then the reality of what was going to happen dawned on the boy and he felt sick. As he watched, the girl removed her scarf and coat, and handed them to one of the women attending her. Then she took a handkerchief and tied it around her eyes. Shakil tried to open the window, but it was stuck. He rattled it in a desperate attempt to get it open, but to no avail. He shouted, but nobody could hear him. He was forced to watch helplessly as the beautiful girl kneeled, then panicked as she couldn't locate the block by touch alone. Shakil watched in horror as someone from the crowd scaled the scaffold, and guided the girl's hands to the chopping block. She calmed down, and lay her head upon it. The masked man stepped out of the shadows and raised his axe.

As the axe came down, Shakil cried out and woke up. His relief that it had only been a dream dissipated as soon as he realised where he was. As his eyes adjusted to the dark, he saw a figure watching him from a corner of his cell. He pulled back, frightened, but then he recognised the girl from his dream. The gentleness emanating from her dispelled Shakil's fear in an instant. Confused, but unafraid, he watched the girl draw closer. He could smell her perfume, and wondered why it was familiar. The girl touched his face and Shakil closed his sore eyes for a moment, then opened them again and gazed into the girl's sad face. He reached out and touched her reddish-gold hair, smiling back when she smiled at him.

The first light of dawn crept into the cell. Pain clouded the girl's delicate features and a thin red line appeared on her pale neck. Shakil watched in horror as the girl put a hand up to her neck, and blood oozed out between her fingers. Shakil started to panic, and the girl held out her free hand to him, trying to reassure him even as she fought to stem the flow of her own blood with her other hand. As she bled, the girl's features became soft and blurred, and she faded away, leaving only a pool of blood on the floor; a second later that too was gone.

Shakil pushed himself back against the cold damp wall of his cell and sat there, shaking. He was still sitting there when the guards came to hose him down.

"We're going back upstairs now," said the Warden, "but bear in mind that this is where we'll be having our little chats from now on if you don't tell us what we want to know."

Shakil's hands were handcuffed behind his back and his ankles loosely chained together. He was speechless following the interrogating officer's demonstration of the rack, unable even to protest his innocence, which he'd done at every given opportunity up until now. The Warden took Shakil's silence to be an admission of guilt, and congratulated himself silently on his first small victory over the youth. The interrogating officer, on the other hand, was still miffed that the plaques about the torture instruments had been removed – along with all the other tourist information – as his urge to try out the Scavenger's Daughter was growing daily, but he couldn't for the life of him figure out how the damned thing worked. If only someone had told him about *Google*.

Back in the interrogating room, the officer ordered Shakil to name the other people in his terror cell. Shakil was still unable to speak, and the Warden thought that perhaps he'd been wrong: the stubborn little shit was not on the verge of spilling the beans after all; his silence was merely a new and irritating resistance tactic. The Warden nodded to the interrogating officer to get physical. The interrogator grinned and was about to take a swipe at Shakil when Pete appeared and informed them in a trembling voice that the body of Bob Dawson had been found in the Bloody Tower – the body, but not the head. The Warden had no choice but to order Shakil to be taken back to his cell.

"You are one lucky son of a bitch," the interrogating officer hissed in Shakil's ear as Pete led the boy out of the room.

Shakil was left alone for the rest of the day, as everyone in the Tower complex was preoccupied with the search for a psycho killer and three missing heads. The boy spent much of the day lying on the hard stone floor. At night he couldn't get to sleep, and when he finally did, he dreamed about the execution again. This time he was right there, standing among the small group of people at the foot of the scaffold. As the executioner moved towards the girl and raised his axe, Shakil started screaming, "Stop! Let her go!"

The hooded monster turned away from the girl and headed towards Shakil.

"Run! Go! Now!" The girl's voice rang out over the agitated whispers of the crowd. She had raised her head from the block and, the blindfold still over her eyes, moved her head around, as if trying to locate Shakil through sound alone. "You can't stop what will happen to me. It will go on happening over and over – as long as the Tower stands."

The executioner went to descend the scaffold, axe raised, eyes on Shakil.

"Run! Please go! Now!" So urgent was the plea in the girl's voice that Shakil ran.

He woke up to the familiar sound of his cell door slamming open. As Shakil was hosed down, his family were preparing to see a woman from Amnesty International. By the time they had arrived at the Amnesty office, and the woman had said that she would try to help them, but it would be a slow and difficult process, Shakil was already strapped to the rack in the basement of the Wakefield Tower.

"I don't know!" he half screamed, half pleaded.

"You don't know their names?" asked the Warden, as the interrogating officer got ready to tighten the ropes one more time. Shakil was stretched out on the iron frame, his feet secured at one end, his hands at the other. The replica of the sixteenth century original worked just fine. The lever on the central wooden roller allowed the interrogating officer to turn the rollers at the head and foot of the rack simultaneously, pulling the ropes that secured Shakil's hands and feet in opposite directions.

"I don't know what you're talking about!"

The interrogating officer was about to turn the roller again, when Pete came running in and informed the Warden that Jeffries was missing. If looks could kill, the filthy look that the interrogator gave Shakil would have dispatched the boy to the next life for sure. "What shall I do with him?" the interrogator asked the Warden.

"Leave him where he is."

Luckily for Shakil, the ropes on the rack were not stretched tight enough to do any serious damage, but as the day wore on, the agony of having his arms pulled taught over his head grew. At lunchtime a fly found its way into the basement, and tortured the sweating, suffering boy by buzzing around his head and sitting on him, again and again; every time he managed to move enough to dislodge it, it would be back. This carried on for about an hour until the fly grew bored and flew off to find some dog shit to feed on. Half an hour later Shakil's nose started to itch for no apparent reason, and the boy squirmed, tried to blow on his nose and did whatever he could to alleviate the itch, but it persisted for a good forty minutes, driving him crazy, and then suddenly it eased. By teatime his muscles began to cramp painfully and Shakil cried out in pain and fear.

As darkness fell, the chamber changed. Shadows moved around Shakil, and he could hear whispers and moans in the dark corners. Despite his great discomfort, exhaustion overcame him and he almost dozed off, but the approach of heavy footsteps brought him wide awake. The night was at its darkest now, and Shakil peered into the gloom near the chamber door with growing trepidation. The footsteps grew louder, the shadows and whispers around Shakil stilled, and a terrible silence fell on the chamber.

Shakil struggled against his bonds as the footsteps came closer. Then the chamber door swung open, and in the scant light from the corridor Shakil saw the silhouette of a massive man. As the giant entered the chamber, Shakil recognised him: it was the hooded monster that had cut off the girl's head in his nightmare – it was the executioner, and he had seen Shakil, and was advancing towards him, raising his axe.

Shakil thrashed about on the rack, crying out and twisting madly from side to side. An image of his parents and his sister flashed into Shakil's head, and he was sure he was going to die. When a white mist formed before his eyes, he thought he was passing out, but the mist quickly solidified and took on human form. It was the girl from Shakil's dreams – the girl who had visited him in his cell – and she now stood between the boy and the executioner, small and slender, but more corporeal and stronger than the other night.

The executioner went for the girl immediately, but she ducked his blow and fled from the chamber, leading him away from Shakil. The boy shouted out in protest, but the executioner and the girl were gone. Shakil struggled on the rack again, terrified for the girl. Eventually he exhausted himself and gave up. Tears for the girl welled up in his eyes, and he closed them. Then all of a sudden there was that perfume again, and a gentle, soothing presence was in the room. The girl was back. She touched Shakil's face and chest; she touched his hands and studied his bonds closely.

Ever since the presence of people in the Tower at night had disrupted the fine balance between the living and the dead, the girl had found herself increasingly able to interact with the physical world. For many years those who walked in the Tower during the day and those who walked there at night had been separate. Now the order was destroyed, and the girl, and the realm of nightmare in which she resided, had entered the waking world. And she had fallen in love again – and again her love was doomed.

Jane Grey had been fifteen when she was bullied into marrying a young man she hardly knew, but she had grown to love him. Nine months after their wedding, she had watched from her confines in the Tower as he was taken for execution and brought back a while later – his rag-covered head rattling around beside his headless body in the horse-drawn cart. An hour later, Jane suffered the same fate. Her crime: being too young to withstand the machinations of her ambitious parents and powerful in-laws, who had made her queen of England for nine days, incurring the wrath of the rightful heir to the throne.

Jane loosened Shakil's bonds and let him down. The boy's body slumped, his arms temporarily useless, and he fell into Jane's arms. Drawing on his life-force to give her strength, Jane led Shakil out of the dark building.

Jones was checking the area west of the White Tower when he spotted the prisoner whose head he'd shaved leaving the Wakefield Tower with a girl in an old-fashioned dress. He raised his weapon, shouting for them to stop, then gave chase.

Jane and Shakil fled towards Traitor's Gate and the River Thames beyond. The only obstacle in their way was the portcullis on the south side of the Bloody Tower. The pins-and-needles had eased, and Shakil had enough feeling back in his arms to work the ancient mechanism that pulled up the seven hundred and fifty-year-old spiked gate. He and Jane ran under the portcullis just as Jones was catching up with them. The guard paused for a moment, taking aim at Shakil's back. There was a loud creaking noise as the mechanism holding up the portcullis gave way, and the two and a half tonne structure came crashing down, its spikes impaling the guard through his head and his shoulders. He held onto his weapon a moment longer, and then it fell from his hand. His body remained upright, fixed by the iron spikes, surprised eyes staring ahead.

Jane and Shakil ran down the steps leading to the water-logged Traitor's Gate. Water levels had risen in the last few years, the river's tides had increased in strength, and the land beneath the water-gate had been worn away. The bottom of the gate no longer rested on the mud beneath the water, but hung free in the water itself, the gate now held up by the solid walls on either side of it. As Shakil inspected the bottom of the gate, he understood why the girl had brought him to this spot.

"We just have to swim under it," he said to her. "I'll go first, then I'll help pull you under the gate."

Shakil lowered himself into the freezing water and went under, using the bars to pull himself down one side, then up the other side of the gate. He came up, gasping for breath, and stood chest-high in water, shaking from the cold. He reached out to Jane through the bars.

"You just have to get down and under the bars, and I'll help pull you up," he told her.

Jane gazed at Shakil, sadness and longing in her eyes. As Shakil watched, her features began to soften and fade. She turned from the boy and fled back towards the Bloody Tower, disappearing before she reached the top of the steps.

"I'll come back for you," Shakil called out to the night.

The Warden and the interrogating officer were returning from the site where Jeffries's headless body had been found. The multiple lacerations on the dead guard's back and the lengthy blood trail leading up to the body suggested that Jeffries had managed to run a fair distance before succumbing to the killer's axe.

"I'm going to have to get the police involved." The Warden looked defeated.

"We'd better get the prisoner off the rack," the interrogator reminded him.

"Christ, I forgot all about him. Let's go and get him ourselves. There are hardly any guards left, for God's sake." The two of them went down to the torture chamber, but Shakil was nowhere to be found.

"Goddammit! Goddammit!" The Warden's vocabulary – never huge – shrank to one word.

After a final search of the Tower complex by what was left of his staff, the Warden finally called the police and admitted to having a terror suspect on the loose and a bunch of dead guards with missing heads.

The executioner was not happy. The pathetic slip of a girl had outfoxed him, robbing him of the head of the traitor on the rack. It was his duty to collect as many heads for the Queen as possible – and he would have to hurry if he was to get a decent quota before daybreak.

Shakil made it home before dawn. His luminous yellow jumpsuit was almost dry, but he had to ditch it as soon as possible. He used the last of his strength to scale a tree at the back of the house, and quietly opened his sister's bedroom window. He gazed at Adara, longing to hug her, but what was the point of waking her up? Things would never be the same again, and it was best not to get her hopes up. He looked in on his parents, also sound asleep. Then he went to his room and changed his clothes. He noticed an old history book from school and quickly flipped through the pages, looking for something. And there it was: a reproduction of Paul Delaroche's painting of the execution of Lady Jane Grey. Recognition and sadness crept into Shakil's eyes. "Jane."

Shakil moved swiftly and silently to his father's study, opened a drawer and took out the keys to his father's office and warehouse. He put on a long, loose-fitting coat, and tucked the jumpsuit under it – he would dispose of it later, away from the house, preventing any repercussions against his family. He took a final look at his sleeping parents, then went into Adara's bedroom and left quietly through her window.

Adara woke up, looked around her room and shivered. For a moment she had the vague feeling that something wasn't right, but sleep quickly reclaimed her and she sank back onto her pillow.

Shakil disappeared around the corner just as the first police cars pulled up.

The Warden and the interrogating officer were on their way to the Warden's office in the White Tower, when their path was cut off by a brick shithouse of a man, carrying an axe in one hand and Jeffries's head in the other.

"Shit!" The Warden froze for a moment, and the interrogating officer was first to draw his gun.

"Drop the axe!" But the giant didn't drop the axe; he raised it and ran at the interrogator. The interrogating officer emptied his gun into the giant's chest, then turned and ran towards the Wakefield Tower. The Warden paused long enough to ascertain that the killer was following the interrogator, then ran as fast as he could in the opposite direction.

The interrogating officer ran down the stairs to the basement. Before he knew it, he found himself in the torture chamber, cowering behind the Scavenger's Daughter and listening to the heavy footsteps coming closer. He'd barely had time to reload his gun when the heavy door of the chamber swung open, its hinges breaking, and the executioner strode in, Jeffries's head still swinging by one side and the axe held firmly on the other.

The guard emptied his gun into the advancing giant's head and chest, then fell to his knees and started to pray. The executioner raised his axe over the guard's head, and then thought better of it. He placed the axe and Jeffries's head carefully on the ground. Then he grabbed the sobbing interrogator by the back of his neck and the seat of his pants, squeezed his head down towards his knees, and thrust him into the Scavenger's Daughter, fastening the iron bonds with ease.

"So that's how it works." The ridiculously inappropriate thought slipped into the interrogator's head before the monster tightened his bonds, forcing blood from his nose and mouth, and cracking his spine.

The executioner contemplated his handiwork for a moment, then picked up his axe and cut off the man's head.

The Warden had locked himself in his office and was calling the police again when he heard heavy footsteps approaching. He put down the phone and stood very still, hoping the footsteps wouldn't stop outside his office door, but they did. There was a moment's silence, and then an ear-splitting thud as the axe came splintering through the thick wood of the door. The Warden thought he was going to have a heart attack. For some reason all he could think of was Jack Nicholson breaking down the bathroom door in *The Shining*. Then he remembered that the door on the far side of his office led to an adjoining chamber, which in turn led back round to the stairs.

When the executioner burst in, the Warden was already leaving through the back and heading downstairs. As he ran for the main entrance leading out of the Tower, the Warden ran straight into the escaped prisoner.

"You're back!"

"Yes, I am." And Shakil opened his jacket, revealing the vast amount of explosives strapped around his waist, and the detonator in his other hand. The Warden turned around, planning to go back the way he'd just come, but the executioner was striding towards him, axe in one hand, Jeffries's and the interrogator's heads in the other.

The Warden turned back to Shakil.

"We can make a deal. I can get you released from here." Shakil looked the Warden in the eye and raised the detonator in front of the man's face. "No!" The Warden raised a hand in protest and backed away as Shakil placed his thumb over the detonating button. "Please, don't. I have a wife and kids." The Warden didn't have a wife or kids. In fact, he hated both kids and women, only using the latter sporadically when his urges got the better of him. But Shakil wasn't to know. The Warden sensed the boy's hesitation. "I have two kids, and a third on the way." Shakil's thumb wavered over the detonator.

The Warden held the boy's gaze. He didn't see the axe rise behind his head; nor did he see it swing down and round. But he felt the sharp pain in his neck and then the world spun, and turned blood red, as the Warden's head went one way and his body went another, flailing arms lashing out in reflex action and grabbing Shakil's hand, pushing the boy's thumb down on the detonator.

Debris flew everywhere: stone, timber, metal, body parts and shards of glass. Among the body parts were severed heads, which fell – some of them burning, all of them thudding – to the ground.

Had there been any witnesses at that early time of the morning, and had those witnesses looked closely, they might have noticed orbs of light and strange wisps of mist rising from the burning ruins and merging with the dawn sky.

Police, fire trucks and ambulances were on the scene within minutes; news vans not much later.

Adara woke to the sound of the news on her television.

"Police are puzzled by the disproportionate number of heads among the remains..."

She sat up, startled, convinced that she'd switched her TV off the night before, and saw her brother standing before her. He wore his favourite leather jacket and smiled at her, pushing a thick lock of shiny black hair away from his eyes. Adara's grogginess was instantly replaced by astonishment, then pure joy. She smiled back at Shakil and reached towards him, but he faded away, revealing the television with the newsman still reporting on the explosion.

Adara cried out and burst into tears.

"The authorities believe that the explosion was an act of terrorism. Many will no doubt be saying that the Prime Minister's new anti-terror legislation has already been justified; some that it is still not enough."

As Adara stared at the television uncomprehendingly, several ravens hopped past the reporter's back and perched on a nearby wall, overlooking the burning wreckage.

DAYLIGHT ROBBERY

DAYLIGHT ROBBERY

Window tax

From Quickipedia, the online encyclopedia

> ! You have reached a cached page. This is a snapshot of the page as it appeared on 7 May 2174 12:07:24 GMT. The current entry has been removed following failure of the Twenty-Second Century Fox Media Corporation neutrality checks.

Initially imposed in England in 1696, before being abolished 155 years later, the **window tax** (pronounced: ˈwɪndəʊ tæks) was designed to levy a tariff relative to the prosperity of the taxpayer, and was easier to enforce than income tax – as citizens were at the time reluctant to disclose their income, but their windows could easily be counted with or without their cooperation. In those days, the wealthier a household, the bigger the house and the more windows.

The window tax was reintroduced in 2046, at which time it was the poorest who lived in massive blocks of flats with vast numbers of small windows. Like the Community Tax or 'poll tax' introduced by Margaret Thatcher and implemented in England from 1990 to 1993, the 2046 tax was a single flat-rate per-capita tax, but one which was imposed on every resident, regardless of age. The tax calculation included not only every window in an individual's flat, but all windows deemed to be communal, such as those in stairwells and corridors. For example, a single person in a flat with three windows, living in a building with 100 windows in communal areas, would be charged for 103 windows. If a family of five lived in the same three-window flat in the same building, they would have to pay five times as much.

The huge tax bills imposed on the poor and desperate led to riots; the incarceration of the rioters and of those who couldn't pay led to more riots; and by the time the windows on the sprawling council estates were bricked up to penalise non-payers, martial law took care of the few still able and willing to fight the system.

Once the riots were forcibly ended and a cruel new status quo was reached, the dark, dingy, rat-riddled estates were left largely to themselves, with poor and migrant families removed from more affluent areas and forcibly resettled in on a semi-regular basis. Such was the case with the South Acton Estate in West London, which had been redeveloped and expanded in the late 2030s into a massive concrete jungle housing 200,000 of society's unwanted. Acton had always been an inclusive, multicultural area, with people of diverse ethnic backgrounds; once they'd shared the experience of relative prosperity in the peaceful London district, now they shared poverty, pollution and darkness, and the scurvy, brittle bones and blindness that followed.

> **Categories**: History of taxation in England, Georgian Era, Economy of Stuart England, Legal History of England, English architecture, Property taxes, Economic History of England, Windows, Community Charge, Poll tax, Poll tax riots, Margaret Thatcher, Twenty-first century, Riots in London, Riots in England, 2046 riots, Protests in England, Civil disobedience, South Acton Estate, Daylight Protocol.

J UST WHEN IT seemed that the window tax had backfired, the deaths began. First one, then a dozen, then the poor were dying out in their hundreds. Malnutrition and lack of basic healthcare and welfare, combined with the blindness that ensued when generation after generation grew up in buildings with no daylight, had finally taken their toll, as parents couldn't cope with their sightless children, and sightless children grew up unable to care for their sick and ageing parents. At last, the problem of society's unwanted was solving itself.

But all was not glum in London town.

Phillip kicked back in his designer armchair and took a sip of Dom Perignon. He'd always hated champagne, but it was expensive, so he bought it and he drank it.

"TV," he said. The life-size three-dimensional holographic projection of a human brain sprang to life in the middle of the room.

"... About the size of a grain of rice, from an evolutionary point of view the human pineal gland can be explained as a kind of atrophied photoreceptor." The television was evidently still streaming content from the library Phillip had accessed the night before to watch sharks mating. "In some species of amphibians and reptiles the pineal gland is linked to a vestigial organ, sometimes known as the parietal or third eye. Like humans, reptiles and amphibians use their eyes to see, but they still utilise their parietal eye to sense light, and the pineal gland to which it is linked regulates their circadian rhythms and helps them navigate, as it can sense the polarisation of light." Phillip downed the rest of his glass and yawned. "Although mystics have attributed supernatural powers to the pineal gland, equating it to a third eye with microscopic and telescopic vision, and the ability to view reality far beyond our own space and time, it is in fact a perfectly natural organ, reacting to light and producing the hormone melatonin, which regulates our sleep patterns."

"Oh, for fuck's sake," moaned Phillip. "Cricket." The streamed television content changed in an instant, displaying the latest test match against Pakistan. England were losing by a mile. "Bastards!" snarled Phillip. "TV, off."

The cricketers disappeared and Phillip sat in silence for a couple of minutes, deciding what to do next. A third-generation purebred designer baby – legal, since the passing of gene selection legislature in 2032, Phillip's designer baby parents had naturally chosen a blue-eyed, blond-haired male, with good bone structure, a high IQ and no genetic predisposition to the diseases that were currently being screened. Perhaps he'd go clubbing and try to get laid. Trouble was, there were plenty of good looking, blond-haired, blue-eyed young men around and, as most people had been opting for boys since gene selection had been legalised, there was a severe shortage of suitable young women. You could buy a girl, of course, but these were usually malnourished, disease-ridden girls kidnapped from the estates and drugged to keep them passive, and half of them were now born with no eyes – only hollow membranous depressions where their eyes should be. Besides, Phillip hated paying for stuff he should be getting for free. Then the perfect solution came to him.

Phillip downed the last of his drink, swapped his lounge pants and T-shirt for an Armani SmartSuit, and took the lift down to the garage. The sensors in the house detected his departure, and the lights dimmed, then switched themselves off. There was no need for any of them to come on in his absence – to fool potential burglars – as the luxury estate in which Phillip's house was situated had all the latest safety features and was heavily guarded to boot. A gated community of top-spec glass houses on the western side of the Metropolitan Green Belt, every wall of every house constituted a giant sheet of reinforced, engineered, high-tech glass, so Phillip and the other members of the exclusive multi-million pound estate only paid tax on five windows each (four walls and the ceiling). The glass could be set to different levels of opaqueness and to different colours; it could simulate sunrise, sunset; there was even a setting that caused the glass to gently change colours so that at any time the houses could glow with any or all of the colours of the rainbow. Or you could have it set to natural transparent glass and watch the tranquil world outside: the green of the trees and shrubs on the estate and the fields beyond it, the azure of the sky or the myriad stars in the night-time firmament – when not obscured by the polluted glow radiating from Inner London. The glass walls and ceilings also worked with the estate's heating system, making the comfort of living in the glass estate nothing short of perfect. There was a water shortage in England that year, but the fountains and water channels running through Phillip's estate were secured by a deal with the Metropolitan Council.

Phillip had never learnt to drive – there'd been no need. The majority of road vehicles had been driverless since before he was born, and Phillip had no more interest in learning redundant technologies than he had in learning redundant languages – like the French, Spanish and German that his robotic home tutor had tried to bore him to death with.

The computer chip in Phillip's sports car crooned to him in a sexy female voice that made him horny every time he hit the road, answering his questions and obeying commands such as "Switch on the TV" or "Open the drinks cabinet." Now she was telling him the outside temperature and weather forecast for the evening, and he was getting more and more turned on. He didn't fancy spending time and money trying to pull a designer babe in a high-end bar. He just wanted swift, violent release, followed perhaps by a couple more leisurely goes on a girl who'd be completely disregarded by the police even if she did report the assault. There was an arts college in Hammersmith; the girls there were relatively clean and well-nourished. They'd certainly be on the young side – teenagers, many of them. And who knows, one of them might even be into the rough stuff. But to get there Phillip would have to drive through the South Acton Estate.

"Riverside College of Art," Phillip told the computer, and the garage door opened automatically as the car rolled smoothly out. Phillip glanced at his nearest neighbour's house – empty since the owner had gone to prison for murdering his great-great grandfather who'd been cryo-defrosted and turned up to reclaim his estate. Since that time, Phillip had spent an inordinate amount of money bribing the head of the local cryo-lab to terminate and cremate all his cryogenically frozen family members.

As the car pulled out of the estate and into what was left of the Green Belt, on its way into West Central, Phillip settled down to watch the latest serving of his favourite brand of perniciously violent porn.

Traffic was at a virtual standstill, as always, but the premier lane – reserved exclusively for those with upwards of seven figure bank balances – was moving steadily, and by the time his car was nearing the South Acton Estate, Phillip had dozed off. He woke to the deafening, jarring squeal of metal, a violent wrench, and sudden pain all over his body. His head felt like it had exploded, something was dripping into his eye, and the unnoticeably comfortable warmth of the inside of his car had been replaced by the cold of the polluted inner city air as Phillip gazed through the gaping hole in the roof at the looming dark contours of the South Acton Estate. Then he blacked out.

"Hello? Mister? Mister!" John touched the unconscious man tentatively, then a little more firmly, trying to elicit a response. The man in the wrecked car stirred and moaned, then passed out again. There was a large bump on his forehead, and a small gash bled into his blond hair. John, one of the very few members of his class and generation lucky enough to have been born sighted, turned to the small crowd that had gathered in the street behind him. Like John, his sightless friends and neighbours had been brought out of Bollo Bridge House – the largest building on the South Acton Estate – by the sound of the crash, but, unlike John, they had little idea of what was going on.

"What is it? What's happened?" Hands reached out towards John, fear and concern in their owners' voices.

"A car has crashed. There's an injured man in it."

"We have to call an ambulance!" John's next-door neighbour Roger turned his eyeless face in the direction of John's voice.

"They'll never send one out here. You know that," responded John.

"Well, the guy must have medical insurance. Unless the car's stolen, he's surely loaded enough to have insurance."

"True," conceded John, "and the emergency services were probably alerted as soon as the car's computer went down, but we need to stop his head bleeding, and I don't like the look of the smoke coming from the motor. I think we should get him out right now and move away from the car... Someone give me a hand."

Roger and several others stepped forward, and John guided their hands and issued instructions. Once they'd dragged the prostrate man away from the damaged vehicle, John tore a strip from his shirt and tied it around the man's head. As he did so, the blind man who'd been tasked with taking the weight of Phillip's left leg when they lifted him started to undo Phillip's shoelace.

"Hey!" John stayed the man's hand. "What are you doing?"

"He doesn't need them right now," the man responded. "Feel them, they're brand new. He can put his old ones back on when he gets home, and he's probably got ten more pairs like them."

John looked down at the sightless man's feet – one clad in a worn-out, hole-riddled sneaker, the other in a dirty plastic bag with some newspaper sticking out of the top.

"Look," he told the man, "I sympathise, I really do, but you can't take a man's shoes. It's not right." John turned to the others. "Let's get him to my flat. I have some water; we can clean the wound."

"Mummy?" A frightened little voice emanated from the corner of the room.

"It's okay, kitten. It's just Daddy and..." Laura paused, unable to see who'd entered the flat with her husband.

"It's Rog, Mrs Clement," the next-door neighbour reassured her.

"What is it, what's happened?" Laura's grandmother – great-grandmother to six-year-old Katie – rose painfully from the mattress on which she'd been resting and squinted at the newcomers through cataract-covered eyes.

"There was an accident," John explained. "A man was hurt. A few of the neighbours helped me bring him here so that we can clean the cut on his head."

"Clean it how?" asked Laura. "We have nothing."

"We have water."

"Tell the bad man to go away, Daddy!" Katie's agitation surprised her father.

"The man's hurt, kitten," John told her. "We have to help him."

"It's the last of our water, John." There was a hint of desperation in Laura's voice. "We need it ourselves."

"We'll get more water, darling," pressed John, while he, Roger and the man with the tattered sneaker carefully deposited the comatose man on the floor.

Laura reluctantly disappeared into the kitchen, returning moments later with a bottle of rainwater. It had hardly rained that summer, and the taps in the estate had been cut off in a government-led initiative to save water. In a perfectly Kafkaesque move the remotely run Council Management Company was instructed to inform residents that during the shortage they should collect (taxable) rainwater, which, of course, was not forthcoming either.

"Make the bad man go away!" Katie was getting upset, and her great-grandmother shuffled over to her and sat beside her, mumbling some words of comfort and stroking her hair. But Katie was adamant, "Make him go away!"

"Katie's right," the old woman piped up in support of her great-granddaughter. It was unlike Katie to react in such a negative way to someone who needed help. She was a kind and empathetic child, who somehow managed to find and tend to injured birds and mice despite her blindness, and frequently needed reminding not to talk to strangers. Her intuition never ceased to amaze her great-grandmother, so if Katie had taken an instant dislike to the man, then surely it would be prudent to get rid of him as soon as possible. "You should get him out of here," the old woman added. "No good ever comes from dealing with strangers."

"Make the bad man go!" Katie interjected once more.

"Stop it!" John was losing patience with his family. "What's wrong with everyone?"

"Here you go." Laura placed a placating hand on her husband's shoulder, handing him the water bottle and a clean cloth.

"Thank you." The silent unseeing gathered in John and Laura's doorway as John lifted the wounded man's head and put the water bottle to his lips, planning to encourage him to drink before attending to the small cut on his forehead.

As soon as the water touched his lips, Phillip's eyes opened wide and he sat bolt upright. So unexpected was the stranger's return to consciousness that it was all John could do to hang onto the water bottle.

"What the fuck?!" yelled Phillip, his horror growing as his eyes adjusted to the dark and he took in the scene around him. The murky, cramped, musty-smelling room, bereft of furniture bar a rag-covered mattress in the corner. The corpse-like remains of a little robot dog, long since broken. A worn one-eared bunny clutched in the hand of a frightened, sickly little girl; hollow, shadowy indents in the membranous skin where her eyes should have been. Next to the girl a grey-skinned woman, sighted, but so old that Phillip wondered why she hadn't been cryogenically frozen or cremated long ago. More emaciated eyeless figures crowding in the entrance to the flat; a man of around Phillip's own age, but gaunt, dishevelled and looking much older, kneeling over him with a plastic bottle, a sightless woman standing behind him. The whole scene smacked of poverty and deprivation that made Phillip want to puke.

"It's okay," the man told Phillip. "You're safe... Here, have some water."

"Get away from me, you filthy pig!" barked Phillip, lashing out at the man and sending the bottle flying from his hand, its contents spilling on the floor. "Don't you touch me!"

Phillip jumped to his feet and threw himself in the direction of the door, elbowing the blind out of his way as he went.

"Get the fuck out of my way!"

Laura cried out as Phillip pushed her to the ground, her cry eliciting a wail of horror from her daughter.

"Hey!" John shouted after the man, while pulling his wife gently to her feet. But Phillip was already racing through the corridor in the direction of what he hoped was the entrance door to the building. "Are you okay, darling?" John took a moment to comfort his sobbing wife. "I have to go after him. Explain that we meant him no harm. We were only trying to help."

"Don't go, Daddy!" Katie rushed over to her father.

"She's right, John. Don't go," pleaded Laura.

"I have to talk to him. Calm him down. Besides, he could have concussion and pass out again."

"Don't go, Daddy!" Katie wrapped her skinny arms around John's waist and started to cry.

"Daddy will be right back." John extricated himself from his daughter's grip and rushed out into the corridor, followed more cautiously by his distressed sightless neighbours. Left behind in the flat, Katie wailed wretchedly as her mother and great-grandmother tried unsuccessfully to comfort her.

Phillip stumbled around the grimy dark corridors of Bollo Bridge House, looking for a way out.

"Suit!" he shouted as he ran. "Voice control! Police!"

Mercifully, the nanocomputer in Phillip's Armani SmartSuit was still working, and he was connected to a police controller in a matter of seconds.

"Yes, Mr Burton-Smith? How can we assist you?"

"I've been kidnapped!" rasped Phillip.

"Don't worry, Sir. We were alerted when your car malfunctioned, and an ambulance is already on its way to you."

"Fuck the ambulance!" shouted Phillip. "I've been kidnapped! The place is crawling with freaks and terrorists! I'm trapped! You've got to get me out!"

"Try to stay calm, Mr Burton-Smith. We're dispatching a helicopter and an anti-terror squad immediately. Are you still inside the building?"

"Yes!"

"Try to find the exit."

"What the fuck do you think I'm doing?"

"Please stay calm, sir," the police controller intoned dispassionately through the tiny speaker in Phillip's SmartSuit. "Once you find the exit, get as far away from the building as you can. If you find yourself in imminent danger, hide."

"No shit!"

A whirring, booming noise, a rush of air, and the Twenty-Second Century Fox News helicopter was on the scene moments before the police arrived. Footage of the South Acton Estate and of Phillip's tiny figure fleeing from the ill-fated Bollo Bridge House, along with a female newscaster's concomitant commentary, was already live and streaming in every living-room in which people cared to and could afford to watch the news.

"Horror in the South Acton Estate, where earlier today an innocent victim was kidnapped by deviant immigrant terrorists! The man, believed to be Phillip Burton-Smith of the Green Dreams Estate, was ambushed earlier today and subjected to an ordeal of torture and perversion by the cannibalistic inhabitants of this vile disease-ridden estate in West London. You can see Mr Burton-Smith fleeing for his life. Let's hope rescuers can reach him before he is recaptured, killed and eaten by the foreign scroungers who are hot on his tail even as you are brought this exciting live action report by me, Tertia Hughes, of the Twenty-Second Century Fox News Channel."

John appeared in the entrance door of Bollo Bridge house just as a large armed police chopper joined the news helicopter above the building, the pumped-up anti-terror officers on board gesturing angrily to the reporters to get out of their way. John's face blanched at the sight of the aircraft, while Phillip, a dozen or so metres away, breathed a sigh of relief as a fleet of armoured police cars also swept in, lights flashing and sirens wailing, and a host of black-clad, heavily armed officers jumped out. One of them spotted Phillip and hastened over to him.

"Mr Burton-Smith?"

"Yes!"

"Get behind the car, please, sir, and stay there."

As Phillip moved behind the car, John stepped from the building, hands raised. Some of his sightless neighbours spilled from the entrance behind him.

"Please!" shouted John. "We meant no harm. We just wanted to help. We just bandaged his head and gave him water. We haven't done anything wrong."

A quick burst of shots rang out and John fell to the ground, then all hell broke loose as the other officers opened fire on the blind people behind him.

"The terrorists have emerged from the building and opened fire on police!" In the Twenty-Second Century Fox News helicopter, blonde-haired, blue-eyed reporter Tertia Hughes could barely contain her excitement. "We can see police and anti-terror troops returning fire!"

At ground level, cries of fear and pain rang out as those residents of Bollo Bridge House who had emerged behind John tried to run back into the building. In their confusion, some of the blind lost their bearings and ran straight into the incoming gunfire. Others managed to get back inside, and screams and shouts resonated from the building as disorientated tenants panicked, trying to get to safety or reach their families. Parents grabbed hold of their children; children tried to protect their elderly parents. In the mayhem, many of the blind were separated from their loved ones. But their ordeal had only just begun.

"Some of the terrorists are armed with explosive vests. The police need to contain the situation quickly so that the terror riot doesn't spread to the rest of the area and beyond." The newscaster's voice rose in pitch, her excitement almost sexual, and streamed to every paying household that could be bothered to watch. "Specialist anti-terror squads have been brought in to quell the terrorist uprising at the estate. And all this brought to you live by me, Tertia Hughes, on Twenty-Second Century Fox News."

Laura heard the shooting outside, and the screaming and shouting in the corridor. She was beginning to fear for her husband.

"Mummy!"

"It's okay, kitten."

"Laura," her grandmother asked, "what's going on?"

"I don't know, but I'm going to look for John."

"Don't go, dear. John will be back soon."

"Something's wrong," Laura insisted. "He might be hurt. I need to find him." Laura made her way to the door.

"No, Mummy! Don't go!" the panic in her daughter's voice stopped Laura for a moment, but she was determined to look for her husband.

"Mummy will be back soon. Mummy's going to find Daddy, and we'll both come back together."

"No, Mummy! Don't go!" The little girl was inconsolable. Her great-grandmother had to use all of her strength to hold onto her, as she tried to stop her mother leaving.

Laura hurried along the corridor, calling her husband's name, bumping into walls and other sightless inhabitants as they fled in the opposite direction, towards what they vainly hoped would be the relative safety of their flats.

"John? John! Has anyone seen my husband? Who's there? Has anyone seen John?" Then an ear-rending whistle and a huge bang, and the last thing Laura felt was the building shuddering, a debilitating blow to her head and a terrible, crushing weight, as the missile struck and the ceiling caved in on top of her.

The news helicopter increased its altitude to avoid the plume of smoke and dust that rose from the building beneath.

"Out here at the South Acton Estate things are heating up as the police are forced to use necessary deadly force to subdue the rioting terrorists," Tertia crooned in delight.

The armed police helicopter prepared to strike again. Phillip ventured out from behind the police van, turned his back to the smouldering Bollo Bridge House, held out his SmartSuited arm in front of him, and took a selfie. Then he hid behind the police vehicle again and instructed the SmartSuit to upload his awe-inspiring photo onto social media.

"We've seen the valiant rescue by police of Phillip Burton-Smith, but will the police be able to keep him safe, or will the foetid locals have one final meal before they keep their long-overdue appointment with their maker? We will continue to bring the unfolding action to you live on Twenty-Second Century Fox News."

The news report now cut from Tertia Hughes in the helicopter to an almost identical Barbie-esque reporter on the ground, giving the bizarre illusion that the immaculate blonde with the perfect teeth was broadcasting from two places simultaneously. The one on the ground was conducting a vox pop with an elegant woman in a pink leather jacket who'd been passing through on her way to the Westside shopping district and had stopped to join a group of gawkers across the street from Bollo Bridge House.

"They're pure evil," the woman told her interviewer. "They're all rapists, and they eat babies and rats. They're filthy – like rats. When rats eat rats, that's like cannibalistic, isn't it?"

But the reporter had already lost interest, and was racing off, cameraman in tow, to her next, freshly spotted interviewee.

Phillip saw the news team coming, adjusted the makeshift bandage on his head, puffed out his chest and pulled in his stomach. He was already grinning his best toothy grin as the reporter and cameraman reached him.

"Mr Burton-Smith! Sir! Veronica Quaid from the Twenty-Second Century Fox News Channel. How are you feeling?"

"Fine, thanks," beamed Phillip, then checked himself and quickly added, "considering the circumstances."

"A lucky escape for you, sir?"

"Yes, I barely got away with my life."

"Can you tell us what happened?"

"Well, I was driving along, minding my own business, when my car was ambushed by terrorists."

"Horrible. What do you think they wanted with you?"

"They definitely wanted to torture and eat me."

"How awful!" The newscaster could hardly suppress her delight. "How did you get away?"

"They were heavily armed, but I fought them and I managed to get away."

"How many of them were there?"

"Many. There was a large group of them. Hardened criminals. You could tell they'd committed a lot of dreadful crimes – just by looking at them."

"Well, sir, you are an inspiration to us all. A true hero."

"Yes."

Veronica turned away from Phillip and positioned herself directly in front of the camera. "This has been Veronica Quaid from Twenty-Second Century Fox News, speaking live and exclusive to Mr Burton-Smith, Hero."

In John and Laura's flat, Katie was inconsolable. She was crying and screaming, and finally managed to free herself from her great-grandmother's grasp.

"Nanna, we got to go! We got to go!"

"No, dear. We have to wait for your parents."

But the little girl would have none of it.

"They're not coming back!" she wailed. Her words hit her great-grandmother hard. So when the little girl said, "We got to go! Now!" the old lady didn't argue. She took her great-granddaughter's hand and they hurried out into the corridor, Katie insisting that they go to the back door, in the opposite direction from that in which Laura had disappeared, and which was now buried under several storeys' worth of rubble. A moment later a second missile hit, and their flat too was gone.

"As you can see, the compound of horror beneath us has been destroyed. The English people have long called for the hotbed of terrorism and depravity known as the South Acton Estate to be wiped off the face of the earth, and perhaps after this latest outrage their wish will be honoured. Perhaps it is time to erase the South Acton Terror Estate once and for all and liberate the Free World from the immigrant deviants within. Perhaps it is time for the Prime Minister to instigate the *Daylight Protocol*. But for now, the innocent have been rescued; the evil vanquished. Another successful battle in the war against terror. God bless you, and thank you for watching me, Tertia Hughes, on Twenty-Second Century Fox News."

When Phillip finally made it home by courtesy car, following a full check-up in a mobile medical unit and two stitches to his head, the holographic billboard at the entrance to his airy, radiant glass estate was lit up like the proverbial Christmas tree. In giant luminous letters it flashed the message: 'The Green Dreams Estate welcomes home our hero, Mr Phillip Burton-Smith!' Images from the news footage of the day's events played out behind the letters, as did a vast reproduction of Phillip's selfie – showing a confident, tanned, blond man with perfect teeth, against the smouldering shell of Bollo Bridge House.

Over the coming days, neighbours to whom he hardly spoke would shake his hand and pat him on the shoulder. But for now he slumped on his designer sofa, drinking Dom Perignon and watching the number of hits on his selfie climb as it went viral on the internet. Later he'd dig his pleasure model android out of the cupboard, where he'd discarded her when he got bored, and rape the hell out of her. It wasn't quite the same as flesh and blood, but it would do for now.

Over the coming days, the Prime Minister's so-called *Daylight Protocol* would be put into practice. Surviving residents of the South Acton Estate, and other poor, blind and undesirable inhabitants of the Greater London Metropolitan Area, would be rounded up and interned in the government's Tower of London Detention and Concentration Facility, which had been created back in the twenty-first century to contain terror suspects indefinitely. The remaining buildings constituting what was left of the South Acton Estate would be razed to the ground.

In the meantime, a little blind girl and a sighted old woman had escaped the carnage.

Katie and her great-grandmother now huddled together in sight of the rubble of Bollo Bridge House, grieving for their loved ones. In a remarkable feat of reverse evolution, the child had been born with a nerve connecting her disproportionately large pineal gland to retinal structures and a lens-like formation near the front of her skull, just inside her forehead, above and between her eyes. Like her great-grandmother, Katie wouldn't survive the round-ups and incarceration that followed the South Acton Estate massacre. Had she lived long enough to reproduce, her children would have been born with a 'third' eye – not only seeing in the dark, but able to perceive things beyond the physical world.

ALSO AVAILABLE FROM
SHADOW PUBLISHING

Phantoms of Venice
Selected by David A. Sutton
ISBN 0-9539032-1-4

The Satyr's Head: Tales of Terror
Selected by David A. Sutton
ISBN 978-0-9539032-3-8

The Female of the Species And Other Terror Tales
By Richard Davis
ISBN 978-0-9539032-4-5

Frightfully Cosy And Mild Stories For Nervous Types
By Johnny Mains
ISBN 978-0-9539032-5-2 (*Out of print*)

Horror! Under the Tombstone: Stories from the Deathly Realm
Selected by David A. Sutton
ISBN 978-0-9539032-6-9

The Whispering Horror
By Eddy C. Bertin
ISBN: 978-0-9539032-7-6

The Lurkers in the Abyss and Other Tales of Terror
By David A. Riley
ISBN: 978-0-9539032-9-0

Worse Things Than Spiders and Other Stories
By Samantha Lee
ISBN: 978-0-9539032-8-3

Tales of the Grotesque: A Collection of Uneasy Tales
By L. A. Lewis
Edited by Richard Dalby
ISBN: 978-0-9572962-0-6

Horror on the High Seas: Classic Weird Sea Tales
Selected by David A. Sutton
ISBN: 978-0-9572962-1-3

Creeping Crawlers
Edited by Allen Ashley
ISBN 978-0-9572962-2-0

Haunts of Horror
Edited by David A. Sutton
ISBN 978-0-9572962-3-7

Death After Death
By Edmund Glasby
ISBN 978-0-9572962-4-4

The Spirit of the Place and Other Strange Tales:
Complete Short Stories
By Elizabeth Walter
Edited by Dave Brzeski
ISBN 978-0-9572962-5-1

Such Things May Be: Collected Writings
By James Wade
Edited by Edward P. Berglund
ISBN 978-0-9572962-6-8

The Black Pilgrimage & Other Explorations
Essays on Supernatural Fiction
By Rosemary Pardoe
ISBN 978-0-9572962-7-5

Shadmocks & Shivers
Tales Inspired by the Stories of
R. Chetwynd-Hayes
Edited by Dave Brzeski
ISBN 978-0-957-2962-8-2